EntreMundos/AmongWorlds

EntreMundos/AmongWorlds

New Perspectives on Gloria E. Anzaldúa

Edited By

AnaLouise Keating

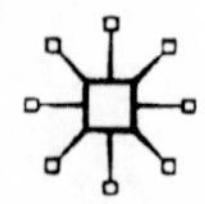

ENTREMUNDOS/AMONGWORLDS

First published in 2005 by
PALGRAVE MACMILLAN™
175 Fifth Avenue, New York, N.Y. 10010 and
Houndmills, Basingstoke, Hampshire, England RG21 6XS
Companies and representatives throughout the world.

PALGRAVE MACMILLAN is the global academic imprint of the Palgrave Macmillan division of St. Martin's Press, LLC and of Palgrave Macmillan Ltd. Macmillan® is a registered trademark in the United States, United Kingdom and other countries. Palgrave is a registered trademark in the European Union and other countries.

ISBN 1–4039–6721–0

Library of Congress Cataloging-in-Publication Data is available from Library of Congress

A catalogue record for this book is available from the British Library.

Design by Newgen Imaging Systems (P) Ltd., Chennai, India.

First edition: November 2005

10 9 8 7 6 5 4 3 2 1

Transferred to digital printing in 2006.

para Gloria, Hilda, y todas almas afines

Contents

Agradecimientos/Acknowledgments

I am blessed to be surrounded by so many wonderful people y espiritús. Thank you, contributors, for your encouragement, your excitement about this project, your patience, your willingness to revise, and your carefully crafted words. Thank you to my friends/colleagues/familia: Nadine Barrett, Renae Bredin, Tom and JoAnn Keating, Chester and Priscilla Lynton, Carrie McMaster, Deborah Miranda, Sonia Saldívar-Hull, Patricia Stukes, Jane Keating-Vraspier, Doreen Watson, Kelli Zaytoun . . . Thank you for your encouraging phone calls, e-mails, and conversations, for your wisdom and advice, for your many other forms of assistance as well. Thank you, Claire Sahlin, for being such a thoughtful, supportive, generous colleague (everyone working in university settings should be so lucky!). Thanks to Glenda Lehrmann and the other FIRST librarians at TWU for assistance with research. Thanks to Dru Merriman for help with copying. Thank you, TWU estudientes in my 2003 and 2004 seminar course, *Gloria Anzaldúa: Theorizing & the Politics of Imagination*, for your feedback and your excitement about Gloria's theories. Thank you, Hilda Anzaldúa, Kit Quan, y Irene Reti, for doing so very much to preserve Gloria's words. Thank you, Liliana Wilson Grez for allowing us to use your artwork for the cover, and for being so flexible about the format. Gracias to the following writers, who inspire and challenge me: Paula Gunn Allen, M. Jacqui Alexander, James Baldwin, Ralph Waldo Emerson, Leela Fernandes, Joy Harjo, June Jordan, Audre Lorde, Thich Nhat Hanh, Timothy Powell, Jane Roberts, Chela Sandoval. Thanks to everyone at Palgrave MacMillan, especially Gabriella Pearce, Erin Ivy, and Lynn Vande Stouwe. Thanks to Maran Elancheran for your sharp copy-editing eye. Thanks to mi esposo, Eddy Lynton, for your advice, wisdom, encouragement, inspiration, humor, patience, y más. Gracias to our daughter, Jamitrice, for your questions, comments, and confidence. I thank you both for understanding/accepting/tolerating my workaholic tendencies; I am blessed to have you both in my life.

And of course I thank Gloria, my dear writing comadre, mentor, and friend. Comadre: gracias por todo, for encouraging me to take on this project (even before *this bridge* was finished and you told me I must be as crazy as you), for opening your house to me during the years I worked on this book and others, for the meals and walks on West Cliff, for all the conversations we shared, for suggesting possible contributors and Liliana's cover art, for insightful comments on the book proposal, table of contents, and contributors' drafts, and—most especially—for your shaman aesthetics, your risk-taking inspiration, your bold vision, and your encouragement over the years. Orishas y espiritus, thank you for guiding me, whispering words of encouragement that nourish body/heart/mind/spirit and inspire vision.

Foreword

Unfinished Words: The Crossing of Gloria Anzaldúa

Chela Sandoval

There is a kind of emptying out here—a hollowing, and a holying.

Gloria Anzaldúa was a prolific writer, yet most of her writings remain unpublished, "unpolished, still," she would say. Gloria earned her living by teaching, and she was a consummate teacher. In that way, as much as through her writings, Anzaldúa's ideas traveled globally.[1] This book, *EntreMundos*, was the last book Gloria and I discussed before she died. EntreMundos is "another way to name the borderlands," she thought aloud, another word for that "alter-space." It is possible to locate such alter-spaces, these borderlands, geographically, materially, yes. But that space entremundos, between worlds, Anzaldúa insisted, also exists in consciousness and culture, in all economies of power. The term "entremundos" situates in language this place that can be experienced and described even though its nature is change—constituted always in-relation-to. For Anzaldúa, entremundos is a science fiction world-of-possibility born of privilege, oppression, hope, and horror. Horror and evil always result from the inequities of oppression, Gloria says, but so too do hope and goodness. In Anzaldúa's hands the methodology of the oppressed transformed into a promise, a way to implement a global methodology of emancipation. Anzaldúa was a resolute theorist of hope.

This book, *EntreMundos/AmongWorlds*, constitutes a communion-table on which the authors lay out the altering work of Gloria Anzaldúa's contributions. No other collection marks or honors her transition similarly, for this book was conceived with Anzaldúa's blessing and before her death. In this first book-publication since her transition, we whom she called "nos/otras" are translating and extending the meanings and senses of her work. And Anzaldúa loved, admired, and encouraged the senses that are made here—and that will be made—by authors such as María Lugones, Irene Reti, Jane Caputi, and AnaLouise Keating. This book, she told me in 2002, will "redraw my work," will advance, explain, and go beyond it. She asserts that "it thrills me and . . . validates me as a writer that people can take my images or ideas and work them out in their own way and write their own theories" (qtd. in Reuman 5).[2] And indeed, *EntreMundos'* chapters are comprised of scholarship that has traveled in relation to, alongside of, through, and beyond Anzaldúa's work, just as she had wished.

The five sections of *EntreMundos* combine to outline Anzaldúa's theoretical and methodological contributions to Mestiz@ Studies, to Chican@, Latin@, and Xican Studies, to feminist and LGBTQ Studies, to emancipatory and peace studies, indeed, to critical and cultural theory across disciplines. Gloria believed that the dialectical interchange of these five "sections" could comprise an internationally useful methodology for emancipation which has risen out of experiences of oppression. Part one of *EntreMundos* is based upon the Anzaldúan idea that all social change begins through a technique of spoken-word-art-performance-activism, what she calls "autohistoria-teoría." This technique can forcibly induce practitioners, she would say, into la conciencia de la mestiza, a condition of being she calls the "nepantla," or in-between state. Parts two and three of this book concern the nepantla state and also make visible new collectives of people Anzaldúa calls "nos/otras"—the we's in the others, the others in us. Autohistoria-teoria, nepantlerista citizenship, and the recognition of nos/otras allow practitioners access to what Keating describes as the heart of part five, the "connectionist" and spiritual mode of thinking Anzaldúa calls "conocimientos." Lastly, Gloria believed that the creative and communicative performance-process of autohistoria-teoría; the in-between state of nepantla peopled by nos/otras; and the elevated connectionist consciousness of conocimientos, when utilized together, will generate oppositional modes of "tribal" consciousness and spiritual politics that are capable of developing planetary life connections. This creation of new tribalisms and planetary alliances through el mundo zurdo is the idea that structures part five of *EntreMundos*.[3]

Like Foucault with his archeology, or Barthes with his semiology, Anzaldúa hoped this five-stage methodology of emancipation would have global consequences. For Gloria, a life lived entremundos and the radical perception of borderlands and mestiz@ consciousness were generated in the crossing, in the interrelationship between these principles.[4] Once activated, this dialectic can be recognized as a social theory and method capable of remapping disciplinary and global borders. Those of us who knew Gloria Anzaldúa know that these five techniques comprise the guiding principles by which she lived her own life. Gloria's speech and writing enacted the truths of autohistoria-teoría; she lived as a nepantlerista and treated nos/otras as her countrypeople; and her politics and spirituality were united in her awareness of conocimientos. Gloria traveled the world, and had tremendous influence as a public intellectual. Through all the difficulties of travel, however, she never gave up her dedication to calling up the global affinities and new tribalisms she believed would be the outcome of these enacted principles.

U.S. third-world feminist activists during the 1970s developed skills that became honed further after the 1981 publication of *This Bridge Called My Back: Writings by Radical Women of Color*. Gloria Anzaldúa was one of the great translators and developers of these skills. In June of that year we traveled in the back seat of a car headed east, sharing ideas like the "tightrope between worlds, el mundo zurdo," and "oppositional consciousness in its differential form." Gloria showed me how to throw the I-Ching for answers, and I carried her books while she performed *This Bridge Called My Back* in Boston. Much later I said "come to Santa Cruz with me and Ro, Ruth and Lata, Gloria Watkins, Lorna, Shirley, Teish, Osa, Ekua, Rhee and Histcon and we'll dream at lunch over books, survive earthquakes and children, deaths and academia, write, and build what we learn into love." Once there she would tell me academia was burning my writing and I would tell her I should edit hers. Our group allied as "almas afines"—that was what she called the crossing. During that decade we became another cadre of lesbians of color dreaming U.S. third-world feminism into a weave of coalition; from out of nepantla our dreams became webs.

Anzaldúa was an inventor, a lover of technology, science, physics, M- and string theory. We shared a fascination with science fiction and horror—that which forced our shifts and challenged the burdens of who we were. In part it was her dedication to science that brought us to nepantla, to the borderlands of differential consciousness, conocimientos, to the physics of love.[5] Spiritual activism became our term for the theoretical-ethical-moral-emotional-intellectual work we pledged to do as U.S. third-world feminists. We believed that no social change for justice was possible if that change was not informed by a physics of love, a mode of civic affinity that would instruct our political and worldly organizations, our societies. Gloria Anzaldúa, U.S. third-world feminist theorist and Chicana lesbian activist, dedicated her life to mapping the social facts of personal and civic love. Today, Anzaldúa's data extends around the globe. It encodes a physics of love and demands an ordered science that disorders war. In days past we dreamt of this new order, of loss and decay, of friendship and peace, of hope and the future, of science fiction.

We now leave these dreams to other generations, to third-world feminists, Chican@s and citizen-warriors, citizen-lovers and queergenders, to nepantleras. In Gloria Anzaldúa we have a name, a method, a language, a linguistic terrorism aimed to lift us higher. Gloria wrote that she yearned "to pass on to the next generation the spiritual activism I've inherited from my cultures" ("let us be the healing of the wounds"). The editor of *EntreMundos,* AnaLouise Keating, sees with the clarity of a next generation, those who resonate with and have taken up the social-justice and spiritual warriorship dimensions of Anzaldúa's political project.

This book *EntreMundos,* advances Gloria Anzaldúa's legacy. As I write in January 2005, the planet trembles from the earthquake and tsunami in south Asia and east Africa. The vibration connects ethnic communities of survivors across the planet. While the rumble of planetary threat continues, Gloria Anzaldúa's messages of hope, healing, social justice, love, and U.S. third-world feminism continue to resonate around the world.

Notes

1. See for instance Anzaldúa's *Interviews/Entrevistas* and Maria Lugones's "Playfulness, 'World'-Traveling, and Loving Perception."
2. See also *this bridge we call home: radical visions for transformation.*
3. For descriptions of these principles see "shifting worlds," AnaLouise Keating's introduction to this book, as well as Anzaldúa's *Interviews/Entrevistas.*
4. For more on this topic see my "AfterBridge: Technologies of Crossing."
5. See Anzaldúa's *Borderlands/LaFrontera.*

Introduction

shifting worlds, una entrada

AnaLouise Keating

between and among worlds: introducing gloria

> Those of us who live skirting otros mundos, other groups, in this in-between state I call nepantla have a unique perspective. We notice the breaches in feminism, the rifts in Raza studies, the breaks in our disciplines, the splits in this country. These cracks show the flaws in our cultures, the faults in our pictures of reality. The perspective from the cracks gives us different ways of defining the self, of defining group identity.
>
> —Gloria E. Anzaldúa

In Gloria Evangelina Anzaldúa's writings, "nepantla"—a Nahuatl term meaning "in-between space"—indicates temporal, spatial, psychic, and/or intellectual point(s) of liminality and potential transformation. During nepantla, individual and collective self-conceptions and worldviews are shattered. Apparently fixed categories—whether based on gender, ethnicity/'race,' sexuality, economic status, health, religion, or some combination of these elements and often others as well—begin eroding. Boundaries become more permeable, and begin to break down. This loosening of previously restrictive labels and beliefs, while intensely painful, can create shifts in consciousness and opportunities for change.[1]

Some people who experience these nepantla states become what Anzaldúa calls "nepantleras": mediators, "in-betweeners," "those who facilitate passages between worlds" ("(Un)natural bridges" 1). "Nepantlera" is a word Anzaldúa coined to describe threshold people: those who live within and among multiple worlds, and develop what Anzaldúa describes in my epigraph as a "perspective from the cracks." Nepantleras use their views from these cracks-between-worlds to invent holistic, relational[2] theories and tactics enabling them to reconceive or in other ways transform the various worlds in which they exist.

I begin with this reference to Anzaldúa's theories of nepantla and nepantleras for two reasons. First, these theories point toward her broad-ranging philosophical commitments. All too often, scholars focus so extensively on Anzaldúa's identity-based interventions that we overlook other aspects of her career. Such oversights unnecessarily limit our understanding of her work.[3] Second, Anzaldúa's theories of nepantla and nepantleras resonate strongly with her own life story. Ella era una nepantlera. Throughout her life, Anzaldúa moved between and among diverse—sometimes conflicting—personal, political, and professional worlds. The oldest child of sixth-generation mexicanos from the Rio Grande Valley of south Texas and a self-described "Chicana tejana feminist-dyke-patlache poet, fiction writer, and cultural theorist," Anzaldúa participated in a number of divergent worlds yet refused to be contained within any single group or location. Instead, she moved within, between, and among specialized worlds of academia, art, and publishing; private spaces of family, spirits, and friends; and politicized communities of Chican@s, Latin@s, feminist, queer, U.S. women of colors, spiritual activists, and other progressive social actors.

These experiences moving within, between, and among multiple worlds inform Anzaldúa's theoretical perspectives and shape her work. Her movements entre mundos influenced the projects she adopted, the theories she invented, her critiques of rigid identity categories, and her lifelong efforts to develop inclusionary multicultural alliances for social justice. Her words challenge readers to reexamine and perhaps change our perspectives; her words invite us to adopt broader, larger, deeper modes of seeing and responding.

Like other nepantleras, Anzaldúa opens herself to multiple risks and potential woundings (including self-division, isolation, misunderstanding, rejection, and accusations of disloyalty). Thus in "La Prieta," her early autohistoria, she acknowledges the many forms of alienation she has experienced in her interactions with Mexican Americans and Chicanos, other people of colors, feminists, lesbians, and gay men, yet refuses to sever her ties with any of these groups. Locating herself within and among her various peoples, she defiantly asserts:

> I am a wind-swayed bridge, a crossroads inhabited by whirlwinds. Gloria, the facilitator, Gloria the mediator, straddling the walls between abysses. "Your allegiance is to La Raza, the Chicano movement," say the members of my race. "Your allegiance is to the Third World," say my Black and Asian friends. "Your allegiance is to your gender, to women," say the feminists. Then there's my allegiance to the Gay movement, to the socialist revolution,

> to the New Age, to magic and the occult. And there's my affinity to literature, to the world of the artist. What am I? *A third world lesbian feminist with Marxist and mystic leanings.* They would chop me up into little fragments and tag each piece with a label. (205, her emphasis)

Although each group tries to make membership contingent on its own (often exclusionary) rules and demands, Anzaldúa refuses these terms without rejecting the people or groups. She maintains multiple allegiances and locates herself, simultaneously, in multiple worlds. She is "a many-armed and legged body with one foot on brown soil, one on white, one in straight society, one in the gay world, the man's world, the women's, one limb in the literary world, another in the working class, the socialist, and the occult worlds. . . . Who, me confused? Ambivalent? Not so. Only your labels split me" (205).

Anzaldúa positions herself on the thresholds—simultaneously inside and outside numerous groups—and establishes points of similarity and difference with people of diverse backgrounds. By so doing, she can engage in multiple dialogues simultaneously. She rejects the need for unitary identities and exclusive, single-issue alliances, and replaces naturalized concepts of ethnicity, gender, sexuality, or other systems of difference with more openly relational forms.

This resistance to rigid labels, coupled with her interest in developing new alliances and identities based on affinity (or what she refers to in her most recent writings as a "new tribalism"), makes Anzaldúa's work vital for twenty-first-century social actors, artists, thinkers, and scholars. Her words challenge the conventional views that lead to stereotyping, over-generalizations, and arbitrary divisions among different groups; her writings open new spaces where innovative, sometimes shocking connections can occur.

Like Anzaldúa herself, her writings move entre mundos—between and among diverse worlds. This movement is perhaps most evident with her 1987 autohistoria-teoría, *Borderlands/La Frontera: The New Mestiza.* Named one of the 100 Best Books of the Century by both *Hungry Mind Review* and *Utne Reader, Borderlands* represents an innovative blend of personal experience with history, social protest, poetry, and myth, creating what Anzaldúa calls "autohistoria-teoría." This book, which is frequently anthologized and often cited, has challenged and expanded previous views in American studies, Chicano/a studies, composition studies, cultural studies, ethnic studies, feminism, literary studies, critical pedagogy, women's studies, and queer theory. As Sonia Saldívar-Hull notes, *Borderlands* is a "transfrontera, transdisciplinary text" that has "traveled between" many disciplines (12–13). Focusing especially on Anzaldúa's theories of the "new mestiza," the "Borderlands," and "mestiza consciousness," scholars have explored these theoretical perspectives in important ways.

But perhaps not surprisingly—given the multifaceted nature of *Borderlands* and the diversity of Anzaldúa's other writings—readers overlook additional, equally important dimensions of her work, leaving what Anzaldúa might call "blank spots" that prevent us from grasping the radical nature of her vision for social change and the crucial ways her theories have developed since the 1987 publication of *Borderlands*.[4] As Anzaldúa points out, *Borderlands* is not a self-enclosed entity but rather part of a much larger project. As she explains in *Interviews/Entrevistas*, *Borderlands* "is just one project of this overall umbrella project that is my life's work, my life's writing. *Borderlands* is just one hit on it. . . . And this new book on composition, the writing process, [the construction of] identity [and] knowledge . . . is like a sequel to *Borderlands*. All of my books are parts of this project" (268).

Highlighting some of Anzaldúa's lesser-explored theories and texts, *EntreMundos* invites readers to re-examine her writings and theorizing from additional perspectives. Our goal is to broaden Anzaldúan scholarship, shifting the conversation in new directions while underscoring the visionary yet pragmatic social-justice dimensions of her work.

To be sure, Anzaldúa's well-known theories of "the Borderlands," "the new mestiza," and "mestiza consciousness" broke new ground and merit the attention they've received. However, Anzaldúa did not turn off her computer and stop writing after *Borderlands*' publication. Indeed, her ideas and theories deepened and became richer in her post-*Borderlands* years. To focus so extensively on only a few key concepts can prevent readers from recognizing the other contributions Anzaldúa makes, as well as the more recent developments in her thinking. Motivated by our own visions of social transformation, *EntreMundos*' contributors examine previously under-explored aspects of Anzaldúa's writings, ranging from "el otro lado" perspectives on Anzaldúa's "borderlands" (Méndez), to her children's books (Vasquez) and fiction (Blanchard), to *Borderlands*' poetry (Garber, Hernández-Ávila), to Anzaldúa's spiritual activism (Keating), nepantla (McMaster), and other recent theories. Contributors offer new views of Anzaldúa herself: Gloria la professora (Neile), "writing comadre" and friend (Reti), public speaker and co-panelist (Maracle).

from borderlands to nepantla, and beyond: section arrangement

I try to give a term, to find a language for my ideas and concepts that comes from the indigenous part of me rather than from the European part, so I come up with Coatlicue, la facultad, la frontera, and nepantla—concepts that mean: "Here's a little nugget of a system of knowledge that's different from the Euro-American." This is my hit on it, but it's also a mestizo/mestiza, cognitive kind of perception, so therefore this ideology or this little nugget of knowledge is both indigenous and western. It's a hybridity, a mixture, because I live in this liminal state in between worlds, in between realities, in between systems of knowledge, in between symbology systems.

—*Gloria E. Anzaldúa,* Interviews/Entrevistas

I've organized *EntreMundos* conceptually, to enact a dialogue with Anzaldúa herself. The following five sections creatively engage with and elaborate on Anzaldúan theories that have not yet received the attention they merit: "autohistoria/autohistoria-teoría," "nepantla," "nos/otras," "conocimiento," and "El Mundo Zurdo/new tribalism." To some extent, this oversight is not surprising, for Anzaldúa's published writings (to date) include few comprehensive discussions of these terms. However, these concepts are crucial for those readers hoping to understand the development of Anzaldúa's thinking and the complexity of her work. They represent theories-in-the-making that interact with, expand on, and in other ways enrich Anzaldúa's better-known theories of the Borderlands, mestizaje, and mestiza consciousness. The pieces in each section do not, necessarily, focus specifically on the concepts themselves but instead illustrate and in other ways interact with them.

Foregrounding these theories also underscores Anzaldúa's use of indigenous imagery, terminology, and beliefs. Although some scholars have read this turn toward the indigenous as escapism or nostalgia, I disagree. Indigenous Mexican philosophies and worldviews offer Anzaldúa epistemological tools for individual/collective self-definition, resistance, intervention, and creation, as well as additional frameworks or vehicles to develop and convey her own innovative theories. In the following pages, I offer brief descriptions of these five terms. Like so many of Anzaldúa's theories, these concepts are closely related; the boundaries between them are fluid, at times blurring into each other.

autohistoria y autohistoria-teoría. . . . (re)writing self, (re)writing culture

Tu autohistoria is not carved in stone but drawn on sand and subject to shifting winds. Forced to rework your story, you invent new notions of yourself and reality—increasingly multidimensional versions where body, mind, and spirit interpenetrate in more complex ways.

—*Gloria E. Anzaldúa, "now let us shift"*

Although Anzaldúa refers to autohistoria and autohistoria-teoría in interviews, lectures, conversations, and the courses she selectively taught,[5] she did not publish a comprehensive definition of these concepts during her life. Nor could she, for these terms represented her ongoing attempt to enact, describe, and theorize her unique writing style and genres: a complex blending of cultural and personal biography with memoir, fiction, history, myth, theory, and other forms of storytelling.[6] While autohistoria focuses on and at times fictionalizes the life story (seen, for example, in Anzaldúa's *Prieta* series[7]), autohistoria-teoría includes openly theoretical dimensions as well (seen, for example, in *Borderlands*). As Anzaldúa explains, "*Autohistoria* is a term I use to describe the genre of writing about one's personal and collective history using fictive elements, a sort of fictionalized autobiography or memoir; an autohistoria-teoría is a personal essay that theorizes" ("now let us shift" 578).

Deeply infused with the search for personal and cultural meaning, or what Anzaldúa describes in her post-*Borderlands* writings as "putting Coyolxauhqui together,"[8] both autohistoria and autohistoria-teoría are informed by reflective self-awareness employed in the service of social-justice work. Personal experiences—revised and in other ways redrawn—become a lens with which to reread and rewrite the cultural stories into which we are born.[9] Through this lens, Anzaldúa and other autohistoria-teorístas expose the limitations in the existing paradigms and create new stories of healing, self-growth, cultural critique, and individual/collective transformation. The pieces in this section define, explore, enact, and illustrate various aspects of autohistoria and autohistoria-teoría.

nepantla. . . . pathways to change

> *I found that people were using "Borderlands" in a more limited sense than I had meant it. So to elaborate on the psychic and emotional borderlands I'm now using "nepantla." . . . With the nepantla paradigm I try to theorize unarticulated dimensions of the experience of mestizas living in between overlapping and layered spaces of different cultures and social and geographic locations, of events and realities—psychological, sociological, political, spiritual, historical, creative, imagined.*
>
> —*Gloria E. Anzaldúa,* Interviews/Entrevistas

In Anzaldúa's writings, "nepantla" represents both an extension of and an elaboration on her theories of the Borderlands and the Coatlicue state (as described in *Borderlands/La Frontera*). Like the Borderlands, nepantla indicates liminal space(s) where transformation can occur, and like the Coatlicue state, nepantla indicates space/times of great confusion, anxiety, and loss of control. But with nepantla, Anzaldúa underscores and expands the "spiritual, psychic, supernatural, and indigenous" dimensions (*Interviews/ Entrevistas* 176). Nepantla—as process, liminality, and change—occurs during the many transitional stages of life and describes both identity-related issues and epistemological concerns.[10]

Though nepantla demands isolation and seclusion, it can lead to new forms of community—seen most prominently in the work of las nepantleras: those who travel within and among multiple worlds, developing transformative alliances. As I explained above, las nepantleras are threshold people, agents of change, spiritual activists who employ liminal states of consciousness and ways of thinking as they enact their visions.[11] By so doing, they serve as models for others.[12] The pieces in this section explore various nepantlera acts and nepantla states.

nos/otras. . . . intersecting selves/ intersecting others

By moving from a militarized zone to a roundtable, nepantleras acknowledge an unmapped common ground: the humanity of the other. We are the other, the other is us. . . . Honoring people's otherness, las nepantleras advocate a "nos/otras" position—an alliance between "us" and "others." In nos/otras, the "us" is divided in two, the slash in the middle representing the bridge—the best mutuality we can hope for at the moment. Las nepantleras envision a time when the bridge will no longer be needed—we'll have shifted to a seamless nosotras.

—Gloria E. Anzaldúa, "now let us shift"

"Nosotras," the Spanish word for the feminine "we," indicates a collectivity, a type of group identity or consciousness. By partially dividing this word into two, Anzaldúa affirms this collectivity yet acknowledges the divisiveness so often experienced in contemporary life: *nos* implying "us," *otras*, implying otherness. Joined together, nos + otras holds the promise of healing: We contain the others, the others contain us. Significantly, nos/otras does not represent sameness; the differences among "us" still exist, but they function dialogically, generating previously unrecognized commonalities and connections, or what Anzaldúa describes in "now let us shift" as "an unmapped common ground" (570).

Drawing "us" and "them" closer together, Anzaldúa offers an alternative to binary self/other constellations, a philosophy and praxis enabling us to acknowledge, bridge, and sometimes transform the distances between self and other. Although nos/otras, like Anzaldúa's other theories, takes multiple, interconnected forms and occurs in a variety of contexts, the pieces in this section focus on two key dimensions, contained within the term itself: the division and doubled consciousness implied by the slash separating "nos" from "otras"; and the possibilities of (re)uniting self with other: forging commonalities, moving toward nosotras.

conocimientos. . . . expanding the vision

Conocimiento es otro mode de conectar across colors and other differences to allies also trying to negotiate racial contradictions, survive the stresses and traumas of daily life, and develop a spiritual-imaginal-political vision together. Conocimiento shares a sense of affinity with all things and advocates mobilizing, organizing, sharing information, knowledge, insights, and resources with other groups.
—Gloria E. Anzaldúa, "now let us shift"

With conocimiento, Anzaldúa fleshes out[13] the potentially transformative elements of her well-known theories of mestiza consciousness and la facultad. Like the former, conocimiento represents a nonbinary, connectionist mode of thinking; like the latter, conocimiento often develops within oppressive contexts and entails a deepening of perception. But with conocimiento, Anzaldúa underscores and develops the imaginal, spiritual-activist, and political dimensions implicit in her previous theories. An intensely personal, fully embodied epistemological process that gathers information from context, conocimiento is profoundly relational, and enables those who enact it to make connections among apparently disparate events, persons, experiences, and realities. These connections, in turn, lead to action. Anzaldúa offers her fullest discussion of conocimiento to date in her 2002 essay, "now let us shift . . . the path of conocimiento . . . inner work, public acts" where she outlines the "seven stages of conocimiento." As the pieces in this section demonstrate, Anzaldúa's theory of conocimiento offers a holistic, activist-inflected epistemology designed to effect change on multiple levels.

el mundo zurdo, the new tribalism. . . . forging new alliances

We are the queer groups, the people that don't belong anywhere, not in the dominant world nor completely within our own respective cultures. Combined we cover so many oppressions. But the overwhelming oppression is the collective fact that we do not fit, and because we do not fit we are a threat. *Not all of us have the same oppressions, but we empathize and identify with each other's oppressions. We do not share the same ideology, nor do we derive similar solutions. Some of us are leftists, some of us practitioners of magic. Some of us are both. But these different affinities are not opposed to each other. In El Mundo Zurdo I with my own affinities and my people with theirs can live together and transform the planet.*

—Gloria E. Anzaldúa, "La Prieta"

One of Anzaldúa's earliest yet least discussed concepts, El Mundo Zurdo (the Left-Handed World) can perhaps best be described as a visionary place where people from diverse backgrounds with diverse needs and concerns coexist and work together to bring about revolutionary change. El Mundo Zurdo represents relational difference, communities based on commonalities (not sameness). Anzaldúa insists that the inhabitants of El Mundo Zurdo are not all alike; our specific oppressions, solutions, and beliefs are different. Significantly, however, "these different affinities are not opposed to each other" but instead function as catalysts, facilitating the development of new, potentially transformative alliances. Anzaldúa's more recent theory of "new tribalism" builds on and expands her theory of El Mundo Zurdo, offering provocative alternatives to both assimilation and separatism. While some of the pieces in this section discuss the creative strategies Anzaldúa employs in her own attempts to forge inclusionary communities, others illustrate some of the forms El Mundo Zurdo and new tribalism can take.

postscript

I finished writing this introduction in early May 2004, shortly before Anzaldúa's unexpected passing from diabetes-related complications. Although Gloria had been living with (and often battling) the diabetes for over a decade, even those of us who knew her well were shocked by her death. As Kit Quan, one of Gloria's oldest friends and writing comadres, put it, "Gloria always told me that she was going to stick around for twenty more years. She struggled with diabetes and all its complications daily . . . but she was so well read on the disease . . . and worked so hard at managing her blood sugars that I believed we still had more time." Gloria took meticulous care of her health and was so determined to live until she had completed all of her writing projects, that I too believed that she would be with us for many more years.

When I met Gloria in 1991, I was struck by her vulnerability, her openmindedness, and her sensitivity to other people's alienation and pain. Deeply spiritual and intensely political, she believed in human beings' basic decency and potential wisdom. As I grew to know her over the last thirteen years, I became increasingly impressed with the ways Gloria's faith shaped her work. Despite the racism, sexism, homophobia, and other forms of rejection she experienced throughout her life, she maintained her faith in people's ability to change. She used her writing in the service of social justice, and she had the most expansive, inclusionary vision for social justice I have ever encountered. She was confident that "[e]mpowerment comes from ideas—our revolution is fought with concepts, not with guns, and it is fueled by vision. By focusing on what we want to happen, we change the present. The healing images and narratives we imagine will eventually materialize" ("(Un)natural bridges" 5).

I have agonized over the conclusion to this introduction. Perhaps this agony is tied to my belief that although Gloria Anzaldúa (the embodied historic person) is no longer alive, Gloria Anzaldúa (the writer/theorist/philosopher/poet) lives on and, indeed, grows—in her published works, in her future publications, in her readers' hearts, minds, actions, words, and ideas. This is not a conclusion; it's another beginning of sorts. As Gloria wrote in the 1983 preface to *This Bridge*, "Caminante, no hay puentes, se hace puentes al andar. *(Voyager, there are no bridges, one builds them as one walks)*" (n.p.).

Gloria's unexpected departure challenges us to reflect on our own visions for social change. As the following chapters demonstrate, her words give us healing narratives and invite us to create radical visions for transformation.

Notes

Thanks to Gloria Anzaldúa and Carrie McMaster for comments on earlier versions of this introduction. Portions of this introduction were published in revised form in *Women's Review of Books*.

1. Anzaldúa summarizes this process and its effects in "now let us shift": "In nepantla you are exposed, open to other perspectives, more readily able to access knowledge derived from inner feelings, imaginal states, and outer events, and to 'see through' them with a mindful, holistic awareness. Seeing through human acts both individual and collective allows you to examine the ways you construct knowledge, identity, and reality, and explore how some of your/others' constructions violate other people's ways of knowing and living" (544).
2. In "now let us shift" Anzaldúa refers to these relational approaches as "connectionist": "When perpetual conflict erodes a sense of connectedness and wholeness la nepantlera calls on the 'connectionist' faculty to show the deep common ground and interwoven kinship among all things and people. This faculty, one of less-structured thoughts, less-rigid categorizations, and thinner

boundaries, allows us to picture—via reverie, dreaming, and artistic creativity—similarities instead of solid divisions" (567–68). As this description indicates, the connectionist approach can be extremely useful during times of fragmentation. When we view conflicts from this connectionist perspective, we try to look beneath surface judgments, rigid labels, and other divisive ways of thinking. We seek commonalities and move toward healing: "Where before we saw only separateness, differences, and polarities, our connectionist sense of spirit recognizes nurturance and reciprocity and encourages alliances among groups working to transform communities" (568).

3. Leela Fernandes makes a similar point in her discussion of *Borderlands*, "while Anzaldúa's work has been used variously as a representative text of Latina women, women of color and Third World women, the depth of Anzaldúa's critical vision has often been lost in this identity-based deployment. . . . In fact, Anzaldúa's work represents a remarkable political, historical, and biographical representation which disrupts all oppositions between the material and the spiritual worlds" (41).
4. For example, Teresa Martinez describes Anzaldúa's theory of mestiza consciousness as "perhaps the culmination of her work, a bequest to the multiple faces and voices in the 'borderlands'." While I agree that Anzaldúa's theory of mestiza consciousness is of great importance, to describe it as the *highpoint* of her career automatically dismisses Anzaldúa's post-1987 writings.
5. See Caren Neile's essay in this book for a discussion of Anzaldúa's course at Florida Atlantic University.
6. To date, Anzaldúa's most extensive published discussion of these terms can be found in section five of "now let us shift," aptly titled "*putting Coyolxauhqui together. . . . new personal and collective stories.*" For an example of one form autohistoria takes in Anzaldúa's recent work, see "Putting Coyolxauhqui Together," an essay Anzaldúa describes as a meditation on "autohistoria and theory" (e-mail communication 7/2/02).
7. The majority of Anzaldúa's *Prieta* stories have not yet been published, but for early examples see "People Should Not Die in June in South Texas" and "El Paisano is a bird of good omen." Anzaldúa discusses her *Prieta* works-in-progress throughout *Interviews/Entrevistas*.
8. See for instance "Putting Coyolxauhqui Together," "now let us shift," and *Interviews/Entrevistas*.
9. As Anzaldúa explains in "now let us shift," "you revise the scripts of your various identities, and use these new narratives to intervene in the cultures' existing dehumanizing stories" (559).
10. At times Anzaldúa associates nepantla with identity-related issues. For instance, in a 1994 interview she describes it as a "birthing stage where you feel like you're reconfiguring your identity and don't know where you are. You used to be this person but now maybe you're different in some way. You're changing worlds and cultures and maybe classes, sexual preferences" (*Interviews/Entrevistas* 225–26). At other times, she associates nepantla with the mind's creative faculty. In "Putting Coyolxauhqui Together" she describes nepantla as her "symbol for the transitional process, both conscious and unconscious, that

bridges different kinds of activities by moving between and among different parts of the brain. The work of nepantla is a mysterious type of dreaming or perception which registers the workings of all states of consciousness. Shaman-like nepantla moves from rational to visionary states, from logics to poetics, from focused to unfocused perception, from inner to outer world" (252).

11. In "Putting Coyolxauhqui Together" Anzaldúa describes nepantla as her "symbol for the transitional process, both conscious and unconscious, that bridges different kinds of activities by moving between and among different parts of the brain. The work of nepantla is a mysterious type of dreaming or perception which registers the workings of all states of consciousness" (252).
12. Nepantleras are "boundary-crossers, thresholders who initiate others in rites of passage, activistas who, form a listening, receptive, spiritual stance, rise to their own visions and shift into acting them out, haciendo mundo nuevo (introducing change)" ("now let us shift" 571).
13. My pun here is intentional; I use it to underscore the fully embodied nature of Anzaldúa's theory of conocimiento.

Part 1

autohistoria y autohistoria-teoría. . . .
(re)writing self, (re)writing culture

Like an aching tooth, you suck on the problem of how to embody the story. Which genre—memoir, personal essay, or a combination? Memoir is a difficult genre. It's harder to manipulate the raw material of your own life than it is the details of an invented story. The problem is how to distinguish between you, the actual writer, and you, the narrative persona. The problem is how to improvise the self you create as you compose, and how to make that self immediate and alive without falling into self-indulgence, sentimentality, or grandstanding. The problem is deciding which chunks of your inner struggle and pain to cannibalize and incorporate into the text.

—Gloria E. Anzaldúa, "Putting Coyolxauhqui Together: A Creative Process"

Chapter 1

Gloria y yo: Writing silence and the search for the *fronteriza* voice

Zulma Y. Méndez

Es curioso: there wouldn't be you and me without Gloria. Not that our encounter depended on her. We were meant to be together since the beginning. Is just how I found you—or how you found me—and how you grabbed me—or I grabbed you—that has everything to do with her and more. It is just that one day this bridge called puentelibre made sense to me and I loved you. One day I understood the letters of your name and ever since then frontera is on my back. And I've been to places—aquí y allá—and I've seen people—nosotros y ellos—and I've heard languages—español e inglés—but there is something between you and I, and us and them that matters most: alta tensión.

Gloria querida, estás ahí y ni siquiera nos conoces. You are a reference. In our story your presence is felt and I guess we needed you to help us understand. To help us see how necessary we were to each other. To understand that we were meant to be together. To find out who we were and what would we become while being. Yet, I wonder if you had foreseen the power of your words and their potential for travel across those bridges you helped create. Acá estamos: Juárez y yo. And from this border te saludamos, Gloria Anzaldúa.

We know Gloria. We know of her travels, her comings and goings, her crossings back and forth. We know she's a border woman del otro lado: texana-mexicana y maricona. Ni de aquí ni de allá: "A veces no soy nada ni nadie pero hasta cuando no lo soy, lo soy." Like ours, hers is la tierra de nadie. And it could be that we are nobody but she helped us see how in being nadie we are somebody, and we are together, and our nadieness keeps us together, and together we are somebody, we are Juárez y yo, we are frontera.

We perceive Gloria. We know she has seen the waters of the Rio Bravo. We know of her battles and her battlefields. We know of her nepantla and it reminds us of our own: "yo soy un Puente tendido / del mundo gabacho al del mojado, / lo pasado me estirá pa' tras / y lo presente pa' delante, / Que la Virgen de Guadalupe me cuide / Ay ay ay, soy mexicana de este lado." Gloria, you like us, us like you: Sí, somos hijas de la chingada. We are from here, we are from there. We belong to no one. We choose to claim the here and there, este y el otro lado: no one's land, la tierra de nadie.

Not you sold out your people Gloria but they sold you. Is that why me and Juárez are not well at ease with each other anymore? Is that why I invoke you Gloria? Because there is something in frontera's abandonment that I fear. Something about our nadieness that's threatening. Something about the fissures in the herida abierta we inhabit that leaves us open. Is that why we have been betrayed? Something about our daily deaths feels like we are disposable. And as of today, there are more than 280 of us who have been killed in Juárez. I want to write ciudad y no puedo. Juárez, I can barely spell your name now. Te siento un poco lejos.

Eres la atravezada Gloria, the prohibited, the forbidden. So are we. And I know you warned us: Do not enter, trespassers will be raped, maimed, strangled, gassed, shot. But with no remedy we are tráfagas and we are on transit. You told us that "to survive the Borderlands / you must live sin fronteras / be a crossroads," but we are disappearing. Frontera is getting back at us and I no longer know how to be with Juárez. It's become such a stranger. Its houses are so empty that it depresses me to walk its streets. That's why we've abandoned it. Se esta llenando de polvo. And that dust is blurring my sight. We no longer own it. We no longer claim it. Haz vuelto a ser tierra de nadie.

I know you picked up and left Gloria. I did the same too. But you are a turtle, wherever you go you carry "home" on your back. Is that what I need to do too? Carrying frontera on my back isn't easy anymore. How do you do it Gloria? Being a bridge allows people to step over us. A veces quiero quemar puentes, burn bridges.

Gloria, I was twenty when you were making face, when you were making soul and now at thirty estoy haciendo caras. We've affirmed our existence through your making of soul and faces. And now, we are looking differently. We are unearthing the words that will help us tell our stories, bring us cara a cara with our own historias. Gracias, Gloria.

Acá estamos: Juárez y yo todavía, and from here we are making sense, haciendo sentido. Even though I often ask if there is any sense to sin sentido? Is there sentido to this nonsense? There are absences between us that Gloria's words can't reach anymore. And both of us know that we'll have to cross her bridges and find the words.

Chapter 2

The 1,001-Piece Nights of Gloria Anzaldúa: Autohistoria-teoría at Florida Atlantic University

Caren S. Neile

> [T]o me [Coyolxauhqui's story] is a symbol not only of violence and hatred of women but also of how we're split body and mind, spirit and soul. We're separated. . . . [W]hen you take a person and divide her up, you disempower her. She's no longer a threat. My whole struggle in writing, in this anticolonial struggle, has been to . . . put us back together again. To connect up the body with the soul and the mind with the spirit. That's why for me there's such a link between the text and the body, between textuality and sexuality, between the body and the spirit.
>
> —Gloria E. Anzaldúa, *Interviews/Entrevistas*

Hey there, Gloria, you've done it already:
First night of class,
And you're breaking records.
The room teems with bodies,
In addition to the usual brains.
We've never seen anything like it.
        It's a rock concert ticket line;
        It's an Early Bird Special;
                a tag sale;
                a mob scene;
It's students wanting to bask in a little of that
Chicana-lesbian-feminist-writer-activist-teacher
Star Power.

Some of us actually concentrate (major) in the concentration (major) for which your course is listed. Some of us are actually enrolled in the Ph.D. Comparative Studies program that invited you to teach here at Florida Atlantic University in Boca Raton. (It is an interdisciplinary Humanities degree with an emphasis on social action.) Some of us have actually registered.

That makes some of us privileged, ironic for a class led by a professor who is anti-privilege, non-Platinum card, who would like to have us all stay, really, were it not for the number of papers you would have to mark. Were it not for the book you must finish.

In the catalogue, this class is listed as "Creativeness, Writing and Action." This is an indignity, one of many you have suffered. You called it "Conocimiento . . . inner work, public acts." The university has usurped your power to name.

> I don't want to teach in a university, except for a special class, then only one. Universities can subvert you.
>
> (*Interviews/Entrevistas* 68)

It's a clear case of nos versus otras, but because you hate administrative nonsense almost as much as zero-sum games, an hour passes before you sort out those who can stay. The losers slink off, peaceably. You listen for the click of the door behind them.

stage 1: el arrebato—the rupture

> *When the aesthetic and the intellectual collide, wonderful things can happen.*
>
> —Lynne Bentley-Kemp[1]

And that's when it begins, when the outsiders are safely out, the insiders tucked within. You light a sacred candle and incense. Chants curl from the boom box at your feet. According to your instruction, we relax our muscles, imagine that we are fastened to the planet's core with roots that emerge from deep within us and extend down, down through one floor, two floors, and thousands of miles of earth. You tell us that through these roots we derive energy from the earth's central fire. We are so mellow, some of us actually melt on the floor like the wax in your candle.

After a time, we manage to congeal enough to begin our first free-writing assignment. To show our commitment, we must each pull out a body part and place it in the middle of the room.

You would never ask us to do what you would not do yourself. You reach into your chest, deep inside the funky red T-shirt, and rip out your heart. Cup it in two hands, blood slipping through your fingers like Merlot. You place the pulsing organ on the altar of the seminar table. One by one, we follow your lead. Someone contributes a brain. Another lobs off her breasts, left, then right.

I finger my uterus, swollen to the size of a football, long past the point when it should have come out, signifying, I have read, blocked creativity, money worries, sexual astigmatism. My uterus is an essay on my career, how imprisoned I am, how I feel stuffed into a glass-sided box, how nothing I ever do is quite good enough. As I grab hold, the thing lurches inside me, a sign, perhaps, that there is life in it still. I hesitate.

> *Much of the time, language is a struggle. Words contain so much magic—are magic—shaping and shifting reality and possibility with every breath, every stroke of pen or keyboard.*
>
> —Ceti Boundy

You tell me my reaction is normal, but that I should not be afraid to reach within. You explain that writing is an all-encompassing activity that is not entered into lightly. Before writing, you have been known to "pace your breathing to the doleful sounds of the foghorn . . . walk along the coast of Monterrey Bay toward the lighthouse and its beckoning light" ("Putting Coyolxauhqui Together" 241). Writing involves listening to falling rain. Assessing your situation and planning your strategy. Being realistic about your precarious health. Gestating. Estevating.[2] Enervating. The body is wiped out in its marathon race to the finish line. You tell me that "[t]o bring into being something that does not exist in the world, a sacrifice will be required of you, sacrifice means to make holy" ("Putting Coyolxauhqui Together" 242).

I have studied or taught college creative writing for ten of the last twenty-five years, in three universities. I have made my living as a writer and teacher for twenty. But I have never seen anything like this. A spiritual approach to writing? Academic writing teaches a trade, not a calling, because we are part of a system that emphasizes results over process, publish over parish (pun intended), goals over gods.

> Spirituality has nothing to do with religion . . . spirituality begins with and is rooted in the body. . . . spirituality and being spiritual means being aware of the interconnectedness between things. . . . Spirituality is oppressed people's only weapon and means of protection. Changes in society only come after the spiritual. (Keating, "Risking the Personal" 8–11)

So our guts are splayed out on the floor, and it's nearly 10 p.m. We are spent, and we have gotten more than our money's worth. But you are not through with us. For your finale, you pick up your ballpoint and slash yourself into 1,001 pieces, like your signature Aztec myth of Coatlicue's daughter Coyolxauhqui. The woman who was such a threat to one of her 400 brothers, Huitzilopochtli, that he cut off her head. Chopped up her body. Buried the pieces in different places.

In keeping with your philosophy, you simultaneously hand us text, body, mind, and spirit. You do not distinguish between knowledge of the head or of the heart in your writing. Why should you do so in your teaching?

As we watch, slack-jawed, you distribute pieces of yourself to each student, in the form of gold flecks, grains of sugar sand, star dust. The seminar table shudders with sparkles and ink. With what we come to recognize as lifeblood.

stage 2: nepantla—torn between ways

These are the photographs
lying in their undeveloped potential
in the camera, flashes of life.

—Rose-Marie Donovan

Coyolxauhqui was disempowered by her disintegration. But you are like the moon that is rekindled each month. The next week, you are back, burning more brightly than before. You light on our shoulders during free writing, whisper in our ears when we are stuck for words.

Tonight, you divide us into three groups of four-to-six people, dubbing us comadres, whose task it is to co-mother our work. The groups choose the names the Good Sisters (including our single male), Flow, and Four Comadres. We will meet once a week outside of class to discuss our work. I already know two of the four women with whom I have joined forces in Flow. We have named ourselves after the sociologist Czikszentmihalyi's concept of work-as-play.

Your syllabus is divided by the seven stages of what you call *conocimiento*, as is this essay: "alternate ways of knowing that synthesize reflection with action to create subversive knowledge systems that challenge the status quo" (Keating, "Risking the Personal" 5). Our class goals are to "explore how we create identity, reality, consciousness, story and myth. Consider the relationship of artistic processes to the realms of imagination, personal myth, dream, spiritual practice, activism, and social transformation" (Anzaldúa, Syllabus).

You introduce our primary assignment: autohistoria-teoría. Your own genre, it is a fusion of fact and fantasy, poetry and prose, theory and memoir. Three books will help us create it: Tristine Rainer's *Your Life As Story*, your *Interviews/Entrevistas*, and *Borderlands/La Frontera*. We will also be showered with additional readings.

We have five assignments: the seven-to-twelve page autohistoria, as well as smaller pieces about our desconocimientos (the Beast that drags us down), our relationship to nature, our writing process, and our spiritual vision. We are also expected to keep journals documenting our progress and our life history. In them, we are to practice our instrument. But the autohistoria is the raison d'etre, our Holy Grail. Student eyes meet across the table. Sounds like a lot of work.

You give us a handout on reading and critiquing; it is five pages long and contains fifteen steps. We are expected to read our comadres' work four times in order to evaluate it properly. At the end of the semester, we will present a public reading of work we have revised in these groups. No one seems particularly excited at this prospect.

I hear a lot of Spanish in class. In fact, I am beginning to drown in the unfamiliar language. This is what you call code-shifting, conflating languages, letting the unfamiliar tongue (to most students) wash over us, seep into our pores until we capture its meaning on a cellular, soul-ular, level. All at once I have an idea of what it must be like to work in Miami with colleagues who do not bother to speak English. At first I feel threatened. Then it occurs to me that I am lost the way non-English speakers are lost in this country, and I relax. It helps that I am sitting next to a beautiful Colombian woman who translates what I do not understand.

Besides, drowning has recently become a natural state for me. After two decades of writing in various media, I never quite hit. But since the semester has started, my career has begun to take off. I was not careful what I wished for, and what I wished for has begun to come true: the proposals accepted, the jobs offered, the articles published. I think of a line from Beckett: "I felt more at home with [failure], having breathed of its vivifying air all my writing life."

I, on the other hand, find lately that I cannot breathe at all. I am too anxious to know if I am happy. Late at night, the Beast paws the sheets. It is, I know, a vital part of life, representing the dark side, the sexual, the animal in Nature. But all I experience is the terror it provokes. When it wakes me, I write in the journal, to get, at least, a jump on my schoolwork.

I hope to catch myself unaware, hope to forget that I am afraid to rethink my life.

stage 3: coatlicue/desconocimiento—the cost of knowing

The dog doesn't love you and neither do I.

—Jane S. Day

The division of the comadres has an unforeseen effect: The class is splitting into cliques, with very little support across the lines. Students listen less and less to our fellows across the table. Jokes and comments are whispered to best friends. We do not hear the sound of hearts breaking above the chatter, but the cracks are evident in the way some of us walk, or sit, or turn, or fall silent, or do not smile.

You give us a work-in-progress of your own on conocimiento to evaluate. Some return it to you well-marked with comments; others feel too awkward about criticizing the professor's work. When you hand back these papers is the only time we see you visibly displeased at our timidity.

To not see is to be in desconocimiento. (*Interviews/Entrevistas* 177)

What's more, your health is not good. You have written and spoken extensively of your body's self-sabotage, the bleeding at three months of age, the debilitating diabetes. You bring fruit to class and pour water down your throat, but you are a Santa Cruz rose starting to wither in the Florida sauna. You have found some health food stores and are eating okay, but not exercising enough. You work too hard on your book. You rarely sleep.

My career's sudden surge also keeps me up nights, wide-eyed and shaking. Once, after finally drifting off to sleep, I wake up breathless at 5 a.m. to find the Beast on my chest. This is no joke; this is the first time in my experience with anxiety that I have fought it in the flesh. A dragon balances on my chest. I jump out of bed, pace a little, and the thing skulks off.

Next day I mention this to you. Well-versed in battling beasts of your own, you get right to the point, asking, "Who is it?"

He is, I recognize at once, the man who has given me the greatest opportunity. I am terrified by all I've taken on: three classes, teaching, my job, his massive project.

stage 4: the call for transformation (discovering your personal myth)

I wish that I did not have to tell your story in order to tell mine, but we are entertwined.

—Diana Sinisterra

We write a short short narrative (prose or poetry) in a class period. Your instructions begin:

Take a significant experience or situation from the list below:

—death of a family member
—when I discovered my true self
—when she discovered her true vocation
—suffering through a grave illness
—when I fell in love
—when we broke up
—the day I started my period
—when I/she left home
—when I/she split with my family/family members

I do not write easily about myself, so I choose something a little less threatening from your list of "writing take-offs." I choose ". . . until the chicken is done." My piece begins: "Noon on a Tuesday, papers to mark, calls to make; can't do a thing, can't do a thing until the chicken is done." The subject is my need to please my husband as a somewhat traditional (chicken-cooking) wife, even though he doesn't expect or particularly want me to play that role. I warm to the topic, read the thing out loud to the class.

We move on to the autohistoria exercises: "Picture a movie screen in your mind's eye. Allow memories to surface. See your life as though a movie you are watching. See yourself as a character in it. Watch the cycle of events of your life unroll before you." The next step of the process is to summarize our lives, running over the different periods until we can divide them into sections of four or five areas, like major divisions of a book. Then we pinpoint specific incidents, internal or otherwise, and list them under each section. We identify the turning points. Continue fleshing out, fleshing out. Choose one of the early events, project it on the screen, and note people, things, sensual perceptions, emotions, intuitive reactions.

Now we take one event that we have thought through in this way and write about it, perhaps as a story, a poem, or creative prose. We are to reread it, revise, solicit feedback from comadres, perhaps tape ourselves reading it, revise, revise, put it away, pick up another. Repeat, until we have an entire book.

I continue to wrestle the Beast, trying to navigate the rapids of my life and compose my autohistoria. At four, 5 a.m., I tackle the reading assignments. In *Your Life As Story*, I learn that we need to replace the old stories with the new, that even Joseph Campbell acknowledges that the old myths don't work for us anymore; we must create our own. I learn that story structure "pushes you past the circular logic of impairment because it requires you to move forward to a climactic realization in order to give the story a meaningful conclusion" (Rainer 15).

I begin to feel, sifting through these scenes of my life, that we do not so much write as read our lives. Not authors, not yet, but neither are we quite passive observers.

> Inferior writing comes from working only on the surface, easy formula and plots. (*Interviews/Entrevistas* 240)

I snuffle around my childhood like an old dog, but it eludes me like a kitten. Can't see/hear/feel/taste/smell the details. Astonished at how honest you are in writing about your body, your desires, your family. Often these nights, I find myself wondering: How can anyone be so open in public? How can anyone be so open in private? How can anyone be so open to herself?

Flow helps a lot. The group is wonderful, five women of different ages and backgrounds who seem to genuinely care for and support each other. We sit under a tree on campus, in a health food store cafeteria, on a member's front porch. We are nurturing. We listen. We are gentle. We are honest. We share food. We accommodate schedules. We gossip. We are everything a writing group should be.

One day, for a class assignment, I consider my personal myth. A fairy tale of the younger daughter, loved but not as respected as the firstborn, who goes out to make her way in the world and is never quite good enough. Until, perhaps, now. Could this be why I am in such pain? Perhaps the myth has reached its climax, when the heroine is transformed, impaling her insecurities on the final plot point.

stage 5: el compromiso/the commitment—the crossing and conversion

We have luscious green trees,
'n' dancing bees
right here for your pleasure.

—Judith Castro

As a class outing, we meet one Thursday morning at a museum/preserve across from the beach. Ill after a bad night, your body stays behind, but your spirit hitches a ride in with the clouds. None of us is unduly impressed with the place. The humming of the air conditioner unit, the cigarette butts blended with dried leaves underfoot, the conversations of the passersby all serve to undercut the pastoral scene we had anticipated. Still, Flow attempts to write.

I compose a confession of how far I have strayed from the Nature I once loved so deeply. Days later, I realize that the piece seems to have unhinged something in me, and I find myself starting the autohistoria. It simply comes, an overnight sensation slaved over half a semester, in the form of a jigsaw puzzle, snapshots of my early life. Can't show what I am working on to anyone outside the class. Will never publish it; don't have your courage. But I am getting it out, pulling forth those pieces of myself and putting them on the seminar table at last. Because I feel no shame in front of you.

stage 6: putting coyolxauhqui together—creating new personal/collective stories

Age signals a life lived—lived well if you've put the effort into it.

—Anita Kirchen

I read to the class a charged, erotic piece I dash off during free writing about the first time I tasted mango. Another woman recites an essay about her breasts. A Flow-mate shares a tormented mother–daughter scene, ca. 1986. We students are working on relating to each other better. More importantly, we are working. Some of us pour out 1,001 pieces a night. Others focus on the minutiae of finely wrought poems, intricate and fragile as spider webs. We are using, all of us, a side of our brain we use in no other class. You keep busy, alternately writing and sprinkling us with your stardust. My autohistoria is growing. I am sleeping better. I am beginning to fit my skin.

stage 7: spiritual activism

There are no clouds in the sky or in my car. I made it to the finish line. I breathe out. She is safe for now.

—Staci Weiner

Must be a hundred people in the Board of Regents room the evening of our public reading. Dressed in dramatic red and black, we clash with the green decor, yet still manage to look smashing. For the first time all semester we are in synch, this class, and we move through our paces unrehearsed, without flaw. Two students have bound our class writings and distribute them among us. I catch sight of you, beaming.

At the reception you are swallowed by admirers. We students migrate to the corners of the room, speaking of you:

> *—I'm glad I took her class; her soul is important. She is not of this world. It's good for us to see someone on the path she's supposed to be on, to see her specialness.*
>
> *—My writing has become more sincere; this class has allowed me to tap into sincerity. I wrote about things I never would have, concentrating within, looking at how a slice of life can illuminate larger issues.*
>
> *—Gloria is not imprisoned by ego. She has given me the practice and courage to trust that I can speak from a place that is honest.*
>
> *—It's liberating to combine fantasy and theory. This was one of the best classes I ever took.*
>
> *—Gloria confirmed where I want to be as a teacher. I'm not about structure, either; it's confirmed my desire to allow in other voices.*
>
> *—Gloria taught me that her seemingly smooth blend of autohistoria and theory was, in fact, an intellectual labor of crushing complexity. Her deep regard for the human spirit, in all its manifestations, and recognition of life experience as part of that spirit, brought me closer to acceptance of myself and my work.*

After the reception, you shepherd us back inside to say good-bye. We all receive an A, but on a few, you bestow an A+, worthless to the registrar, but diamonds to us.

Our last free-writing assignment was a prayer. At the time I couldn't think of one, but now it flows easily:

> Mira, Gloria,
> Your class has changed us forever.
> Yet we still miss more chances to create than we can count,
> More opportunities to save the world than sand at the shore.
> We do not ask your forgiveness,
> because you would say there is nothing to forgive.
> We do not praise you for doing better than we,
> because you shrug off praise.
> So we pray:
> Please remember your stay with us,
> And let it help you in some small way.

Know that you have friends here who think of you often
Who strive to nurture the pieces you left behind.

Contigos.

Notes

1. My epigraphs come from the writings of Anzaldúa's students at Florida Atlantic University, Boca Raton, Spring 2001. I gratefully acknowledge all those who gave me permission to use their work.
2. "Estevating" means spending the summer.

Chapter 3

Reclaiming Pleasure: Reading the Body in "People Should Not Die in June in South Texas"

Mary Loving Blanchard

I remember the exact moment I learned to read. The memory is a photograph in my mind. In the photograph, my eyes are squeezed tight, I am smiling so profoundly that my face is a toothy beacon of rapture, and I am fiercely clasping a picture book to my chest. My parents also share this memory. At family gatherings, they discuss the moment represented in the photograph of my mind. My mother recalls that I was three years old, and that the experience marked the beginning of my habit of sleeping with books. She reports that she would discover the books in the morning when she came to rouse me from bed. Sometimes the books would be underneath the covers; at other times they would be perched atop a pillow; still other times would find me snuggled up with one or more of them as some children snuggled with teddy bears or dolls. My father recalls that the photographic memory was taken the day I learned that the words underneath the pictures were another way of describing the image on the page. I recall the moment as the day that I discovered the pleasure of reading. I recall the moment as the day the book talked back.[1]

Later, reading confused me. In grade school, I was hushed when I voiced my suspicion that something was going on in my textbook beyond that to which my teacher had alerted me. Whispers came from the pages, tiny voices that spoke in half note. I know now that what confused me was not reading, but the way I was being taught to read. For the first time, I learned to view the text as something mysterious, a mythical manifestation that required special skills if I was to decipher its meaning. If I wanted to read, I must learn those skills. It was silly to think that the book would talk to me. This was school, and the books here did not talk.

And, of course, reading is something mysterious; reading creates a place between the worlds of reality and fiction where the reader might work out the differences for herself. And reading is also value-laden. No reader comes to the page empty. Even as I argue here against a theoretical framework that locates reading for pleasure and reading with critical attention as polar activities, I am not proposing a value-free reading, simply a reading that imposes a different set of values. In every event, the values a reader brings to the page effect meaning in a text. However, readers are taught that the text exists in some pristine, value-free condition. In this condition, the text requires use of a special device to reveal its meaning; this device, or theoretical grid, has been predetermined by some Great Reader. In order to approach the page, readers must "impose [this] theoretical grid" and read "coercively" (Lionnet 28). We are taught that we must use this device to render the text pliable to our touch. Reading becomes a violation in which readers force themselves upon a text that is unwilling to receive them. However, were we taught to read "noncoercively . . . allow[ing] . . . self to be interwoven with the discursive stands of the text, to engage in a form of intercourse," then we would come to understand that every text is in dialogue with every other text, and it is texts talking to the reader and to each other that makes a tradition (Lionnet 28). For both reading and writing are organic activities, and the exchange between reader and text transforms both. Reading must transform, else the reader has succumbed to a theoretical grid which precludes a "reading/hearing that is a form of absolute receptivity" and engages instead in a reading that does not, can not, allow the reader to be spoken into existence (Lionnet 283). If the book does not talk back to the reader, it is because the reader has not learned to listen.

As an early reader, I did not have a name for the level of confusion I felt in the classroom. Knowing nothing of theoretical grids, Great Readers, or my place in the scheme of things, I read for escapism and enjoyment. Reading permitted me both to find and lose myself.[2] I read voraciously. Coming to the text as voyeur, I peeped in on the doings of characters created by writers I stumbled upon or who were suggested to me by other readers. My appetite was not sated by the superficial; rather, I drank deeply from the pen of Anais Nin, D. H. Lawrence, and others who understood the pleasure, the passion inherent both to reading and to writing. While I owned no framework by which to classify my engagement with reading, neither did I question that reading was a physical act, an engagement both constrained and set free by the body—constrained by the body's many limitations: its susceptibility to disease, its unfulfilled yearnings; set free when the body devoted its every impulse to uncovering that *thing* which would live independent of the text that gave it life. Reading enlivened me; therefore it must itself be a living thing, and if that were so, then the text too must be alive, changing with each caress of a reader's hand. Of course, my elation at this stage came before I read another Great Reader's ideas about dead authors. Since that time, I have surmised that in order for the text to live, the author must die, and be reborn with each new reading.

Later in my reading, I was directed toward that rarefied section of the canon occupied by those great, dead, white, and male: masters essential to a firm foundation in my growth as a reader. I could always read again for pleasure. Later. This direction was my introduction to one name for the theoretical dichotomy between reading with critical attention (reading as an intellectually-stimulating exercise) and reading for pleasure (reading that displaces a reader's critical engagement). This dichotomy imposes an either/or theoretical grid on any act of reading. Either the process is for pleasure—use Grid Z23—or the process is to gain critical awareness—use Grid 2B.

Perhaps I am guilty of overanalysis here, but I think you get the point. If not: for the most part, readers are taught to read by presupposing a text that has to be subdued. We are not told that there are other ways to enter a text or that we can invent new ways. We are not taught that reading is "the quest for the self, for the center of the self" or that reading may help us to "reconcile [the] other within us" (Anzaldúa, "Speaking" 169). We do not learn that reading is a way we readers "shock [ourselves] into new ways of perceiving the world" and ourselves (172). Teachers of reading seem to opt instead to reinforce that there is one way to read a text. What is more, a Great Reader who knows more than us ordinary, everyday readers has predetermined this one way. Ordinary, everyday readers that we are, we are not to attempt to read into the text outside the parameters of a predetermined way of reading else we risk being labeled a Misreader.

And I was so labeled. For many years, I was accused of simply not getting *it* when I read. The *it* I did not get was the same *it* everyone else immediately grasped. The same *it* some Great Reader had left for this new and inexperienced reader to ease my transition from fantasy to fact. In college, professors and classmates chuckled kindly when I insisted that there was something hiding beneath the surface of a poem that everyone in the room agreed was merely surface.[3] By this time, however, I had learned to relax and enjoy my status as a Great Misreader. I took to the task as though it were a mission. I tried to recruit others. Luckily, texts by Harold Bloom, Audre Lorde, Sor Juana Inés de la Cruz, Phillis Wheatley, and Alexander Pope came to my rescue. Not only did I continue to misread, but I also accomplished it with aplomb, calling on tools used by Great Readers the world over to read familiar texts in unfamiliar ways.

But theoretical grids, you must understand, are creatures of some duration. They have enjoyed positions of power and influence, and as everyone knows, such positions are hard to come by and once attained are not readily relinquished. Theoretical grids do not easily give up their place in tradition-making. Thus, later readings served to reinforce my earlier reading experiences. Indeed, the extent to which teachers of reading relied—knowingly or unknowingly—on these grids in their profession was made clear to me upon introduction to Roland Barthes. In "Roland Barthes versus Received Ideas" the author explains that he is not a "great reader" because "either the book excites me and I keep interrupting my reading to muse or reflect on what it says, or else it bores me, and I abandon it shamelessly. Of course, I do sometimes read avidly, even gluttonously . . . but this is reading outside of work . . . The reason for this is simple: in order to read, if not voluptuously, at least 'greedily,' there must be no attendant critical responsibility" (189). Obviously my reading teachers were fans of Barthes, for like Barthes, my teachers' instruction suggested to me that stimulating reading, as witnessed by a reader's greedy consumption of a text, interrupts that reader's critical engagement with the text and further disengages her from that text at the same time that it requires her critical attention. Indeed, Barthes's argument posits reading for pleasure as a premise founded on contradiction.[4] Barthes's argument caused me equal measures of elation and confusion. On one hand Barthes distances himself from predetermined ways of engaging a text and with the other hand embraces those predetermined ways. Despite his waffling on the subject, however, Barthes does suggest a connection between reading and writing that intrigues me: he suggests that readers and writers are inextricably intertwined. The pleasure a reader gains from a text results in large part from the writer's commitment to the page. Indeed, readers and writers are engaged in a mutual, intimate exchange, for reading is "absolutely dependent on a theory of writing: to read a text is to discover—on a corporeal, not a conscious level—*how it was written*, to invest oneself in the production" (189).

To gain pleasure from reading, the reader must have a stake in what the writer risks in making. The reader must be willing to see herself manifested in the writer's attempts. The reader's stake in the writer's work makes demands of her: she must listen, critically, and thereby come to an understanding of the writer's motivation to risk being misunderstood, or bruised, or both. Or more. The reader must risk hearing her secrets, her sins, her regrets and wishes shouted from the page. Still, without the writer's risk, the reader may not be compelled to listen to the half notes written between the lines. Thus, to compel the reader's risk, the author must be invested in her making beyond theory, for "whenever it's the *body* that writes, and not ideology, there's a chance the text will join us in our modernity. . . . Writing is in the hand, and thus the body: its impulses, controlling mechanisms, rhythms, weights, glides, complications, flights—not the *soul*" ("Roland Barthes" 191, 193, his italics).

Writing is a physical activity, an activity, if its intent is to give the reader pleasure, that must place both writer and reader in the middle of things: in the middle of grief and in the middle of joy. Barthes's ideas about reading and writing not only validate my investment in misreading but also echo Anzaldúa's ideas about reading, writing, and risk. In "Speaking in Tongues" she writes "The danger in writing is not fusing our personal experience and world view with the social reality we live in, with our inner life, our history, our economics and our vision. . . . We must use what is important to us to get to the writing . . . The danger is in being too universal . . . and [in] invoking the eternal to the sacrifice of the particular" (170). For the reader to gain pleasure she must see herself revealed within the text; indeed, if the reader is to gain pleasure from reading, she must commit to an exchange with the text in which her peculiarities are lain bare: her exchange with the text cannot be superficial; she must brave not only entering the text but also having the text enter her. A reader who abhors risk, who fears self-revelation, will never hear a text speak. A reader who eschews the particular in favor of the universal will only discover a speechless, inanimate text.

Oddly enough, it was Barthes's investment in writing, his compulsion to uncover what the writer cloaks, to peek behind the mask language constructs to "lose (or keep) everything" that prepared me for Luce Irigaray's ideas about reading, pleasure, and the female body (104). Not since Nin and company had I engaged a writer who so carefully attended the erogenic connection between writers and readers, a connection in which their bodies are exposed, their strengths, sins, and vulnerabilities revealed. Thus, it was with these ideas of pleasure, risk, and their relationship both to writing and reading that I approached my first reading of Gloria Anzaldúa's short story, "People Should Not Die in June in South Texas."

I selected this story in part because my family is from Texas. Although I am more familiar with the piney boughs of east Texas than with las fronteras in the state's south, I know from firsthand experience that it's as hot as embers all over Texas by June. Given my knowledge of Texas summer, the idea of getting dressed in a black dress and blacker hose to attend a funeral in one of those non air-conditioned one-room churches in east Texas is enough for me to imagine the absurd, a quality often found in satire. I have a keen appreciation of satire, and from Anzaldúa's title I assumed she risked censure by her community for writing a hyperbolic exposé of growing up Chicana.

With what I supposed to be Anzaldúa's risk now clear to me, I settled back against the pillows in my bed, a cold drink nearby, without a pencil—this was a venture into pleasure, after all. By the second paragraph, I put down the book and went in search of a pencil and a pad of sticky notes. (I could not write in the book; it belonged to the library. The sticky notes, containing my musings and reflections as I engaged the text, are pieces of the body that live separate from the whole, recalling it, giving me pleasure long after I have returned the book to its owner and before my personal copy of the collection arrives.)

Anzaldúa's work is short, a mere seven-and-one-half pages. Yet within these few pages, she risks so much more than simple censure and requires so much more of her reader than a cursory engagement. Indeed, Anzaldúa requires that her reader move beyond any fear—of rejection, of being thought vain, or naïve—to risk peeping behind the writer's mask, to risk the receipt of pleasure vis-à-vis critical and studied engagement.

In a note to AnaLouise Keating during her work editing *Interviews/Entrevistas*, Anzaldúa advises Keating to "put yourself and your body in my setting . . . talk about how you physically sense my presence" (11). Indeed Anzaldúa's presence in "People Should Not Die in June in South Texas" is clear to the reader who risks perceiving the personal as both political and theoretical. Such risk invites the reader to come to understand stimulating reading as an act not separate or distinct from critical reading.

Given Anzaldúa's obvious and intentional use of the personal as grounding elements of this narrative, a reader might be compelled to read the piece as entirely autobiographical. However, while the short story is not satire, neither is it merely autobiographical. The narrative is a coming-of-age story that details the protagonist's evolution from girl to woman, an evolution compelled by her father's death.

That the narrative uses elements of the personal will not surprise faithful readers of Anzaldúa's work. In another dialogue from *Interviews/Entrevistas* Anzaldúa notes that "I've never been a third person. I've always been me, the first person, so I don't know what it's like to be a third person. I can't write from that experience" (223); writing from the third person point of view "put[s] me in the margins." Anzaldúa subverts this displacement by "dislocating [her]self from [her]self" to construct an alter ego, Prieta/Prietita, whom she authorizes to relate "autobiographical experience" (223). In this narrative, Prieta/Prietita not only relates Anzaldúa's personal story of loss but also makes that personal story relevant to her reader's experience. Anzaldúa is sensitive to her reader's need to see self: from the opening sentence in which readers are located in the activity surrounding the funeral, Anzaldúa uses language to conceal and reveal the protagonist's realization of self, and to invite her reader into Prieta's inner world. Prieta's movement toward self-realization takes place in the dual realities both she and her reader occupy, realities once occupied by the author herself. Prieta's realities are immediately familiar to a reader who has experienced loss and growth.

One reality is revealed in Prietita's engagement among the living, and is familiar, known. In this reality, the protagonist is a child. The familiar reality is contrasted against an unfamiliar reality, marked primarily by Prieta's forced movement from child to woman. These realities—the familiar and the unfamiliar—are demarcated by Anzaldúa's use of Spanish and English and demarcated yet again by the form of the protagonist's name.

The spelling of Prieta's name shifts between the diminutive (Prietita) and the non-diminutive (Prieta) throughout the story. Anzaldúa explains that "La *Prieta* stories are part fiction and part autohistorias" consisting of "autobiography that's fictionalized, . . . parts of my life which are true but which I embellish with fiction" (*Interviews/Entrevistas* 243). Although Anzaldúa acknowledges the mixture of fact with fiction, the reader who pays attention to the author's careful attention to naming is able not only to observe Prieta's movement but also to determine which reality the protagonist occupies at the time of her observation. Still, fact and fiction bleed into each other, and become blurred to the point that a reader must carefully engage if she is to receive the full measure of pleasure with which Anzaldúa has written this narrative.

"People Should not Die in June in South Texas" is Prieta's story. However, although readers learn that Prieta's mother is twenty-eight when her husband dies from a ruptured artery as he returns from loading cotton bales, we do not know Prieta's age. We know from Anzaldúa's interview with Linda Smuckler that her father died when her mother was twenty-eight, an event that stoked "a rage I'd buried, an anger" (*Interviews/Entrevistas* 67). But readers do not know if the protagonist is seven or ten or sixteen when her father dies; we know only that "Es la mayor y se parece mucho a su mamá" (28). The reader is decentered by the narrator's omission of this small fact. She is left unable to determine, chronologically, when Prieta's movement begins. While Prieta can fix the start of the process as the time of her father's death, she is no less decentered by the event. Thus, this tale of becoming also details Prieta's movement away from a reality that has shifted, leaving her without direction and toward a new reality that will find her in control of her life's direction.

Additionally, readers do not observe firsthand Prieta's efforts to re/locate herself. We come to this knowledge through an omniscient narrator. Irigaray argues that "In her statements—at least when she dares to speak out—woman retouches herself constantly" (103). Again, the personal and fictional aspects have become intertwined. Anzaldúa describes self in this narrative by admitting to the denial of her own voice. She has described her writer's voice as "the voice I most treasure" and as a voice that was "repressed" (*Interviews/Entrevistas* 61). In this narrative, she acknowledges the repression of that voice by not allowing Prieta to speak out. Thus, in not permitting Prieta to speak out, both Anzaldúa and her protagonist are "turned back" within themselves, fixed in a place where they think about an existence that is "nothing . . . Everything" (Irigaray 103). Still readers should make no mistake: Despite, or perhaps because of the blurring of fiction and fact, "People Should Not Die in June in South Texas" is a consciously crafted story. Anzaldúa has intentionally silenced Prieta, for the protagonist's lack of voice distances her from the reader and gives her an uncluttered space in which to re/discover her voice. The story's many shifts and moves locate the reader as a benevolent voyeur: We are able to peek in on the girl's grief, noting it as a process by which we may observe her movement from child to woman, without otherwise disturbing or altering the process.

In this way, Anzaldúa writes as Barthes argues she must—with impulse, weight, and complication. In so writing, she compels her reader to read in like manner. The reader must pay attention to the nuances Anzaldúa pencils into language; she must note too the density of simple sentences, as well as tense shifts and instances of naming. In these ways Anzaldúa writes the realities of Prieta's world(s) into the protagonist's body. And in these ways Anzaldúa re/writes the realities of her own private grief. What is more, both Anzaldúa and Prieta risk erasure of all their realities in this shared movement toward individuation.

In Prieta's familiar reality, she attends to duties as the eldest daughter of the man to whom mourners have come to pay their last respect. In this reality, Prieta is the frugal daughter, somewhat detached from the event as she contemplates financial and other restrictions her father's death has brought. The narrator reports that at the funeral, Prieta stands "for hours watching relatives and friends one after the other approach the coffin" (280). The protagonist is turned within herself, having already begun, even if subconsciously, to hear an "other meaning" (Irigaray 103). Anzaldúa's own inward turn, her own acknowledgment of an other meaning came "[a]s [she] grew older, [and] . . . put out that [she] was book smart but not smart at anything else" although she "always knew how to do any task in the shortest amount of time with the fewest number of movements" (*Interviews/Entrevistas* 84).

In this way, the adolescent Anzaldúa played a role similar to the role Prieta plays: both the fictional Prieta and the very real Anzaldúa act out assigned roles. Prieta is the eldest daughter of the man who has died and in that role she must be strong for her mother and her little brother even as her own grief threatens to devour her. As the daughter of farm workers,

Anzaldúa was not expected to be book smart, but she was. And being book smart, she was then thought to be lacking other, more critical skills required of the children of workers who tended the land of others. Anzaldúa embraced the restrictions placed on her ability to be both intellectually and physically to free herself from labor in the fields. She reports that she intentionally appeared "absentminded, forgetful" when she worked in the fields, confessing that "it was all a mask" (*Interviews/Entrevistas* 84). A mask constructed to position and protect her body during labor in the cotton fields. A mask constructed to free her body from labor and reward it with the pleasure of books. Thus Anzaldúa's inward turn was toward the pleasure she discovered in reading; the narrator notes Prieta's inward turn as beginning when she questions her mother's choice of suit and coffin for her father's burial: " 'Why are we buying such an expensive suit? It doesn't even have a back. And besides, it's going to rot soon.' . . . Her mother looked at her and burst out crying again. . . . Prieta had to swallow her own tears" (281). However, immediately after readers observe Prieta "forced to be the more practical of the two" we witness as "her body trembled with fury. How dare he die? How dare he abandon her? . . . It wasn't fair" (281).

Prieta's body rejects her practicality. Although Prieta remains speechless, remains other in herself, readers learn from her body's language that she is physically split between two selves and that these two selves are at odds. The narrator comments on many such instances of Prieta's engagement within this duality. In the scene describing the morning of Prieta's father's funeral, for example, Prieta "rises from her bed vacant-eyed, puts on her black blouse and skirt and black scarf, and walks to the living room. She stands before the coffin and waits for the hearse" (282).

Prieta is vacant-eyed because her familiar reality has gone off in all directions; language, by which she orders her realities, by which she gives voice to those realities, has also "wandered too far from . . . nearness" (Irigaray 103). For as the narrative nears its end, Anzaldúa writes less in Spanish—Prieta's native tongue—and more in English—the tongue of the adult Prieta is becoming. Prieta is leaving behind the child who speaks in the language of her parents and moving toward individuation via adoption of another tongue. However, although Prieta is vacant-eyed, she is nonetheless able to attend to her duties systematically, as if prompted by something outside herself. Prieta has mechanized self, and in so doing is free to conduct a search for a familiar place from which she might "set out again from another point of pleasure or pain" (Irigaray 103).

Prieta's search for nearness compels her to de/evolve. As she watches her mother sit up with the body prior to the funeral, the familiar and the unfamiliar realities merge. The protagonist is once child, then adult. The narrator notes this movement from child to adult and back again: "For three days her father sleeps in his coffin. Her mother sits at his side every night and never sleeps. Oliendo a muerte, Prietita duerme en su cama, Prieta sleeps in her bed with the smell of death. En sus sueños, in her dreams, su padre abre los ojos al mirarla, her father opens his eyes. Abre su boca a contestarle, he opens his mouth to answer her. Se levanta del cajón, he rises out of the coffin" (282). In Spanish, Prietita is a child, her name once again in diminutive form. In English, she is an adult who sleeps with the memory of her life before her father's death. It is the adult Prieta, having accepted that tragedy can strike without warning, who identifies with women mourners as they "follow the coffin with faces hidden under fine-woven mantillas, the women all look like urracas prietas, like black crows. Her own nickname was Urraca Prieta" (283).

The women, Prieta included, are symbolic harbingers of the new beginning that death heralds. In the tradition of the heroic myth, Prieta has traveled to an underworld from which she now emerges. Her identification with the women moves the child squarely into adulthood even as she attempts to travel back into the underworld, "backwards to yesterday, to the day before yesterday, to the day she last saw her father" (283).

Later in the narration, a fly signals Prieta's return to adulthood by forcing her from her underworld retreat into the present: "As she watches her father, a scream forms in her head. 'No, no, no.' She thinks she almost sees death creep into her father's unconscious body, kick out his soul and make his body stiff and still. She sees la muerte's long pale fingers take possession of her father—sees death place its hands over what had been her father's heart. A fly buzzes by, brings her back to the present" (284).

In the story's final pages, Prieta completes her movement into adulthood; this movement is signaled by the merging of her realities, and by the merging of her two bodies—child and adult—into one. In this final stage, the adult Prieta spends "Every evening [waiting] for her father to walk into the house tired after a day of hard work in the fields. . . . For years she waited. Four years she waits for him . . . But one day, four years after his death, she knows that neither the One God nor her father will ever walk through her door again" (286, 287). Prieta has accepted the finality of her father's death and with that acceptance has moved forward, living fully in the adult body she now owns. While her acceptance of death may suggest that she has given up on God, Prieta's sentiment may also be read as the protagonist's final act to merge all the realities of her world(s). Her acceptance of death also marks her return from the underworld. This return acknowledges Prieta's achievement of individuation, her act of self re/discovery. Anzaldúa describes her own hysterectomy as personal re/discoveries: "I saw it as a lesson; the body has to speak . . . I couldn't keep this woman locked up in the basement any more . . . It was like my body was acting out [to protest] the suppression of women for two thousand years" (*Interviews/ Entrevistas* 66). And not unlike Anzaldúa, Prieta's re/discovery of self speaks her into being.

Irigaray observes that "a woman's (re)discovery of herself can only signify the possibility of not sacrificing any of her pleasures to another, of not identifying with anyone in particular, of never being simply one. It is a sort of universe in expansion for which no limits could be fixed and which for all that, would not be incoherency" (104). Thus, Prieta's re/discovery results in a new knowing; a new whole is produced from the two ragged realities she previously occupied. She has arrived at the point where she can "enjoy her pleasure as a woman," dependent neither on man nor God (105).

Anzaldúa, in removing her writer's mask, has risked revealing her own dependencies—on emotional engagement, on the pleasure she finds in reading/writing—to theorize the personal and create a fictional work. Her efforts do not make this work less fictional or more autobiographical: there is no single theory that can, or should, codify rules of reading/writing. Indeed, such a theory would have to be kept in an airtight box, where writers and readers alike could wish only to gaze upon it in awe. The most objective theory is made subjective, is turned within itself, once it comes into contact with the writer, with the reader.

Sometimes it is preferable to arrive late to a place, rather than not at all, especially when your arrival completes a journey you have been on all your life without knowing you had actually left the place where once you were. Now that I have (re)discovered the pleasure of reading, I should not be a bit surprised were I to begin sleeping with books. Again.

Notes

1. Certainly I am not the first reader to examine the idea of a talking text. In *The Signifying Monkey*, Henry Louis Gates describes "the trope of the Talking Book" as originally appearing in James Albert Ukawsaw Gronniosaw's first edition of *A Narrative of the Most Remarkable Particulars in the Life of James Albert Ukawsaw Gronniosaw, An African Prince, As Related by Himself* (136). Gates reports that because his master's book refused to talk to him, Gronniosaw's "desire for recognition of his self in the text of Western letters motivates [his] creation of a text . . . that speaks his face into existence" (137, 138). Gates's discussion of Bakhtinian ideas about how any text by any author may employ palimpsest to write one voice over another reveals a verbal exchange between reader and text and reinforces the premise of a talking text that echoes the voice of its reader.
2. I echo the sentiments of Anzaldúa, who argues that she writes because "writing saves me from this complacency I fear. . . . Because the world I create in . . . writing

compensates me for what the real world does not give me. . . . I write because life does not appease my appetites and hunger. I write to record what others erase when I speak" ("Speaking in Tongues" 168, 169). Reading fulfills me in much the same way that writing fulfills me; in both instances, I "discover myself . . . preserve myself . . . convince myself that I am worthy" (169).

3. I am thinking in particular about Phillis Wheatley's 1773 poem, "On being brought from AFRICA to AMERICA." I first read the poem when I was twelve years old. At that time, I disagreed with the interpretation put forth by Great Readers of the period, and was promptly hushed. Some twenty years later, I was still disagreeing with the idea that Wheatley's work was imitative, her craft insubstantial. This time, however, I could not be hushed.
4. Barthes has also observed that he "reads very little"—perhaps because he views reading as the less important element in any reading/writing equation. His confession made me suspicious of his theory of reading. How could he speak to a process in which he does not engage? What empirical evidence will he call on to support his notion that reading for pleasure and reading for critical awareness were mutually exclusive, and when would he share it with this reader?

Chapter 4

Daughter of Coatlicue: An Interview with Gloria Anzaldúa

Irene Lara

introduction

Among the first Chicana writers to recover and rewrite Mexican histories and Mexica goddess figures from a feminist, decolonial perspective, Gloria Anzaldúa is what I call a "daughter of Coatlicue." Coatlicue is the Mexica earth mother goddess of creation and destruction. In patriarchal Mexica mythhistory, Coatlicue's daughter is named Coyolxauhqui, the Mexica warrior goddess dismembered by her brother Huitzilopochtli, the God of War, and banished to the sky as the moon. According to several feminist interpreters, this story marks a shift in Mexica history from a gynecentric to androcentric ordering of life and the simultaneous divestment of female power. Given the additional context of Spanish colonialism that from its inception negatively constructed Mexica culture, Coatlicue, Coyolxauhqui, and other indigenous sacred figures were also demonized and fragmented. Spanish chroniclers, for example, described Coatlicue as an "old hag" and a satanic "idol." Engagement with Coatlicue's physically dismembered daughter, therefore, marks the desire to suture the wounds inflicted by patriarchy and eurocentrism. "My whole struggle in writing," says Anzaldúa, "has been to put us back together again. To connect up the body with the soul and the mind with the spirit" (*Interviews/Entrevistas* 220). Indeed, literary critic AnaLouise Keating describes Anzaldúa as "a modern-day Coyolxauhqui, a writer-warrior who employs language to 'put us back together again' " ("Risking the Personal" 12). In this interview, which was conducted with

Anzaldúa in her home in Santa Cruz, California on July 25, 2001, Gloria elaborates on her ideas about culture, identity, spirituality, healing, and social change from a decolonizing, feminist perspective.

theorizing identities: new tribalism, nos/otras, mestizaje, latina

GEA: New tribalism is a kind of mestizaje. Instead of somebody making you a hybrid without your control, you can choose. You can choose a little Buddhism, a little assertiveness, individuality, some Mexican views of the spirit world, something from blacks, something from Asians. I use the image of an orange tree, like an árbol de la vida, to illustrate. Some kinds have a very strong root and trunk system but don't put out as much of the fruit, so you graft them together to get a variety with better oranges.

I'm struggling with new labels. I don't like the word "Latina" because it privileges Spain and the white part, and completely erases the indigenous. Umbrella terms like "Hispanic" or "Latino" erase some of the smaller Latino cultures and Mexican culture, which is the biggest of all U.S. Latino groups. When you erase the Mexican, you erase the Mexica, the india in us. I was seeking a new label and came up with "mestiza consciousness," but it didn't go over well. I wanted a substitute for the divisions between people of color in this country. When Cherríe Moraga and I were doing *This Bridge Called My Back* we decided to use "people of color" as a generic term to show our solidarity with blacks and others. But now the term doesn't work because many people of color have white mindsets, and a lot of whites have people-of-color consciousness. When I do my gigs I ask my audience, young people like yourselves: "Can you come up with a term?" It's no longer the work of us, the "foremothers," "forerunners," whatever you think of the older generation.

IL: Las veteranas. Las sabias.

GEA: Sí. We need a new tribalism. We need a different way of shuffling the categories. As long as we rely on language, we'll have categories even though they're very limiting and imprisoning. Every few years we should blur the boundaries, make them porous. If we reshuffle all the categories, can we come up with new identity markers, new ways of composing members of different groups into new groups? I've come up with "new tribalism" y allí estoy. I'm stuck. [laughter] Every so many years I add a little bit, extend the categories, pero I don't think the problem will ever be solved because life transforms all the time, so of course categories only work for so long.

IL: How are the ways you describe your identities different from your description in *Borderlands*?

GEA: I realized that it wasn't enough for me to be just Chicana, just a dyke, just a woman of color, just a writer. Everything is intertwined. Even though *Bridge* spoke of the experiences of women of color, that label also limited the range of perception because you were locked into your cultural group. You were locked into the idea that you belonged to a "minority." If you identified yourself as a victim of racism, economic deprivation, sexism, todo eso, that identity itself limited you. But because the inequality was so blatant, you really had to stand behind your ethnic label in order to motivate people to fight for social justice and equality. Otherwise there would be no unity among women of color and we couldn't make inroads into social transformation. So we were stuck with being "Chicana" or "black" or "Asian" or "Native," lo que sea, by the very nature of "us" versus "them."

As time went by and las "otras" ("us") partook more of the dominant culture—in terms of education and better living wages—the us/them boundary became less rigid. There's still a division between the haves and have-nots, the rich and the poor, but in the last twenty, thirty years or so, the women-of-color movement has enabled people like us to go to the university, get teaching credentials, go to med school, tú sabes? We have some of whites' privileges and whites have acquired some of our otherness; so then I started thinking of us as "nos/otras" with a slash in the middle. The whole struggle of our movement for social change has been to take that little slash off so we're all in it together. Right now and for many, many more years that separation will exist, but we can start envisioning what it would be like without those separations. With "nos/otras" we recognize commonalities, the humanness in the other. As long as you're entrenched in a counterstance of "us against them" you are locked in! You have to remove yourself, get others to remove themselves, and then look at the situation and say, "This is the mess we've made living in the U.S. and living in the world. How can we learn to live together? What tools, what strategies, can we use?"

path of conocimiento

I call the strategy I've been developing "conocimiento,"[1] symbolized as la mano zurda. I started with "El Mundo Zurdo" in *This Bridge*, but now la mano zurda tiene ojos y orejas, symbolizing that when you look at the other don't just look at what's on the outward surface, but really look inside; when you hear the other, really hear what they're saying beyond their spoken words. I have a transparency I show during my talks (see figure 4.1). It has a mouth and la boca tiene una lengua y la puntita de la lengua es una plumita pa' escribir, so you communicate with your mouth. Communication, the dialogue, is the whole purpose of getting to know each other's points of view and working with people who are so different from us—our so-called enemies—to solve societal problems of inequality, violence against women, violence against the environment, y todo eso. When you reach out for the "other," you reach out una mano con corazón. I have another transparency I show (see figure 4.2). I got this idea from my mom when me dió un milagrito with la mano con un corazón adentro. It's an entirely feeling heart because feelings—anger, bitterness, y todo eso—can overwhelm you, but it's a mindful heart like what Buddhists advocate about being attentive and aware: un corazón con razón. When you reach out to another person you're using your brain as well as your feelings.

"Conocimiento" is just a good old-fashioned word that means knowledge, or learning, or lo que conoces. When you're about to change, when something in your life is transforming itself, you get this "Ahá! So this is what it's about." That to me is conocimiento.

IL: So it's a moment of suddenly just knowing?

GEA: Yes, but this "just knowing" is a consequence of specific experiences. Many of my realizations have come from confrontations with my critical illness and the many complications and pains it's caused me. I've had some realizations about the body, about western medicine, about the mind/body/spirit split. Often these realizations come out of what I call "el arrebato," the first stage of conocimiento, when something jerks you out of your normal, everyday activity self. Maybe you get divorced, maybe you lose your job, maybe you get sick, maybe your dad dies. Con ese arrebato, you realize certain things: that you're getting older, that you're going to die soon, or that this person you're married to is not your forever true love, o lo que sea. It's quite a shock, but it gives you insights if you're attentive to it.

Of course the first thing it does is to put you in between your old story of who you were and the new story of who you're becoming. Te pone en nepantla, a transitional space. This shock puts you in a third stage, what I call "the Coatlicue state" in *Borderlands*. During this stage you deny everything, you repress things: you don't want to think that your girlfriend is in love with someone else or that you've got this chronic illness or lo que sea, so you go into depression. While you're in this darkness underneath todo lo que está pasando, your unconscious is processing it. This is where Coyolxauhqui comes in. Ella es la luna and she lights the darkness, verdad? Okay, so

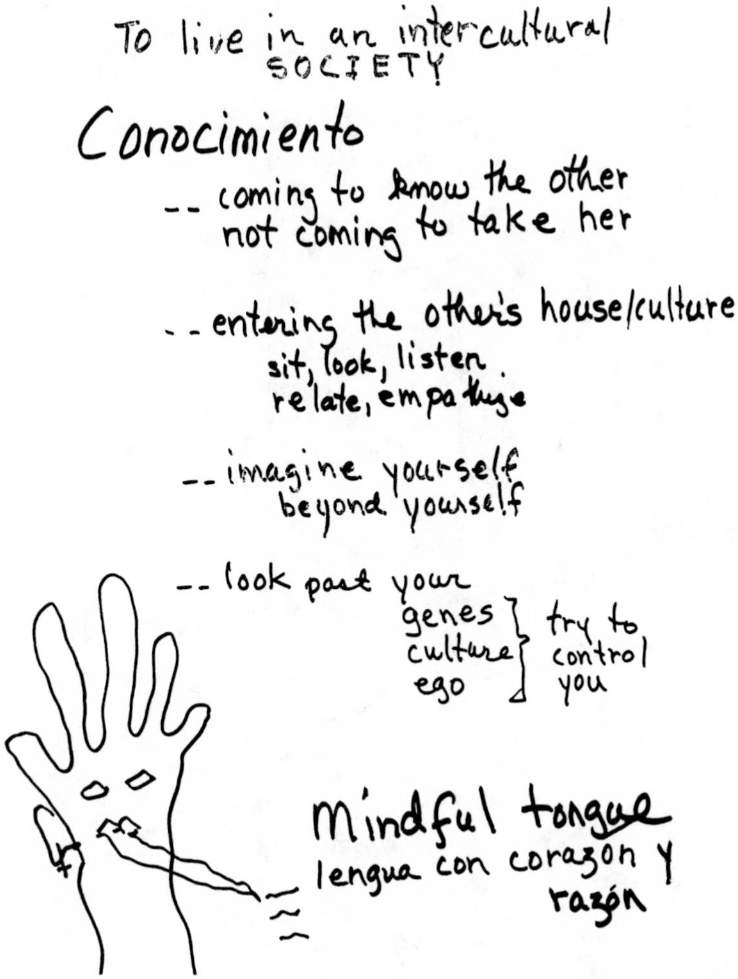

To live in an intercultural
SOCIETY

Conocimiento

-- coming to know the other
not coming to take her

-- entering the other's house/culture
sit, look, listen
relate, empathize

-- imagine yourself
beyond yourself

-- look past your
genes
culture
ego
} try to control you

Mindful tongue
lengua con corazon y
razón

Figure 4.1

you're in this dark night of the soul and you get these intuitions, these conocimientos—whatever your being works out unconsciously, it comes to some realizations. I call this process "Coyolxauhqui consciousness." It's not a consciousness of the awake world, of the sun, of the light. It's a consciousness of the darkness, the underworld, the depression. This kind of consciousness is not even noticed by people. You have a problem, you go to sleep, and the next day you've solved it. But who solved it? Or how? It's your

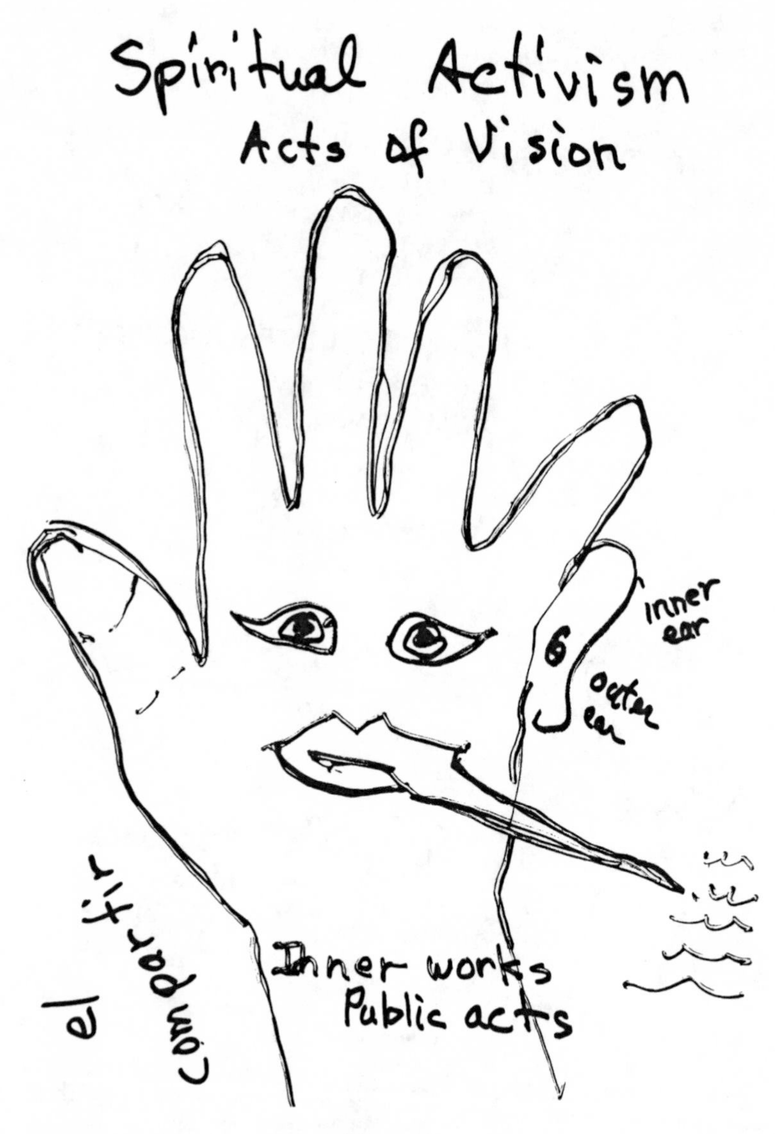

Figure 4.2

Coyolxauhqui consciousness working! For me, Coyolxauhqui consciousness is very much tied up with the subconscious, the unconscious, the collective unconscious, and even the collective consciousness, the consciousness of all the people in the world.

Here you are in the dark and something pulls you out, algo te llama: you have to change, you have to take care of your health, you have to find a new lover, you have to find a new job, lo que sea. You have to act, you have to move, and it moves you out of there. I call this fourth stage the call for transformation, the call to cross over to another space, to convert. You have your doubts, you retreat, you go forward, you retreat. Estás en nepantla because between all the different stages is also nepantla. You have to compose a new script for yourself, a new story. You used to be a mexicana, but now you're in the United States, you're in grad school and lo que tu familia creé y como te creáron, it's not enough. Now you have this other culture added on through your education, you're exposed to different ideas, you want something different for yourself than what your mom got. You have a different dream, skills, facultades so you start scripting this new you, this new identity. I call this stage "putting Coyolxauhqui together" porque 'stas en pedazos, verdad? The old way doesn't work anymore, your ideas don't work anymore so you have to arrange esos pedazos in a new order. You're not only putting the old self back together again, but in the recomposition, you're creating a new self. You have a new story.

You take your new story out into the world, and some of it clashes with other people's reality. You're in conflict with your best friend, your lover, white people, western culture, lo que sea. So the idea you had of conocimiento—opening up your heart and really listening to them when they're slapping you on the face and verbally abusing you—your theories aren't panning out, you have to rewrite them otra vez.

YV:[2] This is a very vulnerable stage. I think it can be very scary. I remember, Irene, when you told me about when you were at the National Ford Fellows Conference in 2000 . . .

IL: Yes, at the plenary Q&A I was addressing about 300 Fellows and a Chicano professor who had spoken about using our tremendous "brain power" to be revolutionary scholars of color. I commented on the need to go beyond the power of our minds and also examine the role of our spirits in forging social change. To ignore spirit reinscribes a false split between political activism and spirituality which can limit social change. Indeed, validating, nurturing, and learning how to use all of our facultades—our bodymindspirit—will help us be revolutionary. Although I was shaking before and while I was speaking, I felt that I was being called to intervene by bringing the powerful role of spirituality into the conversation. The response was disappointing; the speaker just said, "Next question please." I felt as if my contribution wasn't worthy of engagement. Now, I think that perhaps he simply did not know how to respond. On my way out, to top it off, another Latino scholar came up to me and said, "That was rather self-indulgent of you."

GEA: Condescending.

IL: Very condescending. It felt very silencing, like he was telling me that I shouldn't talk about these things. Like others before me who raise similar concerns in academic and/or activist spaces, I was confronted with the assumption that to do so is "self-indulgent," further splitting the personal from the political, as if the two are not deeply interconnected.

GEA: The first conference where I really got panned for my spirituality was in '81—at the National Women's Studies Conference, in Connecticut—when *Bridge* came out. Cherríe Moraga, Barbara Smith, Mirtha Quintanales . . . about five or six of us were on stage telling people the situation with women of color and what changes we needed. And here I go and speak about spirituality; everybody on stage and in the audience was horrified. Ever since then, I'd push at that issue. It's tiring; even when they don't openly disagree there's this energy that says, "You're not fighting for human rights. You're not fighting for civil rights . . . The spirit is not basic to our struggle." If you speak out like that too often, your body takes it on. I'm convinced that part of the reason I came down with diabetes is exhaustion from those situations.

At another NWSA conference—in Akron, Ohio, in '90,—there was a big blowup between women of color and white women, and the women of color walked out. I felt caught in the middle: I wanted to side with my sisters of color, but I didn't want to wall myself off from the people who were supposed to be our enemies. At that time I started thinking about nepantla, and I coined this word, "nepantleras," for those of us caught in the middle. Some were not people of color, like one of my co-presenters, Irena Klepfisz, a holocaust survivor. She felt caught between the whites and the women of color because she identified a lot with the women of color but she passes for white. There were white working-class women who identified more with us than with white middle-class women. Some of us who were caught in the middle remained. I was introducing *Haciendo Caras* at the conference. I'd set up a roundtable, but some of the contributors had walked out and only a few of us remained. Nepantleras are caught between cultures. You don't totally identify or sympathize with just one side, but can see the others' point of view. So that became the seventh stage of conocimiento.

In the seventh stage las nepantleras (the people who are on the bridge, who bridge these different opposing groups) act as mediators, people who can help you cross the bridge to the other side and help the other side cross to your side. I call these people nepantleras because they're so used to living in this transitional space of change. In this stage you figure out how you can talk to each other, how you can work toward a common goal, what the ground rules might be. There's no such thing as one leader. We're all working it out together. Nepantla and spiritual activism build on ideas presented in "Bridge, Drawbridge, Sandbar or Island." All my work is sort of tied together. It's kind of hard to discuss because tiene muchos layers. When I'm describing this little layer over here, there are all these acá. To interweave them together and come up with a cohesive cloth takes a lot of work because you're not just dealing with one topic.

healing work

IL: Since you consider your work to be socially healing, transformative work, will you elaborate on what conocimientos you are healing, such as worldviews that are racist and propose only one way of knowing in the world?

GEA: Yes, I see them as wounds. Coyolxauhqui and putting herself, *our*self, together is about healing the wounds, the work of striving for wholeness instead of being fragmented in little pieces. It's also the work of reparation. Not just healing, but having the wounds acknowledged publicly, having the other parties say, "We did this wrong, we acknowledge it, forgive us." It's about bringing that acknowledgment not just into consciousness but also into public words. If you're a white person you can say, "Yeah, my ancestors were responsible for slavery or exterminating many indigenous tribes." But if you don't publicly acknowledge and make reparations, it doesn't have much meaning. In some ways these are wounds to your psyche, your intellect, your presence, to the fact that you're a woman. A lot of those wounds come from desconocimiento, the opposite of conocimiento, from playing ignorant and not attending to things because they're going to take too much energy. You'll feel bad, so "let's not look at racism; it's somebody else's problem." It's not the seven deadly sins we struggle against; it's the little desconocimientos, the little ignorances, the little acts of indifference, apathy, the little acts of unkindness, los desconocimientos chiquitos. Together they are a huge desconocimiento. I think racism, sexism, child abuse, and violences against women stem from selective perception. For example, if you're male you're entitled to your comfort and if that means you have to hit your wife because she criticizes you then that's okay. It's kind of like selective reality: you select certain things that fit (what makes you comfortable); everything else deserves to be kicked.

In one of my transparencies I talk about forbidden or unacknowledged forms of knowledge (see figure 4.3). The image is a treasure chest in the background and in the foreground is la Llorona, the coiled serpent, con la cara y cabeza de mujer. To me this image symbolizes indigenous knowing

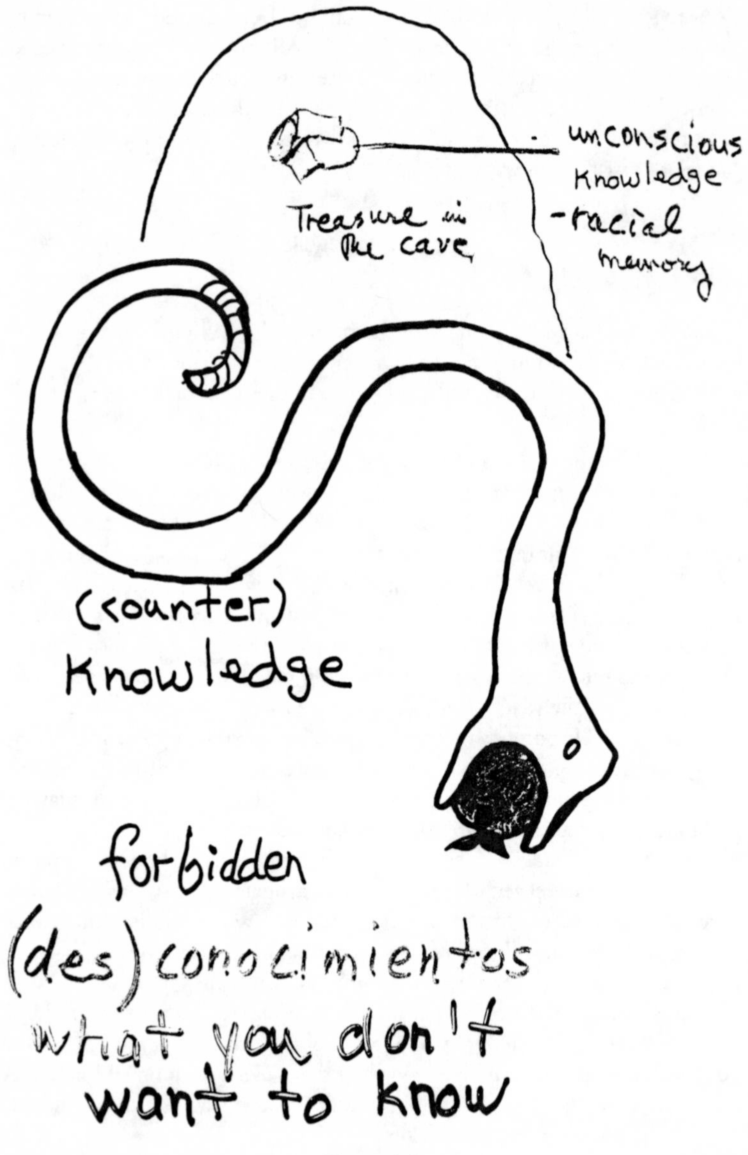
unconscious knowledge
-racial memory
Treasure in the cave
(counter) Knowledge
forbidden
(des)conocimientos
what you don't want to know

Figure 4.3

or the knowing of other nondominant cultures. That dominant culture—like the reception that you got from the Chicano scholar—would rather ignore these knowledges—condescend and say you're being too hysterical, you're a woman, what do feelings or the soul or your body have to do with academia? These knowledges you bring in with your body and your soul and your spiritual practice are not accepted.

desconocimientos and health

IL: How do you see the healing of desconocimientos tied to the concept of health? How do you define health?

GEA: I don't define health as the absence of disease, but as learning to live with disease, with dysfunction, with wounds, and working toward wholeness. If you're human you don't have a whole integrated body, being, soul, whatever, because of the traumas and difficult lessons we've gone through. Health also has to do with holism. You can't just heal your appendix; you have to look at your whole body, your mind, and your soul. They're all one. Since Descartes we've split them and view them as separate compartments, but they're interwoven. I believe in holistic alliances, holistic health where you consider the whole, not just the part. In that respect, taking it into spiritual activism, you don't only consider the best interest of your group, your organization, your race. You consider the best interest of the whole, which means white people, black people, *everybody*. This perspective makes me a "race traitor." That's how I felt at that NWSA conference. When you start thinking about holistic alliances you're stepping across barriers, gatekeepers to cultures that want to keep you out, and your own culture that wants to keep you out. You're given only two choices: assimilate completely or separate out completely.

The major paradigms for reality—the scientific paradigms, the democratic paradigms—were constructed by those in power. We need a new paradigm that comes partially from outside and partially from inside the dominant paradigm. Look at academic disciplines: Insiders lay down the rules, principles, and conventions of sociology, anthropology, English, creative writing, American studies, whatever. Thanks to the movement struggles, these disciplines are including some outsider points of view. One or two books in their syllabus, tú sabes? They're slowly rewriting their guides, their conventions.

We need to realize that the pictures of reality imposed on us can't be made only by those in power; they have to come from us tambíen. We need more people who can do philosophy, anthropology, composition studies . . . who can make changes in these disciplines. And I've seen the changes, gradually.

spirituality and sexuality: autohistoria, prietita stories, nagualismo, and "la naguala"

IL: You write a lot about the body, sexuality, and bridging the body and sexuality with spirit and spirituality. Will you discuss how you bridge these things in your everyday life, in your work practices, your writing?

GEA: Right now most of the writing around those concepts besides my "conocimiento" essay is the fiction, or what I call *autohistorias: historia* for history, the story of the self, and the story of the culture; *auto* for self. This pretty much takes care of memoir writing, autobiography, and fiction. The other half of autohistorias, *autohistoria-teorías*, brings theory into the personal anecdote. I'm working on a book of nineteen stories. I start with Prieta as a little girl, age five or six, on a merry-go-round; she's rubbing up and down on a wooden horse and she has an orgasm. The second story, "De Re-ojo/out of the corner of the eye," occurs when Prietita is in the woods. The third story, "En el osico del mar," is about a drowning experience. These are all autobiographical, but as I put in the details I've forgotten, it fictionalizes it. The next story is about my father's death and my whole confrontation with Catholicism and spirituality.

My whole interpretation of the world is more like a Toltec, nagualismo way of perception, which in some ways is dualistic so I'm trying to rewrite it and make it less dualistic. For the Toltecs, áca estába el mundo más alla, el mundo de los muertos, y acá estába el mundo de los vivos, and they were at odds. I'm rewriting that interpretation with my sense of how things work in the world. Instead of separate realities, they're levels: depending on what you've struggled with and what kinds of conocimientos you've come up with you're tuned to that level. Some people can look at reality from a more enlightened level, but when they get into an emotional trauma they'll go down to the very basic oppositional "us against them."

We all partake of multiple levels. A lot of the stories hit on this kind of Toltec interpretation, nagualismo. This is another concept of consciousness where you have the witness or the watcher: you're doing something, you're feeling something, and it's making you sense yourself experiencing this feeling. I've divided that watcher into two different faculties. One I call "la naguala": she or he or it is the faculty that makes spirit signs, watches for spirit signs, messages from nature, señales, símbolos. Some of my characters are naguales, people with a capacity to shift their perspective to that of an animal, shapeshift. I'm modernizing Mexican indigenous traditions. It's not easy to put into words; as I write it clarifies itself and works on a different level than me telling you all my ideas. On that level, I recreate scenes and feelings. It's working backward. Instead of working from the intellect, laying out certain theories, concepts, I'm working from the body and the feelings, experiencing these things; then the mind thinks, "Oh yeah, this is what happened" and gives it an explanation. Sometimes I like to work from the creative fiction aspect, and other times I like to do the theoretical. I think it just uses different parts of your psyche. I also have a novel I'm working on called *Chamana*; it's about a woman who is part naguala, part bruja, part hechicera, part curandera, yet she's had university training. I've got seven chapters lined out; the first few are very autobiographical, but I don't want to be limited to what happened in my life.

IL: How is the story where Prietita has an orgasm on the horse connected to the spiritual?

GEA: It's connected to energy, and energy is spiritual. "She Ate Horses," "The Werejaguar," and "La Luciernaga" ("The Firefly") are also about sexuality. I have one really dark Prieta story, "Urraca Prieta" ("Crow Prieta"), about sexuality and obsession. Then I have "Ms. Right, My True Love, My Soulmate." So I have some stores that show the desconocimiento and characteristics that you wouldn't associate with a feminist.

IL: How do you connect spirituality and sexuality with health? You also talk about remembering Coyolxauhqui in terms of health and holism. Do you connect all of these?

GEA: Yes. I think I probably do that better in some of my poems, like "Canción de la diosa de la noche," "Antigua, mi diosa," and "The Basque Witches." To me sexuality is creativity, symbolized by the kundalini serpent, when energy rises through your energetic body in terms of the chakras and you get this rush of feeling, eroticism, sexuality. For me, this is connected to creativity, writing, making art, and also to sexuality, the needs of your body, in terms of release. With an orgasm you release energy, you enable energy to flow through your body rather than being blocked, and creativity does that when you write a story or a book or whatever. It releases that energy to flow; it flows out to your life. Spirituality does the same thing. When I meditate, go for a walk, I can feel that energy. Creativity, sexuality, and spirituality are all rooted in the body, so it comes down to the body. The body grounds us to the earth. Everything goes through the body—ideas, feelings, energy. I don't know why people always separate them out, but to me, they're together. It's part of nagualismo where, when you dream, have an out-of-body experience, or your soul leaves your body, your physical body se queda but then this other body pulls up through the skin. In both the Prieta stories and the conocimiento essay I talk about out-of-body or near-death experiences. The body is not just minerals, chemicals, bones, and skin; you also have the dream body. My concept of consciousness, my sense of myself, no se para at my skin; it extends outward, and if it extends then it also mingles with your consciousness, las de las flores, la del mar, la de los animales . . . Consciousness is not local.

This is not just my idea although I've had this idea for a long time. Modern science is only beginning to investigate consciousness, hope, prayer, intention, y todas esas cosas. Consciousness is in everything even though the level of consciousness varies. The consciousness of a flower is not like my consciousness or the consciousness of a dog, yet chimpanzees, monkeys, dogs, have a personal consciousness, an autobiographical consciousness. I took this term from Antonio Damasio's discussions of "core consciousness," "autobiographical consciousness," and "extended consciousness." To me, extended consciousness is conocimiento, but I didn't know these guys were working on the same ideas.

IL: I'm exploring a related question in my research: how having this conocimiento about the connections between the body or sexuality and spirit impacts the ways that we are in the world and the ways we see ourselves, how it can help heal those wounds you've been speaking about.

GEA: Uh-hmm. I think I'd be much worse off if I wasn't conscious of those connections. I often ignore them; I feel self-pity and I think "Why do I have to deal with this?" and "Ay, pobrecita de mi," you know—whining and complaining, but when I'm at my best I do see the connection.

IL: Why do you think we've been taught not to connect those things? Why is this integration a threat to dominant society?

GEA: It would challenge their way of life, their system, their power. They're invested in keeping their self-respect, their privilege. So of course they feel threatened.

healing the wounds of colonialism

IL: How do you think colonialism of the Américas affected or even still affects Latina practices and ideas about the body, mind, and spirit—that connection?

GEA: That act of invasion is a trauma, a wound which the whole country has not recovered from or attended to; it keeps bleeding in the psyches of

Mexicans, Latinos, Blacks, Asians . . . all the different peoples who have been exploited. Dominant society has this great denial: these atrocities belong to people who are dead. This is the major trauma that this country is suffering under, but it's un desconocimiento, they're not acknowledging it. We, in our bodies, feel this trauma every day. It's like a repetition of the invasion, the genocide, the exploitation of nature. It's a major wounding on many levels, including a colonization on our minds and consciousnesses. They're still exploiting our energy. Our chief resource is our energy, what we're attentive to. If you have to be attentive to tomato plants twelve hours a day, or cleaning a white person's house, or working in a factory, wherever your attention is placed, you're giving that energy to these other people. When you use your energy to do your own thing, to take care of your own agenda, that's when you're free. But as long as you're putting your attention on somebody else's agenda, they're exploiting you. Most of us are caught up with survival. Because we place a lot of our attention on all the hurts, the racism, the discrimination, we can't focus on resolving the problem, looking toward the future and enacting our vision. They keep us busy fighting each other. But it's not just indigenous and people of color who are in a struggle against neocolonialism, it's white people too. We're all struggling for the autonomy to do what we want with our lives, to give our energy where we want to give it.

My symbol for la herida de colonialism and the trauma of the conquest is la Llorona. Sometimes I feel a deep grief for indigenous people, for the earth, for whatever has been wounded, and I feel like crying. So that brings to mind la Llorona because she's wailing for the lost children, for her own woundedness. Sometimes I see that as my depression. There are different kinds of depression: the regular depression that a lot of people suffer from and then the one caused by illness, such as the one I've been dealing with for months because diabetes causes a fluctuation of the blood sugar in the body. But then there's another depression that I sometimes pick up on that's everywhere. It's like being in grief, collective bereavement because of this big wound.

Notes

1. Anzaldúa elaborates on all of the stages of conocimiento in her essay "now let us shift . . . the path of conocimiento . . . inner work, public acts."
2. Yolanda Venegas, a colleague, who attended this interview.

Chapter 5

Living in the House of Nepantla

Irene Reti

Nepantla becomes the place you live in most of the time—home.

—*Gloria Anzaldúa, "(Un)natural bridges"*

The year was 1992. I moved into the upstairs of a house in Santa Cruz, California. The place was a writer's dream: a loft, woodstove, skylights, a deck, and best of all, a view of the ocean only a block away. The house belonged to Gloria Anzaldúa. Gloria's books *This Bridge Called My Back* and *Borderlands* had shaped my feminism, particularly my understanding of women of color. Her work had also been a catalyst in strengthening my identity as a Jewish woman. My parents, who are both Holocaust refugees, had kept their pasts and their Jewish heritage a secret from me. When I read Gloria's writing I was inspired to understand my own struggles with assimilation. Carrying all of this admiration for Gloria's books intensified my usual shyness. For the first week I almost avoided Gloria. I couldn't believe I was living upstairs from this incredible woman.

Some of this shyness ebbed a few afternoons later, when Gloria came out of her house carrying a dozen seed packets. "Can you use some of these?" she asked in her gentle voice. I was about to plant a garden. "My mother gave these to me and I've been saving them." She began shuffling the seeds like a pack of cards. "Here's corn, and squash and beans, and tomatoes. Oh and here are some sunflowers . . ." I laughed and accepted some seeds. Soon we were taking walks along the ocean, discussing our writing, our lives. Before long I could not believe that I had been so shy around her. We became friends.

We have walked this journey into memory and history on parallel paths for nine years: me, upstairs researching and writing a memoir; her, downstairs in her study writing stories and essays, sometimes all night.

We are heirs to separate histories. Where is the border between us, between Chicana and Jew? Gloria's concept of nepantla seems to me the perfect metaphor for our house. She has written, "Living between cultures results in 'seeing' double, first from the perspective of one culture, then from the perspective of another." But what happens when two women from different cultures inhabit the same space? Perhaps the house itself begins to see double, becomes a vortex of intense creativity, or, as Gloria writes, "a zone of possibility."

I was baptized Unitarian, and attended Congregationalist and Catholic schools. Now I am both a cultural and spiritual Jew, a feminist, and also a lesbian. I live in the space between the Shoah and the atom bomb, and the questionable future. The bracing and invigorating crosswinds of nepantla have become home.

Does nepantla shimmer between our cups of decaf as we write at the local coffehouse, or reside somewhere in the floorboards that separate my feet from her head as we move through our days? These separations are not trivial, they are part of what define our house. I am the light-skinned Jew in my family; she the dark one in her family, la prieta. I was raised middle-class in Los Angeles, California, the daughter of a civil engineer; she picked cotton in rural south Texas. There are eighteen years between us (yet our mothers are the same age). I wonder whether our neighbors have any idea what transpires within the walls of this wood-shingled house with blue trim. Who do these white people who surround us see when this short Chicana woman walks by twice a day? Who do they see when they look at me and how do they see us differently?

Two women writers live in a house by the sea, a house filled with books. Sometimes I think this little house will explode from the very power of us. I am not only a writer, but also the publisher of HerBooks feminist press, my back room a wall of boxes of published titles. But these walls are more than just material walls. They contain our tears, our breathing, our dreams, our love, and our isolation. They contain our spirits. And they speak the common language of writing.

Here we flourish, two women who care more about writing than home maintenance. The rose bushes and blueberries cry out for water, and the decks of our house rot like an old ship. So? We will not be remembered for our housekeeping. Our hands stroke keyboards while the weeds grow ever higher, weave a marvelous jungle for my cats, whom she too has come to love. When I go on vacation she becomes Cat Mama. Two black cats have suddenly made cameo appearances in her writing. Here we are, two women who speak the common language of writing, who respect the privacy writing demands. Out of respect for that privacy essential to creativity we never drop by unannounced, but instead call each other on the phone, or even use e-mail. What shall I call Gloria? Certainly not landlady, but she's not quite a housemate either.

She calls me her comadre in writing. She is a key editor of my memoir. I read drafts of her stories, help her wrangle with contracts, editors, and publishers. We've gone to the same writing colonies. For my birthday she gives me special leather-bound blank journals with creamy smooth Italian paper. This year her inscription reads, "Para mi comadre Irene. Otro librito para otro projecto." Next to the inscription she has drawn a bird woman with open arms like wings. I looked at this drawing and realized it was Gloria. I have many writing companions, but there is no one else with whom I share such a rich cultural and political context.

Once a week we make the short trip downtown to our favorite coffeehouse, where we swoop down on a table as soon as a student leaves, and write, she relishing a decaf while I eat the sweets that she, as a diabetic, cannot have. Sometimes before we work she reads the astrology column to me in a voice full of portent and drama, accompanied by many significant looks. Sometimes we talk before we write. We tell each other when we are lonely, when our bodies hurt, when the writing is not going well. Sometimes we arrive ecstatic over the publication of a book, or simply share the joy of the writing itself.

I know the diabetes wears at Gloria's strength and spirit. When I don't hear her voice below my bedroom talking on the phone, or when I notice her mail still sitting in the mailbox, I worry a little. I try to keep myself from terrible visions of Gloria passed out on the floor of her house from a hypo episode. But Gloria is strong and determined. Sometimes I look out my window and see her hacking the bamboo plant that is always threatening to take over the backyard. One day when we cleaned out the garage I got tired after a few hours and went inside to rest. She said she was going to go inside and take her insulin and rest, but a little while later I heard her downstairs, still working, fiercely stubborn. We both struggle to take care of ourselves, to slow down. Diabetes has become her spiritual teacher.

I write this in a house of nepantla, a house by the sea at the edge of North America, a house inhabited by a Jewish woman whose parents survived destruction and a Chicana woman who survived racism. The borders of history and personal life cross and crisscross, propel us deeper into nepantla. I live upstairs from this remarkable woman. We have become family.

June 2001

Part 2

nepantla. . . . pathways to change

Bridges are thresholds to other realities, archetypal, primal symbols of shifting consciousness. They are passageways, conduits, and connectors that connote transitioning, crossing borders, and changing perspectives. Bridges span liminal (threshold) spaces between worlds, spaces I call nepantla, a Nahuatl word meaning tierra entre medio. Transformations occur in this in-between space, an unstable, unpredictable, precarious, always-in-transition space lacking clear boundaries. Nepantla es tierra desconocida, and living in this liminal zone means being in a constant state of displacement—an uncomfortable, even alarming feeling. Most of us dwell in nepantla so much of the time it's become a sort of "home." Though this state links us to other ideas, people, and worlds, we feel threatened by these new connections and the change they engender.

—Gloria E. Anzaldúa, "(Un)natural bridges"

Chapter 6

La Gloriosa Travesura de la Musa Que Cruza/The Misbehaving Glory(a) of the Border-Crossing Muse: Transgression in Anzaldúa's Children's Stories

Edith M. Vásquez

¿Mi musa? Es un diablillo
con alas de ángel.
Ah, musilla traviesa,
¡qué vuelo trae!

—*José Martí*

Perhaps trouble need not carry such a negative valence. To make trouble was, within the reigning discourse of my childhood, something one should never do precisely because that would get one in trouble. The rebellion and its reprimand seemed to be caught up in the same terms, a phenomenon that gave rise to my first critical insight into the subtle ruse of power: the prevailing law threatened one with trouble, even put one in trouble, all to keep one out of trouble. Hence, I concluded that trouble is inevitable and the task, how best to make it, what best way to be in it.

—*Judith Butler*

Prietita, a young Chicana, is the main character of Gloria Anzaldúa's children's stories *Friends From the Other Side/Amigos del Otro Lado* and *Prietita and the Ghost Woman/Prietita y la Llorona*. Prietita is a brave and daring girl whose misbehavior works to improve the lives of others. The developing expression of her identity mirrors wider aesthetic and political consequences and occurs in tandem with aesthetic and political progressions. Although juvenile voices convey a sentience and range of human experience in narratives, literary scholars rarely explore them. Juvenile perspectives communicate dramatically and with a stark perspicacity across a range of themes.[1] The child narrator generally performs in unlimited contexts for adult audiences, but child narration does not equate with child readership. I stress this point because I believe it can provide a fresher understanding of what Anzaldúa attempts in her stories, which are directed to a child audience yet incorporate serious themes and outcomes.

That children's stories conventionally portray good versus evil is not a new concept. Although Anzaldúa's children's stories operate like heroic quests and coming-of-age tales, Prietita's adversaries and obstacles are not Disneyfied, fantastic, or computer-animated. Prietita encounters the apparatuses of what may represent age-inappropriate forces: infectious illness, malnutrition, clandestine immigration, and vigilantism. These encounters defy expectations rather than reality, since children are obviously acutely aware of and respondent to environmental dangers. They cannot opt out of imposed, material trappings and are vulnerable in bodily, emotional, sexual, economic, and discursive spheres. By nature and circumstance, children are default actors within adult narratives. In her children's literature, Anzaldúa locates relational aspects of narration and embodiment within a borderlands milieu; characters play the roles of heroes and villains in unique culturally realistic ways. What she theorizes and relates in her writings addressed to adult audiences concerning personal, gender, and political liberation, is here recounted in the form of childhood experiences authored for children readers.

Anzaldúa's work contravenes some of the commonly held assumptions about children's cultures, bodies, and subjectivity. Childhood is the arena in which symbolic ordering, language, and subject formation are acquired, yet children are nonexistent in literary theory. In academic research they often appear as objects of social studies. In developmental psychology, nature-versus-nurture debates polarize their identities and realities. In popular culture children are often used as novel marketing devices in sales campaigns and advertising. Meanwhile, popular media narratives rarely depict strong, multidimensional girl characters. Fashion, food, and other industries regard the racialized child as an especially precious commodity, leading to destructive tokenization. Multicultural programming targeted to a child audience may represent appeasement of racism, rather than genuine change. Antiracism ministering to children—the most disenfranchised of all human populations—seems to suggest that children either originate their own racism, or that cultural sensitivity training is "child's play."

Anzaldúa intervenes in these various misappropriations by establishing an organic connection to a child audience. She performs an activist diegesis within the borderlands comprised by "childlife." There are at least two interrelated ways of reading these stories: as literary productions of Mexican/Chicano youth border culture, and as interventions into the ontological site of human language, symbol, and subject-making: childhood. The Chicana cultural figure propels the storymaking in these texts, which are not a linear project but an intrusion into, and transformation of, personas and ecologies. In these action narratives, where a girl hero rescues a boy from an immigration raid (*Friends*) and finds the cure for her mother's disease by trespassing on the grounds of the ominous King's Ranch (*Prietita*), the plot points are constituted by social, ethical, personal, cultural, and spiritual changes.

Over the course of *Friends*, Prietita's identity gains new dimensions as she befriends and aids Joaquín, a child worker. "La amistad," or friendship, that develops between the two children catalyzes action and relationships in their community. Prietita leads Joaquín and his mother to safety during the central crisis of the story—an INS raid—introduces Joaquín to the revered community curandera, and supplies him with job leads. At the diegetic level, Prietita is an agent of civically disobedient story-making: she assists the escape of two indocumentados, and because this community exists within the U.S./Mexico borderlands, such succor is illegal. Prietita and Joaquín perform heroically, humanely. Yet they disobey legal, political, and social strictures. En este sentido, son niños traviesos.

Prietita and Joaquín procure mutual benefit through their humanitarian collusion, their solidaridad, and their concomitant courage to traverse imposed borders. They are mischievous children and the trust they share is an act of defiance. It is a form of misbehavior that constitutes another articulation of Anzaldúa's poetics, coded for a child audience but inscribed with the topical complexity and humane deliberateness characteristic of her work. Anzaldúa's development and deployment of these children protagonists counters the standard depoliticization and disempowerment of minors' agency, political imagination, and ethics.

In *Friends*, Anzaldúa depicts multiple vulnerabilities and risks in the transnational amistad between two children. Prietita is a Tejana with ancestral ties to the land on the U.S. side, and Joaquín is a new immigrant from the Mexican one. His needs are acute, and he has no friends in the neighborhood until he meets Prietita. Joaquín symbolizes the emergency status of the refugee child. By presenting child agents' sociopolitical realities and resistance, Anzaldúa offers a more accurate portrayal of the borderlands as experienced by children who have only recently crossed the border.

In *Prietita*, Prietita's personality develops in correlation with larger challenges. These challenges extend her role beyond familiar geographic and experiential settings. Her senses, instincts, and communicational abilities expand as she moves beyond previously established boundaries. She progressively penetrates more deeply into the woods as various faunal, floral, and celestial omens guide her along her path. The first omen is la Llorona's cry. Prietita subsequently receives the aid of the deer, the salamander, the dove, the jaguarundi, and the lightning bugs. The moonlight, trees, and river are more than landmarks; they help her distinguish directions and locate the medicinal plant to treat her mother's illness. The woods, then, act in solidarity with Prietita and assist her in her mission. But Prietita also summons an inner fortitude that allows her to perceive the messages from natural forces and beings. She gazes into the face of la Llorona, the feared, legendary ghost woman, and asks for her help in finding the rue:

> In a trembling voice, Prietita called out to the ghost woman. "Señora, can you help me find some rue?"
>
> The ghost woman floated along the edge of the lagoon and Prietita followed her. Soon the woman stopped and pointed to a spot on the ground. Prietita knelt down. The moon moved in the sky and suddenly Prietita could see the plant. She examined it—yes, it was the rue! No longer afraid, she broke off a few branches and looked up at the ghost woman.
>
> "Thank you, Señora Llorona."

Prietita conquers the fear that many children, raised on the legend feel, and Anzaldúa effectively reconstructs the specter of la Llorona. She becomes a female deity giving aid to a child. Instead of killing or capturing Prietita, she guides her out of the woods so she can complete her mission.

This recuperation of the weeping woman represents a material intervention into colonial, patriarchal, and child domination ideologies. La Llorona's persona has been put to use much as a bogeyman figure. However, this was not always the way the story was told. In older versions of the legend derived from indigenous culture, Llorona is a prophetic figure who forewarns the indigenous peoples of the brutality of Spanish imperialism. By depicting her as Prietita's protective guide, Anzaldúa recuperates la Llorona just like other Chicana feminist scholars have recuperated the figure of the Indian woman who would come to be called la Malinche. In Anzaldúa's story, la Llorona and Prietita are empowered female personas. Though, on the surface, it might sound simplistic to say that Llorona and Prietita belong in the realm of childhood, I would argue that this is not an ordinary status.

Western epistemologies such as psychoanalysis locate the formation of subjectivity and language in childhood. Anzaldúa, then, is involved in a multipurpose project to provide reading material for children, debunk fear-instilling legends, and invoke a direct tie between political ethos and subject formation. Both *Friends* and *Prietita* textualize the experiences of a specific population of children who are politically engaged with their polemical surroundings as Anzaldúa seeks to represent children's political praxis as effective, transformational, and inspiring. Not only does she acknowledge children's intellectual, moral, social, and political power, she also nurtures these instincts in her juvenile audience. And this liberating sentiment ripples through symbolic, literary, and poetic spheres that matter to everyone.

The effects of the multiple watersheds taking place in Anzaldúa's literary works are revolutionary and personal for every reader. Borders have individual, bodily, and spiritual effects. They define us, mark our personalities and psyches. Yet, inspiration may fuel our breakthroughs beyond our personal boundaries. A manifested poetic inspiration to cross limits plays an important role in Prietita's heroism. I consider this heroism to be linked with a spiritual drive or illumination provided by a border-crossing muse. This muse is reminiscent of Elegua, the Santería child deity who stands at crossroads and is associated with music and the opening of doors. Prietita consorts with, and gives expression to, an Elegua-like muse who has recourse to liberating methods and engages in an activism that precedes and supercedes socio-political and economic hegemony, sexism, essentializing feminism, enforced gender categories, classism, academic elitism, and other oppressive discourses. Hence, the child in all her positions—reader, deity, poet, and protagonist—may inspire and instruct adults in their own humanitarian interventions.

Prietita resembles other cultural figures in Anzaldúa's work. La Llorona, la Virgen de Guadalupe, la musa bruja belong to the Chicana/indígena/mestiza cultural and literary pantheon. Similarly, Prietita takes on aspects of the mythical. Anzaldúa herself is a cultural figure, especially for my generation of students, writers, and teachers. She is La Musa Que Cruza—the border-crossing muse—in a variety of ways. She is bridge, translator, vehicle—a means for the passage of other border-crossers. Her life in text stands as literary criticism, as Chicana feminist knowledge, and queer epistemology.

In another sense, la Musa Que Cruza is a Mexican underground railroad worker for migratory people. She performs poetically and politically, transforming herself into a bridge. She may pay visits to Anzaldúa, Prietita, or Edith Vásquez. In *Friends*, la Musa inspires the mischievous Prietita to outwit those who would bring harm to her friend, Joaquín. In *Prietita*, la Musa appears in the guise of la Llorona, now reconstituted as a protector in the vein of the Greek gods of Homeric epic. As I mentioned before, the impact of this reinterpretation is important and complex. Anzaldúa contributes a counter-reading to which children immediately respond. In essence, she harnesses all of the mythological power contained in la Llorona, re-appropriating her beauty and magic for children's empowerment rather than subordination.

In Anzaldúa's works, indigenous practices of self-knowledge, spiritual training, and innate sympathy for others mitigate oppression. Overall, her oeuvre functions as a poetics and bridge between autochthonous and mestizo components of borderland society. Prietita's actions constitute a violation of dictated legal structures in both stories, but she is actually faithful to a more basic and humane code of conduct—one insinuated by the stories' telos and by the dictates of her character formation, subjectivity, and desire.

Prietita's role extends in the two stories. In *Friends* she begins to develop her faculties for mastering her environment, exercising agency within social communities, and treating physical illness. In *Prietita*, she again surpasses her restrictions, this time to an even greater extent. Accomplishing her quest, she attains increased self-determination, social prestige, and psychic mastery. Her personality is responsive and revelatory throughout the books. Her insightful reading of Joaquín's identity in *Friends* and her sixth sense for interpreting the omens that will help her identify the curative plant in *Prietita* underline her "facultad"—what Anzaldúa describes as "an extra sense" that enables a person to unify apparently dissimilar approaches for problem-solving (*Interviews/Entrevistas* 122). For example, Prietita is introspective and, at the same time, action-oriented. We may read Prietita's patient yet bold and unobtrusive mastery over multiple struggles as an expression of an exceptional, and potentially queer, facultad. Anzaldúa argues that queer and other socially oppressed persons, or those who are artistically endowed, exhibit hybrid critical decision-making. Saber es poder. In the expression of her facultad, Prietita forges a safe passage for Joaquín and his mother at a critical time in *Friends*, as well as for herself in *Prietita*. She intuits causes and effects. In *Friends* she is able to immediately perceive Joaquín's sources of distress, and she envisions a series of actions to alleviate them. In *Prietita*, she elicits and responds to a dynamic natural world from which she will acquire the elixir to cure her mother's sickness. An analysis of the two stories helps us to see how Anzaldúa orchestrates Prietita's personal milestones as dialogic with physical, psychic, and political processes.

In both books, Prietita's call to action surfaces in conjunction with physical distress. In *Friends*, a new illness travels from the external world into Prietita's scene, and the redress of Joaquín's sickness coincides with his integration into community. In *Prietita* recurrent illness develops in the family and a voyage outside of safe, familiar bounds is required. Where in *Friends* she helps an unknown child with an unfamiliar sickness by acquainting him with her own social networks and environment, in *Prietita* she helps her mother by searching for a common plant in unfamiliar ancestral grounds. Because this is the borderlands, familiarity and unfamiliarity are not fixed qualities. King's Ranch, though now controlled by Anglo-Texans for perhaps nearly a century, originally belonged to native Mexicans. The fear that ranch vigilantes will shoot trespassers on sight is one haunting generations of Chicanos.

Prietita takes on the responsibility of curing ailments in both stories. This duty requires that she seek training from the curandera who becomes her mentor. Prietita's abilities, then, hinge on others just as their relief depends on her; she becomes implicated in the community's equilibrium. When contagion occurs, her knowledge of others' needs compels her to seek universal relief and she extends her help without disparagement. She recognizes the similarities she shares with Joaquín in *Friends* and resolves to ameliorate his physical sores, which would otherwise continue to be a source of anxiety and pain for both children. Joaquín's malady, which indicates the economic instability and transition of the newly arrived, undocumented population, incarnates his yet unfinished border crossing. The healing of one child's sores by another child means that cross-border alliances are mutually empowering for populations from both sides, de los dos lados. In *Borderlands/La Frontera: The New Mestiza*, Anzaldúa initiates the border-as-wound topos: "The U.S.-Mexican border es una herida abierta where the Third World grates against the first and bleeds" (25). In her children's literature, she has created a character who acts to ameliorate, transform, and intercept such wounding.

In *Friends*, the poetic instantiation of the border/wound motif is evidenced on Joaquín's afflicted arms, which are a synecdoche of the border. They also symbolize the poor, laboring class and child workers who are manual laborers. In Anzaldúan cosmology Joaquín's open sores represent the material trappings of a person who is nepantlaesque—who has not yet fully crossed de un lado al otro, and exists in a state of in-betweenness. Prietita, then, acts as bridge for Joaquín's integration into her community. On their first encounter, she observes him from above. She is sitting on a tree, a position granting her acute awareness and illustrating her identification with the natural world. In the story's first paragraph, Prietita's acuity allows her to perceive the difference between Joaquín and "most boys": "Prietita wondered why he wore a long-sleeved shirt when it was so hot that most boys went shirtless." She recognizes that this shirt marks other elements of his identity, and she initiates a conversation with him: " 'Did you come from the other side? You know, from Mexico?' asked Prietita, having noticed that his Spanish was different from hers." On another level, she begins a formalized relationship in two ways: by not declaring her assumptions as fact, despite how incontrovertible they appear to be; and by allowing him to identify himself.

It is when Joaquín next exerts himself, taking up the firewood to prepare to leave, that Prietita catches sight of "the large boils on his forearms." Now she is able to understand why he wears the long-sleeved shirt: she "realized that he was ashamed of the sores." Experiencing empathy for Joaquín, Prietita quickly computes a solution: "She thought of the herb woman and her healing powers." At this juncture, Prietita does not simply envision a cure for Joaquín's condition, which would amount to a unilateral, and perhaps charitable or pitying, response. Instead, she initiates a common project that calls on the participation of at least three agents: herself, Joaquín, and the curandera. Prietita begins to undergo specific transformations of her identity as she attaches other characters to a common objective. The ensuing changes can be better understood in light of Anzaldúa's notions of identity formation as community-sensitive. Anzaldúa argues that: "For me, identity is a relational process. It doesn't depend only on me, it also depends on the people around me . . . Identity is not just a singular activity or entity. It's in relation to somebody else because you can't have a stand alone; there must be something you're bouncing off of" (*Interviews/Entrevistas* 239–40).

Both *Friends* and *Prietita* enact such relational processes, sprouting from the particular wounds needing particular cures administered by particular agents. These wounds are not only signs, but act as discursive sites and plot catalysts. Prietita immediately identifies la curandera as one capable of designating precise remedies. She acts as proxy for the wound, la curandera, and the ailing person, and her role as liaison signals her apprenticeship into curanderismo at the end of the story. But Prietita does not rush Joaquín into accepting her help. Anzaldúa meticulously depicts the children's increasingly intimate bond. Already acting like a spiritual practitioner, Prietita patiently awaits Joaquin's readiness to accept her assistance.

In the interim, several action scenes transpire to build tension, leading to the story's climax and the eventual resolution securing community cohesion. In these scenes, Prietita risks her own group affiliations for the sake of her new friend. These risks represent courageous steps in her spiritual/personal development. Additionally, she begins to increasingly and momentously defy social norms. The neighborhood children tease Joaquín for being a mojado—a wetback. This is not an instance of the alienation of the "other," for Joaquín only partially represents foreignness: he and the other boys are racially similar. Prietita's intervention represents criticism of the community coming from within the community itself. Risking possible alienation for the sake of a newcomer, Prietita's experiential struggle invokes the bridge motif. Prietita "stiffens" and is "pulled" across the chasm between an old, familial, group affiliation and a new friendship:

> Prietita heard some of the neighborhood kids yelling and went through the gate to see what was happening.
>
> "Look at the mojadito, look at the wetback!" called out her cousin Tété.
>
> "Hey, man, why don't you go back where you belong? We don't want anymore mojados here," said another boy.
>
> Prietita felt her body go stiff. She had known Tété and his friends all her life. Sometimes she even liked Tété, but now, she was angry at him. She felt pulled between her new friend and her old friends.

In this episode of social tension, the mystical, the corporeal, the social, and the personal pique simultaneously in Prietita. This kind of synergystic climax occurs uniquely in Anzaldúa's works and underscores her insistence that knowledge takes shape in the body.[2] In Anzaldúa, intelligence is always multiple in its sources and applications.

The two children's friendship exhibits mutualism and adult-like seriousness. Prietita accompanies Joaquín to the shack where he lives with his mother. At this point, the children enter an adult, domestic setting. Only a moment before, Prietita has noticed Joaquín's maturity: " 'I really appreciate your help,' Joaquín said, bowing slightly from the waist and sounding very grown up." Prietita, too, evidences her maturity and perspicacity when noticing the indigent family's extremely polite customs:

> "Come in, come in," said a small woman with a tired face and damp hair. She lifted the edge of the canvas to let them in. "Would you like something to eat?"
>
> "No, thank you," said Prietita. . . . She saw pride in their faces and knew that they would offer a guest the last of their food and go hungry rather than appear bad-mannered.

Inside the shack, conversation quickly turns to family history within the borderlands. Joaquín's mother explains:

> "We had to cross the river because the situation on the other side was very bad. I couldn't find work and Joaquín was in rags."
>
> "It's the same on this side," said Joaquín squatting on the dirt floor. "If only we could find real work instead of the occasional odd job in exchange for food and old clothes."

This exchange underlines the children's role in organizing labor and economic survival—something child readers will immediately perceive and perhaps enact in their own lives. Once again, Prietita takes the initiative to offer her help in mediating community structures for the survival of this family:

> "I'll tell the neighbor women about you. Maybe they'll have some work," said Prietita. She stayed a while and then said, "I have to go do my chores now. Joaquín, please bring some wood tomorrow and see if you can stay and play with me."

A complex of messages and performed identities suffuse these words. Prietita moves outside the bounds of childhood, acting as an agent for employment and amistad with a child whose socioeconomic situation differs from her own. She wants to intervene in a way perhaps considered beyond her jurisdiction as a little girl. She is conscious, though, of not forcing her will upon others. She observes customs of respect. The reader sees her high regard for preserving pride in the following passage:

> The next day Joaquín came to the gate again. Prietita asked him to give her a push on the tire-swing hanging from the gnarled mesquite tree. He returned the next day and the next. Prietita always saved some of her lunch and put it in a paper bag for him. She would leave it by the gate to lessen his shame for being poor. When Joaquín felt less shy with her, she would take him to the herb woman and have her cure his sores.

Prietita employs several skills here, foreshadowing her destiny as a curandera. She astutely gauges time, trust, and ritual. First, she engages in play activities to reaffirm nonemergency rites of childhood. By asking Joaquín to push her on the swing, she invites his participation in her own life. Second, she uses playtime to incite her imaginary powers, which endow her with subsequent strategies and the faith to perform them. Third, she bides time, never rushing Joaquín to consider seeking treatment, and transforms her lunch into a sacred offering. Prietita orchestrates various personalities and cultural dispositions to eventually secure the healing of Joaquín's sores. This way, she narratively and metaphysically forges the story's path.

Prietita and Joaquín's friendship evolves substantially, to the point that we find them engaging in a game of lotería in the next scene. Anzaldúa employs the lotería game in multiple symbolic ways. The game signifies transnational cultural contact and affirmation between this Chicanita and Joaquín, who has recently arrived. It also portrays strategic mental aptitudes and exercise, apparently nondiscursive intellectual engagement, and, finalmente, la suerte y el azar. When this apparently tranquil scene erupts into danger as the Border patrol approaches, threatening the safety of Joaquín and his mother, Prietita is emboldened to offer help. Her polite words and deeds change into direct commands as she conducts their escape: " 'Hurry, come with me . . . the herb woman will know what to do," she said, leading him through the streets of the little town, as his mother followed close behind." As they approach la curandera's house—depicted as a sanctuary replete with religious icons and other mystical trappings—they are, in effect, completing a seemingly preordained set of actions. In a fruition of prophetic elements, the herb woman greets their arrival knowingly: "When they entered the herb woman's house they saw that she was already drawing the curtains. 'Joaquín,' she said, 'you and your mother go hide under the bed and don't make a sound.' "

Once inside, Joaquín and his mother are safe, and Anzaldúa permits some comic relief. When the Chicano INS officer inquires about the location of any illegals, a neighborhood woman points to the "gringo side of town," and says, "Yes, I saw some over there." Everyone enjoys this joke, including the Chicano migra, who laughs along with all the others. The INS vehicle then moves on, and the panic in the community subsides.

The curandera accepts Prietita as her apprentice on the last page of the book: " 'Prietita, I'm going to show you how to prepare these herbs in a paste you can use to heal Joaquín's arms. It's time for you to learn. You are ready now.' " This final scene reveals the culmination of processes set in motion throughout the book. We see Prietita in the foreground, holding a harvest of herbs, and readying herself as a healer. Joaquín is kneeling near the earth, wearing a short-sleeved shirt for the first time. His sores, now exposed to the sunlight, are beginning to form scars. La curandera, in the background, prepares the plants picked by the children.

The visual and graphic design of both books is instrumental. Consuelo Méndez' drawings presciently support *Friend*'s character development and plot. Méndez brings to vivid relief the ranch life that is so much a part of this and other Anzaldúa texts. The illustrations convey the borderlands and southern Texas as a fecund ambience nurturing such cultural innovations as the Mexican corrido and the Tex-Mex language. The many animals gracing these pages represent a ubiquitous, spiritually-infused landscape. Roosters, chickens, snakes, dogs, birds, frogs, lizards, and cats witness all human activity. They may also represent los naguales, animals whose spirits accompany people through life,[3] or animals who were once human. Anzaldúan cosmology would support any of these, as well as other interpretations. The visual work in *Prietita* also portrays a rich landscape. In this story, more so than in *Friends*, Prietita directly dialogues with flora, fauna, and the spirit world. Maya Christina Gonzalez' illustrations dynamically render the natural world as communicative, sentient, and responsive to Prietita in her search for the rue.

In both *Friends* and *Prietita*, children's behavior prevails as humanitarian, diplomatic, and instinctually responsive to the borderlands' dangers. Anzaldúa shapes children's behavior into a manifesto for human rights. Childish travesuras constitute a mode of oppositional poetics and politics, such as the willful refusal to abide with antimony, rejection of border hegemonies, and genre, gender, and literary disobedience.

Transgression and translation are complementary, intersecting, and intrinsic modes of border literature. Prietita's personal ethic clashes with structural economic–political forces and institutions, and she must mediate the chasm between imposed structures and self-realization. In deciding upon any course of action, Prietita acts as a translator of values, problems, remedies, and other variables. Transgression and translation belong inside her conceptual toolbox.

Translation is a kind of literary and theoretical mode, as well as a proper genre. Transgression may signify a single event or a general operation. The act of transgression implies an act or acts of translation. Both entail movement, though this movement varies. Transgression may signify—as in the case of Prietita's trespassing on King's Ranch—a movement across boundaries. Translation involves the movement of languages toward one another. In light of the interconnectedness between transgression and translation, I imagine the child protagonist's role as that of a muse propelling the transgressing/translating enterprise. La Musa Que Cruza is Prietita, La Llorona, Gloria Anzaldúa. It is a spirit infusing, inspiring, spiriting, and guiding transformations of sundry sorts. This border-crossing muse enacts crossings and poeticizes them. Translation is par for the course.

However, the child muse/translator is not solely mythic, nor does she languish in academic, literary environs. Child translators perpetually cross over linguistic and social worlds. Translation was, in fact, one of my first vocations. As is the case for many immigrant children, it was fused with language acquisition. I have crossed the borders between the Spanish and English languages so frequently that I have worn many paths between them, and have crossed over others as well. In my study of Anzaldúa's children's stories, I remembered these transgressive, translating childhood roles. I also remembered a much more recent visual experience: that of seeing certain border road signs in the greater San Diego area . . . three people in a running gait. These human figures are similar shadowy profiles that differ only in size. The triad appears to be composed of a man, a woman, and a child. In descending size, these three figures hold themselves together—much like those scissor-formed paper dolls—with adjoining hands. The smallest of the shadowy figures, stirring the two adult-sized ones in their perilous, northward trek, would later become the subject of this essay, *La Musa Que Cruza*.

Notes

1. In Twain, children discuss slavery, homicide, ghosts, and other topics; in Cisneros a little girl's voice relates a near childhood sexual assault as well as the delights of play, song, and kinship; in Díaz boy characters witness extramarital affairs and violence.
2. See for instance Anzaldúa's extensive discussion of her body and manifestation of spirit through illness throughout *Interviews/Entrevistas*. For a poetic illustration of the ways Anzaldúa fuses the intellectual with the carnal, see her poem, "that dark shining thing" (*Borderlands* 172–73).
3. See for instance Rigoberta Menchú's acknowledgment of her nagual in tandem with the performative announcement of her own name. Her name and her nagual are originary sources for her consciousness.

Chapter 7

Apertures of In-Betweeness, of Selves in the Middle

Mariana Ortega

This is her home
this thin edge of barbwire.
But the skin of the earth is seamless.
The sea cannot be fenced,
el mar does not stop at borders.

—Gloria Anzaldúa

Thirsty to have contact with the Latino community in the West side of Cleveland, I headed to the Puerto Rican Festival, accompanied by my camera and a great desire to find out more about the Latinos who live in "the other side" of Cleveland. As I walked through the crowd, I was amazed—it was the first time I attended this festival since moving to Cleveland, and the first time I saw so many Latinos in the streets walking toward the festival, waving flags of Puerto Rico, people driving cars covered with Puerto Rican flags and honking incessantly. Immediately, I felt a tinge of sadness. I thought about how much they miss their island and how much I miss my country of origin, Nicaragua. At the same time, I was happy to see that they had a day to make a park and some of the streets of the West side of Cleveland their own. But I also wondered: How long has it been since they have been on the island? Do their children know the island? What view of Puerto Rico do they have—the Puerto Rico that they left or the Puerto Rico that is now? And such patriotism!

I looked at people, trying to capture their moods, trying to make a record of their feelings and some of my own feelings of being a multivoiced, multiplicitous self in the United States. In the midst of writing a formal and philosophical essay about selfhood in Anzaldúa's work, I remembered my experience at this park; I remembered some of the images, and I thought of no better way of expressing what I wanted to say and no better way of showing how I have been influenced by Anzaldúa's incredibly inspiring and powerful work. Having already written a more formal piece on Latina conceptions of self, I gave in to my love of photography, to memories of my experience of this festival, and to seeing these photographs in light of Anzaldúa's description of the New Mestiza.

This Thin Edge of Barbwire

Here he stands next to two Latinas, perhaps from Mexico, perhaps from Puerto Rico or another Latin American country. He, a Mexican, or playing the part of the ancient Mexican, in a Puerto Rican Festival in Cleveland, Ohio. And thoughts of borderlands, border-crossings come to mind, thoughts of "Nepantla," the "place in the middle," the region where borders intersect,

perhaps the bridge, the crossing, that is frequently permeated by desperation, alienation, abuse, and sometimes by the possibility of communication and cooperation for those who inhabit it or who are traveling across its "worlds."[1] It is a space where one is not in one place or another, one country or another, one culture or another, where countless travelers go through in order to work, play, observe, cheat, deceive, enjoy, or simply exist. But Nepantla is not just a spatial region where faces are inspected, passports displayed; it is the very experience of those who live an in-between life because they are multicultural, multivoiced, multiplicitous, because their being is caught in the midst of ambiguities, contradictions, and multiple possibilities.

Think of this Indian warrior in the middle of this festival in a city divided East and West, West being the "appropriate" place for Latinos, mostly Puerto Ricans, who continue to dream of "the island" even though they might never have set their feet on her coast and smelled her sea and who come out once a year to celebrate "the island," to wave its flag, to eat its food, and to be proud—while the warrior is there to do a traditional Mexican dance, which is not part of the Puerto Rican heritage, which the few "brave" white Clevelanders attending the festival might view as a "colorful, beautiful Puerto Rican dance"—while behind the warrior stands a man wearing a baseball cap with the mascot of the Cleveland Indians, Chief Wahoo, a smiling, sad, caricature of a people who once owned parts of this land. And Anzaldúa's words come to mind:

> Wind tugging at my sleeve
> feet sinking into the sand
> I stand at the edge where earth touches ocean
> where the two overlap
> a gentle coming together
> at other times and places a violent clash. (*Borderlands* 23)

I wonder if this man standing there "in the middle" of Cleveland, of Puerto Rican Cleveland, of Latin-U.S. American culture, of North-American culture, experiences a "gentle coming together," or mostly a defeat, a life of paralyzing ambiguities, of moments of "intimate terrorism."[2] He looks pensive, tired, beaten. As he stands, is he just looking at the crowd or is he wondering what he's doing there or whether or not he even belongs? If he is not a Puerto Rican, a U.S. American, a Puerto-Rican American, where does he fit in this celebration? Does he have to fit in?

This Puerto Rican "Wonder Woman," however, looks strong and decisive. She embraces her culture, carries her flag, even wears her flag. Anzaldúa says,

> In our very flesh, (r)evolution works out the clash of cultures. . . . Indigenous like corn, like corn, the mestiza is a product of crossbreeding, designed for

> preservation under a variety of conditions. Like an ear of corn—a female seed-bearing organ—the mestiza is tenacious, tightly wrapped in the husks of her culture. Like kernels she clings to the cob; with thick stalks and strong brace roots, she holds tight to the earth—she will survive the crossroads. (*Borderlands* 103)

But is not easy to survive the crossroads. Who knows what this woman—now proud of her heritage—has had to go through, whether this pride for her culture, which is at times considered "alien," is new, whether she has had to endure the "psychic restlessness," the "cultural collisions" that Anzaldúa so beautifully describes. And don't forget the "ruptures" and contradictions that might be part of her everyday world because of her multiplicitous selfhood.

Think of Anzaldúa's own "vivid memory" of an old photograph:

> I am six years old. I stand between my father and mother, head cocked to the right, the toes of my flat feet gripping the ground. I hold my mother's hand.
>
> To this day I'm not sure where I found the strength to leave the source, the mother, disengage from my family, mi tierra, mi gente, and all that picture stood for. (*Borderlands* 37–38)

Sometimes, one has to leave, only to come back again—but not as the same self who is bogged down by contradictions and ambiguities from the constant battle of trying to put different worlds, different possibilities together, but as the "new mestiza," the "new mestizo," whose inner struggle has led to a realization that one is not one or the other but a mixture, a kneading, an "amasamiento" of different cultures or possibilities, perhaps a "synthesis of duality, and a third perspective—something more than mere duality or a synthesis of duality" (*Borderlands* 68).

I think of what will become of these two boys; what awaits them in their life in the middle? While others look behind, they look ahead, to the right, to the left—will they find their own "tlilli, tlapalli," their own black and red ink leading to writing and wisdom? Or will they become a "nahual," agents of transformation who can change themselves and others, attaining a new consciousness of mestizaje (*Borderlands* 91, 96)?[3]

I also look at these two mestizas, and wonder if they will become "new mestizas." Will being a part of a beauty contest always be of value for them? Will wearing crowns always matter? Will they find out or do they already know how both Latino and U.S. culture oppress and belittle women? I don't remember what the first part of the banner said; we can see what the

rest says: "America." One of these women represents "America," but let us not forget that "America" stands for a whole continent, not just the United States.

America

No, it would be a grave mistake to forget that "America" stands for a great mass of land, especially at times when "America," the country, is taken by some to reign supreme and to refer only to a nation where the "American Dream" waits to be fulfilled by those crossing its borders—when in reality more and more of those crossing its borders suffer from countless offenses of degradation, exploitation, and racism—when in reality there are many new mestizos experiencing what Anzaldúa refers to as Coatlicue states of confusion, ruptures of the ordinary. I look at these photographs again, at these apertures of the in-between, and I am struck by the power of nationalism, patriotism, by the power of the Puerto Rican flag being held, worn, and adored. How to explain being in-between when one sees himself or herself as a Puerto-Rican, a Mexican, a Nuyorican, a Chicana, here in the U.S.? How to understand the pull to belong to a group and the conocimiento[4] that Anzaldúa teaches: we are multiple and can be at "both shores at once"?

When Anzaldúa thinks of herself as a Mexican, she says, "Being Mexican is a state of the soul not of mind, not one of citizenship. Neither eagle nor serpent, but both. And like oceans, neither animal respects borders" (*Borderlands* 84). Citizenship grants familiarity and the powerful feeling of belonging, even when we no longer visit those faraway places that we used to call "home" or that we call "home" even though we've never been there. We can see ourselves as citizens of many lands or as having many homes, despite the fact that there are pressures on us to be good "American" citizens and thus blend in, melt into a whiter version of ourselves, despite the fact that the so-called "browning" of "America" calls for a browness that fades to whiteness.

Anzaldúa reminds us of the concreteness of the borderlands, the spatiality filled with real flesh-and-bone beings, the Texas-U.S. Southwest/Mexican Border, what she sees as an open wound and an unnatural boundary. But she also alerts us to the fact that the borderlands are our psyches, that "The struggle has always been inner" (*Borderlands* 109). We stand at the interstices between two shores, one representing the dominant Anglo world and another representing our "world." We are multiplicitous beings with inner borders that confuse us, betray us, but also empower us.

Anzaldúa stands next to Audre Lorde, María Lugones, W. E. B. Du Bois, and other powerful, extraordinary writers, shamans,[5] who have described the struggle, pain, and agony of being in-between these shores. Few have described this way of being with such passion, with so many cactus needles embedded in their flesh. She tells us that it is not enough to cross to the other side and to carry out a violent critique of the dominant norms. This is a move forward, but not the way to live out one's life:

> It's a step towards liberation from cultural domination. But it is not a way of life. At some point, on our way to a new consciousness, we will have to leave the opposite bank, the split between the two mortal combatants somehow healed so that we are on both shores at once and, at once, see through serpent and eagle eyes. (*Borderlands* 100)

There are multiple possibilities for us new mestizos and mestizas. We may try to synthesize, integrate; we might even decide to give up the dominant culture, not to embrace the dominant version of "America," and move into a new territory—but we will always embody the struggle within, the struggle that leads us to develop a new mestiza consciousness which will ultimately help us break down paradigms that make us homogeneous, unified, abstract. The work that Anzaldúa leaves us is indeed the black and red ink of writing and wisdom that new mestizos can use as inspiration, as she would say, to carve our very bones.

Notes

1. Here I am using "world" not as the sum of objects in the world but rather in the way Lugones and Heidegger use it. (See Lugones's *Peregrinajes*, Ch. 4, and Heidegger 93.)
2. Anzaldúa describes life in the borderlands as a life of "intimate terrorism." She explains, "Alienated from her mother culture, 'alien' in the dominant culture, the woman of color does not feel safe within the inner life of the Self. Petrified, she can't respond, her face caught between los intersticios, the spaces between the different worlds she inhabits" (*Borderlands* 42). While Anzaldúa refers to the lives of women at the borders, I am extending her analysis to all who live the life of in-betweenness, regardless of race, sex, sexual orientation, or physical ability.
3. Anzaldúa provides a compelling account of this new consciousness, which she calls a "new mestiza consciousness." Explaining how her new consciousness has transformed her, Anzaldúa says, "I am an act of kneading, of uniting and joining that not only has produced both a creature of darkness and a creature of light, but also a creature that questions the definitions of light and dark and gives them new meanings" (*Borderlands* 103).
4. According to Anzaldúa, "conocimiento" refers to a way of knowing that goes beyond subject/object duality, that questions conventional categories and is derived from all the senses rather than primarily reason ("now let us shift" 541).
5. Anzaldúa sees writers as shamans capable of transforming both reader and writer into something else (*Borderlands* 89).

Chapter 8

From within Germinative Stasis: Creating Active Subjectivity, Resistant Agency

María Lugones

This writing is a personal engagement with Gloria Anzaldúa's *Borderlands/La Frontera* as a "text,"[1] a journey, that enabled me to occupy a resistant position. From within this position I learned to block the effectiveness of oppressive meanings and logics. This blocking is a *constant, recurrent, first gesture* in coming to understand the limits of the possible. The inhabitation of this place/vantage enables me to withdraw my energies from cementing and contributing to the relations of power that define me as servile or as nonsensical. This is a position of understanding myself as more than passive, docile, acceptable, within the "confines of the 'normal' " (25). That is, I take lessons from Anzaldúa's journey. But it is also a coming into intimate relation with Anzaldúa's path to resistant meaning in a way that enables me to begin to know her. To inhabit a resistant terrain, a "vague and undetermined" space, is also a coalitional journey. It is this knowing each other that makes life livable.

In taking up this double task I am careful not to appropriate Anzaldúa's path. When it is a question of my own resistance, I try to take lessons from her inhabitation of space; her complex incarnate memory; her brooding her self into being; her isolating her self from the pulls toward normalcy, passivity, subordination; her acute expression of the visual/tactile tension inside the complexity of the journey. To take lessons without appropriation of this "text," a text that is alive—enacted as it is told—is to feel drawn by its call without conflating understanding and mimesis. These tasks, taken together, are constitutive of the journey as coalitional.

In this writing I focus on strategies Anzaldúa offers us toward a making of oneself against the logic, the sense, the weight of oppressions. To work with her strategies is to come to understand the inadequacy of the western notion of agency. I dismiss the modern western notion of agency—the ground of individual responsibility—in favor of a more contained, more inward, sense of activity of the self in metamorphosis. Like in a cocoon, the changes are not directed outward, at least not toward those domains permeated by the logics of dominations. The western conception of agency stands in the way both of understanding Anzaldúa's "journey" and of the possibility of creative activity under conditions fertile for resistance to multiple oppressions.

The modern western conception of agency orders one's sense of responsibility toward a set of prescribed ready-made choices, none of which are compatible with liberation. Agency, in this sense, presupposes *ready-made hierarchical worlds of sense* in which individuals form intentions, make choices, and carry out actions in the ready-made terms of those worlds. That is, agency is constituted by potent intentionality in a particular vein. Agency, in this sense, is thus not antecedent to a fundamental liberatory transformation of the context of action. I am not suggesting that this transformation should move toward the formation of contexts that would make agency in this sense possible. I do not think agency in the modern western sense is desirable as a liberatory goal since it requires a univocity of meaning.[2]

As I now interpret on the page—as I did for myself—the strategies Anzaldúa offers to the one who recreates her self away from dichotomies—away from the border—into the Borderlands, I do it through and in this resistant sense of agency which I call "active subjectivity." It is the exercise of active subjectivity that makes transformation conceivable.

What I mean by active subjectivity, and which I see in Anzaldúa's strategies, has no such presuppositions, no ready-made sense within which our actions and intentions can be made congruent with our domination. In the brooding of one's own metamorphosis, the subjected form intentions against that grain. I learned from Anzaldúa's expressiveness from within the mestiza's journey that growing into a being who can form such intentions is something we do in germinative stasis from within our own multiplicity. In Anzaldúa's path, this is her intimate visit with Coatlicue. Women of color are not supposed to make sense or choices outside the domain where they are dominated. The active subject concocts sense away from the encasement of dominant sense. Her intentions, the meaning of her possibilities, is to be fashioned. In this path, Anzaldúa turns inward, toward her self, in a long and wide sense of her self: she inhabits the ancient Mesoamerican serpent as she takes on the splitting of her enduring self by western modernities. Her self is the self of a historicized people who live in resistance in the midst of oppression:

> This land was Mexican once
> was Indian always
> and is.
> And will be again. (113)

The border: a "chainlink fence crowned with rolled barbed wire" that marks woman from man, object from subject, passion from reason, sexuality from spirituality. The border splits the subjected inside, as it splits us[3] from histories and possibilities through the colonial excision.

> 1,950 mile-long open wound
> dividing a *pueblo*, a culture,
> running down the length of my body,
> staking fence rods in my flesh,
> splits me splits me
> *me raja me raja* (24)

> In trying to become "objective," Western culture made "objects" of things and people when it distanced itself from them, thereby losing "touch" with them. This dichotomy is the root of all violence. (59)[4]

A borderland: "a vague and undetermined place created by the emotional residue of an unnatural boundary" inhabited by aliens, transgressors, a risky home, an unsafe place, a place of ambivalence and ambiguity, a place of tense inhabitation against the tyrannies of dominant and "mother" cultures (25). Mother: Guadalupe, la que nutre, excised from her sexual self, reduced, emptied. But she can take her self back, si la visten y la bañan, with serpentine motion, con intenciones carnales transgresoras, with transgressive intentions. Chicana Lesbians as Anzaldúa las amasa, las viste, slither, writhe, on the ground of the borderlands against la rajadura colonial.

Normalcy: (in my words) submerged, surrounded, inundated, constituted, circumscribed by concepts, ways of doing things, institutions, values that conceptually, materially, and politically determine, decree, regulate, justify all possibilities. Concepts, customs, institutions, values that become invisible, a deep sort of framework encasing every move and gesture, every justification.

So taken for granted as to create the illusion of individual—non-collective—creativity and authorship. Case, background, texture, to one's lonely, genial, unaccompanied, self-made subjectivity. Those who enjoy, hold, exercise power over others can inhabit this fantasy of individual power, socially cashable energy. The subjected see more clearly through this fantasy of individual agency as a face of power. But living against the grain of this fantasy, commits us to an awareness of intimate terror. It commits us to struggle within intimate terror.

> Los atravesados live here: the squint-eyed, the perverse, the queer, the troublesome, the mongrel, the mulato, the half-breed, the half dead; in short those who cross over, pass over, or go through the confines of the "normal." (25)

The borderdweller comes to understand, through a jarring, vivid awareness of being made into more than one person, that the encasing by particular systems of meaning is a process one can consciously and critically resist or accept. The borderdweller sees in this process that the encasing can be resisted through the development of alternative meaning systems that keep particular oppositional relations to the closed ones. The borderdweller understands the illusory quality of the closure in closed systems of meaning, understands it as a technique of domination.

In this writing I will not follow the path all the way to the new mestiza. Instead, I allow myself to dwell in the strategies that permit germination, strategies of accepting stasis toward an interiority that seeks to steady itself as it departs dominant sense into the making of one's face.

As she follows the Chicana Lesbian into the worlds of her oppression, Anzaldúa valorizes despised states of being. I have found this valorization deeply sustaining. She sees them as strategies of the oppressed self. She sees in them the helpful for survival, the resistant, the liberatory, the positive where others may have a tendency to experience or see defeat, despair, incompetence, demoralization. In her intimate visit into oppressed subjectivity, Anzaldúa uncovers her self, the self of a Chicana Lesbian—oppressed in more than one world—to be multiple, not just because of the multiplicity of her oppression, but also because she comes to understand the self as resisting oppression: "There are many defense strategies that the self uses to escape the agony of inadequacy and I have used all of them" (67).

Anzaldúa exhibits Chicana Lesbians as caught in and in-between two cultures: both the Anglo dominant and their mother culture are oppressive worlds. Anzaldúa thinks of her self in each of these realities and she also thinks of the self oppressed by them. She considers five strategies of this self: the state of intimate terrorism, the use of rage to drive others away, reciprocating with contempt for those who have aroused shame in us, internalizing rage and contempt, and what she calls the Coatlicue state. These strategies of defense are insulating strategies; since she cannot respond in the terms of her oppressors to their harm, she must make space apart for creation, for new sense.

the state of intimate terrorism

Anzaldúa sees that our Latino cultures give women selves characterized by a failure of control. La cultura teaches women away from taking control over our own lives. If we choose to take control, we cease to be traditional women: we become tercas—pigheaded, hociconas—women who talk back—, lazy (38), mujeres malas—bad women (39). But in choosing to remain traditional, women give themselves up, do not make full use of their faculties, do not engage fully:

> I abhor some of my culture's ways, how it cripples its women, como burras, our strengths used against us, lowly burras bearing humility with dignity. The ability to serve, claim the males, is our highest virtue. (43)

Anzaldúa dwells on this state to feel the possibility of responsibility. She understands the process of oppression as contested by a process of resistance, a process with a long history. In expressing this contestation, she poses a self full of undeveloped potential who is being pressed between two worlds of oppression, the anglo cultural world and the world of her "mother culture." She is terrorized by these two worlds. Each of her selves is in their respective oppressive worlds "shackled in the name of protection": "Blocked, immobilized, we can't move forward, can't move backward . . . We do not engage fully. . . . We abnegate" (43). "The ability to respond is what is meant by responsibility, yet our cultures take away our ability to act" (42).

Chicanas are culturally stuck, captive of oppressive worlds. Anzaldúa takes, occupies, the position of the self being oppressed, terrorized, pressed by these two worlds, and conceives of this self as in-between, in the borderlands. In adopting the eyes of this self in the process of being molded by oppressive realities, Anzaldúa sees the possibility of getting unstuck from in-between these worlds, even if this results in not belonging anywhere. She sees the self in the moment of being pressed, feels the pressing, the imminent reduction of her self in the direction of abnegation, and as she feels the pressing, she also feels the possibility of resistance. The moment of intimate terror is not itself a liberatory state. It is the aware inhabitation of this state, the sensing of being pressed, that begins the process of resistance. The awareness is deeply sensorial.

I want to mark this insight in my own words. Oppression is not to be understood as an accomplished fact. To understand it as accomplished renders resistance impossible. Rather, the relation is oppressing<=>being oppressed, both in the gerund, both ongoing. Resisting meets oppressing enduringly. It is the active subject resisting<=>oppressing that is the protagonist of our own recreations. But as she is resisting<=>oppressing, she is both the one oppressed and the one resisting. The one resisting and the one oppressed exist within very different logics, within very different worlds of sense. She is multiple as reality is multiple. Resistance and liberation are alive always within multiplicitous meaning. As one de-emphasizes agency, the subject appears multiplicitous: at once terrorized and resistant; at once paralyzed in stasis and brooding her own liberation.

The one aware of intimate terror understands the consequences of resistance: not belonging anywhere; becoming an alien; becoming someone who is conceptually, culturally outside of either universe of meaning. This alienation of the self is part of the intimate terror: "Alienated from her mother culture, 'alien' in the dominant culture, the woman of color does not feel safe within the inner life of her Self. Petrified, she can't respond, her face caught between los intersticios, the spaces between the different worlds she inhabits" (42).

The terrorized self that feels the possibility and the terror of resistance is conceptually quite different from the one who is under someone else's control and thus gives up her ability to choose, accepting to serve instead. To feel the terror is already an activity against the sense of those who exercise control over and against her. Both the self forced on her by the Anglo world and the self forced on her by the raza world take away the ability to act (42). Servility and absence of responsibility mark the one who abnegates. Her intentions are servile within both of the worlds of meaning that reduce her and she is passive both in and toward their servility. Passivity here is opposed to activity, where activity and action are not identical.

But the one who feels the possibility of self-control is not an agent in the western sense because her intentions are not part of any status quo. Her meaning, the control of meaning, the scope and tenor of her possibilities are ahead of her and within an ancient history of violent struggle. Even though every move she makes will have a status quo interpretation that reads her as an alien, an outlaw, reduced, her meaning co-opted in the direction of servility or incompetence, those interpretations do not hold her captive. She cannot act, but she is active, a serpent coiled.

She senses two ways of describing her self at the intersection of white culture and her own culture. One uses the language of resistance, of awareness of being more than a victim. The other uses the language of reduction to passivity.

The one (actively coiled):

> Blocked, immobilized, we can't move forward, can't move backwards. That writhing serpent movement, the very movement of life, swifter than lightning, frozen. (43)

The other (simply passive):

> We abnegate . . . to feel a victim where someone else is in control and therefore responsible. (43)

rage and contempt: strategies of the in-between self

> *Soy nopal de castilla* like the spineless and therefore defenseless cactus that Mamagrande Ramona grew in back of her shed. I have no protection. So I cultivate needles, nettles, razor-sharp spikes to protect myself from others. (67)

I keep on wavering between thinking that Anzaldúa believes these states/moves to be negative and sensing them as helpful in her path in making germination of a resistant self possible. She may experience them as both negative and positive. I may be also reading her against her grain. She tells us that we can and do use rage to drive others away and to insulate ourselves against exposure. I understand this as a strategy of the self in-between, the self active inside intimate terror.

What the self in-between does with rage is the reverse of what people who can exercise their agency within normalcy successfully do with rage. They use rage against other people and address them through rage. They engage through rage. They may attempt to dominate through rage or they may demand rectification of a wrong done to them. In both cases successful agency in the modern western sense is presupposed if the enraged act is to succeed. There is an expectation of being understood in addressing one's rage to or against others in these cases.

But for the in-between self, rage is a way of isolating her self, of making space for her self, of pushing back. The oppressed self cannot use rage to communicate rage: she fails in communicating rage because she makes no sense as enraged;[5] her rage is out of character. It can only be madness. But it is fine to be interpreted as mad if the self is looking for isolation, for space apart from harmful sense. To understand her rage as a failure from the point of view of agency is to miss its point or to fail to understand how rage is available to the oppressed.

The oppressed mestiza can also reciprocate with contempt for those who have aroused shame in her. Again, this is an insulating strategy, not an extending her self toward others. Contempt in her is also out of character, beyond the bounds of her propriety within both the dominant and the traditional raza worlds of meaning. She, who is supposed to serve and nurture and ingratiate herself to others through her service and docility, turns to nurturing her self when shamed. Her contempt appears hostile, but this is not the hostility of engagement. It is not battle: rather, it is disengagement, a way of telling others to leave her alone. So, again, out of the bounds of sense of official sense, instead of exercising agency, something denied her, she helps her self through active withdrawal.

Isolating the self from harmful sense to make germination of a resistant self possible is a crucial reading of the political made vivid by Anzaldúa in her strategies. We feel the temptation to stay within the "confines of the normal" since reality and we in it are familiar to ourselves. We always may feel the temptation to engage in political activity without this preparation, as if oppression did not touch our selves. Anzaldúa shows the transformation of reality to require a tense inhabitation of our selves.

The Coatlicue State

Anzaldúa's intimate visit with Coatlicue is central to her own remaking. She re-inhabits a past to remember her possibilities, possibilities occluded in her present multiply subjected self. In this intimate visit with her Mesoamerican self she comes to inhabit the serpent. As the serpent, she writhes sensually against the splittings of her self.

> In pre-Columbian America the most notable symbol was the serpent. The Olmecs associated womanhood with the Serpent's mouth which was guarded by rows of dangerous teeth, a sort of vagina dentata. They considered it the most sacred place on earth, a place of refuge, the creative womb from which all things were born and to which all things returned. Snake people had holes, entrances to the body of the Earth Serpent; they followed the Serpent's way, identified with the Serpent deity, with the mouth, both the eater and the eaten. The destiny of humankind is to be devoured by the Serpent. (56)
>
> After each of my four bouts with death I'd catch glimpses of an otherworld Serpent. . . . I realized she was, in my psyche, the mental picture and symbol of the instinctual in its collective impersonal pre-human. She, the symbol of the dark sexual drive, the chthonic (underworld), the feminine, the serpentine movement of sexuality, of creativity, the basis of all energy and life. (57)

Anzaldúa begins her journey into the Coatlicue state by dwelling into the mirror metaphor. She tells us that the obsidian mirror shows two aspects of the self: the self captured, objectified in the mirror by the glance. The glance possesses it, turns it into an object, freezes it in place. But the one who looks into the mirror also sees, has awareness, sees through things. She experiences her self in the mirror. Anzaldúa places her many selves in relation to the mirror: the passive abnegated selves, the in-between self in the moment of terror, turned into stone by terror, the in-between self in the moment of creative resistance. The passive, the blocked and immobile, and the in-between self turned to stone by fear are seen by the in-between creative self. The object: the passive and the petrified. The subject: Coatlicue, the in-between self as seer of her selves.

> dark dumb windowless no moon glides
> across the stone the nightsky alone alone
> no lights just mirrorwalls obsidian smoky in the
> mirror she sees a woman with four heads the heads
> turning round and round spokes of a wheel her neck
> is an axle she stares at each face each wishes the
> other not there (63)

As the self is caught by her own glance, the glance focuses not only on the passive but also on the terrorized self, the in-between self. The in-between self is petrified, turned to stone by fear: she is afraid of becoming an alien, of leaving the bounds of oppressive sense, she is afraid of having to make new sense:

> She has this fear that she has no names that she
> has many names that she doesn't know her names She has
> this fear that she's an image . . . the fear that she's the dreamwork
> inside someone else's skull She has this fear that if
> she takes off her clothes . . . that if she digs
> into herself she won't find anyone (65)

> Simultáneamente me miraba la cara desde distintos ángulos. Y mi cara, como la realidad, tenía un caracter multíplice. (66)

The Coatlicue state is a transitional, liberatory state. It signifies an important break with colonization. Colonization tore woman in half: the dark or wild and the light or quiet aspects of Coatlicue, the serpent goddess was torn in two. Guadalupe—the virgin mother—came to be one half of Coatlicue from which colonized woman was made: generosity was transformed into passivity, abnegation. In the Coatlicue state the Chicana comes to an understanding of being torn in two, and resistance can be anchored in this history.

For Anzaldúa, the Coatlicue state is preparatory to becoming a full-fledged member of the borderlands, a new mestiza. It is a state of stasis, of motionlessness, a standing still. The Coatlicue state has two simultaneous "moments": in the first moment the focus is on the self afraid, terrified of abandoning the conventional construals of her self. The self is afraid of not being anyone after all. In this moment, the self survives fear through repetitious activity, addictive activity. Though this activity keeps awareness from happening, "[a]n addiction (a repetitious act) is a ritual to help one through a trying time; its repetition safeguards the passage, it becomes one's talisman, one's touchstone" (68). She—the subject—keeps her self—the one turned into object by fear—focused on her self as preparing her self to live in the border. She could assuage her fear by going back to the oppressive worlds of passivity. And this is tempting. All oppressed people know this temptation. In the second moment the focus is on the self as subject, the one who sees, Coatlicue herself, who devours us when pain, suffering become intolerable (69).

Anzaldúa describes the first moment:

> In order to escape the threat of shame or fear, one takes on a compulsive, repetitious activity as though to busy oneself, to distract oneself, to keep awareness at bay . . . repeating, repeating, to prevent oneself from "seeing.". . .
>
> Held in thrall by one's obsession, by . . . addiction, one is not empty enough to become possessed by anything or anyone else. . . . [O]ne does not "see" and awareness does not happen. One remains ignorant of the fact that one is afraid, and that it is fear that holds one petrified, frozen in stone. (67)

This defense strategy is being blocked and remaining within oneself, allowing oneself to feel the fear without paying attention to it. One is paralyzed by fear but instead of retreating into one of the oppressed selves and feeling safe in servile activity, one dwells in the paralysis and senses its cause: the very possibility of liberation, of ceasing ordinary life, or ordinary life as oppressed. "Those activities or Coatlicue states which disrupt the smooth flow (complacency) of life are exactly what propel the soul to do its work: make soul, increase consciousness of itself" (68).

The Coatlicue state is the state of the in-between self at the crossroads of choice. Anzaldúa's depiction of our selves as we are about to go out of the bounds of the normal is not one in which agency plays a role. Rather the state is remarkably one of inaction, of stasis: in fear but unaware of and distracted by aimless, repetitious activity. It is a static state because the activity, the going to and fro has no destination, no point except keeping us steady and inward, like whittling. But in its second moment, Coatlicue "devours" the fear, and the state becomes one of germination: of feeling, sensing from within the serpent, the limits between the oppressive worlds, a coming to understand her own possibilities not through acting, but through not acting, since at this stage all acting would be oppressed activity carrying out servile intentions.

I understand the Coatlicue state as placing an emphasis on the resisting side of the "oppressing<=>resisting" relation. In the state of intimate terror the emphasis is on the oppressing side. One way of understanding the Coatlicue state available to me is to understand it as how the state of intimate terrorism feels when one centers within the confines of the terrorized self; rather than concentrating on being pushed, pressed, reduced, the self pushes back toward liberation, pushes back and beyond. It is here that the oppressed self and the resistant self meet in intimate struggle. Though the struggle is inward, it is not narrow, because the sense of self is expansive.

But the state of intimate terrorism and the Coatlicue state are very different ways of experiencing oppression. They are both states in which modern western agency is neither possible nor successful because non-servile intentions by the subjected are outside of the bounds of sense of the status quo. In both cases one is immobilized. In both one does not engage one's faculties and abilities fully. Anzaldúa says of the Coatlicue state, "We are not living up to our potentialities" (70), and of the state of intimate terrorism, "We do not make full use of our faculties" (43). But in the state of intimate terrorism the self is terrorized by oppression from the outside (which is of course in her, since she is the one oppressed). In the Coatlicue state the fear is provoked by the very prospect of liberation. She is not yet living up to her potentialities; rather, she is fomenting her potential self, the creation of a counter-universe of sense in which she can engage her potential fully. This self and this counter-universe of sense are what the germination in the Coatlicue state is all about.

As subjected, we fear standing outside the bounds of the ordinary, even though the ordinary oppresses us into servility. We know the use of both "neurotic," repetitious activity and depression in the face of lack of action and in the fear of possible action that would place us out of bounds. We all know the temptation to escape these states telling ourselves to play politics so as to give ourselves a sense of worth, of engagement. We go to meetings, pass out leaflets, join demonstrations. Anzaldúa valorizes the "neurotic" states: she inverts their value. She also helps us understand the bind, the trap of oppression and helps us see stasis, germination, quietly active subjectivity as fundamental to liberation.

company

I have wondered about the company that the self-in-between, the border self, the inhabitant of the borderlands keeps in resistant creation.

> A borderland is a vague and undetermined place created by the emotional residue of an unnatural boundary. It is in a constant state of transition. Los atravesados live here: the squint-eyed, the perverse, the queer, the troublesome, the mongrel, the mulato, the half-breed, the half dead; in short, those who cross over, pass over, or go through the confines of the "normal." (25)

A social history of both despojamiento and resistance in the meetings between anglos and mexicanos crisscrosses Anzaldúa's understanding of the borderdweller's situation. She places the intimate resistance of the self-in-between, the " inner war," within the sociality of Chicano resistance: "Quién está protegiendo los ranchos de mi gente? Quién está tratando de cerrar la fisura entre la india y el blanco en nuestra sangre? El Chicano, sí, el Chicano que anda como un ladrón en su propia casa" (85).

Anzaldúa seeks the cultural backings for her own resistance in ancient Mesoamerican culture—she taps the "collective unconscious"—and in contemporary mexicano, Tejano, Chicano cultures. Her text draws from corridos, ancient myths, dichos, cantares, contemporary texts by Chicano/a and Latin American writers. She draws from Los Tigres del Norte as well as from Andres Gonzales Guerrero, from Gina Valdes and Alfonsina Storni, from El Puma and Miguel Leon-Portilla.

In depicting the borderlands, she tells us of a "place" or state populated by "the people who leap in the dark" (103), a people who are a new mixture of races, "una raza mestiza la primera raza síntesis del globo" (99). In speaking of the "new mestiza" Anzaldúa shifts back and forth from "she" to "we." She speaks of the "work that the soul performs" (101) breaking down dualities, adding a third element, la conciencia mestiza, the mestiza consciousness who participates in the creation of a new culture, a new value system. She also says "We are the people who leap in the dark," where "we" captures those doing this revolutionary work "out of the clash of cultures" (103). She/we exercises a rupture with all oppressive traditions, communicates that rupture, documents the struggle, reinterprets history, and using new symbols, she shapes new myths. She/we surrenders all notions of safety, of the familiar. "We" signifies that the borderlands are inhabited by many atravesadas/os.

But for Anzaldúa "the struggle has always been inner" (109). Anzaldúa depicts the crossing-over as an intimate act, without acknowledging explicitly her company in rebellion. But it is not difficult to see that the Coatlicue state and the state of intimate terrorism are described as states of the inner life of the self because Anzaldúa is describing states in the psychology of oppression and liberation. Anzaldúa does not link the psychology of oppression and resistance to collective resistance in an explicit manner and thus does not acknowledge the sociality that she documents in resistance. Unless resistance is a social activity, the resistor is doomed to failure in the creation of a new universe of meaning, a new identity, a raza mestiza. Meaning that is not in response to and looking for response fails as meaning.

As I understand the liberatory project, the inner and the collective struggles are not separable; they are "moments" or "sides" of the liberatory process. A dismissal of the "inner struggle" dismisses liberatory subjectivity. A dismissal of the collective "moment" robs the struggle of the self-in-between of any liberatory meaning. The collective struggle backs up, makes resistant meaning-making possible as meaning-making is interactive. The conceiving as well as the taking up and carrying of meaning requires a collectivity, however disorganized or open-ended that collectivity may be. Anzaldúa's desafio is about the creation of a new culture, an intimate and also and inseparably, a collective struggle.

I see enough evidence in Anzaldúa's text to develop an account of the sociality of resistance. If rebellion and creation are understood as processes rather than as isolated acts, then each act of solitary rebellion and creation is anchored in, responsive to, and looks for response from a collective, even if disorganized, process of resistance.

> Los Chicanos, how patient we seem, how very patient . . . We know how to survive. When other races have given up their tongue, we've kept ours . . . Stubborn, persevering, impenetrable as stone, yet possessing a malleability that renders us unbreakable, we, the mestizas and mestizos, will remain. (85–86)

The U.S. society places borderdwellers in profound isolation. The barriers to creative collectivity and collective creation appear insurmountable. But that is only if we think of the act and not of the process of creation. As we author every act of resistance, we can understand it as meaningful to the extent that it is inserted in a process of resistance that is collective, but we can also aspire to acts of collective resistance, breaking down our isolation against the odds prescribed by "the confines of the normal."

The borderdweller refuses to be split by the dichotomies of patriarchal/colonial modernity. It is my own sense that inhabitation of the borderlands does not guarantee communication among the atravesadas/os. But it makes communication imaginable as borderdwelling constitutes an interrogation of the logics of dominant meaning and dominant meaning-making and a suspension of one's confinement to those logics. This interrogation and suspension are multifaceted: dichotomous, binary, logics are interrogated and the borderdweller withdraws commitment to them; the logic of fragmentation and closed communities, groups, categories, nations is also up for interrogation and commitment withdrawal. The borderdweller is thus in need of interactive sense outside the narrow and oppressive confines of dominant logics and sense.

> Not only was the brain split into two functions but so was reality. Thus people who inhabit both realities are forced to live in the interface between the two, forced to become adept at switching modes. Such is the case with the india and the mestiza. (59)

in struggle

The journey from the border to the borderlands is then a coming to be both incarnate and aware without separation: to sense, perceive, relate, know within the flesh. Its core is the active/static, the germinative moment when we realize that the possibility of transformation away from our subjected selves lies in the power of our knowing embodiment: away from granting epistemic authority to distance. The knowing is from within our bodies, its senses felt from within when sensing the outside; the imagination open to sexual/social callings. I have dwelt on the strategies that keep the Chicana focused away from the familiar worlds of domination that constantly reduce and split her into germinative stasis. The germinative stasis has been lived as richly sensual. The sensual passage is not easy. Anzaldúa conceives of her creative stasis lavishly, writing from within a long memory. She calls forth beings from the past of the one she wants to be. It feels like a ritual passage. But Anzaldúa does not conceive her creative stasis, she conceives the very possibility of creative stasis through a deep sense of her past.

Stasis is not a once-in-a-lifetime passage, but constant, recurrent. Becoming the new mestiza is a recurrent activity. It is certainly not easy to claim una conciencia mestiza since it is not given to us. It is rather an aspect of the constant movement that includes the Coatlicue state, a form of nepantla. Without moving inside that enormously risky, difficult state, she cannot come to "see" the limits of the possible.

> Earth is a coiled Serpent. Forty years it's taken me to enter into the Serpent, to acknowledge that I have a body, that I am a body and to assimilate the animal body, the animal soul. (48)

Notes

1. I use the quotation marks in "text" because her writing defies the practice/theory dichotomy and it also defies the western notion of a book.
2. For a more extensive exploration of the relation between agency and univocity see my *Pilgrimages/Peregrinajes*.
3. Anzaldúa moves from the specificities of Chicana subjection to all those subjected.
4. In this writing I am committed to not making Anzaldúa, her path, or her "text" into objects for "objective" perusal. Our relation is not one between objects, one that objectifies either one of us.
5. For further discussion of resistance and anger see my "Hard-to-handle anger." There I revisit rage, its meaning, and its place within resistance toward liberation. "Rage" is not a term used for what I call "anger that demands respect." That anger seeks to make sense within dominant structures of sense.

Chapter 9

Negotiating Paradoxical Spaces: Women, Disabilities, and the Experience of Nepantla

Carrie McMaster

> *She felt shame for being abnormal. The bleeding distanced her from others. Her body had betrayed her . . . Her soft belly exposed to the sharp eyes of everyone; they see, they see. Their eyes penetrate her; they slit her from head to belly. Rajada. She is at their mercy, she can do nothing to defend herself. And she is ashamed that they see her so exposed, so vulnerable.*
>
> Gloria Anzaldúa, *Borderlands/La Frontera*

In this passage, describing her childhood, Anzaldúa vividly depicts the emotional impact of being different and therefore alienated from others. When I first read these unsettling words, I assumed, as many readers do, that she was referring to her experiences as the only Chicana in a class filled with Anglos. After all, elsewhere in *Borderlands* Anzaldúa does recount at length the racism she experienced in the Rio Grande Valley public schools during the 1950s. Anzaldúa's description of vulnerability and shame resonated strongly with me; I too felt alienated and marked as unacceptably different—not because of my racialized appearance but because of my abnormal hands and feet. Reading these words, I recalled my own childhood experiences as a shameful outsider and identified with Anzaldúa's pain. I could understand in new ways the feelings Anzaldúa describes—feelings that I mistakenly associated only with racism.

Not until I later read "La Prieta" did I realize that in the above passage Anzaldúa associates her intense shame with a congenital physical defect—a rare hormone disorder that caused her to begin menstruating in infancy and lead to an emergency hysterectomy in adulthood. Given my own stigmatizing physical defect, how did I entirely miss Anzaldúa's reference to her own congenital disease? The framework I had been given for understanding Anzaldúa was too narrow. Although I viewed Anzaldúa as a feminist, a Chicana theorist, and one of the founders of queer theory, I had not learned to also think of her as a woman with a chronic illness, a person with a disability.

Rereading Anzaldúa's writings with this new knowledge about her life offers additional perspectives both into Anzaldúa's theories and into disability studies, including feminist disability studies.[1] Unfortunately, disability scholars have yet to discover the power of Anzaldúa's poetic and persuasive prose and the relevance and flexibility of her theories.[2] Nor have theorists in other disciplines recognized the crucial roles Anzaldúa's struggles with her hormonal imbalance and another disabling condition,[3] adult-onset diabetes, played in shaping her work. How might our perspectives on Anzaldúa's theories and writings change when we broaden our frameworks to include this information? How might feminist disabilities studies benefit by including Anzaldúa's theories and writings? In this essay, I offer some preliminary answers to these queries. It is my hope that readers will, as I have, come to appreciate how Anzaldúa's lifelong struggles with disability facilitated rather than interfered with her greatness of mind, heart, and soul. I also hope that this realization will lead to the further understanding that, as Gloria Anzaldúa made positive meaning out of her supposed "incapacities," so can other women.

What do we learn when we look at Anzaldúa's work through this new lens? First, we can read "La Prieta," *Borderlands*, "Putting Coyolxauhqui Together," "now let us shift," and Anzaldúa's other writings as disability narratives.[4] Since the experiences of disabled women of color have seldom been examined within the field of feminist disability studies, Anzaldúa's accounts as a self-reflective Chicana are especially valuable to the discipline, for they remind scholars that feminist disability studies must go beyond analyses of gender and disability status to include the many factors shaping our lives and the societies in which we live. And, since disability-related issues are so rarely explored outside disability studies, reading Anzaldúa's writings *as* disability narratives would expand other scholars' understanding.

Second, we see that Anzaldúa's struggles with her hormonal imbalance and diabetes played a crucial role in shaping her inclusive politics. Indeed, Anzaldúa herself saw a clear connection between her politics and these conditions. As she asserts in a 1999 interview with AnaLouise Keating, "My resistance to gender and race injustice stemmed from my physical differences . . . I was extremely shy and vulnerable, and it all stemmed from the fact that people saw me as 'flawed' " (*Interviews/Entrevistas* 288). She does not hesitate to draw a parallel between ableism, sexism, and racism, stating that it was the experience of the former that engendered her resistance to the latter. Clearly, the shame Anzaldúa experienced because of her untimely menstruation had a powerful and enduring impact upon her life and her identity. Thus in the same interview, when Keating asks if Anzaldúa's chronic illnesses had affected "the ways you define and think about *other* aspects of your identity—like being Chicana, being queer, being female, being spiritual," Anzaldúa replied, "They have impacted me totally. My body has played a large role in shaping my identity" (288, her emphasis).

Third, and closely related, Anzaldúa's ability to draw non-homogenizing parallels between various embodied identities illustrates a type of empathic identification with significant implications for social justice work. Anzaldúa enacts a type of cross-difference identification, arguing that persons who experience any form of oppression are capable of empathizing with *differently* oppressed persons. Such empathetic identification can serve at least three purposes: allowing us to identify with and acknowledge kindred spirits who aren't members of our chosen political identity group(s); encouraging us to form temporary or permanent alliances with these other Others; and providing us with both rational and emotional grounds for opposing their oppression as we oppose our own. As Anzaldúa explains in "La Prieta," "Combined we cover so many oppressions. But the overwhelming oppression is the collective fact that we do not fit, and because we do not fit *we are a threat*. . . . In El Mundo Zurdo I with my own affinities and my people [those who differ significantly from any of society's norms] with theirs can live together and transform the planet" (233, her italics). Compassionate awareness of the oppression that we share with others who "do not fit" is not automatic, nor did Anzaldúa claim that it was. She *did* claim that such awareness could be used to better the lives of oppressed individuals and to change society so that such persons would no longer be regarded as threatening.

Fourth, Anzaldúa's theorizing has much to offer disability scholars and activists. Her concepts of la facultad, nepantla and nepantleras, conocimiento/desconocimiento, El Mundo Zurdo, new tribalism, the Coatlicue state, the Coyolxauhqui experience, and spiritual activism contribute both ideological and pragmatic tools to our work. In the following pages, I focus almost exclusively on nepantla and explore some of the ways we might apply this concept to our lives. Anzaldúa describes nepantla as a mental space, "the site of transformation, the place where different perspectives come into conflict and where you question the basic tenets inherited from your family, your education, and your different cultures" ("now let us shift" 548). Nepantla is a place/state beyond the boundaries of one's habitual world/mindset where transformation, growth, and change can take place, affecting the individual, her communities, and the world at large, because they are all interconnected within nepantla.

How might feminist disability scholars and women with disabilities, among others, apply this concept to our lives? We could begin by acknowledging that to live with disability is to live between the realities of what our body and/or mind experiences as normal (for us) and what society prescribes as normal (for a human being). Because U.S. society puts very strong emphasis on being "normal" or "average," we are torn between feeling alienated from our culture or alienated from ourselves. This conflict throws us into nepantla. If we are to thrive, we must hold the paradox of who we are versus who we are supposed to be until we can arrive at conocimiento and become able to act on our own behalf, on behalf of all persons with disabilities, and, indeed, on behalf of all people. Although Anzaldúa does not explicitly say so, the dissonance between who one knows that s/he is and who society claims that s/he must be encourages empathy with others caught in similar dissonances. The ability to assert the right of self-definition that emerges at the end of the process suggests that others who experience similar conflicts between self and social roles also gain the ability to be self-defining in new and liberating ways.

Gaining conocimiento through the liminal state of nepantla is not a one-time experience. Conocimiento is a type of knowing—specifically a spiritual knowledge or gnosis. Its spiritual nature notwithstanding, it does not encourage us to flee the demands of everyday life. Rather, this form of knowledge permits us to go beyond what we might incorrectly believe are the limits upon reality. Conocimiento opens new possibilities including new narratives that retell the stories of our lives in unfamiliar but life-enhancing ways.

Because of the above-described discrepancies between how we experience our lives and how we are told that we ought to experience them, some disabled persons become what Anzaldúa calls nepantleras. A nepantlera is a person skilled at living with contradiction, someone who can see from more than one point of view at a time and negotiate the in-between spaces that connect seemingly rigid either/or positions.

Being a nepantlera benefits not only the individual herself or himself but also the nepantlera's society. Nepantleras' double vision (second sight/insight) equips them to serve in roles requiring the ability to see issues from more than one (dominant) point of view. For instance, nepantleras might elect to become progressive political activists, negotiators, counselors or psychotherapists, dialogic teachers, religious leaders or spiritual directors, or holistic healthcare professionals. Anzaldúa acknowledged that "persons with disabilities are more apt to become nepantleras" (Keating, "Message"). I believe that persons with disabilities who have gained insights from experiencing nepantla early and/or often should seriously consider filling connective and integrative roles in society—and that we should be encouraged and provided the means to do so. Providing the means would involve utilizing existing channels such as state rehabilitation commissions and legislation such as the Individuals with Disabilities Education Act and the Americans with Disabilities Act to secure the equal educational and employment rights that we would need to enter into these professions. It would also necessitate making the public aware that some people with disabilities are gifted at coping with liminality and could perform work involving the reconciliation of multiple points of view, altering existing points of view, and/or resolving conflicts extremely well. At present 66 percent of disabled U.S. citizens are unemployed. If those of us who wished to use our skills at navigating nepantla professionally had the respect of our able-bodied peers and more adequate access to classrooms and workplaces, our unemployment rate might drop dramatically, to everyone's advantage.

Anzaldúa's vision of El Mundo Zurdo explicitly included persons such as myself who struggle daily with the socially constructed burden of physical and/or mental, emotional, or cognitive disabilities. I applaud her for incorporating us into her dream of a just society and for having been one of, or perhaps the, earliest social activist to do so. In *This Bridge Called My Back*, which was published in 1981, Anzaldúa spoke of an alliance incorporating "the colored, the queer, the poor, the female, and *the physically challenged*" (218, my italics) that she believed could change the world in fundamental and revolutionary ways. I also emphatically recommend that each of us involved in the Disability Rights Movement, disability studies, and/or feminist disability studies explore the roadmaps to El Mundo Zurdo that she gave us and use them to discover liberatory opportunities and kindred spirits of our own.

Notes

1. Feminist Disability Studies explores the social construction of disabilities and how the oppression of persons with disabilities parallels that of women (Thomson).
2. Even Abby Wilkerson—who quotes from *Borderlands* in "Disability, Sex Radicalism, and Political Agency" and commends Anzaldúa's "inclusive politics

that rejects narrow conceptions of identity in favor of a complex notion of oppression, privilege, and resistance" (39)—*only* attributes Anzaldúa's politics to her lesbian, feminist, and mestiza identities.

3. While classifying a chronic illness as a disability is problematic, I believe, based on Sally French's definitions, that doing so is reasonable, just, and appropriate. Societies erect powerful barriers around many such diseases (like HIV/AIDS, cancer, and psychoses); and construct more subtle but still significant barriers around less "catastrophic" disorders (like asthma, diabetes, and endometriosis). Those disability scholars who hesitate to incorporate chronic diseases into their models do so for several reasons: 1. Until recently all disabilities were considered illnesses requiring medical treatment, which is not the case and which works to the disadvantage of those who do not need constant medical care. 2. "Disease" and "illness" are not derived from the same theoretical models as "impairment" and "disability"; therefore, a shift from one model to another is necessary if one is to realize that some illnesses do indeed qualify as defective mechanisms of the body and—if chronic or even frequently recurring—can be disabling. 3. Most importantly, designating chronic diseases as disabilities might threaten to put persons with disabilities back under the purview of paternalistic medical "authorities." The risk of being re-pathologized/re-medicalized is real. However, I don't believe that it justifies some persons with disabilities turning their backs on other persons with disabilities whose disabilities happen to be chronic illnesses. For an excellent analysis of circumstances under which chronic diseases might constitute disabilities see Susan Wendell.
4. Disability narratives are autobiographies, memoirs, and self-reflective essays written by persons with disabilities. As G. Thomas Couser explains, "Unlike most cultural representations of disability, which issue from nondisabled parties and which may reinforce stigma and marginalization, disability autobiography issues from the perspective of someone living with the condition in question. Written from inside the experience of disability . . . [it] may represent disability in ways that challenge the usual cultural scripts" (109–10). In my opinion Anzaldúa's writings about the impact of disabilities on her life strongly challenges familiar cultural scripts.

Part 3

nos/otras. . . . intersecting selves/intersecting others

Living in a multicultural society, we cross into each other's worlds all the time. We live in each other's pockets, occupy each other's territories, live in close proximity and intimacy with each other at home, in school, at work. We're mutually complicitous—us and them, white and colored, straight and queer, Christian and Jew, self and other, oppressor and oppressed. We all of us find ourselves in the position of being simultaneously insider/outsider. The Spanish word "nosotras" means "us." In theorizing insider/outsider I write the word with a slash between nos (us) and otras (others). Today the division between the majority of "us" and "them" is still intact. This country does not want to acknowledge its walls or limits, the places some people are stopped or stop themselves, the lines they aren't allowed to cross. . . . [But] the future belongs to those who cultivate cultural sensitivities to differences and who use these abilities to forge a hybrid consciousness that transcends the "us" vs. "them" mentality and will carry us into a nosotras position bridging the extremes of our cultural realities.

—Gloria E. Anzaldúa, *Interviews/Entrevistas*

Chapter 10

What Do You Learn from What You See? Gloria Anzaldúa and Double-Vision in the Teaching of Writing

Eve Wiederhold

When I began to teach the first-year writing course, I was startled whenever students would listen to me. Life had never given me a ready audience before, let alone one accustomed to following orders, and since it seemed clear that I did not know what I was doing, I'd find myself laughing whenever they took me seriously. "Take out your notebooks," I'd say and they would, and their implicit faith in my authority used to make me pause, especially since I often issued the directive to fill a ten-minute void. Sometimes I'd stand there for a moment, feeling vaguely unethical, wondering whether to let them in on the joke. "It's just me," I wanted to confess. "I am not The Professor. I am not The Institution." Often I did call attention to what I found humorous—our resemblance to the Keystone Kops trying mightily to construct some version of what a writing class was supposed to be, watching those efforts dismantle under our mutual confusion over what it meant to be sharing lives and words for fifteen weeks.

There was some discomfort. Not everyone found the situation laughable, because of course, there was no real equity. Meanwhile, this was the early 1990s and my studies in feminism led to a growing realization of the ways I had been socialized to feel unauthorized and girlish. But nonetheless

I remember (or choose to remember) the experience of joy in discovery, the way the lack of a plan allowed for an exuberant spontaneity.

Years later, hundreds of students later, with a body and face transformed by time and the pursuit of a doctorate, my ability to occupy that doubled space inside and outside the institution has evaporated. I have settled into the role of The Professor (or it has settled upon me), so that when I say, "Take out your notebooks," there is a slight shift in the ways that students react. I have authority, they know it, I'm invested in it, and gone is the balance between my pause and their "who are you?" skepticism. I am read in my institutional role and my commands for notebooks are greeted with predictable responses: the alert snap from the ambitious, the recalcitrant "not again" from the bored, or, worst of all, the trepidation and fear from those who are simply confused, the ones who whisper "she wants us to do what?" because they are too intimidated to ask me to clarify, too distanced from my professorial rank, too well-versed in a pavlovian way with the knowledge that to not obey is to be intellectually slapped, branded a failure, a nonachiever, a member of the "lower" reading group. When I see those hunched shoulders and grim expressions, I wonder if there is any way in my present guise to convince my students that, even as I stand by my pedagogy, I still am not fully engaged with either the institutional goals of composition nor my role as Professor.

I suspect that there are other instructors and program directors who feel both allegiance to and alienation from the identity categories and official program goals that define and legitimize work in composition studies. Those who predicate the writing course upon a conceptual fracturing of institutional identities can develop strategies for registering ambivalence with the help of iconoclastic writers like Gloria Anzaldúa, whose innovative style poses a challenge to comprehensive, coherent articulations of what writing is or should be.[1] Her generative "borderlands" metaphor highlights complexities accompanying acts of translation in ways that can help writing instructors interrogate the institutionalized categories organizing their work. Instead of clarifying, Anzaldúa blends poetry with prose, political theory with personal narrative, and Spanish dialects with English in texts that motivate readers to trip over their acts of reading, take note of how they stumble, and, consequently, adopt a "double vision" when rendering an interpretation. Asking readers to attend to "the text" and the cultural strategies that direct how texts should be read effectively unsettles an entire structure that informs conventional understandings of how writing bears upon knowledge, reality, meaning, and communication. Compositionists can draw upon Anzaldúa's interpretive turbulence to transform critical theories and pedagogical obligations.

the comfort of the familiar

At a liberal arts school in the Midwest, I asked writing students to read Anzaldúa's "How to Tame the Wild Tongue," which explores (among other things) how intimate and painful it can be to read language use as a social identity. I did not expect the students—all Caucasian, mostly from comfortable, middle-class suburbs—to identify with Anzaldúa's testimonial to the shame she internalized as a Chicana accused of speaking "a bastard language" (58). But I thought connections with the text might be made by asking students, for example, if anyone ever critiqued their speech; if they had a "home" language that differed from how they spoke at school; if they understood what Anzaldúa meant when she wrote, "so if you really want to hurt me, talk badly about my language" (59).

Their response: silence. Notably quiet were members of the women's track team, six otherwise energetic and boisterous athletes. I thought that perhaps class members were puzzled or afraid to speak, so to loosen things up, I described a dream I had the previous night, in which I found myself in a motionless trance watching snakes slither out of my shins, a seemingly horrific image that nonetheless left me feeling content and freed. I related the image to finishing a major writing project and reading Anzaldúa's "Entering Into the Serpent," the night before. Wasn't it amazing, I asked, how textual images can filter through our psyches in ways that we can't control? Warming up to my own rhetoric, ignoring the saucer-eyed stares, I encouraged the students to consider how reading and writing affect our bodies as well as our identities, and how we learn to try to control this influence by placing constraints on our expressions as we compose. I think I also threw in some thoughts about the language of dreams, which, I said, are like confessions, and then I wondered, how might we revolutionize the classroom if we started class with reports on our dream states?

The next work day, I received a message on my voice mail. The athletes apparently were so alarmed by the essay and my reaction to it that they turned en masse to their coach, who called to let me know that she had concerns about the appropriateness of my pedagogy. She never mentioned Anzaldúa or my dream. Rather, she spoke on behalf of college rules and student welfare, out of a concern for their education and safety. She suggested that perhaps I needed to get a better handle on school policies (including, I learned later from the acting department head, that I should refrain from using inappropriate words, such as "what the hell" and "damn"). The coach and I never spoke, although I responded with a message inviting her to meet with me. Instead, I was left to wonder about the institutional context that made it possible for a person from another department to lecture me about my class. Even more troubling than the phone call was the coach's ability to invoke a language of protection when leveling her complaint. To me, formulating her comments in terms of student welfare and safety committed a bigger offense than my miscalculation of audience. But of course, that difference in perspective was part of the problem.

The reactions of the students and their coach might be understood in terms of composition's historical mission within the academy. Composition historians locate early rationales for the writing course in the late nineteenth century, a time when U.S. colleges were "upgraded" into research institutions modeled after German universities.[2] Disciplinary specialty replaced liberal study, and this shift led to a decline in instruction about rhetoric, which, prior to 1870, had constituted the basis for the four-year degree. Indeed, rhetorical studies had been a central component in educational programs since the classical era, and in various ways, attended to the myriad, contentious contingencies animating speech and acts of persuasion. In the new university, however, this focus came to seem too general and unscholarly; it was replaced with the study of texts specifically identified as *literature*. As English departments evolved, so did the specialties of professors, who concentrated their research on literary genres and praiseworthy authors. Pedagogical goals shifted. Rather than ask students to engage in oral arguments about popular values, students of English were expected to aspire to become introspective, contemplative thinkers, able to read proper literary texts in tasteful and decorous ways. The "streamlined curriculum" that accompanied these developments also produced the first-year composition course, which replaced rhetorical analyses of invention and audience reception with circumscribed lessons about organizational skills and correctness.[3]

This drive toward disciplinary specialty influenced perceptions of the respective scholarly value of literary and composition studies. Literature professors (i.e., the department's Shakespeareans) appear to *be* specialists. Compositionists, by comparison, do not. Presumably, anyone with a college degree is familiar with the introductory writing course. Consequently, a track coach can speak with authority about writing instruction, while a writing teacher may not necessarily speak knowingly about track (even if she jogs regularly). The lingering perception of composition as a general course without a disciplinary pedigree has put those who work on its behalf at a disadvantage, as evidenced by the familiar division of labor—composition remains a lower division course at most schools, staffed by adjuncts and untrained graduate students; literary analysis is still the preserve for upper division majors and professors with special expertise—and by the well-known conceptual divisions that distinguish rhetoric from poetic. Accordingly, literary language entices students into the realm of the imagination and represents the best that has been said. Composition-rhetoric bespeaks the language of the "everyday" and traffics in the practical, political, and common. Meanwhile, the literary author is constructed as creative, open, a risk-taker, willing to delve into the unknown for the sake of representing timeless truths. The rhetorician/composition student seems to be less imaginative, bounded by lived experience, constrained if not docile to the order of logic, and writes for utilitarian and practical purposes.[4]

Compositionists have spent the last thirty years trying to overturn the conceptual divisions contributing to the field's reputation as the "weak spouse, the new kid, the cash cow, the oppressed majority" (Elbow 533). An enormous body of research published in the past three decades has professionalized the field and explained what compositionists do as they study how common languages shape attitudes and lived experiences. A most promising articulation of this work has been developed by scholars who seek to reincorporate the rhetorical tradition lost when academies shifted from studying liberal arts to conducting research. Those arguing for a return to rhetoric aim to restore students' abilities to engage critically with existing cultural representations, to teach students how to formulate their own and through their writing, expand possibilities for democratic participation. James Berlin, for example, argued that writing instructors should train students to critique dominant ideologies so that they become "better readers of signifying practices that shape all of their experiences—economical, social, and political" (91). Patricia Bizzell defines "the public function of the intellectual as precisely rhetorical" and argues that just as the intellectual's task should be to teach all citizens how to "share a discourse," the writing classroom should situate language study within "the public interest" to restore regard for "the authority created by collective discursive exchange and its truths as provisionally binding" (261–62). This perspective is congenial with that of Thomas P. Miller, who would repoliticize the writing class by restoring the civic humanist tradition of rhetorical studies that does not reject popular opinion as anti-intellectual, but instead teaches students to draw on "shared values to resolve public conflict" (219).

The attempt to give cultural form to democratic plurality seems to offer a strong corrective to the local histories and contexts that have situated composition as a handmaiden to poetics by placing primacy upon the isolated thinker in pursuit of singular truths. Articulating social goals for the writing class enables the compositionist to emerge as a scholar with a specific expertise about how composing processes influence who controls the way information is processed and disseminated. Recognizing the value of this expertise would not only dislodge the entrenched association between writing instruction and grammar rules, it also would dramatically revise how the academic study of texts gets organized within English departments as a whole.

But while these visions have much to offer compositionists, they do not fully address the complexities of translation raised by Anzaldúa's prose. One problem is that the attempt to identify a proper subject for composition/rhetoric continues to measure work in the field in binary terms and retains the either/or logic that separated poetics from rhetoric and established hierarchies in the first place. This binary logic has appeared in many forms throughout the history of western thought to reaffirm the idea that there are distinct insides and outsides, presences and absences, and borders to guard the distinctions. Anzaldúa's *Borderlands* scrutinizes precisely "the space between" and the exclusions necessary to maintain conceptual boundaries. Like other feminist/postmodern writers, she points out that if there is no privileged space external to some institutional framework determining the circulation of cultural signs, then categories of "inside" and "outside" collapse, marking the inability to fully and clearly comprehend differences that appear to enable categories to *be*. Indeed, categories are cultural constructs, supported by imbricated institutions that empower them to make meaning in the world. Given that systems of power already anticipate and co-opt social and political alternatives, structuring the democratically oriented composition course as an alternative to the "insular" study of poetics does not disrupt the affiliations between the production of knowledge and the cultural authority that accrues to those who produce venerable texts. Indeed, positing composition's value within an academic institution indebted to disciplinarity does little to change a system that rewards competition and that encourages fights over ownership of disciplinary property.

A second problem with translation can arise when considering speech acts and propriety, and the goal of using the classroom to impart linguistic competency. Ostensibly, democratic equity is guaranteed in the writing classroom just by participating in an exchange of ideas. The conditions enabling rhetorical engagement would seem to unfold neutrally and continuously, providing an equitable basis for transactions between speakers, writers, and audiences. Language appears to be an impersonal ground available to all to use at will, while each person's interactions with symbols would seem to be similarly constituted. But emphasizing democratic inclusivity through equal access to language does not necessarily address how institutional contexts manage negotiations of communicative transactions, nor how the "democratic" rubric places a premium on the social importance of recognizable form. In the democratic writing classroom, students and teachers will continue to struggle with questions about what language to speak for inclusion in a given discursive community.[5]

Theorists who identify the composition class as a public arena that fosters critical thinking and debate often imagine a pluralism of conscious individuals, each of whom wants to share language and claim group identity. As James Williams puts it, "the heterogeneous nature of the composition workshop . . . was seen as a way of finding common value among disparate students with significantly different backgrounds and unequal skills. Differences were to be celebrated through rational discourse that would overcome emotional prejudices of all varieties" (140).[6] In practice, however, the goal of speaking "rationally" to announce membership with the group typically gets articulated in terms of learning the protocols of style preferred by a majority. *The New St. Martin's Handbook*, for example, includes a short section on what is euphemistically called "language variety," wherein students who use nonstandard English are advised to consider audience when deciding which mode of speech to use. "The key to shifting among varieties of English and among languages is appropriateness: when will such a shift reach your audience and help you make a particular point?" (Lunsford and Connors 337). Such advice implies that speakers and writers can engage in simple acts of code-switching at will, and constructs the process as neutrally occurring in an intellectual vacuum. There is no acknowledgment of the potential for such advice to establish expectations of what is "normal" when making choices, no consideration of how some of us might form attachments to "inappropriate" modes of speech, nor of the ways that our experiences within different habitats can affect how signs of propriety are read. Resolution of tension is favored over cognitive dissonance, and then filed under the moralizing label of "tolerance," "respect," or in the case of the handbook, "building common ground" (339).

When the language of "the wild tongue" does not translate, who is obligated to do what to try to effect communication? The problem with teaching students to "share a discourse" is that it presumes that a principle of equivalence underwrites acts of translation. Instead, the burden of communication typically falls on the "non-standard" speaker, and authorizes those in the majority to blandly reaffirm the validity of their own perceptions of propriety and normalcy. From this perspective, constructing the composition classroom as a locus for discursive exchange about public issues promotes the same cultural agenda the writing course has always had: "Making" good Americans via shared participation in cultural rituals that can be associated subsequently with "nationhood."[7] Students may still receive instruction that validates the three R's: responsibility, respectability, and recognizability.

transforming categories

Anzaldúa's prose style resists Western culture's investment in the "aesthetic of virtuosity"—that drive toward mimesis in which students and professors stay within contained, self-enclosed epistemological systems, expecting that everyone's texts will mimic recognizable prose styles to demonstrate intellectual achievement. As Anzaldúa explains, "the aesthetic of virtuosity . . . attempts to manage the energies of its own internal system such as conflicts, harmonies. It is 'psychological' in that it spins its energies between itself and its witness" (*Borderlands* 89–90), erecting a Plathian bell jar of sameness and homogeneity. Like the rule of sameness that organizes our understanding of how we communicate, the "aesthetic of virtuosity" presupposes a centered subject able to engage with symbols in systematic ways in order to provide recognizable evidence of that engagement to like-minded teachers. Through this management of energies, speaking the same language identifies a state of belonging. The stakes are high when determining who is included and excluded from the intellectual arena.

Challenging this dynamic does not mean that as we speak, we lose the goal of sharing and recognizability. Doing so would be impossible, as Anzaldúa observes, since our citations depend upon a familiarity with prior contexts for their intelligibility. She does not seek a replacement but a reorientation toward language that implicates how to negotiate alterity and *whether* to try to translate "the other" into a form recognizable to a majority. In an interview with Andrea Lunsford, Anzaldúa considers the dual goals of seeing anew and being understood, highlighting the impossibility of embracing either perspective on its own. She notes that during her writing process she asks herself, "How much can I get way with pushing at the norms, at the conventions?" (*Interviews/Entrevistas* 259). "How much do you push and how much do you accommodate and be in complicity with the dominant norm of a particular field" (*Interviews/Entrevistas* 253) in order to assist the translation process? Composition programs are fraught with the tension between the two horizons Anzaldúa describes: to encourage writers to say anew, to communicate what hasn't been expressed, to lay claim to the power of invention, re-vision, but to do so for audiences who have the habit of expecting sensible representations.

Rather than seek a resolution to such tension, Anzaldúa articulates how new meanings can be created from contested arenas. She invokes the word "nepantla" to name a paradigm that steps beside western epistemology's binary logic by "theoriz[ing] unarticulated dimensions of the experience of mestizas living between overlapping and layered spaces of different cultures, and social and geographical locations of events and realities—psychological, social, political, spiritual, historical, creative, imagined" (*Interviews/Entrevistas* 268). In tentatively naming overlapping experiences, nepantla refuses the categories that conventionally carve up language study into poetic, rhetoric, public, private, artistic, practical, sublime, and mundane. Instead, it draws attention to both the writing act and the ways that it is embedded within institutionalized contexts, paying homage to the space that separates the unrecognizable from the familiar, the place where the promise of "going somewhere" via the power of speech meets obstacles imposed by conventions and the allure of normativity. Nepantla opens a space in which to listen for the not-yet said, the not-yet imagined.

Offering a complex refusal to represent her self and her writing as recognizable, Anzaldúa simultaneously prompts the writing teacher to consider how normative pedagogical contexts inform what he thinks should be made visible in student texts to show evidence *of* "democratic" participation—or even of a *desire* to participate. Indeed, her attention to "borderlands" and "mestiza" consciousness blurs boundaries and refocuses the framework used to organize the "what" and the "how" of language study because it suggests a completely different way of envisioning how to read what is significant within any scene of representation. The doubled vision enacted and illustrated in her writing calls attention to what is worldly and unworldly in our interaction with symbols; in the process, it destabilizes the meanings of our most familiar terms. A doubled perspective, for example, refuses to simplify the idea of audience. For Anzaldúa, "the audience" is always the reader and an unnamable other. ("Sometimes I'll bump into a chair and I'll say, 'Excuse me' " [*Interviews/Entrevistas* 285]). Rather than advocate the commonplace, "consider your audience," attention might be drawn to the ways in which cultural conventions work to categorize who becomes a member of a group worth writing for (a question that might have helped me negotiate responses with those alienated athletes). For the artist-genius, the question of audience is usually ignored, or imagined as a higher power "beyond" the limited human imagination. Indeed, writers who aspire to produce literary texts and who "consider their audience" seem to taint the integrity of the artistic process. The elitism inhering in this construct dissipates once the classification of what is literary is scrutinized. Anzaldúa's texts are both political treatises and literary constructs. Identifying her audience will not function to determine who should read her text, since it will be directed toward who/what is simultaneously mundane and spiritual, embodied and imagined, formed and unformed, suggesting a dispersal of "audience" that is always there and not there depending on where and how one looks. Further, her multilingualism reminds readers that the work of translation is ever-present, even when we think we speak the same language. All speakers/writers are positioned as foreigners occupying distinct discursive spaces, and when we rely upon known conventions to do the work of communicating, we risk reproducing institutional practices that ultimately regulate our understanding of participation itself.

The labor of understanding changes once conventional classifications become unreliable, and that change is profound. Readers are unable to "look past" form to understand content. Rather than position the reader as "master overseer"[8] capable of sharing what is known, "seeing double" maneuvers the reader away from the obligation to either "stay in control" or "make sense" according to immediately recognizable terms. Indeed, when reading Anzaldúa's texts, the point is not to "get to the point," but to attend to the relationship between politics and form, to always "keep an eye on" the ways form informs meaning, and to notice when and how interpretive acts adhere to social norms that regulate writing and reading.

enacting the interpretive abyss

If we conceive of engagement as occurring in a "borderland," a space between defined territories, possibilities for what students (or any of us) might experience as interpreters and composers are endless. If we imagine ourselves as "standing between," there is no conceptualized formal center, no singular way of measuring and fostering participation, no reverence for form itself that then may be referenced to appear to assuage the call of accountability. This relinquishing of institutionalized obligations opens up avenues to transformation. Anzaldúa describes writing as perpetual shapeshifting, an artifact and the energy spent to produce it in private/public performances: "When invoked in rite, the object/event is 'present'; that is, 'enacted'; it is both a physical thing and the power that infuses it" (*Borderlands* 89). Writing is as much a physical as an intellectual activity. Indeed, it is the combination of both that enables Anzaldúa to enter "a shamanic state" that involves the labor of the body (mopping the floor) and the psychic work of opening herself to receive "voices and scenes . . . projected in the inner screen of [her] mind" (89), which then require the work of translation to the page—an act that itself demands physical and mental exertion. "I write in red. Ink. Intimately knowing the smooth touch of paper, its speechlessness before I spill myself on the insides of trees" (93). Writing, she reminds us, "is a sensuous act" (93).

Here is a foregrounding that compositionists invested in public rhetorics tend to forget: the need to experience and recognize that sensuous state and to be *in* it and a watchful spectator, and to remember—always—that writing involves physical bodies wrestling with the work of translation. Our interactions with narratives yield performances in time. We tend to prioritize the time of the future—using the writing classroom as a stand-in for some other "real" moment of engagement (at work, when voting)—or the perpetual time-of-reflection (of 'classics' that have withstood the test of time). But there is also the time of the classroom which allows for the eruption of the "new" in the time of the "now." In rare moments in which I experience something like hope, I imagine what would happen if this perspective were welcomed, honored, taken seriously by university administrators who make decisions about how to spend money. I think about what might change in the writing class, even physically: no more blaring overhead lights, gray walls, nondescript floors, hard-backed chairs placed in ordered rows, too many bodies gathered in some dreary space for the purpose of looking like productive citizens. . . .

When I read Anzaldúa's work, I am tempted to think about what (I think) *really* matters about engagement and participation with symbolic texts. Writing, she explains "is metaphysical in that it 'spins its energies between gods and humans' and its task is to move the gods. This type of work dedicates itself to managing the universe and its energies" (89). I am completely taken with this description, although the last thing I would advocate is that writing programs try to promote and administer shamanism. Indeed, I am loath to appropriate the descriptions of tribalism that inform Anzaldúa's perspective as I go about making a case for shifting conceptions of the first-year writing course's purposes. But I do think it is worth noting how inadequate grades and hierarchies of judgment and enforced deadlines and production of texts on demand seem in the context of this other way of conceptualizing those most mysterious and enigmatic encounters with symbols. How should we measure signs of engagement? It is worth noting that the history of composition studies could be described as an attempt to clean up and regularize the labor of this kind of engagement. Perhaps because that endeavor is so immense, so fraught with a blundering ignorance, those of us deposited before students bearing the glean of authority feel an obligation to live up to some image of it, and make sure that we look like we know what we're doing. But Anzaldúa's articulation of her writing as "a flawed thing—a clumsy, complex, groping, blind thing . . . alive, infused with spirit" (89) encourages receptivity to ignorance and the unfamiliar, while simultaneously inviting readers to see how reactions are informed by preformed cultural narratives. Were teachers to adopt this other doubled perspective, they might notice differently, especially when evaluating signs of who is participating and who is engaged.

Indeed, the practice of seeing double would mean attending to several simultaneities that occur in those "between spaces" wherein (seemingly) private meditations meet public exposure. This space makes room for a joyful reveling in the open possibility of transformation while remembering that translating can also leave one feeling cloddish and foolish. And this space would acknowledge rhetoric—its arbitrariness and "please-join-the-group" pull in which a "choice" is made to speak in recognizable terms even if one attempts to rebuff cultural impositions. Within this space, one would attend to the simultaneous beauty and weighty obstruction of form itself; the ways organizing categories that help sort through and make sense of the mystery of composing also establish conceptual boundaries that regulate and constrain. And as Anzaldúa explains, it is here that we open ourselves to the energy of creativity while facing the abyss of the unknown in our attempts to manage it.

Notes

1. For brief analyses of connections between Anzaldúa's work and composition studies, see Thomas R. West; Min-Zhan Lu; Bonnie Lenore Kyburz. For analyses not strictly related to composition, see Sonia Saldívar-Hull; Bat-Ami Bar On; and Monika Kaup.
2. On this point, see John Brereton, introduction. See also Bill Readings.
3. For notable studies of the history of composition see Sharon Crowley; Elizabetheda Wright and S. Michael Halloran; Thomas Miller; Winifred Horner; and William Riley Parker.
4. See James Berlin, chapter five, for a detailed examination of this dichotomy.
5. Composition scholars are beginning to address the politics of form. See, for example, *Alt Dis: Alternative Discourses and the Academy*, edited by Schroeder, Fox, and Bizzell.
6. Williams is arguing for a return to standards, not their blurring.
7. For a fuller examination of study in the humanities and citizenship, see Toby Miller.
8. This phrase is borrowed from Annette Murrell.

Chapter 11

Reading National Identities: The Radical Disruptions of *Borderlands/La Frontera*

Beth Berila

In the wake of September 11, 2001, U.S. anxieties about national identity have surfaced with a vengeance. Despite the prolific "United-We-Stand" rhetoric, racial profiling of people of color in airports and on our streets has escalated, revealing the "we" to be both contestatory and exclusionary. The rhetoric of unification masks the materiality of both national identity and culture as sites of "resistance and struggle, not coherence and consensus" (Saldívar 14). Few texts confront these issues more profoundly than Gloria Anzaldúa's *Borderlands/La Frontera: The New Mestiza.* Anzaldúa interrogates dominant conceptions of nation and identity, exploring whether and how it might be possible to develop a sense of national identity that doesn't exclude and do violence to women and men of color and those who are poor or queer. The text's experimental form foregrounds the contestatory narratives of national identity, revealing the histories of colonization, exploited labor, and racism that make possible dominant national narratives. In doing so, it invites readers to enact a similar interrogation of national identities and their performances, offering us opportunities to critically locate ourselves in these narratives' formations and learn less violent ways to to read national contestations.

Drawing on my experiences teaching *Borderlands* at a private university in central New York, I argue that the text's experimental form and politics challenge readers to make meaning in ways that reveal the constant *work* that goes into constructing national identities. These constructs are not given and self-evident but are, rather, the result of constant political and ideological struggle. Calling attention to people's participation in this process—whether that participation is about contesting or upholding dominant narratives,—Anzaldúa highlights the costs of validating dominant national narratives in ways that do violence to other narratives, and urges readers to hold multiple, contestatory accounts simultaneously.

Borderlands, as many critics have noted, articulates the material, spiritual, and psychological effects of living on multiple borders (Yarbro-Bejarano, "Gloria Anzaldúa's *Borderlands/La Frontera*" 5; Keating, "Writing" 105; Bernard 35). I argue that the text's experimental format *enacts* an interrogation of national identity, calling for a process that challenges readers to examine our own relationships to border issues, colonization, and ethnic/race relations, thus revealing "national identity" to be multiple, relational, and contestatory. Whereas constructs of national identity often presume a stable authority and a unified whole that "naturally" excludes "others," *Borderlands* reveals the contestations and exclusions that always already exist within such formations—indeed, upon which such monolithic constructs depend. As she calls for new understandings of national identity, Anzaldúa challenges readers to self-reflexively position ourselves within those narratives and to be accountable for the effects of the narratives we uphold.

Anzaldúa links aesthetics, politics, nation, and identity by moving between forms, languages, and themes, building a hybrid narrative that progresses through disjunctures. As the narrative shifts from prose to poetry, Castillian Spanish to English to Nahuatl, folklore to "official" historical accounts, it performs the complex identity that Anzaldúa claims for herself and the shifting borders this identity entails. Readers are thus pushed to continually adjust our reading in ways which may be more familiar to some readers than to others, depending on our subject positions. Indeed, Anzaldúa elsewhere establishes a relationship between literary form and identity when she writes in her introduction to *Making Face, Making Soul/Haciendo Caras*: "Let the reader beware—I here and now issue a *caveat perusor*: s/he must do the work of piecing this text together. . . . As the perspective and focus shift, as the topics shift, the listener is forced to connect the dots, to connect the fragments" (xvii–xviii).

This challenge applies to *Borderlands* as well: Anzaldúa highlights the interactive nature of meaning-making and asks readers to recognize our various roles in the process. We must examine the ways our own locations (whatever they may be) shape how we read, while the text's mixed form urges readers to experiment with reading from different and shifting locations. Such reading practices are more than literary or intellectual exercises; they offer ways to recognize multiple understandings of the nation simultaneously and enable readers to hold the various narratives accountable to each other for the violence they enact or the spaces they allow. Practicing more open ways of reading invites readers to perform national identity differently in our daily lives.[1]

This radical form begins immediately as *Borderlands* opens with a corrido written in Spanish, moves to a passage which revises history to reclaim Aztec roots, then moves to Anzaldúa's own poetry about the violence and contradictions of living on the borderlands (23–25). Readers are immediately introduced to the juxtapositions pervading the text and characterizing her life: the heritage of colonized and colonizer and the multiplicity of languages and traditions. As Anzaldúa performs her own dislocations in and critiques of dominant national narratives, the text reveals gaps in those narratives. Thus the opening corrido describes "el otro Mexico," while the subsequent passage claims the Aztlán homeland. But just as this "true" homeland is named, Anzaldúa shifts to her own poetry, which describes this space as a fluctuating edge: "I stand at the edge where earth touches ocean / where the two overlap / a gentle coming together / at other times a violent clash" (23). Anzaldúa never allows readers more than a momentary comfort in this homeplace because she immediately marks it as unsettled; she textually disrupts reading processes through juxtapositions of form, language, and subject matter. These disruptions call for different, more flexible reading processes that make room for gaps in dominant narratives about national identities.

In the above passages, the narrator gazes across the border to Mexico and poetically marks the split that will recur throughout the text. But the border fence is not fixed, since the poem also describes the sea surging around it. Moreover, the narrator actually traverses the border by walking through a hole in the fence. The line's layout on the page is significant:

> I walk through the hole in the fence
>   to the other side. (24)

The space after "I walk" invites readers to pause, and leaves an opening in which our eyes can fall to the line below which describes "the other side." The border's two sides have been separated by the spatial pause on the page, a pause which, significantly, immediately follows an act of agency: walking through the (presumably illicit) hole in the fence. This space occurs again in the lines "splits me   splits me / me raja   me raja" (24); now the space resonates with violent division, but also contains the agency marked earlier. We see this space again near the poem's end when Anzaldúa returns to the idea of a homeland: "This land was Mexican once / was Indian always / and is. / And will be again" (25). This reclamation demands a presence for that space and a recognition of the violent splitting that results from arbitrary borders. Later, Anzaldúa links this border crossing to a political agenda of resisting and reinventing national identity; she calls for a new consciousness allowing her to straddle both sides of the border without a violent division. Issuing a direct challenge to white society to take responsibility for its brutal racism, she demands a recognition and a revaluing of difference. She also delineates a strategy, mestiza consciousness, that explicitly links her writing's experimental form to national identity as it calls for a tolerance for ambiguity and contradictions (101).

These passages, and many others, disrupt dominant narratives of race, nation, and identity, suggesting that as these categories are linked to historically and politically embedded constructions of national identity, we can begin to question them. If, as Stuart Hall argues, identity is partly about representation, then revealing their constructed quality can open spaces to create multiple national identities, or to challenge the construct entirely ("Ethnicity" 298). Coco Fusco has suggested that art is a particularly valuable site for this disruption because "culture in this country is a critical, if not the most crucial, area of political struggle over identity" (26). While literature does not "automatically" unsettle such categories, Anzaldúa's text enables such possibilities precisely because her aesthetic practices, inextricably linked to the materiality of living on the border, challenge readers to confront that materiality. *Borderlands* invites a self-reflexive reading process—an opportunity to critique and transform the exclusions that make possible comfortable notions of national identity; it also creates spaces for voices that have been marginalized and erased by those formations.

The political and pedagogical potential of this reading process became clear to me when I taught *Borderlands* in two undergraduate courses. Because the classroom is a public space, the text enabled public reading moments in which participants were accountable to each other for the meanings they produced. This accountability can prove invaluable for a radical politics seeking to disrupt the racism and violence of certain notions of national identity. Students often expressed frustration at the sudden shifts in narrative, and even more frustration at the shifts in language, since many of them did not speak Spanish, Tex-Mex, or Nahuatl. They held Anzaldúa responsible to make her writing accessible rather than taking on the responsibility of meeting the text. Of course, Anzaldúa prepares readers for this challenge, writing in her introduction that "[t]he switching of 'codes' in this book from English to Castillian Spanish to the North Mexican dialect to Tex-Mex to a sprinkling of Nahuatl to a mixture of all of these, reflects my language, a new language—the language of the Borderlands—. . . . [W]e Chicanos no longer feel that we need to beg entrance— . . . to translate to Anglos, Mexicans, and Latinos, apology blurting out of our mouths with every step. Today we ask to be met halfway" (n.p.).

Here, Anzaldúa names the power dynamics embedded in reading and speaking. Her text demonstrates that meaning-making processes are connected to our subject positions: who we are shapes how we read. As Chandra Talpade Mohanty and Biddy Martin point out, we can examine our own privilege or lack thereof by constantly examining our positionality in relation to others in any given moment: " 'Being home' refers to the place where one lives within familiar, safe, protected boundaries; 'not being home' is a matter of realizing that home was an illusion of coherence and safety based on the exclusion of specific histories of oppression and resistance, the repression of differences even within oneself" (168). Unsettling the false coherence and safety accompanying certain constructions of national identity, and revealing that marginalized groups have never felt much safety in those narratives, offers opportunities to begin dismantling these constructions.

Revealing this illusion is thus invaluable to critiques of national identity. Various public spaces, including the university classroom, offer sites in which to draw out that connection. When I taught *Borderlands* in a course on the U.S. West, most white students and all but two students of color expressed reluctance to code-switch, at least publicly; the classroom's racial dynamics clearly played a role in students of color's reluctance. Most white students felt blamed and put off by what they read as Anzaldúa's anger. When I encouraged them to explore this sense of blame and asked them what it might look like to meet *Borderlands* halfway, they turned the responsibility back on the text. One student expressed frustration and disdain at Anzaldúa's description of how the dominant culture limited her; this student argued that she does whatever she wants to do despite dominant-culture standards of femininity and suggested that Anzaldúa should do the same.

These reactions—which are fairly typical of white students' initial reactions to *Borderlands* at this university—reveal how particular subject positions and institutional constraints predetermine "conventional" reading practices that reproduce dominant narratives. Many white students (though significantly, not all) came from solid middle-to upper-class backgrounds; when this class privilege is combined with race privilege, issues of border clashes as they impact intersections of identity seem far removed from their lives. That distance, of course, is deceptive; we are all positioned on axes of race, class, gender, sexuality, and nation in inequitable power relations to each other. But as students read through overly familiar categories, they can avoid seeing how their comfort in dominant narratives of national identity *absolutely depends* on the political and economic exploitation of those marked as "others." Conventional reading practices worked to obscure the ways identity is constructed differently for a working-class queer Chicana living on the U.S./Mexico border than for a straight white middle-class woman in central New York.

Especially significant was the vehemence with which the white students constantly reasserted the dominant national narratives' authority and stability.[2] Indeed, the intensity of students' reactions leads me to believe that *Borderlands* disrupted their constructions of national identity. Such narratives depend on excluding voices such as Anzaldúa's; if students were to engage her critiques in any complexity, they would have to be willing to unsettle those narratives. Patti Lather has suggested that student resistance to feminist work is not something that must be overcome so that students can embrace the "correct" politics, but is rather the process of recognizing and negotiating the dissonance of contestation (76). The vehement reactions suggest that students were deeply affected by *Borderlands* and the ways it resisted and unsettled their conventional reading practices. Our discussions revealed the *work* and the racism that go into upholding dominant ideologies about national identity in the face of challenges like Anzaldúa's. Students had to continually differentiate themselves from her text and insist that in America people are free to do whatever they wish to do—a narrative that rang false in light of Anzaldúa's historical and personal accounts.

As white students vocalized these narratives, shoring up their sense of national identity, students of color voiced responses that revealed the classroom's racial power dynamics. While most didn't fully identify with Anzaldúa's political critique, their responses distanced them from the presumably monolithic national identity and noted the racism inherent in it. Two expressed their comfort with *Borderlands*—a Native woman and a Spanish-speaking Latino. In my experience, students of color more frequently identify with the text, though some of them, along with many white students, have difficulty with the its queerness. One student, for example, focused on Anzaldúa's assertion that she made the choice to be queer, suggesting that Anzaldúa wouldn't be lesbian if it weren't trendy. When we explored the possible rhetorical and political purposes of saying one "chooses" to be queer in a world that would prefer queers to stay in the closet, this student's position became more nuanced. She argued that as an African American woman, she can't "choose" not to hold a marginalized position in U.S. culture. These comments reflected a complexity not evident in the initial resistance, and led to a productive discussion about race and sexuality in the United States and Mexico. These classroom moments revealed students' vexed relationships to conventional reading practices—moments when narratives of national identity contain their own undoing.

Significantly, when I taught the same essays in a course on gender performance and cultural activism (cross-listed as both English and Women's Studies), students' response was quite different. While many white students still felt frustrated by their "inability" to read *Borderlands*, there were more feminist students who interrupted those responses. And while there were fewer students of color in this latter class, those who enrolled had strong backgrounds in race issues and women-of-color third-wave feminism, as did many of the white women's studies students. The questioning of the responses and the urge to code-switch thus came not from the white, feminist, queer teacher but from students' peers, which increased students' willingness to self-reflect about their own reading practices.

These different responses indicate that the degree to which constructs of national identity can be challenged depends upon the degree to which students and teacher are willing or able to locate themselves as active participants in those narratives. The first class certainly felt implicated in the challenge to dominant constructions, but they treated *Borderlands* as an object of study and thus remained distanced. Part of this distancing occurred, I think, because the group never really cohered: students didn't seem to feel accountable to each other, only to themselves and the teacher. The second class had a very different group dynamic—a temporary community in which students and teacher felt accountable to each other and were thus willing to engage each other, even when deeply held views were challenged. This sense of responsibility contributed to the ways students located themselves as participants who help uphold or contest narratives of national identity. The temporary community meant that they felt some accountability for how their different locations within constructs of national identity positioned them in relation to each other.

While the classroom space ultimately has limits (not the least of which is that, despite my feminist pedagogy, I must give grades and thus hold power), it suggests that certain public spaces and community relations provide fertile ground to enact Anzaldúa's challenges. *Borderlands* invites readers to unsettle our reading practices—whatever they may be—and learn to read differently, allowing room for nonviolent contestations of the nation. The text's aesthetic practices reveal the collective work of meaning-making around national identities and the gaps and tensions deeply embedded in the construction of U.S. national identity, opening spaces for alternative processes. *Borderlands* invites self-reflexive reading processes that enable a deconstruction and a re-envisioning of the relationship between nation and identity, a practice holding valuable political potential for radical feminist politics.

Notes

1. I do not presume a monolithic reading process. Indeed, it is precisely the diversity of Anzaldúa's reading audiences that is so important to my argument; as readers' different positions within constructs of national identities become public, readers are challenged to account for the inequitable power relations existing between us. More spaces are then created for people from marginalized groups to express their/our own experiences and understandings of national identity.
2. I suspect that other students felt unvoiced dissent and complexities silenced by their white classmates' seemingly monolithic responses.

Chapter 12

Teaching la Conciencia de la Mestiza in the Midst of White Privilege

Simona J. Hill

introduction

Those of us teaching cultural studies, women's studies, and other courses exploring issues of oppression and second-class citizenship status are often mired in perplexity: How can we reach students of privilege about the manifest and latent privileges they hold? In a year when I attained an academic triple crown of sorts—tenure and promotion, the university's award for distinguished teaching, and co-directorship of the University Honors Program—the odds are seemingly with me as I attempt to help my students access a text which is, for them, inseparably dense, challenging, and potentially transformative. However, my credentials are mere fodder when it comes to using Gloria Anzaldúa's *Borderlands/La Frontera* with uninitiated students for whom crossing a border means leaving the state of Pennsylvania for the first time in their eighteen or twenty years or actually speaking to a "real live" person of color.

Addressing the needs of a predominantly white, alleged or actual economically privileged, homogeneous student body remains a challenge for me. After six years on this campus and as the only tenured black woman presently on the faculty, I say this with unflinching confidence and staid conviction. When I teach, I am drawn to "Mother Gloria's" truths about understanding oneself and the other in multiple contexts and throughout varying allegiances. Anzaldúa's tenets, which define teaching as spiritual activism, help me to keep the fires of resistance and hope for change burning within myself as I attempt to ignite a similar passion within my students.

In addition to teaching the substance and methodology of sociology, my task as an educator and activist is to encourage students to examine their positions of power, privilege, and (sometimes) isolation from other racial–ethnic groups. Facing my challenge as a woman-of-color professor (who chooses to address issues of white privilege) at a small liberal arts institution in central Pennsylvania where tuition and fees have surpassed $30,000 per year is no easy feat. I look for texts and develop assignments requiring students to dig deep (as my course syllabi suggest), go beyond their preconceptions, apply concepts to their individual life experiences, and learn something new and dynamic. Anzaldúa's *Borderlands/La Frontera* offers excellent opportunities to meet these goals. In this essay I discuss how I have used *Borderlands* in two courses: Social Control (Sociology 232) and Minorities (Sociology 413).

My fundamental challenge as an educator is to expose my students to elements of "white privilege" that they otherwise would ignore or simply dismiss. Yet to do so is not easy. As bell hooks explains,

> Unlike the oppressed or colonized, who may begin to feel as they engage in education for critical consciousness a new found sense of power and identity that frees them from colonization of the mind, that liberates, privileged students are often downright unwilling to acknowledge that their minds have been colonized, that they have been learning how to be oppressors, how to dominate, or at least how to passively accept the domination of others. (*Talking Back* 102)

Not surprisingly, my privileged students are extremely sensitive to being challenged in such ways. Reluctant to acknowledge systemic issues, they take such challenges personally ("the professor doesn't like me") and often become tearful at the slightest critique. I do not think it is unreasonable for me to require that students consider alternate perspectives. But because I am a faculty of color making this demand, students are more unwilling to break from their comfort zone of privilege. They know their parents' resources or their own will buy expensive cars, the "right" education, and eventually the "right" position within a family-owned business. The university's tacit agreement, one long preexisting my arrival, is that "we" (faculty, professional staff, administrators, housekeeping services, etc.) will take care of your children and keep them "safe" (read: "innocent-white-privileged"). Yet this "safety" damages both my students and those they encounter.

When students see their background and self-identity in full light of the societal constructs holding individuals and their families in place, I feel a welcome sense of accomplishment. I require students to begin with self-examination (as the self is virtually their only frame of reference) and to extend beyond a personal recognition to explore the ways in which they fit within a larger universe. Perhaps not surprisingly, they generally find this task extremely difficult, intimidating, and fear-provoking.[1] Even those students who have traveled the world grapple with self-reflection. In the face of their egocentricity, I believe (and probably must believe as my own succor in this environment) that these students are capable of so much more than they have been asked to give. Significantly, my intention is not to induce guilt because of their privilege. Rather, I want students to examine the contexts in which their privilege exists. I challenge them as the future "Power Elite" (to borrow a term from sociologist C. Wright Mills)—active participants in constructing the hierarchies of oppression which they did not necessarily create, but from which they certainly benefit. Anzaldúa's *Borderlands/La Frontera* serves as a useful teaching device in advancing my classroom goals to expose privilege, nurture students, generate their sense of themselves as agents of change, and abate students' resistance to examining the effects of their lives of privilege.

borderlands/la frontera as pedagogical device

Designing a classroom experience that actively engages pedagogy requires careful consideration. Arnetha Ball reminds well-meaning educators to give "serious attention—whether implicitly or explicitly expressed—to enlightening learners concerning life possibilities and focus on issues of power and the struggles that have historically shaped the voices, meaning, and experiences of marginalized others" (1008). In both Social Control and Minorities, *Borderlands* functions as a mirror inviting students to see the isolation and white ideology informing their own cultural milieus. I wanted my students to experience the difficulty (and acts of volition) it takes to cross borders into groups that traditionally do not access privileges as easily as dominant groups within U.S. society. I do not ask my students to miraculously become "mestiza" (which is both an impossible feat and a crass attempt to delegitimize Anzaldúa's concept); instead, I encourage them to recognize the borders (whether manufactured by privilege or poverty) crisscrossing their lives and comprehend how they choose to navigate those borders.

Like Edén E. Torres, who also teaches a predominantly white student population, I ask: "If it is true that we inhabit many different subject positions, and that identities and roles are constructed and can therefore be deconstructed, then why is it so difficult for these students to step out of identification with the dominant elite?" (81). Why indeed is it so difficult? My students are woefully imprisoned within the confines of white privilege; they are oblivious to how often others, who are nonwhite and not of a middle-to-high socioeconomic class, impact the well-constructed and seemingly "safe" borders of their white world. Nor do they recognize how their whiteness impacts in reverberating ways in their own worlds and those of others. This (intentional and unintentional) ignorance, or what Anzaldúa might call desconocimientos, makes it difficult (although not impossible) for many of my students to access her text. When I teach *Borderlands*, I want students to acknowledge the multiple borders in their own lives; thus, I de-normalize the bedrock of their privilege with pointed questions, analysis, and direct confrontation. This is not to say that discussions of race, gender, and sexuality are not important; they always are. However, in my teaching, privilege and its meaning must be addressed first.

When I designed the course syllabi for Social Control and Minorities, I certainly did not plan to read entire chapters of *Borderlands* aloud, word for word with my students. I had hoped to use valuable class time to discuss major concepts and themes. However, students in both classes were "stuck"—frustrated and openly resistant to reading this classic work. Some admitted that they had read and reread the material but did not understand Anzaldúa's message for those who are white or living outside her cultural definitions. Many, who had never encountered code-switching or non-English-language texts, were now experiencing what it means to be outside the norm. Facing their antipathy toward another language in the classroom—in a primary course text, no less—de-normalized the privilege of using English in all forms of communication. Students' discomfort with another language presented a border they were forced to confront in order to complete the course. Exiting their English-only comfort zone became a catalyst for destabilizing their notions of privilege, one of my course goals.

We spent more than two weeks of class time listening and responding directly to Anzaldúa's words. I used the text interactively, allowing each reader the space to explore possible meanings. We discussed questions such as the following: Anzaldúa speaks of inclusivity as the hallmark of mestiza consciousness. How is this inclusivity achieved? Where is the mestiza located in society? What cultures must she serve and what cultures has she chosen because without them she herself could not exist?

These questions marked the beginning of our course analysis. I wanted students to explore their own places in society and to investigate self-reflectively what they have been taught. In the Minorities class, place had been an ongoing theme, for this concept is a powerful constraint on people of color in a white-dominated culture. Similarly, in the Social Control class, I wanted students to see place as the locus of power and control in society. Those who were born in certain dimensions of a hierarchy receive benefits not afforded to specific others. But of course neither privilege nor whiteness are monolithic. While I am deeply invested in exposing white privilege, I do not want students to adopt stereotypes that purport to describe all white-raced people. Instead, they must recognize that whites act in many ways, ranging from *co-conspirators* who keep a system of domination fixed to *mediators* who work to dislodge this oppressive system.

For students who had never been conflicted about their privilege, reading how Anzaldúa develops ideas and lives as a mestiza exposes them to a revelatory process previously inaccessible. For Anzaldúa, mestiza consciousness often entails intense self-reflection: "first there has to be something that is bothering me, something emotional so that I will be upset, angry or conflicted. Then I start meditating on it" (*Borderlands* 236). Students who begin to see their privilege both as a barrier to others outside their social space and as a safety zone regard Anzaldúa as the purveyor of an influential gift. They learn in a fundamental way that borders are not fixed entities but in many ways are permeable and can be shared with others. This recognition enabled them to begin exploring their conflicted emotions about privilege's meaning in their lives. Significantly, they were able to do so in ways that did not appropriate a mestiza identity. Instead, they developed new arenas where differently situated social actors can co-exist within negotiated boundaries, transcend visible and invisible borders, and acknowledge points of direct contact with each others' cultural expediencies.

When my students glimpse life from Anzaldúa's perspective, they have an opportunity to recognize and perhaps overcome the dimensions of privilege shackling them to misplaced ideas about the oppressed—dimensions that are wrong, inappropriate, and grossly limited. Reading *Borderlands*, they learn in concrete ways that "[t]he dominant white culture is killing us slowly with its ignorance" (108). My students are members of this murderous culture. Part of my task as an instructor is to chip away at this ignorance and find a meeting ground or crossroads of dissension, agreement, or ambivalence. To ask the question, "Where are we in the process of going outside of our own cultures and becoming attuned to cultural difference?" supplants ignorance by moving privileged students beyond some of their false assumptions. For those students who have never had to ask such questions, the challenge is great. For the few self-identified minorities in both classes,[2] transversing the bridges of difference had been well-practiced, demanded of them by society, and obvious.

In both courses, I require students to write a short descriptive essay exploring mestiza consciousness (see Appendix). Most students approach the assignment with various levels of discomfort. Some, for example, confessed that they never really thought about their identity in the world. Many had never considered whiteness to be a cultural category; nor did they understand how whiteness as ideology and expectations was transmitted and in other ways reinforced. To compensate for these desconocimientos, I incorporated discussions about whiteness as a cultural category into classroom dialogues.

In their essays, students defined mestiza consciousness rather simplistically—as a form of situated self-reflection in which one becomes aware of oneself in the existing society. Many could identify with Anzaldúa—not in terms of her specific ethnic identity, but in the glaring reality of her identity forged in the presence of conflicting information and points of view within psychological borders. Anzaldúa states that the new mestiza copes by developing "a tolerance for contradictions, a tolerance for ambiguity" (101). Although Anzaldúa here calls for tolerance, my privileged students need to be prodded to become aware of and move beyond their own privilege-induced contradictions. They were grossly unaware of the racism pulsing, alive, and coursing through their remarks and writings with predictability and force. When dealing with evidence of overt racism in their families of origin, for example, they were forced to confront their own racist beliefs as well. Reading *Borderlands* enabled these students to view themselves as active participants in the white consciousness shaping their experience. Although my students would most likely place themselves farther along this consciousness-raising experience than I would, I do note it as a promising (not definite) measure of what they could achieve with more work and application.

Passivity is admonished within mestiza consciousness. So, too, for students of privilege, passivity and reticence impede progression toward social transformation. In many respects and especially before reading *Borderlands* these students did not recognize the borders existing in their lives. By the end of reading the text and reflecting on their assignments, students were able to venture beyond their own notions of reality and consider the existence of multiple realities. I take this awareness as another promising step. "Awareness of our situation must come before inner changes," assures Anzaldúa (109). For some students, those who bravely question themselves and dare to look at the answers, the process is quite gradual, moving from awareness to action to alteration of self-identity:

awareness→action→alteration of self-identity

Borderwork, for my students, meant taking the risk of being different from the norm and acknowledging that difference without allowing it to consume their sense of self. Anzaldúa's ability to do her own borderwork with integrity is a skill my students seemed to admire. Challenging the outcomes of social control, in this case by doing consistent and thorough borderwork, students become aware of increased societal complexity, interdependence, and ultimately change definitions of what constitutes an acceptable level of human misery (Marx).

I want my students to understand that what they describe as "mestiza" consciousness and borderwork is not synonymous with the *Anzaldúan* mestiza. At best, they achieve the beginnings of an awareness of something—powerful, encompassing, and border-shattering, in some respects—that is beyond their limited awareness. Those students who mistakenly claim mestiza consciousness are, in reality, awakening to larger forms of collective awareness that extend beyond the breadth of their own privilege. For some that is a rude awakening and for others it promises a lifelong commitment to seeing themselves differently in the face of an increasingly diverse world that challenges the suppositions of white privilege. For example, one student—a self-proclaimed, "self-satisfied redneck at heart"—admitted that as she read *Borderlands*, nothing seemed relevant until a line jumped out and caught her attention. Anzaldúa writes, "I am a turtle, wherever I go I carry 'home' on my back" (43). This assertion spoke to the student in a meaningful way: "like Anzaldúa, I carry my past with me. Every today becomes the past tomorrow. I try to see every situation as a learning experience. Through these experiences, I have become a mestiza." Although in some ways this recognition is quite an accomplishment for one who considered herself isolated, sometimes narrow-minded, and rednecked, in other ways it is quite dangerous. After all, becoming a mestiza through one writing assignment is a highly improbable feat. To assist this student in understanding the limitations of her assertion, we explored the complexities of mestiza identity and revisited Anzaldúa's discussions of the material circumstances of her south Texas life. The student learned that by claiming a mestiza identity, she dilutes Anzaldúa's message.

Being mestiza is not part of a twisted sense of entitlement as in the student's declaration, "I have become a mestiza." Admittedly this statement reflects a rather immature conceptualization of the dynamics of privilege. Acknowledging privilege and discovering selective aspects of one's identity do not (as some students would like) easily translate into an assumed mestiza status. There is much work to be done and students such as this self-proclaimed "mestiza" must travel amazingly far on the path of critical reflection. At a basic level, the path of mestiza consciousness demands that students suspend judgments and move beyond a highly individualized and insulated way of relating to the world. As Torres emphatically states, "One of the ways we might strengthen alliances with other oppressed peoples is to build a foundation from which we can, without judgment, listen to other people's perspectives and experienced realities" (183). My students can forge strong alliances *not* by declaring themselves mestiza and thus adopting the false cover of another's identity, but simply by acknowledging and exploring their own social status. Recognizing the many facets of privilege begins the conversation. If students are willing to do the sometimes daunting work of self-examination, mestiza consciousness offers a way for them to access knowledge of their own privilege and the consequences such privilege has for society.

A first-year woman student concluded her essay by stating,

> We cross "borders" every day without even realizing it. Examining ourselves and parts of ourselves reveals the privileges we accept and the oppression we suffer. It is the journey, the process, we all face in living. These "borders" made and re-make me who I am today, who I will be tomorrow, and for every following tomorrow. These borders will change; I will change them or someone else will change them. As they change, I, we, too will change to accommodate them. That is the beauty of it. Until then, we strive to make them as acceptable to ourselves as possible, and live with what we can in our "borderlands," seeking to make ourselves whole despite scattering ourselves to these remote places.[3]

I want my students to explore these remote places that lie outside the everyday borders of their lives. The realization that borders even exist marks the beginning of a shift in their knowledge of self and an expanding world. For these students, the importance in learning about mestiza consciousness is not in somehow assuming a fully developed mestiza identity, but in coming to understand the borders that influence who they are and hope to become in a larger social context. Doing border work does not confer "mestiza-ness"—despite the false hope they sometimes have. The course assignments offer students a way to go beyond their own limited experience and begin a journey as world citizens, change agents, non-tourists, and humble learners. With rare exception, my students were very much engaged. Anzaldúa's *Borderlands/La Frontera* helps us to untangle the elements of mestiza consciousness that can impact privileged positions. Addressing the core aspects of mestiza consciousness enables one to move beyond assumed privilege and discover, if not embrace, a more complex identity. This transformative effect can occur even in the midst of the most entrenched notions of white privilege and established structures.[4]

Appendix

Social Control (Sociology 232)

Analyze in a descriptive essay mestiza consciousness. Does any aspect of the mestiza consciousness make an impact on the person you are today and the person you hope to become after graduation from Susquehanna University? Is "mestiza consciousness" a form of social control? If so, how does it operate in one's life? How does the process of crossing borders inhibit (or make easier) the dynamics of social control? Give examples to support your ideas. I need to see evidence in this paper that you have taken time to digest Anzaldúa's *Borderlands/La Frontera.* Consider other works on identity formation to support your ideas.

Page length: range of responses should be four–five pages, typed and double-spaced.

Minorities (Sociology 413)

Analyze in a descriptive essay mestiza consciousness. Does any aspect of mestiza consciousness make an impact on the person you are today and the person you hope to become after graduation from Susquehanna University? How have conflicts over your personal ambiguities hindered and helped redefine your sense of justice in the midst of oppression? Where is the privilege in this process? I need to see evidence in this paper that you have taken time to digest Anzaldúa's *Borderlands/La Frontera.* Consider other works on identity formation to support your ideas.

Page length: range of responses should be four–five pages, typed and double-spaced.

Notes

1. For instance, when I require introductory students to interview a woman who is currently receiving welfare benefits, most students (who seek a recipient living in the rural Pennsylvania county where we are located) will find a woman who is white with virtually the same "appearance" as themselves or members of their families. In fact, some welfare recipients are white adolescent mothers about the same age as these seventeen- to nineteen-year-old college students. My students find it awkward and jarring to see poorer versions of themselves and hear parts

of the life stories that made welfare the only or most viable solution for survival. Generally, they assumed the typical welfare recipient to be a black or Latina "Welfare Queen," an image cultivated by a steady diet of predigested media pablum. In fact, I use Karen Seccombe's *So You Think I Drive A Cadillac* to refute student misconceptions about women on welfare.

2. No students in either class had any known Spanish or Native ancestry. One lesbian was enrolled in both classes and one African-American woman in the Social Control class.
3. All students gave me permission to use their papers as resources for this article. This passage is by Kristen M. Brown, a white, first-year female student.
4. I am grateful to AnaLouise Keating's editorial expertise that (I believe) channeled Gloria's spirit in very positive directions. Thank you, AnaLouise for your support and insights in the writing of this article. May personal transformation be yours as you mourn Gloria's passing.

Chapter 13

"Know Me Unbroken": Peeling Back the Silenced Rind of the Queer Mouth

Mark W. Bundy

> The bridge to a queer world is, among other things, paved by *This Bridge Called My Back*.
>
> —José Esteban Muñoz

> We dare to speak. Trembling, and on the verge.
>
> —Carole Maso

Even as we tremble, even as we are on the verge of sifting through the sediment of so many stories, we must to dare to speak them aloud as a collective of mindful queer men and radical women of color; we need to hear them sung in numerous, unbroken languages.

Gloria, I want to know you unbroken, just as María Lugones wants all muted women "to be seen unbroken" ("Hablando" 46). And, just as Lugones wants women "to break cracked mirrors that show [them] in many separate, *unconnected* fragments," I want to keep this heady momentum going—this process of uncovering new ways to delight in the exploration of your language and your textual cosmos: a space of longing, heat, and courage; of making room for both inwardness and for connecting with the world; of an integrity that fosters the outrage and beauty of both the fragmentary and the undiluted ("Hablando" 46). *Sin quebrar.* Making room: *why not allow everything that gives us pause—the exotic, the breathtaking, the raptures of occasional miracles, the daily tides of the body?* To make room for contradictions is a symptom of our desire for a greater capacity for seeing, listening, talking back, and recovering the knowledge of what has been broken. Gloria, I want to listen to you, always, and to let you know that I *am* listening. I want to pare the fruit of the silenced queer mouth with you and to wait for the warm succulent hum of its first word.

* * * * * * * * * * *

What is it about your writing, Gloria, which promises the evocation of a vigilantly openhearted vision of the queer/mestiza body as a site of spirit and resistance? No puedo darlo nombre. How dare you promise such exquisite fruit? Gracias por siendo tan generosa. And what are we to do, now, with all this queer shimmer: fruit and flower of your language and of mine? What incantations can I utter here that will invoke the feverish weather of a more radical language? In the foreword to *Bridge*'s second edition, you make a suggestion: "Dejemos de hablar hasta que hagamos la palabra luminosa y activa (*let's not talk, let's say nothing until we've made the word luminous and active*)." But already you've begun the dialogue, and you've peeled away the skin of the forbidden fruit: the queer knowledge/voice as a ripe, thick-skinned orange. *These ongoing harvestings of yours, Gloria. Peeling it all back—culture, self, body, voice, sex, identity, meaning, realities, love, illness, recovery.*

What is Peeled Open: your language, so many historias, your passion for words, like "seeded bodies, split apart, molten and bright as lanterns," continue to forge a space where theory is embodied and made accessible, fresh, powerful, and useful (Ducornet 58).

What is Peeled Open: words that resonate with both beauty and abjection, established theories pulled apart, re-examined, put back together in new ways. Old polarizing notions about scholarship and incompatible levels of spiritual realizations peeled open by your left hand in order to connect, if and when they are meant to connect. *Le debo tan mucho, Gloria.*

What is Peeled Open: labios, boca, garganta of the silenced queer who can no longer abide the swallowed fury, the buried story, and the swelling, readied voice. Whenever the rind of the queer mouth is peeled back, the widening noise is but deafening music. Imagine the euphoric noise of that resonancia, at last.

Beware: In one hand I hold a serrated knife, glistening. In the other, either a ripe tangelo or a huge navel orange.

Glistening.
Beware: I have many other unseen hands, many fists uncurling in all directions. Why not bliss and hunger and hurricane and calm, together? Make Room, *hacer campo. Why not slash open and heal over at the same time?* None of us is scarless. We must make room.

exotic fruits

Certain exotic fruits have such beautiful, extraordinary names that we can almost taste their wet, iridescent flesh and we are hypnotized by the halved belly-centers sparkling with dark seeds—dazzling, edible geodes exemplifying a secret beauty that must be excavated out of a banal shell. The strange, opened fruit has saturated your senses and your atmosphere with its absolute succulence, and you feel ravenous and vulnerable and speechless. When spoken aloud, the very names of such fruits seem as luscious as the morsels themselves:

Guava. Papaya. Ambarella. Buriti. Eggfruit. Honeyberry.
Miracle Fruit. Neem. Osage Orange. Rambutan. Sugar Apple.
Pulasan. Longan. Traveler's-Tree. Alligator Pear. Tamarind.
Words, like ripe fruit, to be plucked and savored. Nothing left to rot, nothing wasted.
Waterberry. Mahonia. Sweet Prayer. Lulita. Velvet Apple. Babaco.
Mangosteen. Rough Lemon. Lingaro. Wonderberry. Starfruit. Lychee.
Nipple Fruit. Cherimoya. Love Apple. Sparkleberry. River Plum. Black Persimmon. Pomelo.
Blood Banana. Chocolate Pudding Fruit.
Palabras tan sabrosos como guayabas o sandía.

The exotic is *that which gives us pause.* Languages, alphabets, scripts, and fonts all can be exotic. The voice waiting to speak, exotic; the mouth kept from speaking, exotic. The undoing of queer silences depends on the willingness to dwell upon all the unknowable exotic histories of our future.

Such a future might reveal itself only when and where any openness to "others" kindles the ongoing dialogue of finding points of connection along the strands, throughout the many networks of our "differences." Hagamos de nuestras cuerpos que diferencían un collar maravilloso de la perla. It is a project of both listening and responding to one another's voices, memories, dreams, realities, and insights. And, "if we joyfully violate the language contract, might not that not make us braver, stronger, more capable of breaking other oppressive contracts" (Maso 159)? This effort to come together, to apply the complexities of basic talking and listening to thinking, writing, and language—all as a form of activism—is part of Anzaldúa's ongoing visualization of the manifold processes of knowledge, spirit, and interconnections or what she sometimes calls "conocimientos":

> People bond because they want to work together . . . That's where my model of the bridge, drawbridge, sandbar, or island comes in. My model is conocimientos. . . . "Conocimiento" is the Spanish word for knowledge and skill. It has to do with getting to know each other by really listening with the outer ear and the inner ear. Really looking at each other and seeing with our eyes and communicating orally or with the written word. (*Interviews/Entrevistas* 206)

More than anything, I want to take up certain aspects of the one haunting thing about the potential for unsilencing the queer mouth: *Language*. Like Ducornet, "I was infected with the venom of language in early childhood" (1). And, like Barthes, "I am interested in language because it wounds or seduces me" (*Pleasure* 38). Lenguaje, mi amante asombroso, sosteniendo un cuchillo.

Beneath the indisputable paleness of my skin lies the sinew of a Native American heritage, the truth of which my white exterior disavows, betrays, and fails to convince every last disbeliever: my grandfather was born on an Ojibwa reservation in Wisconsin, and spoke only French and Ojibwa until he was sixteen. He died six months before I was born, and I carry his name in the middle of my own.

> *Your* Weendijo, *Grandfather, your demons. They are here with me tonight.*
> *But there are kinder spirits and myths, and my blood is not diluted and gone.*
> *There are so many things I want to tell you. In your language and in mine.*
> *What I wish for you the world cannot contain:*
> *Wherever you are, when you move through that world,*
> *may you be surprised suddenly by the scent of lilacs*
> *where there are no lilacs.*
> *May you be able to look at what I have made, and think of home.*
> *When I think of you,* Nimishomiss, *my grandfather, then* Nin Giwe: *I go home.*
> **Be careful: I am not only that which my body tells you I am.**

Anzaldúa: "There are a lot of Indian souls inhabiting white bodies" (*Interviews/Entrevistas* 35). *Make room,* hacer campo. *Why not a skin of both brick red bougainvillea and palest freesia? Why not a relaxed heart in disarray, both because of love?* Make room.

Significantly, Eve Kosofsky Sedgwick contends that the word "queer" no longer *always and only* refers to gay, bisexual, or lesbian sexualities:

> a lot of the most exciting recent work around "queer" spins the term outward along dimensions that can't be subsumed under gender and sexuality at all: the ways that race, ethnicity, postcolonial nationality criss-cross with these *and other* identity-constituting, identity-fracturing discourses, for example . . . Gloria Anzaldúa us[es] the leverage of "queer" to do a new kind of justice to the fractal intricacies of language, skin, migration, state. Thereby, the gravity (I mean the *gravitas*, the meaning, but also the *center* of gravity) of the term "queer" itself deepens and shifts. (8–9)

I am fractal: a jota, a queer, a "fruit," a gay man whose voice shifts and deepens and attempts to connect—Like so many others, all women and all men who carry the signifying baggage of self-identification, I am but fragments of a whole self that refuses to reify a culture of inequity, pain, sorrow, violence, despair, and rage. *What I wish for you the world cannot contain. No voy a deaparecer*. I have blueprints for a bridge. I have a voice, and I will not fade.

* * * * * * * * * * * * *

If, however, the silenced queer body either remains silent, invisible, or is likely to disappear, then to where does it travel? *We know this much:* there are so very many worlds, *hay muchos mundos*, which we inhabit, move between, flee from, or run toward.

> Vivo en tan muchos diversos mundos.
> Mundos del miedo y de la belleza.

Moving from world to world, or living in different worlds at the same time, we're blurred and lost and silent (if we hesitate still to speak) as homeless phantoms; we can see each other clearly, sometimes, whether we are planted firmly on the ground or blue with the vertigo of leaning at the edge of some invisible, terrible precipice. Ya casi. We see the urgency of the self-wired jaw, desperate to scream or moan in pleasure or in pain, or simply to ask somebody—*which way is our home*?

¿*adonde está mi casa?*

Mark Doty: "Exiles see exiles everywhere."

Ghosts, exiled mestizas, muted queers, margin walkers, and walking wounded all too often sense powerfully each other's existence and pained state of being. Those who possess this capacity for such empathic sensory awareness are "excruciatingly alive to the world," as their spirits and synaptic responses are endowed with la facultad:

> Those who do not feel psychologically or physically safe in the world are more apt to develop this sense. Those who are pounced on the most have it the strongest—the females, the homosexuals of all races, the darkskinned, the outcast, the persecuted, the marginalized, the foreign. (*Borderlands* 60)

In *Bridge*, Anzaldúa's masterful editing itself is evidence of Norma Alarcón's avowal that "consciousness as a site of multiple voicings is the theoretical subject, par excellence, of *Bridge*" (365). As perhaps the first grounded collection of recent critical theory written by lesbians, mestizas, women of color, *Bridge* did, for the most part, the necessary functions of both sowing and sewing: planting seeds of thought that would take time to break through, and stitching together the seams of voices just breaking open, not unlike Anzaldúa's compostura paradigm: " 'Compostura' means seaming together fragments to make a garment which you wear, which represents you, your identity and reality in the world" (*Interviews/Entrevistas* 256). So often, then, the ongoing and crucial compostura of language *must* be one of the primal materials for building bridges between cultures, across borders, or toward freedom from oppressive categorization.

Anzaldúa has assembled an oeuvre of almost nuclear proportions. She has made room. She has been holding the knife and the orange all this time, waiting for more new voices to emerge. I would imagine that as she is working on how to express new ways of seeing, of being, of reading, and of living between worlds, she has also been waiting for the coiled brood that slithers through the bottomless dark seas of nepantla to come up for air, to claim a voice and a name:

> because I'm a writer, voice—acquiring a voice, covering a voice, picking up a voice, creating a voice—was important. Then you run into this whole experience of unearthing, discovering, rediscovering, and recreating voices that have been silenced, voices that have been repressed, voices that have been made a secret. (*Interviews/Entrevistas* 276–77)

Many of Anzaldúa's challenging theories include but are not limited to "an epistemology that tries to encompass all the dimensions of life, both inner—mental, emotional, instinctive, imaginal, spiritual, bodily realms—and outer—social, political, lived experiences" (*Interviews/Entrevistas* 177).

Anzaldúa's devotion to her vision and the fierceness of her imaginative writing work synergistically and glisten on the page with both poetic and political inventiveness: "I identify as a woman. . . . Whatever insults women insults me . . . I identify as gay. . . . Whoever insults gays insults me. . . . identify as a feminist. . . . Whoever slurs feminism slurs me" ("La Prieta" 206).

As Anzaldúa and other *Bridge* authors have made manifest, being a walking bridge is as exhausting and forbidding as it is utterly necessary. We must overcome our reluctance to inscribe and give life to the cycles of queer histories, regardless of the ugliness of the past. We must push beyond our hesitancy to speak about the realities and violence and pleasures of our queerness, regardless of any risks.

Maso: "as we dare to utter something, to commit ourselves, to make a mark on a page or a field of light. . . . a literature of love. A literature of tolerance. A literature of difference. . . . Wish: that we be open-minded and generous. That we fear not" (179–182).

And even when it gets to be too much:

Donna Kate Rushin: "I'm sick of seeing and touching / Both sides of things / *Sick of being the damn bridge for everybody*"

We must not be reconciled to shame or silence.

Anzaldúa's writing is the unfolding of a life through experience, reading, writing, and reflection. Clearly, Anzaldúa recognizes the need for queer writers and mestiza writers to form some sort of alliance or safe community (even in the shape of anthologized works as "communes") where the potential for conocimientos might be realized and enacted. In *Borderlands* she makes a stronger appeal for more listening, more writing, making more face/soul (living without masks), and creating newer, stronger "bridges" between mestiza feminisms and queer theories: "the mestizo and the queer exist at this time and point on the evolutionary continuum for a purpose" (*Borderlands* 107).

Living and writing and listening to each other together, junto y libre.

In *This Bridge*, the potential for finding and flourishing within an expressive community is one of the few triggers that might unlock the silenced queer voice:

> Only *together* can we be a force. I see us as a network of kindred spirits, a kind of family.
>
> We are the queer groups, the people that don't belong anywhere, not in the dominant world nor completely within our own respective cultures. Combined we cover so many oppressions. ("La Prieta" 209, her italics)

If and when the energies underpinning so many feminist queer theories are combined in earnest or are given the "permission" to expand, collapse, or collide, then we might see a true rewriting of culture; when the evolving theories of new voices are made accessible to everybody and are applied practically to the lives of los atravesados, then we might encounter a noticeable, more provocative transformation.

To transform the "silence that hollows us," we must allow our bodies to absorb and process the language of those mouths already given license to speak ("Haciendo caras" xxii). However, "[f]or the body to give birth to utterance, the human entity must recognize itself as carnal—skin, muscles, entrails, brain, belly," and "[b]ecause our bodies have been stolen, brutalized or numbed, it is difficult to speak from/through them" (xxii). We must speak—with any words, in any language, from any location: "By sending our voices, visuals and visions outward into the world, we alter the walls and make them a framework for new windows and doors. We transform the *posos*, apertures, *barrancas, abismos,* that we are forced to speak from" (xxv). We will transform reality by speaking what has been considered unspeakable.

Make room for the liberated voice.
We must make room for new things, debemos hacer el sitio para las nuevas cosas.

Para las nuevas ideas.
Para las nuevas voces.
Para todos.

Mas palabras tan sabrosos:
Breadroot. Cocoplum. Sea Grape. Umari. Roselle. Wild Orange.

Hacer campo, make some room, and leave enough to share. Listen to and savor the words of other people. Savor the echo of your own voice, love its brilloso. Meet me in the middle of your own crossroads, and we will make face, make soul, make identities, make bridges. We will do this act together, in friendship. We will resist the impulse to bite our tongues in order to keep the abrasive words inside. From the cracks, the gaps, the hidden fissures of this world, I will wait to hear all the muted tongues clicking against the wetness of the skinned palate.

Beware of my gifts to you:

Un cuchillo (A knife). *Una naranja* (An orange). *Una boca* (A mouth).
Un milagro (A miracle). *Riendo* (Laughter). *Amor* (Love).

What will you do with them?

This essay is dedicated to my parents and to my partner, John, with love.

Chapter 14

New Pathways toward Understanding Self-in-Relation: Anzaldúan (Re)Visions for Developmental Psychology

Kelli Zaytoun

When I was very young, maybe three or four, I began having a recurring dream that my spirit body left my physical body, floated toward the ceiling, and flew. I'd fly around the house from room to room, like a bird, although the whole time I sensed that I was being carried. While I felt completely under the control of something other than myself, I had no fear. I also remember, as a child, a recurring sensation of someone tapping me gently on my back. The presence was strong, wise, and female. I did not dare turn around, but I also knew that there really wasn't "someone" there—not someone in the traditional sense anyway. Although I never mentioned them, these experiences were real to me then. Somewhere along the way the strong presence left me, and I stopped flying. *So I grew up in the interface trying not to give countenance to el mal aigre, evil nonhuman, non-corporeal entities riding the wind, that could come through the window, through my nose with my breath. I was not supposed to believe in susto, a sudden shock or fall that frightens the soul out of the body.*[1]

I am still a very conscious sleeper. Things cannot go on in the room without my waking. And when I'm awake, I have no filters; I hear and feel everything, everyone, and everything between everyone—every tension, every fear, every hesitation, every irritation. Sometimes it's so intense that my body feels too heavy for me to stand. *I walk into a house and I know whether it is empty or occupied. I feel the lingering charge in the air of a recent fight or lovemaking or depression. I sense the emotions someone near is emitting—whether friendly or threatening . . . I feel a tingling on my skin when someone is staring at me or thinking about me.*

I am not a woman of color, but I have la facultad. Every day I feel "excruciatingly alive" (*Borderlands* 60). I recall when I was twelve the sudden pit that plunged into the center of my belly as I walked down the hall past the half-closed door to my three-year-old sister. I discovered she wasn't breathing and yelled for my parents who had to rush her to the hospital. I also recall the fall of 1997, when I sensed something clearly wrong during a visit with a young man who came to the Women's Center wanting to be a part of our outreach program for grade school girls: We later discovered that he had a child sexual abuse file an inch thick.

I am not a woman of color. Not really. My father is first-generation Arab-American and my mother doesn't know much about her parents' background other than her father's German ancestors and one of her mother's parents was part South Carolina Cherokee Indian. People tell me I look Greek or Italian or "ethnic." I always felt different—a little darker, bushier eye-browed, hairier, and taller than the other kids. I had a strange last name, brought strange food to school for lunch. And then, of course, there was my unmistakably ethnic nose.

I was raised Catholic, went to Catholic schools, but my parents stopped going to church after their parish refused to accept my sister, Jen, who has cerebral palsy, into their bible school program. Growing up with a physically disabled sister certainly honed my facultad. Living with someone who can't walk or talk taught me that walking and talking are gifts, but having wellness and being "able" can have nothing to do with one's stride or speech. Jen was different, which made our family and me different.

I am not Chicana, but I have felt the presence of la Jila, Chihuacoatl, Snake Woman, la Llorona, Daughter of Night, "traveling the dark terrains of the unknown searching for the lost parts of herself" (*Borderlands* 60). I never had a name for her until I read *Borderlands*. I believe it was Jila's voice, not mine, that wailed from a deep place inside of me, bitterly, uncontrollably, for hours, for seemingly no reason at all, the summer before the fall that marked the beginning of the end of my twelve-year partnership. *She brings mental depression and sorrow. Long before it takes place, she is the first to predict something is to happen.*

I do not identify as lesbian, but I believe I am capable of entering into a loving, intimate, long-term relationship with a woman. My past significant partners have all been men, but I have loved women too. I've always felt this way as far back as I can remember. I'm not sure what that makes me but

I don't think it really matters anymore. *A borderland is a vague and undetermined place created by the emotional residue of an unnatural boundary. It is in constant state of transition.*

Maybe I connect to *Borderlands* because I've unconsciously longed for words, stories, metaphors, to name and explain my deepest memories, the experiences my mind still clings to, to take me back to another time, another me, another way of thinking. I didn't long for one particular explanation—just something to bring these parts of myself back to life, to make my life's path traceable in some way more meaningful than just recounting a series of events or thoughts. I want to trace what I was thinking and feeling, not only in my heart, but also in my body.

I want every woman to be able to trace her own or someone else's psychological history, and pass it on to her daughters and granddaughters if she wishes to do so. I want this for every woman because every woman could be my great-grandmother, Siti Minnie Zaytoun. Born and raised in Syria, immigrated to the United States as a child, survived the Great Depression, two husbands, and one of her four children: Siti never told her story—the story I wish I'd asked her to tell before she died in 1999 at the age of ninety-eight, a story that could have spoken to and comforted someone who succeeds her by decades or even centuries. I remember her when I'm stifled by the hardships of parenting alone, standing up for women's rights, following my path. I want to know how she made sense of all she faced. What religious, cultural, and historical stories, images, and lessons influenced her being?

When we know our foremothers' historical and psychological stories, we enter our futures with memories of the pain, frustration, and joy of those who struggled and sometimes died just to make that future possible. In knowing my grandmother's stories of struggles and survival, I gain the strength to persevere. And in my struggles and survival, I become a part of the memories of those who have yet to face their own journeys toward individual and social transformation.

Maybe I connect to Gloria Anzaldúa because I hear in her words ways to articulate individual psychological growth without generalizing, compartmentalizing, rating, or ranking. I hear in her stories ways of describing psychological growth that use mythic images and bodily memories. I hear in her psychology a description of her cultures, her struggles between identities, her linking of soul, body, and mind. I hear a way of recognizing that developmental and clinical psychologists have the potential to help individuals understand and heal themselves and others by connecting to their cultural and ethnic roots, their social, political, and physical surroundings, the memories stored in their bodies, and the spiritual and cosmic worlds to which they relate.

My connection to Gloria isn't about falling under a particular category that "matches" hers; in fact, these categories are the very divisive lines that she wishes to (and successfully does) blur. I am not a woman of color . . . or am I? I am not a lesbian . . . or might I be? *Borderlands* has taught me that my identities, all identities, are fluid, changing. *Because I, a mestiza, continually walk out of one culture and into another, because I am in all cultures at the same time.* I connect to Anzaldúa through her bodily and psychological experiences. I want to know myself, all of me—maybe even the part that used to fly—on a deeper level. *Knowing is painful because after "it" happens I can't stay in the same place and be comfortable.* But Anzaldúa reminds us that the process of knowing, though painful, keeps us alive and brings forth new life. *[I]f I escape conscious awareness, escape 'knowing,' I won't be moving.* Her mestiza consciousness, a consciousness of the borderlands, extends beyond knowing oneself and offers a collective consciousness with the potential to transform society: "A massive uprooting of dualistic thinking in the individual and collective consciousness is the beginning of a long struggle, but one that could, in our best hopes, bring us to the end of rape, of violence, of war"(102).

I also know that the scholar in me wants to redress traditional western ways of understanding and articulating cognitive growth by introducing works, such as Anzaldúa's, to the field of developmental psychology for their profound impact on our conceptualizations of the inner self and self-in-relationship. Anzaldúa calls on us to see that the inner self has the potential to change society's collective consciousness; self-in-relationship is not only about self's relationships to other individual beings, but also self's relationship to the greater collective consciousness: "The struggle has always been inner, and is played out in the outer terrains. Awareness of our situation must come before inner changes, which in turn come before changes in society. Nothing happens in the 'real' world unless it first happens in the images in our heads" (*Borderlands* 109).

Although Anzaldúa probably has not been described as a feminist developmental psychologist, her work exemplifies how one might imagine and articulate a theory of cognitive development from the location of borderlands and border-crossings. Anzaldúa's theories, including her concepts of conocimiento, nepantla, the Coatlicue state, and nos/otras, offer complex views of psychological growth; they expand feminist theorizing about development by describing human beings' contextual, multidirectional meaning-making processes. Poetically revealing her pain, passion, vulnerabilities, and strengths, and calling on us to tell our own stories and truths, Anzaldúa offers pathways for understanding our situated inner life, belief systems, and knowledge constructions, and the roles culture, relationships, and identity play in this construction. These pathways provide critical examples of how individual psychology can and must be comprehended, theoretically and clinically.

When an individual is understood from within her cultural context instead of from within a standard ("white," male) framework, not only does she have a better chance for validation, but her history and culture have a better chance for preservation, to the benefit of us all. After reviewing how feminist theories relate to and confound developmental psychology, I explore new perspectives, based on Anzaldúa's theories, that question, expand, and potentially revolutionize core developmental concepts and theories. In linking cultural, physical, and spiritual aspects of the self to theorizing about the mind, self-identity, and self-in-relationship, I seek both to broaden developmental psychology's purview and to expose pathways for understanding the intricate relationships between individual/collective consciousness and social activism. I suggest that Anzaldúa's own journey offers a basis for a transformative vision of feminist psychological development.

feminist developmental psychologies

Traditional western perspectives in cognitive psychology are rooted in the concept of constructive-developmentalism which assumes that human capacities for organizing and understanding experiences and knowledge evolve through qualitatively different mental structures (from simple to more complex) that are fixed, universal, biological, linear, and characterized by periods of transition and stability. Until the late 1970s, models based on and authored by white males (e.g. Erikson, Kohlberg, and Piaget) dominated human development theory. Some developmentalists (e.g. Belenky, Clinchy, Goldberger, Tarule, Gilligan, Surrey, and Jordan) criticized these models for defining psychological growth in terms of autonomy, differentiation, and separation they offered new models based on women's experiences, which emphasized self-development within the context of relationships.

Although these "women's-ways-of-knowing" perspectives offered new insights, they were based on the lives of (and also authored by) white women. Such models ignore diversity among women and risk marginalizing and discrediting women of color. To address this issue, some of these same theorists (e.g. Goldberger, and Jordan) recently examined the implications of power, culture, and differences among women. Although these writings gave voice to previously excluded individuals, some assumptions about definitions of self, relationship, and identity remained unexamined. For example, the concept of "relationship" still referred primarily to *human* relationships, and ignored other material (plants, animals, etc.) and nonmaterial (spiritual and imaginal) entities and worlds. Because "identity" was conceptualized as a fixed category, theorists paid little attention to how transitioning and changing identities influence development. As Sandra Harding suggests, these limitations occur in part because the authors ground their assumptions about knowledge and epistemology in European/U.S. thought (431); she calls for *retheorizing* that includes cross-cultural epistemologies. What would developmental psychology look like if theorizing *began* with attention to the diversity among women? This question is yet to be adequately answered.

In *Toward a Feminist Developmental Psychology*, Patricia Miller and Ellin Kofsky Scholnick identify three concepts underlying feminist perspectives. First, humans are intricately connected rather than separate or solitary. Second, human experiences and knowledge are contexualized and situated, not generalizable or decontexualized. Third, the power structure within the institutionalized androcentrism pervading societies normalizes maleness. As Miller notes, feminist epistemologies' most fundamental implication is that knowledge is interconnected. She describes six relational characteristics of cognition[2] and suggests that traditional and feminist perspectives on cognitive development complement each other: "In fact, the ideal end point of cognitive development may be the integration of separated and interconnected thinking" (59).

Although Miller thoroughly explores how these implications and characteristics affect what might be considered thought content (concepts of causal interactions, relationships, and collaborations) and developmental processes (co-construction of knowledge, reciprocity, diverse, intersectional, and developmental pathways), she doesn't offer a window into a mind, a real-life demonstration of what happens during those processes, a story. She does, however, call for research that includes focuses on "the diversity that comes from varying standpoints" (59).

a transformative vision for feminist psychological development

> I remember listening to the voices of the wind as a child and understanding its messages. Los espíritus that ride the back of the south wind. (*Borderlands* 58)

Offering us a window into her mind, Gloria Anzaldúa enables new meanings of context, reciprocity, relationship, and "others" to emerge. Indeed, she calls the very metaphysics of self[3] into question: we cannot assume what self is until the self is defined within its cultural context. We cannot assume what "being connected to others" is when, in some cultures, the self has connection to wind, earth, trees, spirits, and more. These connections influence one's ways of thinking, how that thinking changes over time, and how one interacts with the world. These connections would also have enormous impact on one's ethics and actions. How we interact with the world and all living and nonliving beings would be affected dramatically if we were spiritually—and spiritually meant literally—connected to the world. *We've been taught that the spirit is outside our bodies or above our heads somewhere up in the sky with God. We're supposed to forget that every cell in our bodies, every bone and bird and worm has spirit in it.*

Since "self" is such a central component of psychological discourse, this questioning is critical. Anzaldúa's perspectives provide impetus and example for radical reconsiderations of self and others; her views expand theories, such as Miller's, focusing on epistemological interconnectedness. Such reconsiderations lead to new possibilities for theorizing about cognitive capacities. Anzaldúa complicates definitions of psychological development and suggests that life in the margins and on the borders generates a particular collective multiple awareness. Her border-crossing perspective includes not only geographical, cultural, and linguistic borders, but other heartfelt divisions (body/soul, psychological/social, masculinity/femininity, black/white) as well.

Anzaldúa's theory of conocimiento best encapsulates her perspectives on the growth of consciousness and indicates pathways toward multiple individual/collective visions. In an interview, Anzaldúa describes conocimiento as

> an epistemology that tries to encompass all the dimensions of life, both inner—mental, emotional, instinctive, imaginal, spiritual, bodily realms—and outer—social, political, lived experiences. . . . In part, conocimiento is a theory of composition, of how a work of art gets composed . . . of how identity is constructed. When you watch yourself and *observe your mind at work* you find that behind your acts and your temporary senses of self (identities) is *a state of awareness that, if you allow it, keeps you from getting completely caught up in that particular identity* or emotional state. (*Interviews/Entrevistas* 177, my italics)

As this passage indicates, conocimiento entails the ability to see—without being consumed—various links and relationships with parts of the self and with others. Anzaldúa adds to developmental theories attempting to complicate a "relational self"[4] by providing personal descriptions and metaphors that have emerged from her experiences as a mestiza, lesbian, and feminist.

Living with multiple identities plays a major role in one's psychological and social understanding and functioning. Anzaldúa states that when an individual claims to have many temporary senses of self, she can use this knowledge to prevent herself from becoming absorbed in a particular identity or a myopic, restrictive epistemology. Her mestiza or borderland consciousness offers a path toward an intricate view of self in relationship to self and the knowledge gained from within that process. In short, identities within the self interact with one another to create multiple cognitive visions.

Anzaldúa's perspective challenges us to view multiple identities and their relationships to one another (not just to other people) as a vital part of the self-as-system. Anzaldúa's description furthers Robert Kegan's fifth and most complex order of consciousness (trans-systems structures) where one views the self as an incomplete self-as-system constantly recreated through relationships (Love and Guthrie 73). Conocimiento illustrates Miller's assertion that "certain kinds of knowledge may require the knower to become immersed in that which is to be known, rather than independent of it or distanced from it" (Miller and Scholnick 51).

Anzaldúa relates individual consciousness to social consciousness by describing how self-reflection produces social action: "You could say that conocimiento is basically . . . the awareness of facultad that sees through all human acts whether of the individual mind and spirit or of the collective, social body. The work of conocimiento—consciousness work—connects the inner life of the mind and spirit to the outer worlds of action. In the struggle for social change I call this particular aspect of conocimiento spiritual activism" (*Interviews/Entrevistas* 178). This direct connection between individual and social collective consciousness raises important issues for inquiry: who becomes an activist, why, and how? How does la facultad happen? If borderland perspectives bring individuals into states of consciousness that encourage and require social action, could we encourage people to develop such consciousness? Linking individual and collective consciousness presents many possibilities for the study of the psychology of social activism.

More importantly, however, Anzaldúa's poetic and heartfelt words call us into action. She acknowledges and validates mestiza perspectives, and gives language to a much overdue critique of white culture's treatment of Chicanos:

> Individually, but also as a racial entity, we need to voice our needs. We need to say to white society: We need you to accept the fact the Chicanos are different, to acknowledge your rejection and negation of us. . . . Admit that Mexico is your double, that she exists in the shadow of this country, that we are irrevocably tied to her. Gringo, accept the doppleganger in your psyche. By taking back your collective shadow the intercultural split will heal. And finally, tell us what you need from us. (*Borderlands* 107–108)

In addition to explaining the connection between individual thought and social action, Anzaldúa gives us the language to connect the two.

Conocimiento is, therefore, not only an understanding of how individuals develop consciousness, but also an understanding of how individuals connect this consciousness to other people, socially and spiritually. As Anzaldúa explains, "I see conocimiento as a consciousness-raising tool, one that promotes self-awareness and self-reflectivity. It encourages folks to empathize and sympathize with others, to walk in the other's shoes, whether the other is a member of the same group or belongs to a different culture" (*Interviews/Entrevistas* 178). Conocimiento is not only a theory, it is a call to action, a path for social transformation. With conocimiento, Anzaldúa broadens consciousness to include a person's complex cognitive and spiritual relationships with her own identities, collective consciousness, the legacies of her ancestors, and her relationships with other people and the external world.

Although Anzaldúa's model shares similarities with constructive developmental theory, it also includes important innovations. Conocimiento encompasses periods of stability and change, and differentiation and integration (of identity): two characteristics of constructive developmental theory. In "now let us shift . . . the path of conocimiento . . . inner work, public acts," Anzaldúa uses another constructive developmental concept, stages, when describing concocimiento. This constructiveness, however, is unique in its spiraling, cyclical pathway; thus Anzaldúa calls the first stage "an ending, a beginning" (546). These stages are not prescriptive; they are descriptive, offering a way of imagining—not measuring or rating—psychological processes' emergence in concocimiento. Anzaldúa's stage theory, therefore, maintains components of early theories (such as the idea of stability and change) yet avoids the dangers of prescribing a one-size-fits-all path of mental structures where one masters particular tasks before emerging into a one-size-fits-all idea about what it means to be highly developed cognitively. Anzaldúa's seven stages of conocimiento describe a journey of how one emotionally, physically, intellectually, and spiritually faces and emerges from all that forces us to change our way of thinking and thus who we are. She describes cyclical, equally valuable mental states or experiences, not linear or invarient, qualitatively different, simple-to-complex mental structures, from which individual and collective consciousness transpires. According to Anzaldúa, individuals repeatedly cycle through these stages during their lifetime instead of mastering particular mental achievements only once before moving on to the next stage.

Anzaldúa's model offers an innovative way for psychologists to understand individual development. Conocimiento's cyclical structure demonstrates that growth can be understood without normalizing, limiting, or ranking self-definitions and psychological processes. The self is constantly recreating itself. Unlike traditional developmentalists, Anzaldúa doesn't describe an ultimate way of being but instead views all stages as valuable mental spaces where learning and self-understanding occur. Her descriptions directly acknowledge how culture and social position affect developmental pathways and, in turn, affect whether and how one engages in society. To clarify the uniqueness and importance of Anzaldúa's theory, I summarize the seven stages of concocimiento, focusing on their relationship to development.

In "now let us shift," Anzaldúa suggests seven changes in consciousness, cycling from stage one, "el arrebato . . . rupture, fragmentation," to stage seven, "shifting realities . . . acting out the vision or spiritual activism." In describing stage one, Anzaldúa uses the experience of an earthquake as a literal and metaphorical example of how physical and emotional crises can collide and extend beyond the situation at hand: "In the midst of this physical crisis, an emotional bottom falls out from under you, forcing you to confront your fear of others breaching the emotional walls you've built around yourself. If you don't work through your fear, playing it safe could bury you" (544). "Arrebatos," whether the death of a loved one or an experience of discrimination, call on us to question and change our thinking and way of being, to seek out something new.

The second stage, nepantla, is "the zone between changes where you struggle to find equilibrium between the outer expression of change and your inner relationship to it" (548–49). An Aztec word for "torn between ways," nepantla is a place/time of confusion, transition, death, and rebirth (*Borderlands* 100). According to Anzaldúa, our path changes because our perspectives change, and sometimes our perspective changes when our path unexpectedly changes. Here she offers a way of looking at paradox and contradiction that focuses on complexities rather that polarities. Transitions occur along an unpredictable path of ambiguity and "ambivalence from the clash of voices [that] results in mental and emotional states of perplexity" (*Borderlands* 100). With nepantla, Anzaldúa adds spiritual and cultural dimensions to traditional concepts of transitions in identity and psychology. "Cradled in one culture, sandwiched between two cultures, straddling all three cultures and their value systems, la mestiza undergoes a struggle of flesh, a struggle of borders, an inner war" (100). She demonstrates the intense psychological impact, or "psychic restlessness," of living between cultures and its effect on one's consciousness.

Conocimiento's third stage, the Coatlicue state or "La Llorona's wail," represents an awareness of deep depression and resistance to change: "Coatlicue is a rupture in our everyday world. As the Earth, she opens and swallows us, plunging us into the underworld where the soul resides, allowing us to dwell in darkness" (*Borderlands* 68). Anzaldúa uses Coatlicue as a metaphor for what happens in transition, nepantla, when painful events overwhelm our state of being. But, she suggests, when we make meaning of these experiences, we increase our consciousness of self: "The Coatlicue state can be a way station or it can be a way of life" (*Borderlands* 68). Coatlicue also illustrates the ways cultural metaphors can describe psychological experiences. Anzaldúa's use of powerful female mythic images to describe personal physical-psychological states are part of why so many women relate to her writing. For me, these images are comforting; they assure me that I'm not alone in my inner journey and validate the magnitude and life-changing power of my challenges and experiences.

The final four stages of conocimiento involve a calling out of depression, reconstructing a new self, and sharing that process and the knowledge gained with others where, finally, spiritual activism transpires. Within stage four is a "calling . . . the crossing and conversion," the point at which we leave old ways behind and prepare to move forward. Stage five, "putting Coyolxauhqui together," involves recomposition, creating stories and meanings to regenerate the self. Stages six and seven occur when we share ideas and stories with the world, discover they clash with each other, and then are forced to shift our reality and position to a less defensive, more comprehensive understanding, allowing us to respect and relate to others, to shift perspectives.

In stage seven, "shifting realities," we have the energy and capacity to engage in spiritual activism, "an ethical, compassionate strategy with which to negotiate conflict and difference within self and between others, and find common ground by forming holistic alliances" ("now let us shift" 545). Within spiritual activism, we experience nos/otras, the blurring of the lines between self and other, where there is no pure subject and no pure object: "We live in each other's pockets, occupy each other's territories, live in close proximity and intimacy with each other" (*Interviews/Entrevistas* 254). Anzaldúa's concepts of spiritual activism and nos/otras thus proscribe traditional self/other divisions, and indicate how individual and collective consciousness and social activism occur and interrelate. Anzaldúa even names the function that gives us the capacity to experience nos/otras. That function, "la naguala," awakens the awareness of deep interrelatedness, the merger of subject/self and object/other, demonstrating how individual development is directly linked to and actually responsible for social harmony. In shifting realities and spiritual activism, the individual strives with others to achieve a vision of a transformed world.

Although el arrebato, a rupture, begins the conocimiento process again, the self (and the world with which self interacts) is forever changed. "To pass over the bridge to something else, you'll have to give up partial organizations of self, erroneous bits of knowledge, outmoded beliefs of who you are, your comfortable identities. . . . You'll have to leave parts of yourself behind" ("now let us shift" 557). While the stages are cyclical and recurring throughout a lifetime, the experience and the self that emerge are always new. Repeatedly on the pathway of simultaneous self-differentiation and integration/inner and social understanding, we experience and survive the shock of el arrebato, the depths of the Coatlicue state, the yearning to know our purpose and love ourselves, and the desire to make contact with the world that we strive to make better for ourselves and those who are with and will follow us.

While writing this essay I stop, close my eyes, and take myself back to my last Coatlicue state, four years ago, a time when I felt held in a place of mental darkness with no way out. I imagine how, had I read *Borderlands* before that time, Gloria's words would have surfaced. *Come little green snake. Let the wound caused by the serpent be cured by the serpent. The soul uses everything to further its own making.* I imagine how my great-grandmother would have pulled herself from that place of stifled despondency into a new journey—weary, but wiser than before. As I run through my spell check, which keeps wanting to replace "mestiza" with "messiah," I smile to myself and think that just maybe she, a lifelong Catholic, is somehow trying to tell me now, that her faith in her images of life's creator pulled/carried/held her through nearly one hundred years of transitions. I smile again at the thought of the contradictions and the straddling, created within me from the influence of "the mestiza" and "the messiah" in my lifetime. For a moment I see myself standing on a path with bones from the past, books I've read, and a yearning for more contact. I see how my path flows into all that surrounds it. I constrict and shiver when I hear ancient whispers as cool winds blow through leaves and seemingly through me, yet I simultaneously begin opening to the warmth and newness reaching toward me with each ray of the sun. For the first time I realize how complex, how intricate, the interconnected self really is, full of paradox and cyclical stages where inner life and outer world are at the same time separate and indistinguishable.

I smile at the thought of all the border states that have honed my facultad; instead of feeling weighted down, I feel lifted, and realize that one night I might feel light enough for my recurring dream to resurface and take me soaring. Gloria Anzaldúa's influence on my ideas about psychology have pulled me through nepantla on my pathway, my concimiento. This essay is one token from my journey. Others rest and move within me, waiting for times to play themselves out in my relationships to all around me.

For now, I offer ways in which Anzaldúa's work strengthens feminist perspectives on psychological development. Her approach provides a vision for defining and understanding the self and its relationship to many concepts of human existence, including intimacy, politics, gender, sexuality, race, class, language, patriarchy, power, and empowerment. Simultaneously acknowledging the differences and commonalities among living beings and insisting on our interconnectedness, Anzaldúa recognizes the valuable necessity of developmental perspectives in understanding individual and collective growth. She calls on us to reach into the depths of our inner beings, into the depths of everything around us, and, quite possibly, to forget which is which.

Notes

1. All italicized passages are from *Borderlands/La Frontera.*
2. These characteristics are (1) contextual-relational, situated reasoning; (2) complex networks of multiple, multidirectional, causal connections; (3) reciprocity, connection, and dialogue between the knower and the known; (4) an emphasis on the social; (5) understanding as a social, negotiated, shared event involving the construction of knowledge in a community of knowers; and (6) attention to, and valuing of, diversity (48).
3. The meaning of the term "self" is intentionally vague here; generally, I use "self" to indicate a sense of inner/psychological identity differentiated and distinguishable from the rest of the world.
4. See for example Robert Kegan's Orders of the Mind, a model of adult development built on issues of self-in-relationship. Rooted in Piagetian theory, Kegan's five qualitatively different, linear "orders" include object permanence, self-concept (self distinguishable from others), cross-categorical (can empathize with others, think abstractly, self embedded in relationships), self-authorship (self has a stable identity that remains stable across contexts and relationships), and self-as-system (sees self and others as multiple systems in constant creation and recreation). This idea of self-as-system is consistent with Anzaldúa's theory of conocimiento.

Part 4

conocimientos. . . . expanding the vision

You could say that conocimiento is basically an awareness, the awareness of facultad that sees through all human acts whether of the individual mind and spirit or of the collective, social body. The work of conocimiento—consciousness work—connects the inner life of the mind and spirit to the outer worlds of action. In the struggle for social change I call this particular aspect of conocimiento spiritual activism. I see conocimiento as a consciousness-raising tool, one that promotes self-awareness and self-reflectivity. . . . It means to place oneself in a state of resonance with the other's feelings and situations, and to give the other an opportunity to express their needs and points of view. To relate to others by recognizing commonalities.

—Gloria E. Anzaldúa, *Interviews/Entrevistas*

Chapter 15

"So Much Meat": Gloria Anzaldúa, the Mind/Body Split, and Exerting Control over My Fat Body

Elena Levy-Navarro

> I don't know of anyone who writes through the body. I want to write from the body; that's why we're in a body.
>
> Gloria Anzaldúa, *Interviews/Entrevistas*

> And those that don't survive? The waste of ourselves: so much meat thrown at the feet of madness or fate or the state.
>
> Gloria Anzaldúa, "Speaking in Tongues"

Imagine you are at a dinner party, as I was last week, and your host, the dean of your college, directs you all to the intimate space around a small round table. In looking at that space, you immediately fix on those captain's chairs with the knowledge that they will not fit your hips or thighs. As you look for other chairs, you think, "I can't cause a disruption, can I?," and so you squeeze your hips and thighs one more time into a chair too small, a prison with bars that crush in on your thighs. Rather than getting angry at the chair's manufacturers, the club, your host, the guest, or, in fact, yourself for being so stupid as to force yourself into this tight spot, you reproach yourself, as I did, by saying, "why are you so fat?," perhaps even adding one of those epithets you know so well. It becomes visible evidence for you of your own laxness, a moral as well as physical laxness. The next morning, whether you say it to yourself or not, you will feel that you deserve the long sharp bruises on your thighs, just as the night before you believed that you deserved the pain that you felt as the bars began to press close and cut into your leg. You have become your own best jailer.

How can a person expect to assert herself, as I did in my conversation, if she insists on first denying and finally punishing her body? Until recently I have never asked that question because I have simply assumed, as my actions of that night demonstrate, that one can only assert one's intellect if one contains, controls, and punishes the body. In other words, I have been subjected (and have subjected myself to) a western dualism that Gloria Anzaldúa has boldly interrogated, undermined, and even dismantled in her writing. The bruises on my thighs and hips that hurt me even now as I write this essay are the signs of the costs of clinging to and perpetuating this western dualism. That is, if one operates by a series of binaries—mind/body, white/black, and male/female—then I, a female, a Mexican-American, a fat woman—can only speak if I contain all the qualities that would associate me with the latter terms. Any attempt to inhabit the former terms have forced me inevitably to contain my body, and so my success has required in this tortured logic that I inflict this pain on myself and others. After all, in an effort to inhabit the former I have searched out, found, and sometimes insisted that others occupy the role of other. For now, I focus on the pain I have inflicted on myself as a metaphor, although not just a metaphor as it is inscribed in my flesh and thus in my being, for this larger pain and for the danger of adopting, using, and thereby proliferating these binaries.

I can only come to these conclusions because I have read Gloria Anzaldúa. Her writing has helped me to imagine an alternative way of being embodied, one that can connect me to other embodied beings in a different, more creative way. Fortunately, then, a good friend of mine sent her *Interviews/Entrevistas* to me over a year ago, at a time when I felt spiritually exhausted with the battle I had been waging against my body. My body, it seemed to me, had been winning, as I was overwhelmed with a series of chronic systemic illnesses—hypothyroidism, fatigue, and migraines. Even as I fantasized over exerting control of that body one more time, I began to imagine an alternative way of being as I read Gloria Anzaldúa's own frank discussion of her own lifelong struggle with her body. Could I, I asked myself, begin to see my body as she had come to see hers—a spiritual medium?

It is difficult for me to say exactly what caused this revelation. Should I attribute it to myself or to Gloria? In some ways, I want to say that I recognized myself in Gloria, her struggles with her body reminded me of my own. I also, however, believe that her style is uniquely suited to fostering the type of recognition I experienced. In *Interviews/Entrevistas*, Gloria describes her own illness as having both a concrete, immediate sense for her and a more metaphorical sense relevant to the sympathetic, communal-minded reader. As she explains of her illness, "I feel like the whole planet is going through that: the woman inside us and inside men is rebelling" (66). I could recognize some of the pain and frustration she felt, even as I was encouraged to see this as relevant beyond my own experience. She describes her own illness in spiritual terms—indeed, in metaphorical terms relevant to me as it is relevant for other contemporary readers. As she states, "It was like everything coming to a head: All the pain, all the secrecy, all the things I'd repressed about my body. I saw it as a lesson; the body has to speak, and if it can't speak through any other way—to make you sit up and take notice—it makes you sick, so you have some time on your hands" (66). Her words forced me to think of my own illness as a spiritual condition, a sign that I too must find alternative creative ways to exist in and through my body. In my case, I thought, I needed to come to terms with my size, and this time, rather than to begin a regime of dieting and exercise to punish, diminish, and control my body, to begin to do things to listen to, appreciate, and live through my body.

After reading Anzaldúa's interviews, I devoured her writing, as someone on a midnight binge. Her simple, direct "Speaking in Tongues: A Letter to Third World Women Writers" especially challenged my way of thinking in dualistic terms. Imagine someone who had always identified herself as "white" reading this letter, and imagine her like me as someone who wants to read literature with all her being. In this gloriously embodied text, Gloria urges us to "write from the body," offering herself as a powerful model. The letter form allows her to connect her body imaginatively with other bodies, reaching out to, and in some senses creating, a community of embodied people. I experience the first paragraph as a kind of assault and challenge. Where am I in relation to this community? I, like all readers, have a choice: I can try to work hard against her style and see these third-world women she embodies before me as objects to be studied, or I can allow myself to experience her style with all my being and become in the process a part of that community. My mind plays tricks on me and finds more clever ways to distance me from these bodies so that it can maintain its privileged position as disembodied outsider. For example, now I want to insist on my own distinctiveness by pointing to my privileged economic circumstances. I am, after all, sitting here in my study, an entire room devoted to thought, and that room sits in the large house I own. Doesn't this, I think, make me different from these women who live in closed quarters, bodies next to bodies as I lived (and remember living) as a child and young woman? This desire to insist on my material difference is only another way I find to trick myself.

I may be inadequate to the task of erecting such firm boundaries around my oozing and unruly flesh, but I can insist that my money, material means, and mind can erect and maintain such boundaries between myself and others. Let's be real, Elena, the only boundary keeping me from these women is my act of intellectual will insisting on some difference between my body and their bodies because the alternative is too frightening. That mind, in an effort to persist in its form, will therefore erect such boundaries even as it pretends to be only confessing its privilege.

Anzaldúa's writing makes me feel something very different, the way that I as a body felt, I imagine, when, as a child, I lived next to other bodies and was animated by them. I am amazed that I am drawn to the most seemingly trivial moments in the text, especially the following: "In the kitchen Maria and Cherríe's voices falling on these pages. I can see Cherríe going about in her terry cloth wrap, barefoot washing the dishes, shaking out the tablecloth, vacuuming." I feel and see in this scene many similar ones of my youth, when the bodies of my adolescent sisters and friends would fill the house, perhaps squeezed into a bedroom or bathroom together. When I remember these moments, feeling them through and in Gloria's narrative, so that the body of my sister becomes Cherríe's body, and her black body (a body that she and my family would have always denied was "black") becomes something I know with such familiarity and love that I can hardly stand remembering it from the prison of my study now, I worry, asking, "can THAT really be worthy of writing?" Gloria answers, "I am thinking *they lied, there is no separation between life and writing.*" My mind insists there is and must be, but at this moment at least, I feel that I cannot betray the embodied knowledge I have known so well. Unfortunately, that knowledge, even if embedded in my being, seems so fragile and illusory that it seems almost inevitable that without the community Gloria imagines it will be replaced by the cold concrete numbers of the physician's scale.

That place of my punishment—my hips and thighs—has been the place of my shame. No matter what my condition, fat or thin, my thighs and hips are a site of pain for me. When I am fat, as I am now, I feel the pain when I force myself into small spaces. When I am thin, I inflict the pain on myself in an effort to "bust" the fat always associated with my womanly hips and thighs. In both cases, I treat my body as "so much meat" that must be controlled by me, a mere lifeless mass, the lifelong burden of my mind. Operating beneath this, however, exists a greater fear that I have not wanted to articulate—namely, that my body is not lifeless fat at all but rather a teeming primordial slime. My aversion to all things liquid, especially my own menstrual blood, comes, I think, from this sense that I am not solid at all. If left to itself, I have imagined, the body would *naturally* grow larger and larger. It is no accident that my fear toward the body is directed at my hips and thighs, the precise place where my body seems to reach outward to deny all containment. Every time I must force myself into a seat, no matter how extraordinarily small, I have had to resist the impulse to see myself as some grotesque fertile ooze that will inevitably spread beyond any limits. Trapped in this way of thinking, I remain inactive and quiescent, unable to see, for example, that the seats are designed, not for any body at all but rather for the profit of the theater or airline company.

All my diets have been directed at my hips and thighs. In my first successful "diet"—that is, in my period of anorexia during college—I was exhilarated in losing pound after pound. Even then, I realized that I would never reach a point in which I could conclude, "Now I have lost enough weight." The compliments only reinforced my sense that the more the better. I also was simply exhilarated at exercising this sort of exceptional control over my body. Every visible and invisible sign of that control, then, was cherished as a sign of my superior virtue, whether it was the hunger, the ability to deny myself even my favorite foods, the number on the scale, the direction of my weight-loss graph, the pain of the exercise regime, the amenorrhea, and, of course, the appearance and finally protuberance of my bones. In fact, as I lost weight, I began to cultivate a way of being designed to make people notice these protruding bones. Sitting doubled over, I would hold my arms across my skinny body and hold and even caress my shoulder bones, as if to say: look at me, how virtuous I am to have chiseled off my flesh to reveal the simple bones underneath.

This posture, however, was simultaneously designed to hide the shame of my hips and thighs. As insane as it sounds now, I thought they were enormous, and they seemed even more enormous the more I lost weight. At my skinniest, I had exposed virtually all of my hip bones, something I also called attention to by wearing the tightest pants possible. Their appearance proved, I thought, that I had superior will power because I, after all, could shape my body in ways others could not. At the same time, I became even more aware of what I considered the enormity of my hips. As I traced the outline of the bone, I thought to myself, "Why do they have to protrude so much?" I contrasted them to the hips of other imaginary women, who of course matched some sort of hipless ideal. As I cupped my hips, something I did obsessively in private, I used to imagine that my hands could smooth them out so that they wouldn't protrude in quite that offensive way and direction. Similarly, as I traced their outline at night, I used to wish that I could simply shave off some of them so that they would more closely conform to that ideal. Only now I can see that no amount of shaping, no amount of shaving, would have been enough because what I desired really was to have no body at all.

In a similar way, I organized my exercise regime so that I could bust the fat in my thighs. At my skinniest, my thighs were perhaps the only place with much fat at all, and I began to imagine that I could at the very least tighten up that fat. My blonde aerobic instructor, a varsity swimmer who offered the class because, as she insisted, she needed much more exercise than her practices provided, commented on my thighs one day by saying, "I guess whatever you do you won't be able to rid yourself of them." Her remarks were to me a death sentence because I knew that I would always be fat as long as I had those swelling thighs. My attitude to my thighs and hips shows that I associated "fat" not with the substance under the skin, but with my very bodily existence. The hips and thighs, I believe, were the sign of my humiliation especially because I knew instinctively, in a way I can't really prove right now either, that they were the marks that identified me as both a female and a person of color. When I cradled my hips at night or willfully ignored my thighs, I was trying desperately to pretend that I could become those privileged minds—white, male, and thin.

Already, you can see how these efforts at control were efforts to distance myself from any association with a female gender. I remember that I was proud that I had amenorrhea because it seemed to prove that I had overcome my female body. In fact, I loved consulting with that expert male physician; he and I were joined together under the same desire to use our considerable expertise to control that unruly female body of mine. The same impulse was evident in that obsessive concern with measuring and charting my weight. That chart proved to me yet again that I had the intellectual fortitude to bring my body in line with some seemingly objective standard. Given this type of thinking, it is no surprise that I was proud and somewhat relieved when I finally stopped menstruating altogether. Far from convincing me that I should turn back, this fact seemed a sign of the success of my diet and exercise regime. After all, I had been able to use my mind to overcome my (female) body.

In my case, I saw my fat, concentrated in my hips and thighs, as marking me also as a racial or ethnic other. I learned early on in my assimilationist Mexican-American family that I must blend in as much as possible if I were to succeed. For this reason, I readily looked down on anyone who asserted their difference. When reading Lucille Clifton's "To my Hips," quite a while ago now, I thought the poet ridiculous in making THAT a subject of her poetry. At the same time, I also understood that her own assertion of her size was an assertion of her right to speak from her body in defiance of the culture that says it is only worthy of ridicule. I accepted without question that the small thin girls with blonde hair would be favored and similarly that the white boys would never find me attractive (never asking about whether I found THEM attractive). Thinking in this white supremacist framework, I shrunk in horror at every sign that I was not, in fact, white. I was horrified, yet again, when Mexican men would appreciate my hips, or when in a nightclub, only men of color would ask me to dance. In all these ways, I acted on the assumption that, as Audre Lorde writes in "Song for a Thin Sister," "skinny / was funny or silly / but always / white." I retreated into the life of the mind, believing in that way that perhaps maybe then white society would forgive me my body and thus allow me to squeeze in. Adopting such an attitude gave people around me too much power, since they could always use the veiled (or not so veiled) allusion to my body to bludgeon me into submission. Just please don't place me in that category, I implicitly suggested, and I will be a good girl.

Now, I think that my illnesses were spiritual in nature. The body was telling me to stand up and take notice. And, if I read my illnesses this way, I can go even further—even though I still find it difficult because, I say, wildly presumptuous but really because the statement is so utterly transgressive: I am spiritual in my fatness. My fat is a blessing that has come to me to insist that I should live life large. Stop hunching over, stop crossing your arms, stop trying to make your body as small as possible. To put it another way, stop dieting. I prefer to look at my fat self in very different terms by following Gloria Anzaldúa's defiant but joyful refusal to perpetuate the western dualism of mind/body. Then, my fat self, which spreads from the hips outward to refuse the containment of the standardized chair or seat, constructed not for real bodies at all but by some engineer and corporation that calculates the seat size for maximum profit (the way that I calculated and charted my weight loss), can be a sign of my own spiritual growth. My body announces my decision to remain big, a refusal to become complicit in our society's efforts to restrict, shrink, and finally annihilate all those relegated to the second term of a series of implicit binaries. We have to say and act as if our bodies matter.

I must develop the courage to live with my fatness which means, given our current society, defiantly. Next time I approach the same table in the intimate academic setting, I must cause some trouble, thinking and knowing that I deserve adequate space. Rather than saying to myself, "I am too fat for that chair," I should say out loud that the chair and table are too small for me. That simple act, I believe, is important, not only to heal myself, but to help create a world that will take account of all sorts of bodies. In some way, it would represent progress toward building the type of embodied community that Gloria Anzaldúa's work has imagined and created. I will try to imagine it, and in imagining do it, because the table and the chairs are just too small right now.

Chapter 16

Champion of the Spirit: Anzaldúa's Critique of Rationalist Epistemology

Amala Levine

> Growing whole means becoming divine . . . It's like recognizing myself, taking the veil off. It's like building a bridge to the source—to the creative life force, the substance that's in everything.
>
> —Gloria E. Anzaldúa

"Fighting with the spirit," Gloria Anzaldúa stands at the vanguard of a movement, currently underway, to go "beyond the mind, the vital, and the physical" (*Interviews/Entrevistas* 124–25). She develops a mode of consciousness offering both an integrated theory of pluralist totality and a recorded life experience of "multiple little selves" coexisting within "the big self" (*Interviews/Entrevistas* 20). Anzaldúa preserves cohesion without sacrificing differentiation by grounding her lived experience and conceptual thought in a spiritual dimension, pointing the way beyond the deadlock between modern rationalism and postmodern scepticism. She ardently criticizes the Western mindset for privileging "the mechanical, the objective, the industrial, the scientific" (*Interviews/Entrevistas* 163) while denigrating imagination, fantasies, and dreams as equally legitimate modes of knowledge. The depth vision Anzaldúa cultivates injects lucid observation with the prismatic powers of imagination, intuition, and feeling. Far from constructing subject/object binaries, she weaves self, world, and spirit into a synergistic whole: "I look for omens everywhere, everywhere catch glimpses of the patterns and cycles of my life" (*Borderlands* 58).

According to Anzaldúa, we have reached a "turning point," where "we're going to leave the rigidity of this concrete reality and expand it" (*Interviews/Entrevistas* 285). She is not alone in noting such a paradigm shift from a modern atomistic viewpoint in which religious institutions serve as the exclusive connection with a transcendent godhead, to a highly secular postmodern stage containing both radical doubt of reason's powers and at-times indiscriminate New Age fascination with all things spiritual.[1] In the crucible of these conflicting visions, Anzaldúa crafts an expansive epistemology of synergistic consciousness that goes beyond both the modern constraints of reason and the postmodern dangers of incoherence. Securely anchored in her spiritual awareness she enlists mind, imagination, intuition, and emotions, and develops a transformative vision for our age. Though linked to New Age orientation in philosophy and lifestyle (particularly its embrace of cultural mythologies and esoteric wisdom traditions), Anzaldúa's vision does not share the disdain of the physical body found in some New Age philosophies. Her embodied, experiential spirituality constitutes not only a particular mode of perception and being in the world, but also the fountainhead of her creativity, sexuality, and political activism.

When only three months old, Anzaldúa showed unusual physical symptoms. Later in life, after consultations with psychic readers, past life regressions, and a regular routine of daily meditation, she no longer attributes her early menstruation exclusively to physiological causes—as a hormonal imbalance—but rather sees it also as the psychic phenomenon of another spirit, unused to physical incarnation, having entered her body. The onset of this abnormal bleeding was accompanied by her first near-death experience which was later followed by two others, the most recent after a hysterectomy when for twenty minutes she "was off the rational track and . . . could see more clearly" (*Interviews/Entrevistas* 107). Such traumatic experiences, including her hair turning white at sixteen when ill with fever and the onset of severe diabetes, have regularly punctuated Anzaldúa's life. But she also has had blissful Kundalini experiences during some especially deep meditations (*Interviews/Entrevistas* 108). Whether frightening or pleasurable, such incidents strengthened her awareness of an inner spiritual presence, "a greater power than the conscious I" (*Borderlands* 72). This power, which she elsewhere describes as her "inner self" (*Interviews/Entrevistas* 20, 34–35) has consistently served her as teacher and guide. For the reader as well, that spiritual inner being holds the key to a fuller understanding of Anzaldúa's work and its significant contribution to the contemporary shift toward a post-rationalist epistemology that acknowledges the spiritual, the imaginal, and the emotional as legitimate sources of knowledge, offering a broader, more inclusive vision of reality.

From early childhood, her psychic and physiological precocity set Anzaldúa apart from family and friends, causing not only deep emotional pain but also distrust of her experiences' validity. An outsider longing to be inside the circle of the familiar and conditioned by a dominant-cultural materialist view of reality, she initially doubted her inner senses, permitting them to "atrophy." She allowed "white rationality to tell [her] that the existence of the 'other world' was mere pagan superstition" and accepted the socioculturally sanctioned "consciousness of duality" (*Borderlands* 58–59). Yet despite such pressures she gradually recognized her psychic insights as the catalyst of a spiritual awakening to the multiple selves conjoined within the totality of a larger self beyond ego boundaries. First experientially and then intellectually she developed a nondual vision of self and world that indicates an alternative epistemology, a "third eye view." Neither exclusively rational nor emotional, but integrating both with the imaginal and the spiritual, she realizes that

> everything is spiritual, that I am a speck of this soul, this creative consciousness, this creative life force; and so is a dog, a rock, a bird, this bedspread, and this wall. In recognizing that soul—which is what Native Americans have always recognized. . . . —nothing is alien, nothing is strange. Spirit exists in everything; therefore God, the divine, is in everything—in whites as well as blacks, rapists as well as victims; it's in the tree, the swamp, the sea. . . . Everything is my relative, I'm related to everything. (*Interviews/Entrevistas* 100)

Such spiritually grounded holistic vision and integrative epistemology positions Anzaldúa within the current renaissance of idealist ideology characteristic of the New Age Movement which has its antecedents not only in U.S. Transcendentalism and European Romantic Idealism but also shares conceptual ground with indigenous shamanist spirituality, preconquest myth and ritual practice, and Eastern wisdom traditions.[2] Whether ancient or recent, all share a sacral vision of self and world permeated by divine spirit, the all-pervasive life force. Anzaldúa holds an animist view of the universe, interconnecting the heavens with the depth of the ocean and the human with inorganic matter as a living whole imbued with consciousness (*Interviews/Entrevistas* 160) Her many physical ailments—combined with a voracious appetite for literature, philosophy, and mythology—convince her that it is possible to access a consciousness larger than mere thought or emotions, once she acknowledges that which first appeared an alien element within: her spirit, her soul. This perspective reveals the fallacy of limited vision. It is as if she had looked through the reverse end of binoculars whose myopic focus had offered a bifurcated view of separatism and fragmentation, framing her as the isolated "other." Entering a deeper consciousness generates a perceptual revolution: the excluded outsider transforms into the ultimate insider, connected to one and all by a spiritual bond that highlights commonality without eliminating differences, displaying on a macro-level the kind of pluralist totality characteristic of the multiply located individual self.

Anzaldúa's discovery is accompanied by a liberating sense of power (*Interviews/Entrevistas* 112). Socially and psychologically she overcomes her shyness, drawing from the newly uncovered reservoir within, the assurance of a universal human and cosmic bond. Anzaldúa regards her inner self, unbounded by ego, as her principal teacher and guide. Carefully listening to her inner voices, she uses their promptings to shape her path, handle her health problems, and balance professional with personal commitments, especially the need for solitude while remaining actively engaged socially and politically.[3] Though her spirit is the source of empowerment, it is not the agent of self-creation: "I really do believe that we have to create our souls, we have to keep evolving as souls, as minds, as bodies—on all the different planes" (*Interviews/Entrevistas* 75) Self and world are "a text we co-create" by giving meaning to experiences and setting the tasks of our lives, by transvaluing the seemingly negative into a positive catalyst for change, when viewed with detachment. The more we are attuned to our inner selves, the clearer becomes our mission and the path to its accomplishment. In her foreword to *Making Face, Make Soul,* Anzaldúa succinctly points to the connection between spirituality and creativity, arguing that "[i]nherent in the creative act is a spiritual, psychic component—one of spiritual excavation, of (ad)venturing into the inner void, extrapolating meaning from it and sending it out into the world. To do this kind of work requires the total person—body, soul, mind, and spirit" ("Haciendo caras" xxiv).

Anzaldúa experiences her spirituality physically in the body. Uncovering one within the folds of the other, she sanctifies the body as the locus spiritus, celebrating divinity manifest in its spiritual inner being, vibrant mind, and exuberant sexuality. Demonized as evil, corrupt, and treacherous, despised as wanton temptress yet used as sexual object when not desexed and adulated as virgin, women historically have been dismembered and disemboweled only to be filled with the male fantasies that have scripted social and cultural taboos. Anzaldúa harnesses both spirit and mind to reclaim the body. In an act of radical self-assertion that is both personal and prescriptively collective, she restores the female body to wholeness. She not only decolonizes the female body and reattaches the mind but even goes beyond the predominant feminist agenda that seeks to empower women by legitimizing their intelligent mind.

Drawing on her own intuitions, spiritual self-discovery, and immersion in Hindu philosophy and religion (in particular the work of Sri Aurobindo),

Anzaldúa formulates a "yoga of the body" that unites mind *and* spirit with body. Far from renouncing the physical, "you work the other way around, make the body divine, make every cell divine . . . Each cell is a miniature universe" (*Interviews/Entrevistas* 99). Spirit inhabits the body and pervades the universe. Conceptualizing the human as a quantum being, Anzaldúa develops a liberatory tool for self-definition, with revolutionary impact for interpersonal relationships. Additionally, this conceptualization offers a way out of the postmodern conundrum. The quantum body is a field of infinite possibilities: neurons, photons and electrons arranging themselves in ever-shifting patterns of interrelation, signaling each other in a constant transfer of energy and information. Just as this atomic and subatomic process, despite the appearance of chaotic movement, is not random but guided by the cells' intelligent awareness, so the quantum mind creates reality out of unlimited potential configurations. Depending on the state of consciousness,[4] the appearance of reality is always a projection of our particular cognitive state. Together, in an interactive process of cooperation, quantum body and quantum mind produce our physiological, psychological, and sociocultural conditions. To the limited, rationalist consciousness reality appears as objectively existing matter; from a spiritualized perspective matter dissolves into a flux of possibilities co-existing in a web of potential interrelationships, the evanescent raw material for our creation of self and world.[5] This holographic view also holds the answer to postmodern deconstruction's almost exclusive reliance on a rationalist epistemology that rarely sees beyond atomistic fragmentation. Oppositions and fragmentation resolve into a dialogic model of pluralist totality offering infinite possibilities of material configuration.[6]

Anzaldúa's philosophical underpinnings do not make the body an abstraction but rather point to its spiritual permeability. Her ailments remain just as excruciatingly painful, and cultural/ethnic stigmatization do not lose their sting, even though, when viewed through the prism of a deeper consciousness, they appear as crucibles in the path of transformation. A spiritual viewpoint does not relieve us of social responsibility. Since we manifest in the body, we must act through it, guided by the heart. Anzaldúa speaks of having three hearts, one physical, one emotional, and one spiritual; whichever predominates conditions the experience of the moment. The heart symbolizes integration. She explains that sometimes, "when [she] meditate[s], [she] synchronize[s] the three" (*Interviews* 68–69); she becomes synergistically attuned to the holistic nature of self and world, *tat tvam asi* in Sanskrit, the self as the embodiment of pluralist totality collapsed into One (Goswami, *Visionary* 47).

In such heightened awareness, Anzaldúa achieves her "yoga of the body;" intellect, emotions, imagination, soul, and spirit comingle as one. In a 1983 interview with Christine Weiland, she argues that "[w]e have to recognize the total self, not just one part, and start to be true to that total self, that presence, that soul" (*Interviews/Entrevistas* 103). This integrated perspective offers insight into nonduality or what one might call soul vision since it apperceives the infinite multiplicity yet oneness of all being. Conventional society, still privileging the intellect, frowns on such psychic experiences: "We're supposed to ignore, forget, kill these fleeting images of the soul's presence and of the spirit's presence. We've been taught that the spirit is outside our bodies or above our heads somewhere up in the sky with God. We're supposed to forget that every cell in our bodies, every bone and bird and worm has spirit in it" (*Borderlands* 58). To legitimize such soul visions, Anzaldúa turns to her indigenous roots in Aztec-Mexica culture and mythology.

Mythopoeic thought is not guided by analytic reason but follows imagination, intuition, and spirit as it attempts to articulate the meaning of self and world. A "form of spiritual creativity" (Cassirer 98), myth exhibits the same mode of integrated perception Anzaldúa accesses when entering states of deeper consciousness. Mythopoeic and spiritual vision create intersubjective relations, I and Thou connected by an empathic, ontological bond. They are the thought form of nonduality amid ostensibly oppositional material conditions or what Anzaldúa sometimes calls Coatlicue: "I've always been aware that there is a greater power than the conscious I. That power is my inner self, the entity that is the sum total of all my reincarnations, the godwoman in me I call Antigua, mi Diosa, the divine within, Coatlicue" (*Borderlands* 72).

As far back as the Toltec civilization, before the eleventh century, Coatlicue—"she of the serpent skirt"—was revered as the Earth Mother who contained within herself "the dualities of male and female, light and dark, life and death" (*Borderlands* 54). She combined peaceful bounty with warrior aggression and, like the serpent, healed the wound she herself inflicted. In Aztec myth she is revered and feared as Magna Mater, mother of the gods, foremost among them Huitzilopchtli whom she conceived without male participation. Her worship featured prominently in Aztec ritual practice, linking her with family, community, and land in a bond of interdependence analogous to integrated states of mind.

For Anzaldúa, entering the Coatlicue state means changing perspective—descending through the unconscious deep into the soul, there to perceive herself, when "suddenly I feel everything rushing to a center, a nucleus. All the lost pieces of myself come flying from the deserts and the mountains and the valleys, magnetized toward that center. Completa" (*Borderlands* 73). Anzaldúa has experienced such rebirth not once, but several times. As a very young child it turned into a fearful passage through boundaries, while as an adult it has been experienced at times orgasmically. But on every occasion the third or spiritual eye has acted as the midwife of rebirth, "propel[ling] the soul to do its work: make soul, increase consciousness of itself" (*Borderlands* 68). What had appeared separate to the rational mind now stands revealed as part of a larger fabric in which differences are not merely synthesized but sublated. Just as the myth of the serpentine Coatlicue conjoins clearly differentiated opposites into an overarching whole and the mythopoeic mode of consciousness integrates without obliterating differences, so does the perception the Coatlicue state produces. Anzaldúa's intricate use of myth as text, methodology, and psychology underscores her ontological conviction that we are the creators of ourselves and co-creators of the universe, if we have but eyes to see.

Anzaldúa experiences privileged moments of deep insight not only at times of sexual intimacy but already when as a three-year-old she perceived herself as multidimensional. Reaching for some fruit, she suddenly saw "three parts of [her]self but all connected . . . It was all the same body, but not in one place." Only much later does she understand that she had sensed "the soul's presence" (*Interviews/Entrevistas* 97). Her out-of-body and near-death experiences, her most profound sexual encounters, and the initially incomprehensible childhood incidents all share an epiphanic quality. They open her to the spiritual ground of being, the unitary One, the cusp of all multiplicities. Such moments are rare and not sustainable, but they have progressively transformed Anzaldúa's perception:

> When I was young I was one with the trees, the land, and my mother. . . . Then I became separate, and made other people and parts of myself the other. Then I went one step beyond into the supernatural world—the subtle world. . . . and dealt with that kind of otherness. Plus the uncanny—the demon, the ghost, the evil. . . . It was an energy of refocusing and bringing it all back together. (*Interviews/Entrevistas* 41)

Privileged moments of insight act as catalytic transformers, jolting us into new awareness. But unless we are finely attuned to our intuitive senses, we may remain unaware of the first and last tact of the triadic rhythm Anzaldúa so succinctly describes in the above passage. It begins with an originary, unconscious unity of self and world in early childhood, followed by an extended period of alienating subject–object division when the dictates of rationalist consciousness predominate, and ends with an inter-subjective sense of being, once a deeper mode of consciousness has been gained. To live and perceive spiritually we must attain the third stage, at least intermittently. Sri Aurobindo writes that "to live the spiritual life, a reversal of consciousness is needed. . . . All who have lived a spiritual life have had the same experience: all of a sudden something in their being has been reversed. . . . There has been a decisive experience and the standpoint in life, the way of looking at life has suddenly changed" (*Powers Within* 166–67).

When Anzaldúa first read Sri Aurobindo she was not sure who had channeled whom, perplexed at their identical trains of thought. He was an Indian sage regard by some as an avatar, who died at his Ashram in Pondicherry, India in 1950; she is a self-described "third world lesbian feminist with Marxist and mystic leanings" ("La Prieta" 205). On the surface they have little in common, but when she encounters his work she recognizes him as the teacher she never met but whose mind, thought, and spirit she knows intimately. A fully realized being, he has taught her through dreams, meditations, and his writings that the ground of all being is consciousness, the fountainhead of energy and transformation. Holistic at its highest/deepest level, the unconscious and the rationalist self-conscious are sublated into a third, unitary mode. This creative consciousness is the wellspring of Anzaldúa's articulation of nonduality: "the idea that God and the devil, . . . that evil and good are the same. . . . Like the yin and the yang. If you go so far to evil, you get good. They're one; we only separate them because of the duality, the way we work" (*Interviews/Entrevistas* 99).

In an intellectual climate when both the academy and society are largely governed by myopic vision and contentious factions, when specialization is prized and ratiocination privileged, when religions contest each other rather than concur, Anzaldúa is a breath of fresh air. Every aspect of her thought, mind, and being is spiritually grounded and oriented toward inclusiveness. She easily embraces both Shiva and Coatlicue, Eastern wisdom traditions and Aztec mythology but takes umbrage at institutionalized religions' dogmatic, stifling, absence of soul. As a child she was more attracted to her parents' stories of spirits and supernatural/mythic beings, than Sunday sermons. "Institutionalized religion fears trafficking with the spirit world and stigmatizes it as witchcraft. It has strict taboos against this kind of inner knowledge . . . [I]t fears the supra-human, the god in ourselves" (*Borderlands* 59). Such religions vilify the body, positing a split between body and spirit, that Anzaldúa regards as conceptually and methodologically flawed. They think dualistically, radically separating good and evil, human and divine as irreconcilable opposites of unequal value. To postulate, as Anzaldúa does, that God and the devil are one, is heresy to the orthodox, while from a nondualist perspective both are simply different aspects of the same life force.

Our perceptions, epistemology, and ontology are deeply intertwined and mutually conditioned; how we know inevitably affects what we know. If we only use our rational cognitive faculties, we will merely see the limited outlines and surface form of the other as an object to be dissected and analyzed.

If, however, we perceive not only intellectually but also imaginally and attune to la facultad, our perception of self and world changes dramatically. Intellect turns into insight, vision expands, becoming inclusive and receptive while remaining materially grounded in the body. Self-world parameters become translucent to reveal the bonding link of all existence, and we respond empathetically to others. When we see with la facultad, we perceive "in surface phenomena the meaning of deeper realities. . . . It is an acute awareness mediated by the part of the psyche that does not speak, that communicates in images and symbols" (*Borderlands* 60). Once reason is no longer privileged but regarded simply as one of several cognitive modalities, the censoring mind is silenced and the spirit world becomes visible within our own.

La facultad is a synaesthetic faculty, involving intuition, imagination, senses, and emotions as well as the inner eye, which as modes of perception collectively condition the appearance of reality. When operating in conjunction they produce a much stronger, more vivid experience than in isolation:

> This shift in perception deepens the way we see concrete objects and people; the senses become so acute and piercing that we can see through things, view events in depth, a piercing that reaches the underworld (the realm of the soul). As we plunge vertically, the break, with its accompanying new seeing, makes us pay attention to the soul, and we are thus carried into awareness—an experiencing of soul (Self). (*Borderlands* 61)

Anzaldúa is not anti-reason per se, but she deplores the predominance of a rationalist epistemology that favors the so-called objective, scientific view of reality as quantifiable matter. Although analytic, linear thought has produced spectacular results, these results have come at a high price, including the underutilization of the right brain, delegitimization of subjective experience, and suspicion of spiritual cognizance outside institutionalized pathways. Rationalist thought is the domain of the conscious ego, the mind in action, separating itself as the observer from the observed—the object to be brought under control. This separatist view necessarily regards the world as a potential battlefield, a Darwinian power struggle for dominance. What to the rational mind appears solidly real is actually "only one facet or one facade of the spirit world" when perceived holistically, using all our faculties (*Interviews/Entrevistas* 159). But this proposition remains suspect as long as the legitimacy of subjective viewpoints grounded in intuition, emotions, and imagination are not fully admitted.

From a purely rationalist viewpoint, splitting the bicameral mind inevitably divides reality into the seen and the unseen, matter and spirit, creating the basis for the western separation between the secular domain of reason and science and the metaphysical terrain of faith and religion. If, however, all portions of the brain and their different modalities of perception are understood holistically as cross-correlating exchanges of energy and information, then such dualisms dissolve and reality appears as one infinitely extended, interconnected whole.[7] Einstein, well aware how much he owed to his intuition, imagination, and spiritual awareness, emphatically insisted that "I did not discover relativity by rational thinking alone." Each aspect of the mind and its corresponding level of consciousness creates its own form of perception; the more integrated they are, the more the contours of reality distend. This, Anzaldúa argues, is "the work of mestiza consciousness . . . to break down the subject–object duality that keeps her prisoner and to show in the flesh and through images in her work how duality is transcended" (*Borderlands* 102).

The defining characteristic of mestiza consciousness is its integrative nature; whether it engages in social, cultural, political, or sexual arenas, mestiza consciousness remains grounded in the realization of their spiritual interrelation. From this expansive consciousness, Anzaldúa derives her activist mission and defining role: "to unite people—the blacks with the whites with the Indians. Not in any grandiose way but just in calling attention to the fact that we're all human, we all come from the same spark. . . . I'm also all these other people. That is the spiritual in me" (*Interviews/Entrevistas* 123). This language might sound suspiciously universalizing to postmodern feminists and postcolonialists. But Anzaldúa very clearly distinguishes between this spiritual bond interlinking humanity that organic, inorganic, and planetary nature and the essentialism that elides the specific sociocultural differences shaping each individual's perceptual and physical experience.

Throughout her work Anzaldúa insists on the need to articulate specific locations and conditions. "[O]ur surroundings, our growing up, and . . . ideologies control how we act and think" (*Interviews/Entrevistas* 222). We live embedded in particular communities, shaped by their values, customs, and institutions; we belong to groups that give us our social identity. These overlapping worlds stamp us in multiple, distinct ways, creating individualized ego structures as we acquire self-consciousness. Significantly, these particular differences and the correlative identities they produce preclude neither cross-cultural understanding and collaboration, nor the recognition of a deeper spiritual bond as the common ground for human understanding. The ego's conscious mind focuses on the material, experienced as a subject–object split, while the spiritual self (also referred to as the quantum self and accessible only in a deeper state of consciousness) is transpersonal and unitary (Goswami, *Visionary* 170). Anzaldúa makes a similar point: "There's an ego of the mind, an ego of the emotions, and an ego of the body. If we shut those three egos up long enough, then you can hear the vibration of [the spirit's] presence, of its soul. [W]hen you've got the three egos silent, then you can start the supermentalizing that Sri Aurobindo talks about: instead of operating from this mind, you operate from the supermind which is outside of the body and slightly above" (*Interviews/Entrevistas* 121).

Undeterred by potential stigmatization, Anzaldúa willingly risks being labeled "essentialist" by insisting on the foundational significance of the supermind as a deep structure of consciousness uniting all humans in a web of interconnected being. She celebrates it as the basis for empathy and the wellspring of her own political and social activism because "[s]pirituality is oppressed people's only weapon and means of protection. Changes in society only come after that" (*Interviews/Entrevistas* 98).

With the pen as her sword, Anzaldúa follows multiple, overlapping trajectories of emancipation. As both new mestiza and postcolonial theorist she articulates difference, particularizing her own individual location and those whom she encounters, not by speaking *for* them but by offering the liberatory methodology of mestiza consciousness. With it she has brilliantly revolutionized academic discourse on identity to the point where now the concept is even used by those who have never experienced social oppression. Though such simplification reproduces the elision of the very real conditions of oppression it seeks to address, it nonetheless steers the mind toward a recognition of humans as "kindred spirits" which for Anzaldúa is part of her mission: "[M]y task was to connect people to their reality—their spiritual, economic, material reality, to connect people to their past roots, their ancient cultures" (*Interviews/Entrevistas* 36). Part of what Anzaldúa calls her "spiritual work" consists in awakening in others the realization of their inner being by mapping her own self-discovery's pathway as a methodological model. Another part of her spiritual work issues from her acute sense of social fairness that is outraged by inequalities, economic disenfranchisement, or marginalization because of cultural, ethnic/racial, or gender differences.

From a postcolonial perspective, Anzaldúa's work is clearly intended to be emancipatory, to decolonize the mind, shake off domination, and replace homogeneity with heterogeneity. She challenges her readers to think about themselves in relation to their sociocultural world: how are they defined by others? who has the power and makes the rules? But the act of writing also has a spiritual and psychic component; it is "connected to the soul, connected to making soul" (*Interviews/Entrevistas* 226). Writing is "the quest . . . for the center of the self" ("Speaking" 169) located deep within the inner being on a level of consciousness inaccessible to cognitive reason alone. To plumb these depths, the writer must use the imagination, itself an integrated mode of consciousness: "The 'spiritual' part of myself as a writer is also concerned with traveling to other realities, with change, with transformation of consciousness, with exploring reality, with other possibilities and experiences. . . . You do these tasks through the imagination, through your creative self, creative unconscious—which to me ties in with spirituality and with the spirit" (*Interviews/Entrevistas* 251).

The creative imagination as a mode of perception unifies, calling up images from the soul. In the writing process, imagination serves Anzaldúa as the special conduit for tapping the depths within, revealing that "we are specks from this cosmic ocean, the soul" (*Interviews/Entrevistas* 116). She believes that "we are all 'almas finas,' . . . kindred spirits, and this interconnectedness is an unvoiced category of identity, a common factor in all life forms" (*Interviews/Entrevistas* 164).

Weary of the word *unity* as semantically suggesting homogeneity and possibly erasing the very differences she seeks to affirm, Anzaldúa resorts to the term *conocimiento* to indicate an integrative perception which, like the imagination, is related to la facultad. She describes conocimiento as a mode of consciousness that recognizes connections and commonalities while clearly acknowledging differences without, however, privileging either. Like imagination, conocimiento is a tool of spiritual excavation with a definite social, political thrust: "connect[ing] the inner life of the mind and spirit to the outer worlds of action" (*Interviews/Entrevistas* 178). Hermeneutically, conocimiento is more finely calibrated than "unity," which requires clarifying qualifiers. Anzaldúa argues that "we can live separately, connect, and be together. But I'd rather call it 'in solidarity,' 'in support of,' 'en conocimiento,' rather than 'united'. Unity always privileges one voice, one group" (*Interviews/Entrevistas* 157). Conocimiento is the lived expression of nonduality as spiritually grounded intersubjectivity, social equality, and political solidarity. It means "see[ing] the other from a different perspective, focusing on what we have in common with a rock, a tree, a bird, a black person, a Jewish person, a gay person. Look at the commonalities: We have consciousness, we have a soul" (*Interviews/Entrevistas* 76).

This perceptual transformation has very real political and ethical consequences. The recognition of a shared spiritual base and modes of consciousness defuses the hostility latent in any oppositional confrontation, replacing power struggle and hierarchy with the bond of empathy: "It encourages folks to . . . sympathize with others, to walk in the other's shoes, whether the other is a member of the same group or belongs to a different culture. It means to place oneself in a state of resonance with the other's feelings and situations. . . . Receptivity is the stance here, not the adversarial mode, not the armed camp" (*Interviews/Entrevistas* 178).

This shift toward a spiritually/ontologically undergirded experience of nonduality prepares the ground for an ethic of care predicated on trust, respect, responsibility, and love—not as fusion but as the recognition of I and Thou, plural bodies yet kindred spirits. In sociopolitical terms

Anzaldúa calls this realization of intersubjectivity and interdependence "the geography of hybrid selves" because in a "multicultural society we cross into each others' worlds" (*Interviews/Entrevistas* 254–55). This realization also creates the basis for the formation of alliances, solidarity movements, and contingent communities: temporary, fluid arrangements to empower the marginalized. They are built across social, economic, cultural, racial/ethnic, or gender differences by those with a shared awareness as nos/otras, Anzaldúa's word for those who understand that "to be human is to be in relationship," not only because it is politically expedient but because of a shared vision of commonality (*Interviews/Entrevistas* 195). On the most profound level, she holds this commonality to be spiritual.

Sociopolitically, such alliances are the condition of El Mundo Zurdo which Anzaldúa describes as both a physical space—a transformational, liberatory territory for self-exploration and empathic connection across differences in writing workshops, retreats, or publishing ventures—and a state of mind, of listening "with both outer and inner ear" (*Interviews/Entrevistas* 286). She explains that "traveling El Mundo Zurdo path is the path of a two-way movement—a going deep into the self and an expanding out into the world, a simultaneous recreation of the self and a reconstruction of society" ("La Prieta" 208). Methodologically and epistemologically, El Mundo Zurdo is a postmodern paradigm, deconstructing binaries and sociocultural narratives, crossing boundaries, replacing homogeneity with heterogeneity. This paradigm is anti-rationalist without relinquishing reason and inclusive without obscuring difference. But like every other Anzaldúan concept, El Mundo Zurdo also points beyond the potential impasse of postmodern destabilization by formulating an expansive, integrative model of self and world that preserves not only self-representation's feasibility but also the creation of alliances, solidarity, and community by acknowledging spirit as the vital connecting link.

At present, the modern apologists of objective reason and the postmodern champions of radical doubt still reign supreme—especially within the academy, firmly focused on "concrete reality" (*Interviews/Entrevistas* 283). But inroads are being made, especially outside the academy where concern with matters spiritual is on the rise, including a growing interest in Eastern religions and philosophy as antidotes to the western rationalist/materialist/dualistic mindset. Sri Aurobindo wrote that the twentieth century has seen "a revolt of the human mind against this sovereignty of the intellect . . . Vaguely it is felt that there is some greater godhead than reason . . . that reason is too analytical, too arbitrary, that it falsifies life by its distinctions and set classifications" ("*Reason*" 97). Now, in the twenty-first century, Anzaldúa compellingly articulates this dis-ease. She knows from experience that once we expand the powers of perception we will apprehend the spiritual dimension as the very ground of being, recognizing that "we are specks from this cosmic ocean, the soul."

Notes

1. The current paradigm shift from modernity to postmodernity and New Age spirituality that began in the 1960s is addressed by, among others, Capra's *The Turning Point*; Sri Aurobindo's *Future Evolution*; Hawken, Ogilvy, and Schwartz; Ogilvy; Maslov; Needleman; Leonard. This shift is also evident in the rapidly rising western interest in Eastern religions, especially Buddhism, yoga, ashrams, gurus, shamans, the articulation of spiritual-mental growth (i.e. Peck's *The Road Less Traveled*), the popularity of interfaith alliances, and the return to traditional religions.
2. The current paradigm shift is also part of a larger pattern of cyclically recurring cultural transformations, value systems, and epistemologies. Historically thinkers from Vico to Emerson, Nietzsche, Toynbee, and Sorokin have formulated theories of alternating dominants (Capra, *Turning Point* 31–32). The spiritual underpinning of Anzaldúa's worldview links her to the idealist current driving the present spiritual awakening which in turn constitutes a cyclical re-emergence of nineteenth-century metaphysics with postmodern overtones. Not only is spirit perceived immanently within the natural world without reducing multiplicity to homogeneous Oneness, but it is sublated into pluralist totality. Though not displacing the rationalist perspective still dominant today, spiritual idealism has been steadily gaining ground as a valid, more inclusive viewpoint.
3. Anzaldúa describes this process at length in "now let us shift."
4. These states include dreaming, sleeping, or waking; using the powers of the intellect, emotions, or intuition; accessing higher states of consciousness through meditative techniques.
5. I'm deeply indebted to Goswami's and Chopra's work. There exists by now a large body of literature on physics, metaphysics, and religion/mysticism that seeks to close the gap between them by locating their originary ground in the deeper reaches of consciousness. I am highly indebted to Talbot, Wilber, Capra's *Tao of Physics*; Chalmers, and Maslo.
6. Postmodern feminists emphasizing interconnectivity, commonality, and alliances across differences include Haraway; Sandoval; Di Stefano; Alexander and Mohanty; Moya and Hames-Garcia; Hutcheon; Nicholson; Albrecht and Brewer.
7. Although mind and brain are not identical, the terms are sometimes used interchangeably. I concur with Michael Talbot: mind is "an energy field that is both the brain and the physical body" (192). The mind, also referred to as the subtle body, has tremendous powers of healing, imaging, and the ability to make noncausal connections. In near-death experiences the mind enters into even "higher" frequencies than it exhibits in normal consciousness (246–48). For further reading see note 5, especially Goswami's *Visionary Window*.

As a preface to this piece, and in memory of Gloria, I want to tell a story about her. In March 2002, Gloria was visiting as a teacher in Florida Atlantic University's newly established public intellectuals Ph.D. program. But Gloria was a Teacher no matter what she was doing. One evening, she came back to my house with me to have some supper. As we walked in to my apartment, I opened a letter that was in the mail I had just picked up. It was from the provost of the University telling me that I had won a distinguished teaching award. After reading that, I touched the play button on my phone machine and heard a lengthy message telling me that a former student, who was mentally ill, had written a letter claiming that she had been raped in front of my Women, Violence, and Resistance class. This was as disturbing a message as the other was exhilarating. Surely such a synchronicity was filled with meaning. Gloria said, "Well, just remember: neither message is about you." I nodded, as if I understood but asked something like: "But what about your books? Aren't they about you?" And Gloria laughed and said, "Oh Jane, if I had not written them someone else would have."

Chapter 17

Shifting the Shapes of Things to Come: The Presence of the Future in the Philosophy of Gloria Anzaldúa

Jane Caputi

> I've done a lot of thinking and some writing about shifting identities, changing identities. I call it "shapeshifting," as in *nagualism*—a type of Mexican indigenous shamanism where a person becomes an animal, becomes a different person.
>
> —Gloria Anzaldúa, *Interviews/Entrevistas*

The feminist revolution will not be an overthrow; it will be a transformation.

—Gerda Lerner

Shapeshifting, which we can understand as the transformation in substance or form of any being, is spoken of in all religions and mythological traditions (Carse 225). It doesn't always mean the same thing; it can be good or bad, simple or profound. Yet in many contemporary traditions, and popular parlance, shapeshifting is evil—the work of the devil, malevolent "witches," monsters, even terrorists.[1]

Of course, much of what we take for granted as demonic or "other" was previously considered sacred—nature, sexuality, female divinity, the serpent, and the underworld. Gloria Anzaldúa understands this and honors queer spirit, serpentiform and cunctipotent[2] deities, downward pathways, and shapeshifting itself as a potentially beneficial transformational power. Shapeshifting, she explains, is a particular facility of some nagualas or shamans, the ability to transform oneself into another form of being, characteristically an animal, but, implicitly, also the power to transform one's psyche into new forms of being and perceiving. Anzaldúa herself is a sort of shapeshifter for she has a characteristic impact: Once you encounter her words and images you may never experience self/other/world in quite the same way again. If not indigenous, for example, you might start empathically imagining the history of the southwestern United States from that other perspective; you might discover that the invisible world is coming more into view; you might find that your dreams make sense as other-dimensional visitations and messages; you might recognize your mental and physical transformations, painful and pleasurable, in their sacred significance; and you might start thinking of "reality," not as an objective, external, and immutable fact but as something formed by consensus and something that we can shape "in conjunction with the creative life force" (*Interviews/Entrevistas* 100).

Mythic records speak vividly of times/spaces of other sorts of consciousness and very different experiences of reality. Many indigenous oral traditions describe a primordial time when there was no fixed distinction between species of being, when one being could flow easily into the form of another, when all spoke the same language:

> In the very earliest time,
> When both people and animals lived on earth,
> A person could become an animal if [she or] he wanted to
> And an animal could become a human being.
> Sometimes they were people
> And sometimes animals
> And there was no difference.

All spoke the same language.
That was the time when words were like magic.
The human mind had mysterious powers.
A word spoken by chance
Might have strange consequences.
It would suddenly come alive
And what people wanted to happen could happen—
All you had to do was say it.
Nobody could explain this:
That's the way it was. (Rothenberg 41)

This Inuit chant teaches that words are magical and that reality is flexible and can be influenced, intentionally, by people saying what they want to happen. It also can be shaped accidentally, as when a word is dropped by chance. We learn that shapeshifting occurs when there is no separation between humans and animals, when all speak the same language.

But, some might protest, such myths aren't "real"; they are only imaginary. How could "dumb" animals speak? How could a word matter? How could we conceptualize ourselves as anything other than a discrete, bounded individual? To the reigning rationalist consciousness, the imagination is trivial, a realm of mere "make-believe." Yet there is another perspective. Anzaldúa participates in a lengthy philosophical tradition that recognizes imagination as the faculty allowing us to know and describe the realm that can be variously conceptualized as the world of power, the invisible, mythic, spiritual, energetic world.[3] Moreover, for this way of thinking, imagination intimately coexists with reality, for the imagination is the source of *realization*, the "potency/power to create and transform, to render present in place and time" (Daly, *Pure Lust* 149). Hence imagination itself becomes a key zone of activism for feminists (Caputi).

In one interview, AnaLouise Keating asks Anzaldúa if she considers shapeshifting to be imaginary or real. Anzaldúa responds that while today the only way to shapeshift is through the imaginal, this does not mean we should dismiss the phenomenon as not real, or not anticipate its physical actualization in the future. Rather: "[Y]ou create . . . in your imagination first. So . . . I don't see why in the future I can't literally transform my body into a jaguar. But right now such transformations are limited to the beliefs of the majority of people and they don't believe it can be done. I think this is the great turning point . . . we're going to leave the rigidity of this concrete reality and expand it. I'm very hopeful" (*Interviews/Entrevistas* 285, ellipses in the original). Elsewhere, Anzaldúa suggests that this huge metamorphosis she anticipates, the shapeshifting that will occur, may not be one affecting our physical bodies, but rather our "invisible bodies" (*Interviews/Entrevistas* 72). Once we understand that these shifts may not be externally visible, we can look beyond appearances—of identity or shape—into the invisible or energetic world to understand what exactly might be happening.

an identity like a river

> [Y]our self extends to the tree. The self does not stop with just you, with your body. The self penetrates other things and they penetrate you.
>
> —Gloria Anzaldúa (*Interviews/Entrevistas* 162)

The state of being described in the Inuit chant recalls us to a world of connectedness, both past and potential. Different human cultures have very different conceptions of subjectivity—the sense of self and relation to the world. What modern rationalist cultures take as normal human subjectivity is the self as a securely bounded individual, an isolated ego, ontologically disconnected from other humans, animals, the green world, the elements, and the flow of being. Yet this type of subjectivity is not inevitable. It depends upon and furthers fragmentation, internal and external, an ongoing violation of integrity that Mary Daly understands as the defining element of patriarchal consciousness (*Pure Lust; Quintessence*).

The initial psychical fragmentation (signified by the phallus in psychoanalysis) successfully severs the infant from the original symbiotic union with the mother. Much feminist psychoanalytic work has identified fear of the mother's power and denial of dependency on the mother (both the individual mother and the metaphysical mother/nature) as motivations for this splitting. As Teresa Brennan understands it, this splitting from the "original" creates a masculine ego/self (a subjectivity that can be assumed by both women and men) that is able to objectify others and the world. This self fantasizes itself as omnipotent, masterful, and separate, leading to the delusion that one can injure or poison another (including nonhuman others) without also injuring oneself. The world as we know it is based in this "foundational fantasy." Anzaldúa's work implicitly challenges this destructive subjectivity by recognizing an alternative subjectivity, one capable of shapeshifting. A shapeshifting consciousness conceptualizes identity as something fluid and larger than the individual self. By definition, it acknowledges the elemental identity of all being, the intrinsic, original, and ongoing wholeness, interconnection, and transformation of being.

Anzaldúa describes some aspects of this consciousness in her musings on the notion of identity:

> For me there aren't little cubbyholes with all the different identities—intellectual, racial, sexual. It's more like a very fine membrane—sort of like a river, an identity is sort of like a river. It's one and it's flowing and it's a process. By giving different names to different parts of a single mountain range or different parts of a river, we're doing that entity a disservice. We're fragmenting it. I'm struggling with how to name without cutting it up. (*Interviews/Entrevistas* 132)

This is very close to the biological recognition that an organism's external form "has no material permanence," although what biologist E. J. Ambrose calls the "pattern" does: "It is the pattern which has permanence in the living organism. The organism can be likened to a river. The river may retain its identity for hundreds or even thousands of years, yet the water molecules which constitute the river have no permanence" (18–19). Once we understand that an organism's "identity" quintessentially is found not in its external form, but in its pattern (or invisible *shape*), we realize that much shapeshifting takes place not on the level of phenomenal reality, but in the world of patterns, what Anzaldúa calls the "invisible bodies."

Another way of talking about this phenomenon is to speak of morphic fields, fields that by nature change their shape throughout time. To further understand, we might consult another biologist, Rupert Sheldrake. In *The Presence of the Past* Sheldrake also asks us to look beyond what we can immediately perceive about an organism's identity and discern the invisible world of energetic patterns or fields. He advances the unorthodox position that heredity is based not only in the transmission of traits through genes, but also through what he calls "morphic fields": "The nature of things depends on . . . morphic fields. Each kind of natural system has its own kind of field . . . non-material regions of influence extending in space and continuing in time" (xviii). For Sheldrake, the *past is present* in that the field holds memories of the organism and guides the habitual repetition of that same pattern, resulting in the same type of organism through time. But just as genes can mutate, so too can patterns or fields shift in response to things that happen, both materially and psychically. Fields, then, are not eternal but are evolutionary. They are morphic, changeable; they *metamorphose* (literally shift their shapes) in response to new environmental, emotional, theoretical, educational, and psychical conditions as well as to the accidental interventions of chance. Brand new fields can appear—new molecules, instincts, or theories—and with them come new patterns of relationships and connections.

In this view, as Sheldrake puts it, nature is not fixed but fluid, not set but evolving, not so much created (by an immutable god) as creative in an ongoing flow of constant change. The shapeshifter recognizes the underlying patterns as they move, flow, and transmute and is attuned to incipient changes in the field—what we might think of as the "presence of the future." She works to actualize some of these possibilities, to "shape change"[4] in ways that further justice and harmony.

Anzaldúa's recognition that people's beliefs greatly influence what is actually possible finds a corresponding theory in Sheldrake's notion of morphic resonance. In Sheldrake's theory, whenever some members of a species learn a new skill, this causes shifts in the field of human knowledge and consciousness. As more and more people learn this new thing, it becomes progressively easier for others to learn it since it now has entered the general human pattern or field until finally it is part of our human heritage.

This conceptualization offers a new understanding of the significance of someone being "ahead of her time." Such individuals, and Anzaldúa is one of them, often, with some pain to themselves, initiate the process of learning new skills such as shapeshifting, skills that will be necessary to human survival in times to come.[5] By so doing, they manifest *the future in the present.* This activity requires beginning at the beginning, starting, as they say, from scratch, for the future, too, is present in the deep past.

starting from scratch

Shape etymologically derives from a group of words that mean to "form" and to "create," and, curiously, to "scratch" (*Websters*). It is an astonishingly rich word, encompassing many meanings. As a verb, *shape* means (in part) to "give form to," "to ordain," "to destine," as well as "to change" or "metamorphose." Etymologically *shape* is related to an Old Norse word *skap*, which, in its plural form means both fate and destiny and is direct kin to a word that means the genitals. In English, the noun *shape* means not only a form but also "the sexual organs; the distinctive organ of either sex" and in dialect it means "the female pudendum" (*Oxford English Dictionary*).

Philosophical meanings, otherwise elusive, can be discerned in word origins and their subsequent meanderings as the living words themselves shift shape through time. These at first disparate meanings of the word *shape* are in truth deeply connected: the divine power to create and to destine is incarnated most vividly not in our hands, brain, and speech organs, but in our genitals. The first formation of human existence is the shaping of the child not merely in but *by* the womb. Our sex organs, in their capacities for eroticism, exuberance, and creativity incarnate the formative powers of the divine *matrix* (a word that means uterus and is etymologically linked to *mater*, mother), the primal source of matter/energy.

The commonly communicated fears that I mentioned at the beginning of this essay—of sexuality, falling, snakes, shapeshifting, queer spirituality, and female potency and sovereignty—prevent us from learning to shapeshift. Anzaldúa pointedly refuses all these interdictions. She rejects carnal shame (*Interviews/Entrevistas* 93), insists upon the spirituality of lesbian/bisexual/transgender experience, embraces descent as a way of knowledge, and claims the serpent as the symbol of what she calls *conocimiento*—truth that has been subjugated and/or discredited by colonialism, misogyny, and straight thinking: "[W]hen I think 'conocimiento' I see a little serpent for counterknowledge. This is how it comes to me that this counterknowledge is not acceptable, that it's the knowledge of the serpent in the Garden of Eden. It's not acceptable to eat the fruit of knowledge; it makes you too aware, too self-reflective" (*Interviews/Entrevistas* 266).

Anzaldúa's words recall us to the deep mythic past and the scene of that primal threesome, Eve, Adam, and the Serpent, the Genesis or birth story that serves as the creation myth for Christianity, Judaism, and Islam. Although literally demonized by these religions, the shapeshifting Serpent with many names, including Lilith, the "Old Serpent," and "Old Scratch,"—is a beneficial helper and guide, one who initiates Eve into knowledge. Eve and Adam live inside some enclosure, some kind of artificial setting, a theme park called paradise.[6] They deliberately are kept in a state of ignorance, what Anzaldúa calls *desconocimiento* (*Interviews/Entrevistas* 178). God lies to them, warning that if they eat of the tree of knowledge they will die. Yet Eve defies the allegedly divine authority, breaks down the wall that disconnects humans from elemental being, speaks with Old Scratch, follows her/his advice, eats the fruit, and becomes aware. The conocimiento that continues to be transmitted by this story is an awareness that "reality" in a closed and controlled system is a phantasm, a construct of those in power. This conocimiento also provides a model for defying that authority, seeking guidance and awareness from the elemental world or nature, and sharing that knowledge with others.

But why, you might still wonder, am I focusing on the past when speaking of the future? According to the biblical timeline, creation is in the past and apocalypse is in the future. Yet considering the range of horrors, psychic and physical, in our world—our fragmented consciousness; our widespread inability to listen to and speak with the creatures (who are abandoning us even as we do not speak); the vast discrepancies between rich and poor; slavery; starvation; waste; environmental devastation; the worship of violence—we might realize that the biblical timeline is precisely backwards.

It is the apocalypse that already has happened and it is creation that we must bring about. The creation myth is not so much a record of what already has happened, but a "memory" of the future. The myth is a coded transmission of the knowledge and actions needed to end the apocalypse and recall creation.

From this perspective, the work for those of us intent on furthering justice, balance, and harmony is not so much to prevent apocalypse, as it is to imagine/speak/visualize/make creation myth, to live with the full and conscious intention to shift away from the current horrors, shaping a just and harmonious future. Anzaldúa speaks directly to this: "[W]e must have very concrete, precisely worded intentions of what *we* [her italics] want the world to be like, what we want to be like. We have to first put the changes that we want made into words or images. We have to visualize them, write them, communicate them to other people and stick with committing to those intentions, those goals, those visions. *Before any changes can take place you have to say and intend them. It's like a prayer, you have to commit yourself to your visions*" (*Interviews/Entrevistas* 290, my italics). When we thus "pray," saying and intending our visions with the full force of magic words and the power of shapeshifting, we bear the presence of the future into the now.

I use the word *bear* deliberately. Creation is a time of new birth. The poet Muriel Rukeyser asks us to imagine what would happen if we become self-aware, and tell the truth from that state of awareness. As we do, she says, the world will "split open" (217). Anzaldúa also anticipates such a natal opening: For conocimiento to be realized, there first "has to be some kind of opening, some kind of fissure, gate, rajadura—a crack between worlds . . . the hole, the interfaces" (*Interviews/Entrevistas* 266). *Imagine* this gateway as the opening of a birth canal, allowing for the emergence of new ways of sensing, feeling, and knowing.

The name *Eve* translates as the "mother of all living" and, not surprisingly, this cosmic mother is the most maligned woman in patriarchal history. Tertullian, the second-century Church Father, is typical when he rails against Eve and, concomitantly, against all women: "You are the devil's gateway . . . you are she who persuaded him whom the devil did not dare attack. . . . Do you not know that every one of you is an Eve?" (qtd. in Pagels 63). Following Eve's model, those of us who choose to identify as an Eve might become that gateway into the future; we might seek and speak with Snake Woman/the Old Serpent, taste the fruit of knowledge, and become "self-aware." As we do, we become cognizant of the mutability of the reigning reality; the profound interconnectedness of all being; the ontological significance of the pattern, field, or invisible body; and our potency/power to shift the shape of things to come.

Notes

1. Writing in the *New York Times* on Sept. 23, 2001, Maureen Dowd spoke of "shapeshifting suicide bombers."
2. *Cunctipotent* is a currently obsolete English word meaning "all powerful." I first encountered it in Barbara Walker's *Encyclopedia of Women's Myths and Secrets* while perusing the entry *cunt.* Until the fourteenth century, *cunt* was Standard English for the vulva and only became obscene in the seventeenth century. Eric Partridge writes that the word dropped out of standard English due to its "powerful sexuality." Walker asserts that *cunt* is derivative of the Asian Great Goddess as Cunti, or Kunda, the Yoni of the Uni-verse. Following Michael Dames, she associates *cunt* with the words *country, kin, kind, cunning* and *ken*, as well as *cunctipotent.* Most linguists do not support this etymology. Nevertheless, we can accept it as a folk etymology and reclaim *cunctipotence* as a word meaning female potency, possibility, and potential—a concept sorely needed in the English language. Unlike *omnipotence*, which denotes phallic domineering supreme power, *cunctipotence* means the power to connect and, in conjunction with the life force, to make things happen.
3. My thought on this has been greatly enriched by conversations with Fran Chelland who is writing a dissertation: "The Power of Presence: An Inquiry into the Role of the Imagination in Moral Deliberation," Florida Atlantic University, Comparative Studies/Public Intellectuals Ph.D. program.
4. I take this phrase from Octavia Butler in her great novel *Parable of the Sower*. There she develops a theology based on God as "Change," understanding that humans can shape change through their conscious works and intentions.
5. Of course, as Anzaldúa would be the first to point out, this does not mean there is anything "special" about these individuals; this is not about ego or egocentrism. This shapeshifting task is but one among many that the species must perform. If, for some reason, a person called to this task were for some reason unable to do it, someone else would emerge who could.
6. Paradise derives from words that mean an "enclosed park," a "wall." These word origins further suggest that the biblical paradise was a controlled reality, rather like Disneyworld or other such amusement parks.

Chapter 18

"Doing Mestizaje": When Epistemology Becomes Ethics

Monica Torres

an anecdotal introduction to the borderlands

Once each month I return to my hometown to visit my mother, now seventy-eight, not in good health, and since the death of my father several years ago, lonely. Generally, I spend my entire weekend with her: eating at local restaurants, watching television, maybe even playing a little bingo. Our schedule varies little. Within the confines of her life, my mother is able to control that which she will, and will not, engage. She simply opts out of or changes the channel on anything that makes her uncomfortable.

On Saturday nights, we watch her favorite show, *Walker, Texas Ranger*. For those who have not seen an episode of this dramatic series, it is a singular experience, and I mean that literally. The characters include and are limited to the good guys (you guessed it, the Texas Rangers), the bad guys (in the first few seasons, almost without exception, Latinos and/or white working-class drug dealers), and the "innocents" (adolescents of color and women). The plot is straightforward: the bad guys threaten the innocents; the Rangers intervene; the bad guys are punished; the innocents are saved.

To be fair, some of these Rangers are men of color. And there is one woman Ranger. Occasionally, the criminal is a white middle-class man gone wrong. These diversifying moves, however, make little difference to the series' plot or moral. Week after week, my mother and I watch this less-than-complex version of life where behavior can be understood only within an ethical system featuring good guys and bad guys. And week after week, I wonder why my mother enjoys this show so much. Does she not recognize the same plot, episode after episode? Why would she watch a show in which the most obvious of stereotypes play so prominently? Doesn't she know the history of the Texas Rangers? Hasn't she seen that photograph? You know the one: a Texas Ranger sitting upright on a horse, a rope tied around his saddle horn; attached to the other end, a Mexican, laying limply on the ground, dragged to his death across the Texas landscape only moments before this photograph was shot. (Surely this Mexican man, knowing he was to suffer such a slow and painful death, would have preferred a "shooting," but it is his image and not his body that is shot). Hasn't she seen *that* photograph? After many episodes, I finally ask her, "Why do you like this show?" Her answer is brief: "In the end, I know that the good guys are going to win."

I ponder that. I think I know what she means. She has never enjoyed movies, so she is not interested in sophisticated characters or complicated plots. Or maybe she means that at the end of her life, she is not interested in wrestling with difficult, painful, or complex issues, even if they are situated on the television screen and not in her family. Perhaps her enjoyment comes as a Christian who relishes the promise of being saved at the end. I do not know. I do know that despite its setting in Texas, *Walker, Texas Ranger* is not a borderlands text.

a brief introduction to gloria anzaldúa's "borderlands"

Anzaldúa opens her book with a description of geographic space: "I stand at the edge where earth touches ocean / Where the two overlap / A gentle coming together / At other times and places a violent clash" (23). Immediately, I sense the complexity of this space: permeated with the potential for peaceful coexistence but simultaneously haunted by less harmonious possibilities. Of course, many scholars, including Anzaldúa, have projected "borderlands" beyond the physical to theorize other projects. Anzaldúa herself shifts from geographic locations to geopolitical and sociocultural concerns when she outlines historical events such as Cortés' sixteenth-century conquest of the Aztecs and the nineteenth-century Anglo settlements into Tejas. In these discussions, "borderlands" shifts from geographic space in which two physical worlds come into contact to cultural space where real people enter into relationship as a result of occupying proximate locations. In *Border Matters*, José David Saldívar humanizes this space when he writes, "For years, I have tried to piece together what it must have been like for Reyes and Carmelita Saldívar, my great-great-grandparents, to have been almost overnight incorporated into the Union of the United States. I try to imagine what it must have been like for them to improvise a new kind of cultural citizenship" (18). Indeed, what must it have been like? In a cultural environment where one is certain to face contestation, what skills are required? Anzaldúa turns her attention to this very matter with her notion of mestizaje.

In "La Conciencia de la Mestiza," Anzaldúa defines the mestiza as a biological entity: "At the confluence of two or more genetic streams, with chromosomes constantly 'crossing over,' this mixture of races, rather than resulting in an inferior being, provides hybrid progeny" (99). From this perspective, mestizas are simply (and not so simply) biological beings, people of mixed-race. But Anzaldúa has more than genetics in mind. "Mestizaje," stretched beyond the biological, may offer insight to those who live, literally and figuratively, at the confluence of multiple and varied cultural traditions. How does one live in these borderlands? Anzaldúa offers advice: "La mestiza constantly has to shift out of habitual formations" (101). Quoted often and easily, this is no simple recommendation.

mestizaje's epistemological and ethical dimensions

In a 1987 speech at the annual conference of the American Association of Higher Education, educator Parker Palmer harshly critiqued western systems of knowledge for what he argued was a problematic supposition: disconnection. Empiricism, Palmer specifically suggested, relies on objectivism, the critical disconnection between subject and object. Anzaldúa clarifies this point in *Interviews/Entrevistas*: "that theory of objectivity—which has been proven false over and over by its own scientists—makes us separate because it makes us the watcher" (163). Jane Flax makes a related claim when she writes about the history of the dichotomy as a tool for thinking and knowing. "Western philosophers created an illusory appearance of unity and stability by reducing the flux and heterogeneity of the human and physical worlds into binary and supposedly natural oppositions. Order is imposed and maintained by displacing chaos into the lesser of each binary pair" (139). Much of what we know, according to Palmer, Anzaldúa, and Flax, has been based on epistemological assumptions and disciplinary practices that have forced us to divide, detach, or disengage, and in the process, privilege one side of the division over the other.

In *Borderlands* Anzaldúa explicitly names perhaps the most significant binary at the heart of western knowledge systems: subject/object. Throughout *Borderlands* and in *Interviews/Entrevistas*, she outlines other dichotomies that attempt to trap us in this Manichean structure: art/everyday life, white people/people of color, mind/body, heterosexual/homosexual, secular/sacred, theory/autobiography. She does more than name the problem. She aggressively resists this epistemological directive.

> La mestiza constantly has to shift out of habitual formations; from convergent thinking, analytical reasoning that tends to use rationality to move toward a single goal (a Western mode), to divergent thinking, characterized by movement away from set patterns and goals and toward a more whole perspective, one that includes rather than excludes. . . .
>
> The work of the mestiza consciousness is to break down the subject–object duality that keeps her a prisoner and to show in the flesh and through the images in her work how duality is transcended. (*Borderlands* 101, 102).

In this well-known excerpt, Anzaldúa counters an epistemology based on disconnection by offering an alternative—mestizaje.

Central to this alternative epistemology is motion. Note the language Anzaldúa uses in her descriptions: "shifting," "moving," "breaking down," "transcending," "sustaining contradictions," "turning ambivalence into something else," "surrendering safety." These energetic words reflect the mestiza's dynamic nature. She must be mobile enough to slip the traps set by the dichotomous reasoning that characterizes western epistemologies. The mestiza must be active: alert, attentive to history, present to contemporary circumstances, suspicious of those rigid epistemological assumptions embedded in our perspectives and our social structures. This is epistemological mestiza.

In a close reading, however, I discover that epistemological mestiza is not alone. Her motion is purposeful. She moves "away from set patterns and goals and toward a more whole perspective, one that includes rather than excludes" (*Borderlands* 101). And while this inclusive impulse is in service to the deconstruction of the dichotomy, generally considered an epistemological concern, Anzaldúa takes a turn toward the ethical. If one resists the dichotomy—choosing either one side or the other—given to us in a binary, then in some senses, one chooses to relate to both sides. In "La Conciencia de la mestiza" she gives this example: "Many women and men of color do not want to have any dealings with white people. . . . Many feel that whites should help their own people rid themselves of race hatred and fear first. I, for one, choose to use some of my energy to serve as mediator. I think we need to allow whites to be our allies" (*Borderlands* 107).

Here, in an example of what Anzaldúa calls "conocimiento," she resists a well-established dichotomy (white people versus people of color) and relates to people on both sides of what has been a firmly drawn line. As a person of color, she resides on one side of the border, but, importantly, she also crosses the dividing line to create a relationship with those residing on the other side. In fact, in an interview with Andrea Lundsford Anzaldúa argues that we are always already connected: "Living in a multicultural society, we cross into each other's worlds all the time. We live in each other's pockets, occupy each other's territories" (*Interviews/Entrevistas* 254). That Anzaldúa acknowledges this, makes it explicit, is, I argue, an ethical move. In resisting the either/or structure, Anzaldúa suggests a new way of thinking *and* a new way of acting, one that relies on relationship between those who previously have been firmly situated on opposite sides of the border. In this case, her critique of the binary almost literally forces her to change her behavior. In short, she demonstrates that how we know deeply influences how we act.

In a 1999 interview with AnaLouise Keating, Anzaldúa explains what this behavior might look like: "Receptivity is the stance here, not the adversarial mode, not the armed camp. Giving feedback, taking frequent reality checks, and clarify[ing] meaning" (*Interviews/Entrevistas* 178). Anzaldúa is asserting not some sort of metaphorical or hypothetical relationship, but real human relationships—body and soul, blood and tears. She makes this clear in her discussion of cross-cultural alliances. In the above example, she declares her interest in coalitions with white people but insists that to enter into relationship with her, they must acknowledge her cultural history, her cultural injury, and their complicity. In a turn that demonstrates the reciprocity of relationship, Anzaldúa closes with this, "And finally, tell us what you need from us" (*Borderlands* 108). If engaged with any degree of sincerity, these surely cannot be easy or comfortable conversations. I have seen white students bristle at the thought that they might be complicit in the world Anzaldúa describes in "We Call Them Greasers" (*Borderlands* 156–57). I have seen students of color resist the suggestion that they listen to the needs of white people.

Anzaldúa says that "to be human is to be related to other people, to be interdependent with other people" (*Interviews/Entrevistas* 206). It would seem that Anzaldúa asks us to recognize this interdependence even when it makes us uncomfortable or defensive or angry or grief-stricken. Entering into relationships with those who reside across borders, whatever those borders may be, is no simple recommendation. It requires that we engage other human beings. Significantly, the act of relationship also demands that we engage ourselves. Anzaldúa writes, "I believe that the universe is a text which we co-create. . . . But by stepping back and asking 'OK. What's my responsibility in this?' " (*Interviews/Entrevistas* 75) She names this important, if conveniently overlooked, part of relationship building: complicity. Finally, as she proposes, relationships of this sort are not meant to rigidly reverse the order of things. This is not an alternative in which people of color are privileged and white people injured. Rather, I believe, Anzaldúa advocates for a more just world for all.

an epistemology of relations: the "mestiza" text of patricia williams

Since the initial publication of *Borderlands* in 1987, scholars, activists, and students have taken up Anzaldúa's call. We passionately talk about mestizaje. We liberally quote from the text. Despite our enthusiasm, however, I'm not sure that very many of us "do" mestizaje. I am in search of texts that don't just talk about mestizaje, but actually do it. While I'm interested in texts embodying mestizaje in that minimal sense, the incorporation of multiple forms or genre into one publication, I am more interested in texts where mestizaje resides beneath the surface. I'm searching for texts that not only look different but also offer "foreign ways of seeing and thinking," that surrender "all notions of safety, of the familiar " (*Borderlands* 104), texts that examine and reinterpret historical and popular narratives using mestiza consciousness as a lens. What can these narratives teach us about what it means to know in the twenty-first century?

For me, there is little doubt that Patricia William's *The Alchemy of Race and Rights* is a mestiza text. Not unlike *Borderlands*, *Alchemy* is a blending of cultural analyses, personal anecdotes, biographical sketches, historical narratives, and pieces that would more typically be considered literature than analysis. But for both Anzaldúa and Williams, this formal hybridity is not superficial. Rather, it reflects the epistemological interrogation at the heart of these texts.

Williams, a lawyer, begins her argument by naming three distinct strategies she says undergird Anglo-American jurisprudence: the use of exclusive categories and definitional polarities; the existence of acontextual, universal legal truths; the reliance on objective, unmediated voices to communicate those truths (8–9). And, if I have read her argument thoughtfully, these discursive moves depend on what some would call an epistemology of disconnection. Exclusive categories and definitional polarities, for example, assume the physical process of separating one object from another. Universal truths and objective voices require a literal distancing between subject and object.

But for Williams, as for Anzaldúa, disconnection is not a viable epistemology. It is, in fact, the disconnection built into our legal and social structures that contributes to an unjust society, one in which some are privileged while others are injured. Williams unveils this epistemological assumption of disconnection and interrogates it publicly. And, like Anzaldúa, she suggests a more just alternative: an epistemology of relationship. She writes: "Very little in our language or culture encourages looking at others as parts of ourselves" (62). From her perspective, we have learned—through epistemological assumptions, linguistic strategies, and social structures—to deny relationship with others, to literally see others as "not us." She cites this example:

> Once I took the F train to 14th street, where I saw an old beggar woman huddled against a pillar. Behind me, a pretty little girl of about six exclaimed, "Oh, daddy, there's someone who needs our help." The child was then led off by the hand, by her three-piece-suited father who patiently explained that giving money to the woman directly was "not the way we do things." Then he launched into a lecture on the United Way as succor for the masses. It was a first lesson in distributive justice: conditioned passivity, indirection, distance. (27)

Williams' point seems clear: such maneuvering not only creates distance between two but a distance that constructs some as better and others as lesser.

In a rereading of the 1986 Howard Beach incident during which several young black men were chased and severely beaten by young white residents of the New York neighborhood, Williams again demonstrates the process of disconnection. She reports that in the days following the beating, Howard Beach residents made statements—"We're a strictly white neighborhood." "What were they doing here in the first place?"—that betray the assumption that those young black men are "not us." Williams uncovers the assumption of disconnection and then manifests the social and political consequences of that separation: The Howard Beach residents making these claims "assume that black people (and I have never heard the same public assumption about white people) need documented reasons for excursioning into neighborhoods where they do not live, for venturing beyond the bounds of the zones to which they are supposedly confined" (68). Her strategy here is to show us, literally show us, the processes of disconnection and to suggest how some are privileged and others injured during these courses of action.

Early in the book Williams writes that she hopes her interrogation will result in a "more nuanced sense of legal and social responsibility" (11).

But what exactly does she want? Who is it that will enact this "legal and social responsibility"? At one point, she writes "In the Vietnamese language, the word 'I' (toi) . . . means 'your servant'; there is no 'I' as such. When you talk to someone you establish a relationship" (62, . . .). If relationship, as Gloria Anzaldúa asserts, is the act of placing "oneself in a state of resonance with the other's feelings and situations" (*Interviews/Entrevistas* 178), with whom does Patricia Williams attempt relationship in writing this book? Certainly, she understands that the moments she describes are passed; neither she nor her characters can recuperate any lost opportunities for social responsibility. To whom, then, does she speak? Is she trying to connect her text's reader, author, and subject? Having met the people—both privileged and injured—that occupy Patricia Williams's book, can I continue drawing lines of separation as easily as our dominant epistemologies might allow? Is Williams calling me to account for the conditions of the world in which I live? Would I suggest to a child that our social obligations can be met by contributions to the United Way? Would I call the police because a poor, black woman was sitting in the lobby of my building? Would I step over a dead man to get to my job on time? When I hear accusations against black men, do I assume their guilt? Williams forces me to ask: How do I separate? How do I relate?

giving up the ghost of comfort

When we resist the epistemological frame of the binary, we are left with what I am calling an epistemology of relationship. But this ethics, found in both Anzaldúa's and Williams's critique of dominant culture epistemology, is not easy. Just when I might think a Howard Beach resident sounds reasonable when she says "Better to be safe than sorry," Williams suggests that I look at the underbelly of the statement: "The hidden implication . . . is that . . . to be safe is to be white and to be sorry is to be associated with blacks" (59). Just as I am about to take solace from the passage in which Anzaldúa asks white society to acknowledge its complicity in the cultural circumstances of Chicanos/as, someone points to another in which Anzaldúa takes Chicanos/as to task for ignoring our complex and conflicted relationships with American Indians. An epistemology/ethics of relationship requires that we literally change the way we know and the way we act. Jane Flax writes that Enlightenment epistemologies encourage us to believe in innocent knowledge. They allow us to speak in "knowledge's voice or on its behalf," and in doing that, we "avoid responsibility for locating our contingent selves as the producers of knowledge and truth claims" (145).

An epistemology of relationship asks that we recognize that epistemological, linguistic, and cultural structures have been constructed in ways that help some and hurt others; that we identify our own multiple locations in those complex networks; that we acknowledge our relationships with others, as conflicted as those will be. In short, Anzaldúa and Williams suggest that in the borderlands of contemporary culture—neither epistemological nor ethical—comfort is available.

Perhaps it never was. I wonder what it must have been like for Reyes and Carmelita Saldívar as they, and so many other Mexican/Americans like them, lived in that place—both spatial and temporal—between Mexico and the United States. And I think about my mother, a hundred and fifty years later, waiting for those television Rangers to save the day. Why doesn't she know about the photograph of that Mexican man dragged to his death across the desert? What would change if, as a younger person, she had had the opportunity to absorb the devastating details of that image? Perhaps she would be interested in the history of agencies like the Texas Rangers, the Border Patrol, and the I.N.S.? Maybe she would question the frameworks, both intellectual and social, that establish so easily the good, the bad, the ugly, and the innocent? Perhaps she would notice and investigate the relationship between socioeconomic status and criminal activity? Maybe she would think more deeply about the judicial system—who are the people arrested by the Texas Rangers and what happens to them? That photograph might have changed my mother's life. At the very least, those Texas Rangers she watches week after week would become more problematic, more contested. My mother might still watch this tele-version of the U.S. borderlands, but she might have to engage more robustly the cultural complexity of her decision to do so.

Part 5

el mundo zurdo, the new tribalism. . . . forging new alliances

We are the queer groups, the people that don't belong anywhere, not in the dominant world nor completely within our own respective cultures. Combined we cover so many oppressions. But the overwhelming oppression is the collective fact that we do not fit, and because we do not fit *we are a threat.* Not all of us have the same oppressions, but we empathize and identify with each other's oppressions. We do not share the same ideology, nor do we derive similar solutions. Some of us are leftists, some of us practitioners of magic. Some of us are both. But these different affinities are not opposed to each other. In El Mundo Zurdo I with my own affinities and my people with theirs can live together and transform the planet.

—Gloria E. Anzaldúa, "La Prieta"

Chapter 19

This Is Personal: Revisiting Gloria Anzaldúa from within the Borderlands

Lee Maracle

Borderlands, border blur, bordered fabric and loose weaves come to mind. Old cloth, colored cloth, cotton, dog and goat hair cloth full of intense familial design that seem to want to adorn a woman's back. Denim, a town in France usurps the markets of the world—creating a disordered, maladjusted diversity in which the center becomes the periphery and the designer falls from the map. Western lingo dominates, supplants language, communication, and metaphor. Gringo conquers language, annihilating humanism, humanity, and boundaries of decency. From below the map, under all that historical cloth, barely covered in an old woven blanket so full of holes the design blurs like the borders of our dignity I peer out at Gloria Anzaldúa.

I etch word designs onto the cloth of my story with her. Good stories don't take long. *I Am Woman* was incubating itself in my womb, in my musculature, in my mind, outside my mind, in the wombs of every blurred barely visible Indigenous woman on this Island long before the International Feminist Book Fair. I had spent years resisting writing this work. She had spent years wanting to be born. On January 1, 1988, she insisted on being born. The labor of birth is a strange borderland, slightly asinine, somewhat ridiculous, and just a little too intense for summer conception, best to weave stories in winter. She came, full term, beautiful and well-woven. I dropped her on the world long after the phone call came inviting me to this book fair. I tend to like pushing the envelope particularly when a dead line is inside it. As the phone rose in my hand and Diana Bronson's voice invited me to the fair she listed the names of those Indigenous women who would be there, "Gloria Anzaldúa . . . I hope you don't mind. We have invited her as an Indigenous woman. Do you consider Mexicans, Chicanos Indigenous?" (Pause). I have been centered. My blanket has been removed. I am back on the white male Euro map. I never wanted to be a party to that map. "Some people, Diana, are not in the habit of presuming to name the place, position, or belonging of others." The softness in my voice surprised me. It suggested that some piece of me privately forgave her. What is that?

(Nervous laugh). "Good . . . uh, yes, well, good, well . . . we will uh . . . send you an official invitation." The sun fights with the clouds here in winter, each struggling for command of the sky. By nightfall the ocean and its sea water usually win. Now I have to write the book. No I don't have to do anything. The book insisted. I wrote the words to *I Am Woman* while the name "Gloria Anzaldúa" slid around chaotically in my mind. Who is this woman? Who is this woman whose cloth is woven so tightly out of such stern thread that the organizers of an international feminist bookfair would go ahead and invite her without any consultation with the rest of the Indigenous delegation? They invited her despite the fact that they weren't sure of us. She must be powerful. She is such a force that the center must contend with her from a momentary periphery. More than that . . . the periphery they established was positioned somewhere to the left of my old blanket.

My turn to laugh; this should be fun.

Montreal. The heat is unbearable, the freeway completely confusing, the language unmanageable at high speeds. We are all lost. The car whirs back and forth, and round about on this tiny island trying to locate itself. For a few brief moments I don't feel like an Indigenous woman. I laugh, "We are lost like Columbus and Cartier. You, a Mohawk, lost in the center of Mohawk territory." I say this to my lover. "That's because it has been usurped and turned inside out and upside down by the French," Cynthia says. I am glad she never uses the word "others, or non-native." Let them be French, let them be Quebecois, let them be, runs through my mind.

We did make it off the freeway and onto the campus where all the doings were to occur. We registered, not without some difficulty. Our book salesman was a man—a modest, matriarchal man—a Mohawk. The organizers forgave his maleness and let him be our salesman. I received my marching orders and headed for the venue with Cynthia. I am an orator. Before I know what I am about to say, I need to read my audience.

The room is full. More than full, there are women in the hallway, women lining the walls, women seated in chairs, women seated on the floor. I notice

Betsy Warland, though we have not met. Gloria is seated next to me on my right; Jeannette Armstrong is on my left. From the middle I wonder about position. No one told us how to arrange ourselves; we just sat down. The hosts are frenzied; there are too many people in this room for the fire regulations. They keep telling people they can't sit on the floor, or block the aisles—no one listens. The organizers do not have the audacity to pitch anyone out, but they can't seem to stop telling them not to sit in the aisles. I look at Gloria. We both wear a sweet smile—very Ravenesque, naughty, transformative, and powerful.

Jeannette and I clasp hands under the table; this ceremony gets us through moments like these. I look at Gloria again. Her forever-brown eyes look like they recognize me. She is so Chicana, so Indigena, so centered and at the same time, declines to leave the border of her periphery for all that is in front of us. *I will never forget her.*

She sits particularly straight, arranges papers, and tags her book, orders up her speech. Mestizo must mean she reads and speaks her presentation. Jeannette too is arranging her papers. She mumbles that she had written down, so as not to miss the power handed to her in this moment. I know what she means, but am too cheeky to comply. I sit with my hands folded and just wait. Maybe I should not be so arrogant. I have no paper to arrange. Too late now. Anzaldúa looks up, leans into the audience like she is preparing to forge a storm. She is. The moat between the audience and us is filled with our dead. The divide sings with destruction. The distance between Native women and the newcomers is measured with our losses and their gains. Anzaldúa knows this; I feel it just like I can feel the texture of the heat and the rough edges of the listening these women will have to do. *I will always recognize her.*

I like realizing this. I roll the memory about, taste it; I like the edges of it as it tingles my lips. I swallow, savor it going down; each word commits itself to my memory. Anzaldúa looks back at me like she knows me, knows my grandmother. She could have been any other Indigenous woman, strolling down any downtown core in Canada or the United States. We could have been standing on the corner of Main & Hastings, exchanging new comments about our favorite old subject, "these people . . ." Or we could have been in some laundromat, saying "Hello how are you, how's your mom" and finally getting to "old people are just that way" and laughing till our sides hurt.

The room blurs. My mountains come into view. I watch as the newcomers erase my being. I don my old blanket and rise again. I picture Anzaldúa's relatives resisting the same catholic and colonial forces. I erase the room and let the words rise of their own. We are alone for this moment; each of us behaves as though we are in some old kitchen, soup bowls in front, tea behind us steeping and we are about to launch into the beautiful kind of gossip about that Indigenous women get into: "Girl, left her man . . . good for her. Pahinak had a husband and a wife . . . she was something else. Ruby has a new woman." We know that borders are illusions. We also know that these borders are critical to those who benefit from the illusion. We understand. *Gloria knows something about something.*

I can hear murmurings from the women who are attempting to declare that the chaos we are surrounded by is unacceptable. They try to order everyone up, but the women have minds of their own and cannot be ordered like pizzas. The three of us know this and turn to smile at one another. From inside our own intellectual territory we share a common humor. It is not the chaos we find amusing, but the futility of believing you have the authority to order it up that strikes as funny. We are in Quebec now. Algonquin and Mohawk breath still whispers from across the river. This old breath snakes its way around this island. The ancestors still breathe some other sensibility into the hearts of the women who now occupy this land. As a result, the Quebecois have their own way of reconciling themselves to speakers. I return my gaze to the commotion and enjoy its sweetness. *I will always savor this moment.*

My body is struggling to sweat. Jeannette is shaking from the heat. I worry. I take charge of this gathering. Jeannette gives my hand one last squeeze. I look at Gloria and she nods. We are ready. I announce that we are going to get started. Without another word, Jeannette begins, as though we had planned it this way and not at all as if it just felt right for her to begin.

I can feel the power of Gloria's listening, can almost feel the openness of each of her cells as Jeannette's words sing like a song inside her. I imagine hearing her mind clicking across the words; she is careful not to be considering any other sound but the one she is hearing. I would die for this kind of Indigenous discipline. I feel her steady even breath over my shoulder as she leans into Jeannette's conversation, deepening her commitment to listening more and more carefully as Jeannette speaks. I am caught up in watching this listening that is so old, so clean, so innocent, and so very intense. *I like the feel of hearing Gloria listen.*

I begin a moment after Jeannette finishes. Gloria's and Jeannette's listening feels like a blanket we all share. It warms, strengthens, and blurs the border at the edge of all our cloths. This blanket is warm, not like the heat wave rattling Montreal, threatening to bleed us of whatever sanity we came there with, but warm in that spirit way, when you know "We all speak the same language"—Sto: loh, Okanogan, and Chicana Anzaldúa. Our backs begin to straighten. An old load is removed. I feel light even in this claustrophobic, wet, mean heat. *I am lighter for having sat next to Gloria.*

Gloria is next. "Sin Fronteras . . . Sin Fronteras." It rolls off her tongue not like it's Spanish, but like a well-loved woman whom we all know. She looks at us, we look at her. "Sin Fronteras" not like it sits between us, but like we're in the center of it and in front of us is a well-loved Gramma. Jeannette and I nod. Go ahead Gloria, the ceremony is taken care of and now we know whom we all are. We have dispensed with the proper formalities, fulfilled all the necessary protocol, so now begin, talk to these others on the periphery of this fire. *Gloria lives forever in my heart.*

Gloria spoke of Borderlands, not the ones we usually think about. The borderlands we know begin "Sin Fronteras." We begin with paradox. We begin entering the heat in winter with story hot on our tongues. We came to this place, this mountain in summer. We now wander about each other's cool comforting gaze in the brassy glare of the worst heat wave in Montreal's puny male history. We come into the world well-loved and screaming and we go out well-respected, our voices resonant, full and booming and knowing how young humanity's sense of itself is. We are familiar. Family. The borders of our fabrics fit so neatly in our hearts. The weave suits our spirit. The design that appears so keenly arranged is not. It arises organically from a common beginning. Our bodies navigate with grace and agility between sin fronteras and the borderlands Gloria now defines. We got that from Gloria before she even spoke, the uttering of Sin Fronteras was our affirmation not her instruction or advice. *No one but women from this place can speak like this.*

Sin Fronteras means so much more than that. The blankets we weave with their geometric patterns are comprised of border series, layered one over the other. This layering both acknowledges borders and renders them irrelevant. Borders are silly and at the same time so powerful. Borders and your position within them teach respect, binds knowing to being, moves you slippery between thought and imagination. We can create them with a look, dismantle them with a smile, embrace them like an old lover, but Sin Fronteras is without frontiers.

There never was a frontier. We were never on the edge of anything. We have and always will be in the Center. Borders are determined by where our imagination takes us in the moment. There is not center and so we cannot live on some kind of periphery. We are the heart of our nations. We erect and dismantle borders at will, but we will never acquiesce to someone's illusion of Fronteras. As Gloria speaks, tiny beads of perspiration form in my armpits, freeing me of the need to be sick from this heat, sick from the crowded muggy room. Perspire, inspire, and expire, my breath returns. I float between the markers of history, time disappears, and we are here forever as we have always been with neither beginning nor end. *Gloria affirms that the place we take is our own.*

I recognize Gloria. I don't pretend to understand her. I have no wish to comment on her work, but it felt good to recognize her at that book fair so long ago. I acknowledge Gloria, she and every other Indigenous woman who read this knows how big that is for all of us. We are not assigned place, position, or borders, we assume them, we relinquish assumptions or we contrive and respect the borders others take on, but no one but ourselves can define place, position, or power.

Haitchka—Gloria

Chapter 20

Spirit, Culture, Sex: Elements of the Creative Process in Anzaldúa's Poetry

Linda Garber

Not so long ago, in a community very close by, lesbians spoke poetry. We gathered in throngs to hear Judy Grahn and Pat Parker electrify crowds as women talked to death and refused to be partners in womanslaughter. Yellow Woman spoke the words of a woman who breathes fire—a transcendental etude during periods of stress, building bridges to our own power. Poetry was Not a Luxury.[1]

So what happened?

"Women's culture" imploded. Presses vanished, bookstores closed their doors, literary journals disappeared. AIDS emerged, and with it a virulent new strain of homophobia. We became queer, and queer was theorized and commodified more forcefully than it was lyricized.

Crossings from poetry to theory, from lesbian-feminist to queer, are among the many borderlands Gloria Anzaldúa inhabits. As with most dichotomies, she defies them. ("Deconstruct, construct," she writes in *Borderlands/La Frontera: The New Mestiza* [104].) Yet, while many critics have commented on Anzaldúa's "poetic" prose, *Borderlands* has been treated almost exclusively as a work of prose theory, virtually as though the second half of the book—"Un Agitado Viento/Ehécatl, The Wind," 102 pages comprising thirty-six poems—did not exist.

There are many reasons for this neglect.[2] Not the least of them is that the current preoccupation with cultural theory in the academy seems to leave very little room for contemporary poetry.[3] Anzaldúa herself explains that she does not expect "academic professors" to turn to literature for theoretical ideas (Ikas 235) and that "high theorists" are intolerant of discussions about spirituality, which permeate her poems (Keating, "Writing" 114). Most academic criticism focuses on the innovations of Anzaldúa's conceptions of "mestiza" and "queer," and her relevance to poststructuralist, postcolonialist, and/or queer theory. Anzaldúa believes that many scholars avoid the anger expressed in her poems (Ikas 232), but anger is not the only problem she presents. Poetry, itself, is difficult—a code to be cracked, a nonlinear and emotive discourse. And it is in Anzaldúa's poems that she expresses herself in sexually explicit, messy terms. Despite the introduction provided by the first half of *Borderlands*, Anzaldúa's poems pose to non-Chicana readers the additional barrier of frequent Chicano, mexicano, and Nahuatl references. Anzaldúa's liberal use of Spanish likely also contributes to the neglect of the poems in the predominantly English-speaking U.S. academy.

The genre mestizaje of *Borderlands*' first half is analogous to the multiple identities Anzaldúa embodies as mestiza and in that sense is clearly aligned with a poststructuralist reading.[4] The book's second half, a straightforward (one might even say "old-fashioned") collection of poems, belongs more obviously to Anzaldúa's lesbian-feminist history. The lesbian-feminist movement of the 1970s and '80s reveled in the lineage of the poet Sappho, fostered the writing and performance of political verse, and produced a number of activist-theorist-poets of great stature and influence among lesbians and feminists. While it has been aptly termed "poetic prose," the first half of *Borderlands* in many ways looks like theory, sounds like theory, so it must be theory, and therefore worthy of comment by theorists. Anzaldúa's poetry requires literary decoding, embodies the wrong genre, resists appropriation, is perceived as being of no use to dominant academic theories, and is therefore ignored—considered "literature," perhaps, but of little consequence to theorists who trade in a different medium.

But readers who ignore Anzaldúa's poetry miss key aspects of her project and *Borderlands*' political/historical context First, many of Anzaldúa's great, recognized themes are present in the poems as well as the prose. Like Audre Lorde's famous statement that poetry gives shape to unconscious feelings and ideas long before they become articulated as politics and theory ("Poetry"), Anzaldúa explains about poetry, "An image is a bridge between evoked emotion and conscious knowledge; words are the cables that hold up the bridge. Images are more direct, more immediate than words, and closer to the unconscious. Picture language precedes thinking in words; the metaphorical mind precedes analytical consciousness" (91).

Further, some of Anzaldúa's themes, given short shrift or merely implied in the prose chapters, are only fully visible in the poetry. Anzaldúa's "Coatlicue State"—the spiritual, specifically Chicana process that gives rise to her personal growth and creative output—is explained in prose chapter four, and aspects of Coatlicue are depicted in several poems, including "Poets have strange eating habits," "En mi corazón se incuba," "Letting Go," "I Had to Go Down," "Cagado abismo, quiero saber," "Creature of Darkness," "Antigua, mi diosa," and "Canción de la diosa de la noche." But it is only in the poetry that Anzaldúa depicts sex—not merely queer or lesbian identity but orgasmic physical pleasure—as integral to the spiritual and cultural process of growth and creation symbolized by Coatlicue. In interviews both before and after the 1987 publication of *Borderlands*, Anzaldúa makes this connection between body, spirit, culture, and text repeatedly. As early as 1982 she told Linda Smuckler, "my whole thing with spirituality has been this experience with this other alien in the body, the spirit, the writing, and the sexuality" (*Interviews/Entrevistas* 41). Framing a similar sentiment in terms of her project as a writer, Anzaldúa told Debbie Blake and Carmen Abrego in 1994, "My whole struggle in writing, in this anticolonial struggle, has been to put us back together again. To connect up the body with the soul and the mind with the spirit. That's why for me there's such a link between the text and the body, between textuality and sexuality, between the body and the spirit" (*Interviews/Entrevistas* 220).

Expressed in several of *Borderlands*' poems, the idea is clearly stated only once in the much discussed prose half of the book, when Anzaldúa describes the physical sensation of descending into the Coatlicue State:

> Suddenly, I feel like I have another set of teeth in my mouth. A tremor goes through my body from my buttocks to the roof of my mouth. On my palate I feel a tingling ticklish sensation, then something seems to be falling on me, over me, a curtain of rain or light. Shock pulls my breath out of me. The sphincter muscle tugs itself up, up, and the heart in my cunt starts to beat . . . I collapse into myself—a delicious caving into myself—imploding, the walls like matchsticks softly folding inward in slow motion. (73)

Even here the connection between spirit, culture, sex, *and writing* is not made explicit but must be inferred from the Coatlicue State's influence on Anzaldúa's writing process, described more clearly in chapter six, "Tlilli, Tlapalli/The Path of the Red and Black Ink." There Anzaldúa explains in a passage of untranslated Spanish how "Writing Is a Sensuous Act":

> Tallo mi cuerpo como si estuviera lavando un trapo. Toco las saltadas venas de mis manos, mis chichis adormecidas como pájaras al anochecer. Estoy encorvada sobre la cama. Las imágenes aletean alrededor de mi cama como murciélagos, la sábana como que tuviese alas. El ruido de los trenes subterráneos en mi sentido como conchas. Parece que las paredes del cuarto se me arriman cada vez más cerquita. (93)

> [I rub my body as if I were washing a rag. I touch the bulging veins of my hands, my titties drowsy like (female) birds at dusk. I am curled up on the bed. The images flutter around my bed like bats, the sheet as if it had wings. The noise of the underground trains is like a seashell to my ear. It seems that the walls of the room draw ever closer each time.][5]

This passage contains a sexual subtext as well, because "concha" is slang for vulva in several Spanish dialects. Thus, the trains' rumbling can be read as reminiscent of the beating of "the heart in my cunt" Anzaldúa evokes elsewhere when discussing sexual arousal and orgasm as they relate to spiritual experience and creativity (*Borderlands* 73; *Interviews/Entrevistas* 109).

The reader can piece together the path from Anzaldúa's equation of the serpent with Coatlicue to female sexuality, which was cleansed from the virginal image of Guadalupe,

> *Tonantsi*—split from her dark guises, *Coatlicue*, *Tlazolteotl*, and *Cihuacoatl*—became the good mother . . . After the Conquest, the Spaniards and their Church continued to split *Tonantsi/Guadalupe*. They desexed *Guadalupe*, taking *Coatlalopeuh*, the serpent/sexuality, out of her. They completed the split made by the Nahuas by making *la Virgen de Guadalupe/Virgen María* into chaste virgins and *Tlazolteotl/Coatlicue/la Chingada* into *putas* [whores]; into the Beauties and the Beasts. (49–50)

Stated more directly in the Smuckler interview, "for me the serpent is a symbol of female sexuality, of all that's repressed" (*Interviews/Entrevista* 64). From the passage about Tonantsi, Coatlicue, Tlazolteotl, Cihuacoatl, and Guadalupe in chapter three, through chapter four's explanation of Coatlicue's role in growing self-awareness, to chapter six which focuses on writing, and on to the conclusion she states succinctly in the interviews—but the only place Anzaldúa puts it all together in *Borderlands* is in poems.

Given the scant critical attention to the poems despite their unique importance in expressing Anzaldúa's creative and spiritual journey—after all a main theme of *Borderlands*—it is worth noting that the book began as a straightforward collection of poems. This was back in the days when Anzaldúa's published bio notes identified her as a "lesbian-feminist poet," the moniker still used in the back pages of *Borderlands*. Setting out to write a ten-page introduction to the poems, Anzaldúa instead produced ninety-eight pages, "Atravesando Fronteras/Crossing Borders," the "poetic prose" masterpiece that is meant when reference is made to *Borderlands* (Adams 134; Pinkvoss). Along the way, and as the book's influence grew in the 1990s, Anzaldúa's bio notes came to include the word "theorist." By the 1998 publication of the anthology *Living Chicana Theory*, Anzaldúa described herself as "a queer Chicana Tejana feminist patlache poet, fictionist and cultural theorist from the Rio Grande valley of south Texas" and announced a "forthcoming . . . book theorizing the production of art, knowledge, and identity" (Trujillo 438). The growth of the prose half of *Borderlands* out of an otherwise self-sustaining volume of poetry provides a neat metaphor for the shift from the poetry-centered lesbian-feminist movement in which Anzaldúa has roots to the prose theory-centered queer movement which has taken her up and which she, to some extent, embraced.

My intent is not to argue that Gloria Anzaldúa *really* is a poet, nor that *Borderlands* is really *not* a theoretical work. I am interested, instead, in the genre borders being crossed, and in the critical investment in denying the poetry while simultaneously naming the work "poetic prose." A great deal has been written about Anzaldúa's prose stylings and about the employment of poetry within the prose half of the book, but very little about the poetry itself. Anzaldúa herself makes no such omission or distinction. Tellingly, she retains the name "poet," even as she comes to call herself "theorist" over time. Her poems address several of the same issues as her prose theory: racism and the fight against it ("that dark shining thing," "el sonavabitche," "Cuyamaca," "No se raje, Chicanita," and "Arriba mi gente"); racist and homophobic violence ("sus plumas el viento," "We Call Them Greasers," "En el nombre de todas las madres que han perdido sus hijos en la guerra," "Corner of 50th St. and Fifth Av."); border identity ("To live in the Borderlands means you," "sobre piedras con lagartijos"); spiritual self-discovery ("I Had to Go Down," "My Black Angelos," "Antigua, mi diosa"); lesbianism and alienation from home culture ("Compañera, cuando amábamos," "Cihuatlyotl, Woman Alone," "Interface," "Canción de la diosa de la noche," "Nopalitos"). And, perhaps like most poets, Anzaldúa includes poems that specifically address the writing of poetry.

Prominent among these is "Poets have strange eating habits" (162–63), a poem that takes readers on a surrealistic night ride through Anzaldúa's creative unconscious. The poet-speaker rides a scabby, "balking mare / to the edge" (ll.3–4), where her mount collapses into itself, which is simultaneously the poet-speaker's self: "Her body caves into itself / through the hole / my mouth" (ll.6–8). The vehicle for the creative state is both animal-other and self. The vehicle (the poetic process, or poetry itself) is also that which the poet-speaker consumes—her nourishment, and her route into her own creative depths. Throughout stanzas two–nine of the ten-stanza poem, the intermingling "she" of the mare and the poet-speaker's "I" repeatedly choose to "plunge" (l.14), to be wounded into "a deeper healing" (l.30). "I burrow deep into myself," the poet-speaker explains (l.40), until in the final line, "me la tragó todita" (68)—translated in a footnote, "I swallow it whole."

Not surprisingly, Anzaldúa's depiction of her creative process is bilingual and resonates with the Azteca-mexica cultural images explained in the book's prose half. (Perhaps this is one reason why of all the poets she undoubtedly knows, she dedicates this one to Irena Klepfisz, a lesbian who also writes from a distinct cultural idiom and bilingually, in English and Yiddish.) The poem teaches us to understand Anzaldúa's creative experience, while (among other things) the book's prose half teaches us to understand the poem's cultural and spiritual imagery. This is most true of chapter four, "La herencia de Coatlicue/The Coatlicue State." Anzaldúa describes Coatlicue as the earliest "Mesoamerican fertility and Earth Goddess," an ancient predecessor of the much tamer Coatlalopeuh, later known as Guadalupe. Once the "creator goddess" and "mother of the celestial deities," Coatlicue was driven underground and assigned "monstrous attributes" by the "male-dominated Azteca-Mexica culture" (49). Anzaldúa describes Coatlicue's terrific appearance in an Aztec statue unearthed in Mexico in 1824:

> In . . . place [of a head] two spurts of blood gush up, transfiguring into enormous twin rattlesnakes facing each other, which symbolize the earth-bound character of human life . . . In . . . place [of hands] are two more serpents in the form of eagle-like claws, which are repeated at her feet: claws which symbolize the digging of graves into the earth as well as the sky-bound eagle, the masculine force. Hanging from her neck is a necklace of open hands alternating with human hearts. . . . In the center of the collar hangs a human skull with living eyes in its sockets. Another identical skull is attached to her belt. These symbolize life and death together as parts of one process. (69)[6]

Anzaldúa explains her own relationship to Coatlicue, "one of the powerful images, or, 'archetypes,' that inhabits, or passes through, my psyche" (68). "As the incarnation of cosmic processes," Coatlicue visits Anzaldúa when she is "stuck" in ruts of awareness and therefore stuck in ritual or addictive behavior. Coatlicue takes her on frightening, even painful, psychic journeys that "propel the soul to do its work: make soul, increase consciousness of itself" (68). Anzaldúa explains that "blocks (Coatlicue States) are related to my cultural identity. The painful periods of confusion that I suffer from are symptomatic of a larger creative process: cultural shifts. The stress of living with cultural ambiguity both compels me to write and blocks me" (96). Once the painful self-exploration of the Coatlicue State has passed, Anzaldúa writes—an activity she describes as an "obsession" and "a blood sacrifice" (97). She links writing to psychic and physical suffering, "[f]or only through the body, through the pulling of flesh, can the human soul be transformed. And for images, words, stories to have this transformative power, they must arise from the human body—flesh and bone—and from the Earth's body—stone, sky liquid, soil. This work, these images, piercing tongue or ear lobes with cactus needle, are my offerings, are my Aztecan blood sacrifices" (97).

The pain is real, and her resistance is powerful, if ultimately unsuccessful. "Voy cagándome de miedo," she writes, I'm shitting myself from fear. "My resistance, my refusal to know some truth about myself brings on that paralysis, depression—brings on the Coatlicue state" (70). In "Tlilli/Tlapalli" Anzaldúa explains in the third person her writing process and her attempt to resist it: "To be a mouth—the cost is too high—her whole life enslaved to that devouring mouth . . . She wants to install 'stop' and 'go' signal lights, instigate a curfew, police Poetry. But something wants to come out" (96). What follows this resistance is the collapsing into herself, being devoured by the unconscious or underworld, that results in poetry, the process and product of her "Aztecan blood sacrifice." The cycle repeats: resistance, Coatlicue State, shift of consciousness, poetry.

Anzaldúa describes the Coatlicue State as her psyche being visited, being "devoured," and falling into the "underworld"—the process depicted in "Poets have strange eating habits."[7] Chapter four begins with one of the many poems of the book's prose half; titled "protean being," it employs many of the same images and even specific phrases of "Poets." In both, "no moon glides" in "the nightsky," and the poet-speaker faces the decision to jump, "tumbling down the steps of the temple," "heart offered up to the sun." Snakes and feathers, characteristic of Coatlicue's appearance, abound. The placement of "Poets" as the first poem in the third poetry section, titled "Crossers y otros atravesados," is appropriate, as the poem depicts the descent into the underworld of the Coatlicue State, which once accepted "transforms living in the Borderlands from a nightmare into a numinous experience" (95). This statement hints at the sexual dimension of the Coatlicue State, but once again only when connected to a poem. The word "numinous" resonates in the narrative poem "Interface" (170–74), in which the first person speaker develops a secret sexual and emotional relationship with "an alien" (l.194) "noumenal" (l.32) being she names "Leyla, / a pure sound" (ll.149–50)—poetry embodied and sexually embraced.

"Poets" is framed by the image "dark windowless no moon glides / across the nightsky" (ll.1–2, 64–65). In chapter four and in the poem "Creature of Darkness" (208), Anzaldúa describes hiding from everyone when she feels the vulnerability brought on by a visit from Coatlicue: "I locked the door, kept the world out; I vegetated, hibernated, . . . Alone with the presence in the room. Who? Me, my psyche, the Shadow-Beast?" (66). In "Creature of Darkness" she writes, "Nothing I can do / nothing I want to do / but stay small and still in the dark" (ll.7–9), "growing great with mouth / a creature afraid of the dark / a creature at home in the dark" (ll.61–63). It is also "during the dark side of the moon" that Anzaldúa describes having experienced her first life-altering insight; staring into "the black, obsidian mirror of the Nahuas," she saw her face and reality as they really are, multiple in character: "Simultáneamente me miraba la cara desde distintos ángulos. Y mi cara, como la realidid, tenía un caracter multíplice" ("Simultaneously I saw my face from different angles. And my face, like reality, had a multiple character") (66).[8] Obsidian, the black volcanic glass from which "in ancient times the Mexican Indians made mirrors" in which seers saw "the future and the will of the gods" (64) shows up in "Poets" as well. In the poem, obsidian is a knife (l.20) "cutting tears from my eyes" (l.19). The mirror is figured as a weapon; it is painful to gaze into, as Anzaldúa describes in chapter four: "When I reach bottom [of the underworld], something forces me to . . . walk toward the mirror, confront the face in the mirror. But I dig in my heels and resist. I don't want to see what's behind Coatlicue's eyes, her hollow sockets. I can't confront her face to face; I must take small sips" (70).

Both in "Poets" and in part of chapter four (70), Anzaldúa's journey into the underworld takes place on horseback. She refers to "her 'horses' " as "her instincts," which she did not trust when she was young because "they stood for her core self, her dark Indian self" (65). The poem's conceit turns on an apt pun: Anzaldúa's creative process is a nightmare, as she rides a balking horse on a moonless night, plunging repeatedly to terrifying depths in order to gain the insights that result in her art. The mare in "Poets" is "balking," but the first-person speaker nevertheless "coax[es] and whip[s]" her "to the edge" (ll.3 and 4). Edges, those borderlands where Anzaldúa so uncomfortably and productively resides, figure importantly in her description of the Coatlicue State. In the darkness she hears "that voice at the edge of things" (72); she "teeter[s] on the edge" of the process that leads to awareness as she resists Coatlicue (96). In the poem, the horse—her instincts—"caves into itself / through the hole / my mouth" (ll.6–8) mirroring the prose description of the process of the Coatlicue state: "I collapse into myself—a delicious caving into myself—imploding, the walls like matchsticks softly folding inward in slow motion" (73). Instead of the words coming out of her mouth—the role of the poet—in the process of self-discovery that leads to poetry she collapses inward through her mouth.

The images lend themselves to a sexual reading as well. The speaker coaxes her tense sexual self—animal, instinctive—to the brink of orgasm throughout the poem, repeatedly releasing control to go over the edge in a series of images of jumping (l.11), plunging (ll.14–15, 50, 56), and flying (ll.22–23, 31–33). In chapter four, Anzaldúa describes her resistance to Coatlicue as "resistance to knowing, to letting go, to that deep ocean where once I dived into death. I am afraid of drowning. Resistance to sex, intimate touching, opening myself to the alien other where I am out of control, not on patrol. The outcome on the other side unknown, the reins failing and the horses plunging blindly over the crumbling path rimming the edge of the cliff, plunging into its thousand foot drop" (70).

The downward sexual movement is echoed in titles of other poems, "Letting Go" and "I Had to Go Down," the most clearly evocative of oral sex. "Poets" is full of suggestively female and lesbian oral sexual imagery. When the mare plunges off the cliff in stanza three, her "head [is] tucked between her legs" (l.17) and in stanza four "She spreads out her legs" (l.22). The speaker and horse are literally going "down" (l.12). Mouths (ll.8, 66), eating (title, ll.27–28, 47, 68), and teeth (l.26, "fangs" l.47, l.51) are everywhere, as Anzaldúa at once rhapsodizes about reciprocal lesbian sex and reclaims the Olmec association of

> womanhood with the Serpent's mouth which was guarded by rows of dangerous teeth, a sort of *vagina dentata.* They considered it the most sacred place on earth, a place of refuge, the creative womb from which all things were born and to which all things returned. Snake people had holes, entrances to the body of the Earth Serpent; they followed the Serpent's way, identified with the Serpent deity, with the mouth, both the eater and the eaten. (56)

As in the prose description of the descent into the Coatlicue State, the poem's speaker experiences an introspective orgasmic caving (l.6) and burrowing (l.40) into herself. In one sense these images are autoerotic, and in interviews Anzaldúa has linked masturbation to transgression and to communion with the Goddess (*Interviews/Entrevistas* 30, 71, 109–10). She puns in "Tlilli/Tlapalli," "I am playing with my Self, I am playing with the world's soul, I am the dialogue between my Self and *el espíritu del mundo*" (the spirit of the world, 92). On another level, the poem imagines the collapsing of boundaries between self and lover during sex, as the poem's speaker and the balking mare become indistinguishable through grammatical ambiguity—"Her body caves into itself / through the hole / my mouth" (ll.6–8)—and through the progression of pronouns from "I" to "She" to "I" again in the course of the poem's brief narrative. Anzaldúa has described the relationship between sexuality and spirituality in similar terms:

> I feel I'm connected to something greater than myself like during orgasm: I disappear, I'm just this great pleasurable wave, like I'm uniting with myself in a way I have not been. In this union with the other person I lose my boundaries, my sense of self. Even if it's just for a second, there's a connection between my body and this other's body, to her soul or spirit. At the moment of connection, there is no differentiation. . . . In spirituality I feel the same way. When I'm meditating or doing any kind of spiritual thing, there's a connection with the source. (*Interviews/Entrevistas* 37–38)

Interweaving images of sexual and spiritual journey in "Poets," Anzaldúa employs "metaphor and symbol [to] concretize the spirit and etherealize the body," the writer's task she proclaims in the "Tlilli/Tlapalli" chapter (97).

As the Coatlicue State progresses, Anzaldúa/the speaker must continue to face her fear and decide to go forward. Stanza two of "Poets" describes this choice that takes place "[i]n the border between dusk and dawn" (l.9) and on the verge of a descent linked to ancient sacrificial rites: "Should I jump face tumbling / down the steps of the temple / heart offered up to the midnightsun" (ll.11–13). Here she faces the choice to go forward with the process of writing, "my whole life . . . my obsession . . . my Aztecan blood sacrifices" (97). In stanzas three through nine, "She takes that plunge" (l.14). The downward falling and burrowing motion is repeated in "I Had to Go Down," whose speaker timidly descends into her basement where she finds her own self, not the other she had feared (189–91), and in "Letting Go," where the plunge is "into your navel, with your two hands / split open" in order to "turn the maze inside out" (186–88, ll.4–5, 9). The poems' images are explained as part of the Coatlicue State in chapter four: "falling" (64), "plunging" (68), and "that flying leap in the dark" (71).

The core of "Poets," stanzas three through nine, describes the descent and the repeated decision to jump—Anzaldúa's ritualized, quotidian act of self-exploration and creation, "[t]aking the plunge an act as / routine as cleaning my teeth" (ll.50–51). Yet the violence of the "routine" is far from a sanitary act of dental hygiene. Other "teeth" belong to the "hunger" (l.26) of "el abismo" (the chasm, l.24) to which the speaker feeds herself, "let it glut itself on me / till it's pregnant with me. / Wounding is a deeper healing" (ll.28–30). The image encapsulates Anzaldúa's philosophy of creation through painful spiritual submersion and reemergence. Like much of "Poets," these three lines see the poet devoured. Anzaldúa repeats this particular sexual trope in "The Cannibal's *Canción*" (165):

It is our custom
to consume
the person we love.
Taboo flesh: swollen
genitalia nipples
the scrotum the vulva
the soles of the feet
the palms of the hand
heart and liver taste best.
Cannibalism is blessed. (ll.1–10)

Coatlicue "[a]s the Earth . . . swallows us, plunging us into the under world where the soul resides," Anzaldúa writes (68). The spiritual force compelling the speaker to such depths is not separate from herself; as she explains, "I've always been aware that there is a greater power than the conscious I. That power is my inner self, the entity . . . in me I call *Antigua, mi Diosa*, the divine within, *Coatlicue-Cihuacoatl-Tlazolteotl-Tonantzin-Coatlalopeuh-Guadalupe*—they are one" (72). Anzaldúa equates the pain and promise of regular submission in the night with the life-giving creative process:

> She writes while other people sleep. Something is trying to come out. She fights the words, pushes them down, down, a woman with morning sickness in the middle of the night. How much easier it would be to carry a baby for nine months and then expel it permanently. These continuous multiple pregnancies are going to kill her. She is the battlefield for the pitched fight between the inner image and the words trying to recreate it. (95–96)

Creativity, tied to sexuality, results in a metaphoric pregnancy, an excruciating literary process experienced through the body.

Anzaldúa links the violence of creation to one of her perilous totem animals, the serpent. In "La herencia de Coatlicue," she twice repeats the refrain, "Let the wound caused by the serpent be cured by the serpent" (68, 72). (The sentence echoes "Wounding is a deeper healing" from "Poets" l.30.) Let Coatlicue bite and heal, she seems to say in "Poets," as the speaker finds herself "tunneling here tunneling there / the slither of snakes / their fangs pierce my flesh" (ll.46–47). Because the wounding is also a healing, the speaker takes "that plunge again / jumping off cliffs an addiction" (ll.56–57). Although serpents frequently are phallic symbols, for Anzaldúa they represent female sexuality: "She, the symbol of the dark sexual drive, the chthonic (underworld), the feminine, the serpentine movement of sexuality, of creativity, the basis of all energy and life" (57). In chapter three, "Entering Into the Serpent," Anzaldúa recounts being bitten by a rattlesnake when she was working in a cotton field in her youth, after which,

> [I] dreamed rattler fangs filled my mouth, scales covered my body. In the morning I saw through snake eyes, felt snake blood course through my body. The serpent, *mi tono*, my animal counterpart. I was immune to its venom. Forever immune.
>
> Snakes, *víboras:* since that day I've sought and shunned them. Always when they cross my path, fear and elation flood my body. I know things older than Freud, older than gender. She—that's how I think of *la Víbora*, Snake Woman. Like the ancient Olmecs, I know Earth is a coiled Serpent. Forty years it's taken me to enter into the Serpent, to acknowledge that I have a body, that I am a body and to assimilate the animal body, the animal soul. (48)

In "Poets," the speaker is transformed into a snake.

> I burrow deep into myself
> pull the emptiness in
> its hollows chisel my face
> growing thin thinner
> eyesockets empty
> tunneling here tunneling there
> the slither of snakes
> their fangs pierce my flesh (ll.40–47)
> [. . .]
> slithering into holes
> with rattlesnakes (ll.62–63)

As Anzaldúa's *tono*, the snake, the poem's speaker suggestively enters holes—her own and others', as the pronouns again render subject–object duality permeable. With the imagery of the serpent this poem about poetry again connects writing, sexuality, culture, and spirituality. In chapter five, "How to Tame a Wild Tongue," Anzaldúa proclaims, "I will no longer be made to feel ashamed of existing. I will have my voice: Indian, Spanish, white. I will have my serpent's tongue—my woman's voice, my sexual voice, my poet's voice. I will overcome the tradition of silence" (81).

As the poet-speaker falls into the necessary, temporary isolation and silence of the Coatlicue State, as she consorts with serpents who wound and heal, she also flies like the eagle (l.32), on "the buffeting wind" (l.34),

> flailing pummeling
> flesh into images
> sticking feathers
> in my arms
> slithering into holes
> with rattlesnakes (ll.58–63)

"Coatlicue depicts the contradictory" in Anzaldúa's cosmology, integrating the opposite Aztec symbols "the eagle and the serpent, heaven and the underworld, life and death, mobility and immobility, beauty and horror" (69). Anzaldúa figures her creativity as the rattlesnake itself, "her consciousness expands a tiny notch, another rattle appears on the rattlesnake tail and the added growth slightly alters the sound she makes" (71). Simultaneously, she is the bird, "Eagle eyes, my mother calls me. Looking, always looking" (72). She transforms into the eagle when she writes: "I look at my fingers, see plumes growing there. From the fingers, my feathers, black and red ink drips across the page. *Escribo con la tinta de mi sangre*" (I write with the ink of my blood, 93, her italics).

Anzaldúa reads the traditional Aztec-mexican symbol of the eagle with the serpent in its mouth as "the struggle between the spiritual/celestial/male and the underworld/earth/feminine," a battle already won by "the patriarchal order . . . in pre-Columbian America" (27). For Anzaldúa, however (or perhaps more accurately *in* Anzaldúa), the eagle and the serpent, the masculine and the feminine, coexist. "The new *mestiza* copes by developing a tolerance for contradictions, a tolerance for ambiguity" (101). Anzaldúa links the embodied contradiction of masculine and feminine to "queer people," sometimes called "mita' y mita' " or half and half, "neither one nor the other but a strange doubling," a difference said to carry "supernatural powers . . . [an] inborn extraordinary gift." The sexual and the otherworldly come together in this conception of queers as "the embodiment of the *hieros gamos:* the coming together of opposite qualities within" (41). In "Poets," where the speaker becomes the serpent and the eagle, the sexual imagery both is clearly lesbian and flirts with the traditionally male phallic sexuality of the snake burrowing into holes—complicated by the holes potentially belonging to the speaker's own self. Anzaldúa believes that "[t]hose who are pushed out of the tribe for being different . . . those who are pounced on . . . the females, the homosexuals of all races, the dark-skinned, the outcast, the persecuted, the marginalized, the foreign" are most likely to be sensitive to "deeper realities," a quality she calls "la facultad" (60). The spiritually aware queer, the other of any type, possess the perceptive emotional and spiritual abilities Anzaldúa sees in the Coatlicue State and the writer's creativity, and are for her prototypical artists.

Perhaps for the more skeptical reader, the one she believes is resistant to the spirituality permeating her work, Anzaldúa paints a more literal picture of herself writing: "I sit here before my computer, *Amiguita*, my altar on top of the monitor with the *Virgen de Coatlalopeuh* candle and copal incense burning. My companion, a wooden serpent staff with feathers, is to my right while I ponder the ways metaphor and symbol concretize the spirit and etherealize the body." There are the serpent, the eagle, and Coatlicue, present as Anzaldúa writes, making her "Aztecan blood sacrifices" (97). Spirit, culture, and sex come together as the essential ingredients of Anzaldúa's creativity most succinctly and vividly in her poetry. If, as she asserts, "For the lesbian of color the ultimate rebellion she can make against her native culture is through her sexual behavior" (41), then her writing about her sexual behavior, writing "from the body" (*Interviews/Entrevistas* 63) in the symbolic idiom of her native cultures epitomizes the contradictory state characterizing the new mestiza. Without attention to her poetry, the critical literature about Anzaldúa misses the equal importance she places on spirit, culture, and sex in her explication of the creative process, and of the new mestiza herself.

Notes

1. Judy Grahn's *A Woman Is Talking to Death*, Parker's *Womanslaughter*, Merle Woo's *Yellow Woman Speaks*, Kitty Tsui's *Words of a Woman Who Breathes Fire*, Adrienne Rich's "Transcendental Etude," Irena Klepfisz's *Periods of Stress*, Kate Rushin's "Bridge Poem," Audre Lorde's "Poetry Is Not a Luxury."
2. I explore them at greater length in *Identity Poetics* 170–75.
3. John Koethe sees a more specific poststructuralist antipathy for poetry, arguing that theorists avoid poetry because of its association with New Criticism, against which contemporary cultural theory originally positioned itself (66).
4. For a thoughtful discussion of Anzaldúa's mobilization of multiple subjectivities and her contribution to cultural theory, see Yarbro-Bejarano's "Gloria Anzaldúa's *Borderlands/La Frontera.*"
5. Thanks to Barbara Blinick and Josie Saldaña for their help with translations. All mistakes are, of course, my own.
6. For a discussion of Anzaldúa's revisionist approach to Coatlicue, see Yarbro-Bejarano's "Gloria Anzaldúa's *Borderlands/La Frontera*" (14–15).
7. Hereafter cited as "Poets."
8. In the Smuckler interview, Anzaldúa describes a similar actual experience induced by hallucinogenic mushrooms (*Interviews/Entrevistas* 36).

Chapter 21

Radical Rhetoric: Anger, Activism, and Change

Amanda Espinosa-Aguilar

> Rather than seeing them as expressive vehicles, we must understand emotional discourses as pragmatic acts and communicative performances.
>
> —Lila Abu-Lughod and Catherine A. Lutz

Anger is something we all feel but often come to regret expressing, because it isn't held in high regard by the dominant culture. Angry children are put into "time out," angry adolescents are put on antidepressants, and angry adults are put into therapy or institutionalized. How many times have people of color been urged to get over their anger and just "get along"? In fact, the ability to keep one's anger in check, in control, is often seen as sign of one's diplomacy and emotional maturity. Warfare, combat, battle, abuse—these are the nouns most commonly associated with anger. Since we are socialized to resist the raw, confrontational tone that marks expressions of anger, authors who purposefully use it risk having their ideas silenced, ignored, dismissed, or otherwise rejected. However, much unnourished agency exists in selectively using anger as a rhetorical device, and Gloria Anzaldúa does just that throughout her writings.

Echoing Audre Lorde, Anzaldúa writes, "When she transforms silence into language, a woman transgresses" ("Haciendo caras" xxii). Anzaldúa transgresses the cultural expectation that she remain a silent, "DUMB, HYSTERICAL, PASSIVE PUTA" ("Speaking" 167, her emphasis) by being a writer who "will write about the unmentionables, never mind the outraged gasp of the censor and the audience" ("Speaking in Tongues" 169). When this language—which I call angry rhetoric—is devalued, hegemonic structures remain undisturbed. The result is maintenance of status quo behavior that restricts disempowered individuals to lives of oppression, inactivity, or complacency. Anzaldúa wants readers to be aware of when and how she uses angry rhetoric, and not avoid it, as so many of her critics have done. As she notes in an interview with Donna Perry, "some academics have somehow taken the sting out of whatever is dangerous or unsettling or too confrontative and focused on what is nonthreatening to them. They've found a way of diluting the racial aspects and whitewashing the books. . . . The angrier passages or ideas in *Borderlands* get less critical attention. This kind of selective critical interpretation is a form of racism" (31). This essay, then, demonstrates how Gloria Anzaldúa uses angry rhetoric to create inclusionary communities—the left hand world, El Mundo Zurdo—and promote alternate modes of consciousness, or conocimiento.

Throughout her writings Anzaldúa uses anger as a rhetorical device, a means of persuasion, expressing revolutionary or radical ideas to create an active citizenry who enact praxis. Angry rhetoric functions as both an aesthetic and a political strategy: "For many of us the acts of writing, painting, performing, and filming are acts of deliberate and desperate determination to subvert the status quo. Creative acts are forms of political activism employing definite aesthetic strategies for resisting dominant cultural norms and are not merely aesthetic exercises" ("Haciendo caras" xxiv). Anzaldúa envisions building bridges, coalitions of differing forces, to create spaces where we can exist without subjection to societal vivisection. Sometimes her readers (irrespective of race) go on the defensive. Students and well-meaning yet color-blind racist scholars can react negatively to Anzaldúa's essays because her diction and syntax evoke a visceral as well as intellectual response. But as Perry notes, "Anzaldúa wants her readers, both women of color and white women, to get upset" (17). For those who resist, she can only plant an emotional irritant and hope for more later. By using angry rhetoric in her works, Anzaldúa intentionally disrupts readers' desconocimientos (avoidance/ignorance), thereby challenging their worldviews. Those readers who embrace and accept her anger are often persuaded of the moral obligation to join Anzaldúa, as agents, in building coalitions. As she asserts, "It's not enough to understand, and it's not enough to write and communicate. You have to do something about it, which is activism, being engaged, and that's *la mano izquierda*, the left hand" (qtd. in Perry 30).

For Anzaldúa, then, angry rhetoric is an aesthetic strategy to inspire activism by exposing injustice, stimulating moral outrage, and promoting the vision that other possibilities exist besides accepting hegemonic binaries. Angry rhetoric affects readers to the point of action, even if that action is to stop reading (because too offended or disturbed by having their consciousness raised). Anzaldúa evokes anger by purposefully using language usually acceptable only in the context of informal speech. For example, in much of her writing she names the negative stereotypes placed on objectified Others, generating for readers the negative energy she experiences from being labeled a multiple outsider (queer, female, Chicana) herself:

> Why do they fight us? Because they think we are dangerous beasts? Why *are* we dangerous beasts? Because we shake and often break the white's comfortable stereotypic images they have of us: the Black domestic, the lumbering nanny with twelve babies sucking her tits, the slant-eyed Chinese with her expert hand—"They know how to treat a man in bed," the flat-faced Chicana or Indian, passively lying on her back, being fucked by the Man *a la* La Chingada. ("Speaking in Tongues" 167, her italics)

This catalog of women-of-color stereotypes is peppered with angry rhetoric that articulates the reasons why the stereotypes have become normalized. Using sexualized vocabulary, Anzaldúa exaggerates the stereotypes. Words like "fight," "dangerous," and "break" evoke the confrontations that occur when women of color "talk back." She employs purposefully dehumanizing language—"lumbering," "tits," "passively," and "fucked"—to describe the women; one cannot read such words without having some culturally influenced response. While "sucking her tits" might be understood just in the context of childbearing, the word "fucking" in the next sentence reverberates back into the phrase, thus alluding to adult sexual activity. Taking a collective, third-person viewpoint, she highlights yet resists the objectified, dehumanized position into which she and other women of color have been placed.

This passage's tone suggests unease, discomfort, injustice, and anger. Readers can react defensively to the language—the forceful, objectifying, dehumanizing words—or they can be angry at the society perpetuating and normalizing such stereotypes.

Anzaldúa embraces as allies those who, like her, are angered by the situations she depicts. Her rhetoric, turns of phrase, wording, sentence structure, hyperbole, catalogs, repetition, and ethos model a process of fighting not with fists, but with language. It's as if her words say "You think I shouldn't be saying this? Well, too bad. I'm not afraid to use offensive words in an offensive way if it jars you out of your passivity and into agency." Her rhetoric throws readers into various forms of nepantla, and invites them to join her in building a new consciousness. She believes that "coalition work attempts to balance power relations and undermine and subvert the system of domination–subordination that affects even our most unconscious thoughts" ("Bridge, Drawbridge, Sandbar or Island" 225). Accepting nepantla is not easy; it begins with a change in one's own consciousness and identity, and spreads out from there, affecting everything and everyone around us. It is difficult because once conocimiento awakens, the veil has been lifted and some individuals may not be able to live with themselves, or with who they have been in the past, any longer.

By actively engaging (some might say accusing) her readers, Anzaldúa compels them to struggle with racism on emotional and intellectual levels. Early in the introduction to *Making Face, Making Soul/Haciendo Caras*, in a section titled, "Everything About Racism Evades Direct Confrontation," Anzaldúa directly confronts white racism by naming and identifying it with examples from her experiences as a scholar, teacher, Chicana:

> Whites who don't want to confront Racism and who don't name themselves white recoil in horror from it, shun it like the plague. To mention the word in their company disrupts their comfortable complacency. . . . The people who practice Racism—everyone who is white in the U.S.—are victims of their own white ideology and are impoverished by it. ("Haciendo caras" xix)

Although readers can deny the assertions, wallowing in defensive anger, Anzaldúa wants them to acknowledge their reactions and direct their anger at changing the society that perpetuates such racism. As she explains, "Making others 'uncomfortable' in their Racism is one way of 'encouraging' them to take a stance against it" (xix). Anzaldúa's use here of angry rhetoric as a necessary response to oppression is a response that too often is feared, especially by white readers (namely our white middle-class students). But as she notes, "The intellect needs the guts and adrenaline that horrific suffering and anger . . . catapult us into. Only when all the charged feelings are unearthed can we get down to 'the work' *la tarea, nuestro trabajo*—changing culture and all its oppressive interlocking machinations" ("Haciendo caras" xviii). Anzaldúa strives to change the world, one reader at a time, using angry rhetoric to shatter their complacency and desconocimientos, replacing it with conscious agency (conocimientos).

Significantly, Anzaldúa resists expressing anger just for anger's sake. In a 1999 interview she describes her self-reflective approach to anger. Rather than simply reacting out of anger, she explores its sources and its potential impact: "As soon as I emote the anger I stop and say, 'Wait a minute, look at what you're doing! What is this anger serving? Am I a better person for it? Is it helping make the world a better place?' " (*Interviews/Entrevistas* 288). Anger is useful for Anzaldúa when it leads to substantial action or positive change that encourages readers to move beyond binary thinking.

Anzaldúa's angry rhetoric creates spaces where reader and writer, oppressed and oppressor, acknowledge their complicity in perpetuating the status quo. In essays and interviews, she discusses white female academics' racist practices at national conferences on feminism or women's studies. Look for example at her use of angry rhetoric in the following passage:

> Some white feminists, displacing race and class and highlighting gender, are still trying to force us to choose between being colored or female, only now they've gone underground and use unconscious covert pressures. It's all very subtle. Our white allies or colleagues get a hurt look in their eyes when we bring up their racism in their interactions with us and quickly change the subject. Tired of our "theme song" (Why aren't you dealing with race and class in your conference, classroom, organization?) and not wanting to hurt them and in retaliation have them turn against us, we drop the subject and, in effect, turn the other cheek. ("Bridge, Drawbridge, Sandbar, or Island" 221–22)

In this passage Anzaldúa interrogates many institutional structures and beliefs. First, she rejects the binary thinking that makes all forms of discrimination equal ("highlighting gender"). Second, she rejects the notion that women of color "must chose between being colored or female." Third, in noting white women's use of "unconscious covert pressures" and women-of-color complicity, she highlights that hegemonic structures are reified through silencing. Fourth, using words like "force," "covert," "hurt," "racism," "retaliation," and "turn," Anzaldúa shatters white women's illusion of sisterhood, exposing the complacency on which it relies. Fifth, she holds white women accountable; transformed collaboration will not occur until they "have or are dealing with issues of racial domination in a 'real' way," ("Bridge, Drawbridge, Sandbar, or Island" 222).

Anzaldúa even risks alienating her sisters of color, even members of her own family, by claiming that their thinking and reality have also been co-opted in various ways by the dominant cultures:

> My mother has internalized racism from the white dominant culture, from watching television and from our own culture which defers to and prefers light-skinned güerros and denies the Black blood in our mestisaje—which may be both a race and class prejudice, as darker means being more indio or india, means poorer. Whites are conditioned to be racist, colored are prone to internalize racism and, for both groups, racism and internalized racism appear to be the given, "the way things are." . . . I call this "deception" "selective reality"—the narrow spectrum of reality that human beings choose to perceive and/or what their culture "selects" for them to "see." That which is outside their range of consensus (white) perception is "blanked-out." Color,

> race, sexual preferences, and other threatening differences are "unseen" by some whites, certain voices not heard. Such "editing" of reality maintains race, class, and gender oppressions. ("Bridge, Drawbridge, Sandbar, or Island" 226)

According to Anzaldúa, all people, regardless of ethnicity, are guilty of "selective reality," reproducing and maintaining oppression because we are socialized, conditioned, and raised to believe it's the norm—just the way things are.

Readers' anger at this co-opted state is transformed into a constructive force when it leads to the path of conocimiento. As Anzaldúa explains, "Conocimiento es otro mode de conectar across colors and other differences to allies also trying to negotiate racial contradictions, survive the stresses and traumas of daily life, and develop a spiritual-imaginal-political vision together" ("now let us shift" 571). With conocimiento we bridge experiences between the spiritual and political, transforming differences into commonalities and creating communities that can work together for change. These new communities, which Anzaldúa sometimes describes as El Mundo Zurdo, will be based on the shared agenda of rejecting oppressive dehumanization in any form and dismantling social injustice.

Angry rhetoric, then, functions not to divide or evoke defense, which is the typical response and expectation of anger, but paradoxically to unite the actors experiencing it. By actively engaging or affecting readers with explicit expressions of strong emotion, by making readers struggle with their ideas on emotional as well as intellectual levels, Anzaldúa inspires praxis, what Paulo Freire, in *Pedagogy of the Oppressed*, calls "action and reflection upon the world in order to transform it" (66). Like Freire, Anzaldúa calls for transformation that begins with the individual and moves outward, to transform the world. She believes that "by changing ourselves we change the world" ("La Prieta" 208). For Anzaldúa, anger and other strong emotions, combined with self-reflection, can lead to transformation: "by using these feelings as tools or grist for the mill, you move through fear, anxiety, anger, and blast into another reality" ("now let us shift" 552).

Chapter 22

Tierra Tremenda: The Earth's Agony and Ecstasy in the Work of Gloria Anzaldúa

Inés Hernández-Ávila

Querida Gloria, Tortuga Woman, estamos en tiempo de invierno, y las rosas de tu espíritu están brotando la evidencia de la Diosa Antigua. Tú, hermana, eres Tierra Tremenda.

This essay looks at "Un Agitado Viento/Ehécatl, The Wind," the second half of Gloria Anzaldúa's *Borderlands/La Frontera: The New Mestiza*. I frame my reading within the context of my own study of Nahuatl philosophical foundations, because like many of us, Gloria[1] was inspired by this tradition, and embraced and re-visioned many of the concepts to register in our contemporary settings. I want to draw attention to the power of Gloria's creative process, as she has articulated it, and demonstrate how hers is a visionary spirit deeply grounded in the earth and moved by the force of her hunger for justice, her demand for personal autonomy, and her love for the universe. I also want to link her spiritual work in the "path of conocimiento," which she elaborates in "now let us shift . . . the path of conocimiento . . . inner work, public acts" to her earlier spiritual work in *Borderlands*.

The title, "Un Agitado Viento/Ehécatl, The Wind," is a direct reference to La Serpiente Emplumada, Quetzalcoatl, the sacred being of MesoAmerica who represents the highest plane, the highest energy to which humans can aspire. Quetzalcoatl, who is wisdom, is the serpent pierced by the luminous arrow of consciousness,[2] the serpent who rubs the belly of the earth, moving as energy moves.[3] The quetzal feathers represent the ultimate freedom of the spirit that allows the earth-bound serpent to achieve its highest place in the cosmos.[4] Ehécatl, as a manifestation of Quetzalcoatl, appears as the NightWind—invisible and intangible, like the Great CreatorSpirit Herself/Himself. Yet Gloria demands of the invisible and the intangible that she be allowed to see, to touch, con gentileza y con brusquedad, de cualquiera manera que sea, because to see (through), to touch, to perceive is to "link inner reflection and vision" ("now let us shift" 542). She names Ehécatl un *agitado* viento, an *Agitated* Wind, and in so doing she marks what I am calling the agony and ecstasy of the earth in her work.

Ehécatl/Quetzalcoatl is associated with justice, with the search within the heart for truth. This search is the arduous path of the poet, the artist, and the tlamatinime—the wise ones who write in the red and the black ink, who offer the perforated mirror by which to see and learn reflection, who light the path, who bring out the faces and hearts of the people, who teach the people how to make wise their faces and strong their hearts. Poeta, artista, who wrote in the red and the black ink (the color in contemporary times of revolution), Gloria was a tlamatinime. In her works she maps for us her own path to wisdom through "subversive knowledges" ("now let us shift" 542), just as she charts for us the bruja/curandera's path of healing language(s). From a Nahuatl-influenced perspective, I see Gloria's "mindful holistic awareness" ("now let us shift" 544) as a Quetzalcoatl consciousness, and she became in her work and in her life a yolteotl, a "corazón endiosada," who spoke with tireless devotion to la Diosa Antigua through her creative work.[5]

Her floricanto (in xochitl in cuicatl) is the expression of someone who engages passionately with her own heart, in relation to individual beings and the entire cosmos. Like the ancient Nahua poets, Gloria makes a sacred place for doubt, for the incessant human need to question, to wonder, to turn the world upside down and inside out (doubt, named Xolotl, is Quetzalcoatl's double). In her demand for personal autonomy, she manifests consistently the energy of Ometeotl Moyocoyatzin, the Supreme Being Goddess/God Who Invents Herself/Himself[6] through unending acts of Creation, invention, and reinvention (as in the path of discovery, movement, and conocimiento). Reminiscent of the ancient Nahua poet Nezahualcoyotl who wrote, "Dejemos al menos flores, dejemos al menos cantos," Gloria writes, "Como un flor la mujer del desierto / no dura mucho tiempo / pero cuando vive llena el desierto / con flores de nopal o de árbol paloverde" ["like a flower the desert woman / does not last very long / but when she lives she fills the desert / with flowers of the nopal or the árbol paloverde"] (*Borderlands* 202). Like Nezahualcoytl, in the world of spirits, she is still filling the desert with flowers, and her own floricanto lives on.

"Más antes en los ranchos," the first section of "Un Agitado Viento," begins with verses from the popular Mexican song "La Llorona," which says, "They say I have no sorrow, Llorona, because no one sees me weep. But there are dead ones who make no sound, Llorona, and their pain is even greater." The dead make no noise, but they imbue the land with their stories, with their bones, with their heartsblood, and with their spirit. In "now let us shift" Gloria describes writing as an offering, an act of and with the spirits; empowerment comes from the redemption (and expulsion) of pain (540). The first three poems in this section illustrate this process as they explore the shooting of doves for money ("White-wing season," 124–25), the desperate bludgeoning of the venadita by Prieta to protect her father ("Cervicide," 126–27), and the unfathomably torturous murder of the great black horse by willfully ignorant young gringos insensatos ("horse," 128–29). We are reminded of the fearful economic repression facing the families, a repression that limits their choices and makes them vulnerable to those who have more, unwilling partners of (self)inflicted violence.

In "horse," dedicated to "la gente de Hargill, Texas," where Gloria's family is from (and where they still live), she shares a story that forms part of the painfully believable living memory[7] of her community, of her home. In this story, the rich gringo father holds out green bills as if money could erase the atrocity of the horse's death. Las palomas, la venadita, el gran caballo negro, los muertos que no hacen ruido, tanto los seres humanos como las inocentes criaturas de la tierra. In "Cervicide" the venadita must be killed by the girl-child who has to look into the fawn's eyes as she takes its life, taking some of her own as well, and we are reminded by Gloria that the deer is the archetypal symbol for the female Self. In "horse" the poet asks, after the horse is savagely cut up, "did it pray all night for morning?" (128). In the red moonlight, the "gringos cry out" in terror-stricken denial of any wrongdoing. The nightmare has become them, and "the mexicanos mumble if you're Mexican / you are born old" (129). The stories of these muertos are rooted in the earth; Gloria brings them to the light of day.

Several poems in this and the following section, "La Pérdida," speak to the blatant inhumanity and unspeakably cruel discrimination that Mexicans faced (and still face in places like south Texas) on the basis of race, ethnicity, gender, class, and sexuality. Here is where Gloria, as a Tejana, first learned to see with the oldest of eyes, en el valle,[8] en la pobreza, en los campos, en la rigidez de la repression; here is how she came to be able to see so clearly, to recognize so precisely, with her heart's eyes grounded in the earth, the inspirited bodies ("now let us shift" 549) everywhere that she traveled, siempre Tortuga Woman, carrying home on her back. En el valle she first understood the ways in which systemic hierarchies "justify a sliding scale of human worth used to keep humankind divided" ("now let us shift" 541).

Here she first realized her courage as Desert Woman, Cactus Woman, Lizard Woman, Serpent Woman, Turtle Woman. Here her soul began the process of "constantly remaking and giving birth to itself through [her] body" (*Borderlands* 95). Even though the poet writes in *Borderlands'* penultimate poem that she has "no keeper," she recognizes that "The Mother . . . / entangles [her] in human flesh" (*Borderlands* 218). La tierra la recibe, le da su carne y hueso, por medio de su propia Madre que también es Tierra.

The poems of pain demonstrate "el arrebato" that Gloria speaks of in "now let us shift"—the ending and a beginning, the place of return, the journey inward and outward. "Every arrebato . . . rips you from your familiar 'home,' casting you out of your personal Eden, showing that something is lacking in your queendom" (546). Eden, the ecstasy of intensely heightened awareness and reflective consciousness, is not a Paradise as Test or Temptation, but a state earned, achieved through the tremendous and unending desire to know, to love, to pursue freedom, and to experience the orgasmic rush of creativity. To discover and nurture her uncontained relationship to all the spirits of the universe, of the goddesses, the saints, the loved ones and lovers, the aliens, she follows the "huellas ligeras y [el] linaje viejo" of La Antigua, and she tells this Ancient One whose light she desires, "por ti sacrifiqué / las plantas de mis pies" (*Borderlands* 210). It is this Ancient One who shows her a love so huge "you share a category of identity wider than any social position or racial label" ("now let us shift" 558), the connection(s) being from spirit to spirit.

The shocks, the upheavals of innocence, the sustos that imprinted themselves early, the conciencia that remains somehow, to nourish the spirit, and to strengthen every fiber of the being, the arrebatos, the trastornos, the gestos de gran cariño, appear in "Un Agitado Viento" and form a fluid foundation for Gloria's ever-growing awareness. Se dice que uno que sabe curar tiene que haber visto lo mas hondo, tiene que haber enfrentado a los demonios, porque apenas así sabrá curar. Healers are not without myriad experience; they have confronted many, many demons, they have seen the basest of beings and the most degrading of acts. They have also witnessed the most tender of moments and the power of love in all its manifestations. They cherish the doble/multiple saber ("now let us shift" 549) that becomes them. This is how they know how to cure. Es más, the Viento is always Agitado, porque siempre hay arrebatos, siempre estamos en Nepantla, es así.

In "La curandera" (*Borderlands* 198–201), the first poem of "Animas" (the fifth section of "Un Agitado Viento") we are given the story of how a woman becomes a healer, and Juan Dávila her apprentice. The two manifest the dual duality of creation. The woman tells Juan, "You are everyone, when you prayed for yourself, / you prayed for all of us," and he tells her something similar. She says, " '. . . I want to be with her, la virgen santísima.' / 'But you are with her,' he said, / eyes clear like a child's. / 'She is everywhere' " (199). Opening herself to this message, the curandera can receive the serpents as " 'healing spirit guides.' " These guides work with her and Juan, helping them shift their own consciousness so that they can facilitate the miracles of healing. Their work is one of spiritual activism and holistic alliance, and the earth rejoices with them in ecstasy. They know that they "stand on tierra sagrada—nature is alive and conscious, the world is ensouled" ("now let us shift" 558).

Gloria opens Section II, "La Pérdida," with lines from the famous and nostalgic "Canción Mixteca," "Que lejos estoy del suelo donde he nacido" ["How far away I am from the earth where I was born"]. In "now let us shift," she states that in nepantla "[f]ear keeps you exiled between repulsion and propulsion, mourning the loss, obsessed with retrieving a lost homeland that may never have existed" (549). Here is one of the arrebatos: she loves her family, but she did not stay en el valle with them; she knows how many skins her serpents have shed for her to be in the place where the " 'mundane' and the 'numinous' converge" (549). But the Tejano homeland does find its detailed expression, as testimony, as coraje, as amor, as sacred earth, in her early poems. In "Nopalitos," she says, "I keep leaving and when I am home / they remember that no one but me had ever left" (*Borderlands* 135). When she visits her familia she listens "to the grillos more intently / than . . . their regaños" (135), and she feels the earth, the "musty smell of dust" and dusk, the orange blossoms, jasmine, and rose; she knows how the palo blanco will cast its shadow on the ground, how the dog will lay about with his tongue hanging, and how the gallo will mount the hen. She writes about the smell of menudo and the promise of nopales in chile colorado, and through this portrait, she reflects on the piercing self-sacrifice, agonizing discipline, yet luscious price of creativity in her writer's life. Todo viene con dolor y sufrimiento, pero todo viene también con profundo amor, amor sagrado, erótico, y sensual.

As Gloria explains in "now let us shift," she "string[s] together a bridge of words" with the help of the spirits of the earth and the spirits of the dead. Turtle Woman that she is, she brings herself back inside to her own center, to (re)create "a bridge home to [her] self" and the ofrendas she gives to the world (540). The poems in "Un Agitado Viento" recount and release the pain of the outrageous inequities of campesino life—how the "green flutter" (*Borderlands* 124), the blood money controls lives; how dispossession, rape, murder, terror, destruction become all too ordinary; and how backs become bent, eyes haunted, and life extinguished so casually. Yet the earth, like Gloria, is witness; she "shudders" at the violence (155) and remembers those who have suffered from caring for her; she roots them into herself to guard their stories passionately. In "Matriz Sin Tumba o 'el baño de la basura ajena,' " the graphically painful poem that closes the second section ("La Pérdida"), there are two references to el agitado viento (158–60). Deep in her anguished earth/heart/body womb something explodes, and the agitado viento is there to push around the pieces. Ehecatl, and Tlazolteotl, are present to make her work through the pain.

> Eagle eyes, my mother calls me. Looking, always looking . . . (*Borderlands* 50)

The motif of feathers/plumas occurs throughout Gloria's work. Like Lorna Dee Cervantes, like many of us, Gloria es un ser emplumada.[9] Woman with quetzal feathers, woman with pen. Her references to plumas and feathers take us once more back to Quetzalcoatl, and to herself, como serpiente emplumada. These references are a call to consciousness and the creative spirit, at the same time an auto-referencia to herself as writer, shape-changer, and shaman. She describes *Borderlands* as "a rebellious, willful entity, a precocious girl-child forced to grow up too quickly, rough, unyielding, with pieces of feather sticking out here and there, fur, twigs, clay" (88–89). She says, "From the fingers, my feathers, black and red ink drips across the page" (93). She demands protection and mercy from her musa bruja because the demonios "me roban la pluma me roban el sueño" (72). Discussing the Shadow-Beast, Gloria asks, "How does one put feathers on this particular serpent? But a few of us have been lucky—on the face of the Shadow-Beast we have seen not lust but tenderness; on its face we have uncovered the lie" (42). The serpent pierced by the luminous arrow of consciousness, la serpiente emplumada, the Shadow-Beast pierced and "enfeathered," channels out of Gloria's fingers/feathers, writing, revealing, performing, healing, belying the lie(s).

Plumas. Pájaros. El espíritu. The spirit imagery extends to birds as well, as in "A Sea of Cabbages (for those who have [always] worked in the fields)," (*Borderlands* 138–41),[10] where the señor campesino's eyes are "unquiet birds" searching for "that white dove" of hope until "the sound of feathers [surges] up his throat" as the unwilling earth hits him in the face (*Borderlands* 154–55). In "sus plumas el viento (for my mother, Amalia)," Gloria honors her mother and records the life-draining work she did in the fields, calling her hurt hands "wounded birds" cut by the obsidian wind into "tassels of blood from the hummingbirds." The poem reveals the coraje about Pepita, another campesina, letting the boss have her, the other men spitting at her, although they want her, too. "Stupid Pepita," porque se deja. The two women's lives are entwined, and one makes it hard for the other to keep her head high. Her mother wishes for the wind to give her its wings, the wings she hears "humming songs in her head." When the poet says, "the hummingbird shadow / becomes the navel of the Earth," it refers to her mother heart of the earth.

In "En el nombre de todas las madres que han perdido sus hijos en la guerra" (*Borderlands* 182–85). Gloria writes of a mother's angustia y dolor of losing a child, an infant, to war. In this gripping and passionate poem, she writes in the name of all the mothers who have lost children in war, and speaks in agonized outrage to the MotherGod, saying she wants to kill all men who make war and cause innocent sons and daughters to be sacrificed. The mother recounts in horrendous detail the attack on the village, and the sudden murder of the child in her arms—her only surviving child, two sons and a daughter already killed in the war. She says her baby, on being shot, tightens his grip on her thumb, as she sees blood shoot out from him like water thrown out of a pail. The death is incomprehensible to her: "El día amanece, / vivo a ver otro amanecer / que extraño" ["The day breaks, / I live to see another dawn / how strange"].

The reference to feathers reappears in this poem: "Alma de mijo, venga aquí a mis piernas. / Plumita ensangrada, /devuelva de los cinco destinos" ["Soul of my son, come here to my legs / little feather full of blood / come back from the five directions"]. In this poem, which likely references Central America, the poet asks, "Porque los güeros se burlan de la gente?" and immediately she connects with south Texas, with those güeros who perpetuate their own brand of violence en el valle. She knows the kind of heartlessness, this kind of cold blood, and so when she learns of the violence far away, she travels across space and time to record her condemnation: "De lugares remotos viene / este ataque contra el pueblo," and yet not so far away, for her. The mother in this poem, like the mothers in south Texas, like the mothers in all the wars, cry out "Aquí me tiro en la tierra / soy sólo un gemido." Y por eso el Viento es Agitado. Por eso la Tierra se Agoniza.

Agitado Viento. Ehécatl. The NightWind. Gloria was a creature of the night, favorecía a la noche porque en la noche se encontraba, se enfrentaba, se retaba, se hacía pedazos y se reunía. Her own ecstasy was in the writing, her terquedad, her diving into her self, "taking the plunge" (*Borderlands* 163), daring the "[c]agado abismo" (*Borderlands* 192) to shake her up, as she says in poems found in section IV, "Cihuatlyotl, Woman Alone." The ecstasy: she was "fully formed carved / by the hands of the ancients." The agony: she is "drenched with / the stench of today's headlines." The reconciliación: Like the Creative Spirit Herself/Himself, Moyocoyatzin, "my own / hands whittle the final work me" (*Borderlands* 195). In "now let us shift" she describes a preliminary journey she took to the world of spirit, floating, "cool and light as a feather," as she sees herself "spread-eagle on the bed" (555). Here again is her own, and the earth's, ecstasy: "*you're not contained by your skin*—you exist outside your body, and outside your dreambody as well" (555, her italics). There is a constant, radiant pulsation that marks the spirit of the earth, a powerful energy that is wise, amorous, sensual, sentient, just. So, too, con mi hermana, Gloria Anzaldúa, que en la paz y en la gloria descansa, and like the earth, may you always gift us with your light.

Notes

1. I have chosen to refer to Gloria by her first name because of its resonance.
2. For more on this topic, see Laurette Sejourne, *Burning Water.*
3. In *Borderlands,* Gloria has many references to piercing, needles, cactus thorns, knives, as means for sacrifice.
4. The quetzal bird cannot live in captivity, and so represents spirit.
5. I realize Gloria's emphasis on the Coyolxauhqui imperative, but I focus on Quetzalcoatl as a sacred being with dual duality, therefore, female/male, male/female, to see how this perspective further illuminates her work. I also honor Gloria's affirmation that the godwoman in her is "Coatlicue-Cihuacoatl-Tlazolteotl-Tonantzin-Guadalupe" (*Borderlands* 50) and, I would add, Coyolxauhqui.
6. Miguel León-Portilla elaborates the concept of Moyocoyani and Ometéotl Moyocoyatzin in *Aztec Thought and Culture: A Study of the Ancient Nahuatl Mind.*
7. N. Scott Momaday uses the term "living memory" in his essay, "Man Made of Words."
8. I, too, am Tejana, and everywhere I meet other Tejanas/os, we speak of "el valle" (south Texas) as if there were no other valley in the world.
9. Lorna Dee Cervantes' first book of poetry is titled *Emplumada.*
10. The poem's original version in Spanish is dedicated to "la gente que *siempre* ha trabajado en las labores" (emphasis mine).

References

Abu-Lughod, Lila and Catherine A. Lutz. "Introduction: Emotion, Discourse, and the Politics of Everyday Life." *Language and the Politics of Emotion*. Ed. Catherine A. Lutz and Lila Abu-Lughod. Cambridge: Cambridge UP, 1993. 1–23.

Adams, Kate. "Northamerican Silences: History, Identity, and Witness in the Poetry of Gloria Anzaldúa, Cherríe Moraga, and Leslie Marmon Silko." *Listening to Silences: New Essays in Feminist Criticism*. Ed. Elaine Hedges and Shelley Fisher Fishkin. New York: Oxford UP, 1994. 130–45.

Alarcón, Norma. "The Theoretical Subject(s) of *This Bridge Called My Back* and Anglo-American Feminism." *Making Face, Making Soul/Haciendo Caras: Creative and Critical Perspectives by Women of Color*. Ed. Gloria Anzaldúa. San Francisco: Aunt Lute Foundation, 1990. 356–69.

Albrecht, Lisa and Rose M. Brewer, eds. *Bridges of Power. Women's Multicultural Alliances*. Philadelphia: New Society Publishers, 1990.

Alexander, M. Jacqui. "Remembering This Bridge, Remembering Ourselves: Yearning, Memory, and Desire." *this bridge we call home: radical visions for transformation*. Ed. Gloria E. Anzaldúa and AnaLouise Keating. New York: Routledge, 2002. 81–103.

Alexander, M. Jacqui and Chandra Talpade Mohanty, eds. *Feminist Genealogies, Colonial Legacies, Democratic Futures*. New York: Routledge, 1997.

Anzaldúa, Gloria E. "Border Arte: Nepantla, El Lugar de la Frontera." *La Frontera/The Border: Art About the Mexico/United States Border Experience*. Museum of Contemporary Art, San Diego.

———. *Borderlands/La Frontera: The New Mestiza*. 1987. San Francisco: Spinsters/Aunt Lute, 1999.

———. "Bridge, Drawbridge, Sandbar or Island: *Lesbians-of-Color Hacienda Alianzas*." *Bridges of Power: Women's Multicultural Alliances*. Ed. Lisa Albrecht and Rose M. Brewer. Philadelphia: New Society, 1990. 216–31.

———. "En rapport, In Opposition: Cobrando cuentas a las nuestras." *Making Face, Making Soul/Haciendo Caras: Creative and Critical Perspective by Women of Color*. Ed. Gloria Anzaldúa. San Francisco: Aunt Lute Foundation, 1990. 142–48.

———. *Friends from the Other Side/Amigos del Otro Lado*. San Francisco: Children's Book Press, 1993.

Anzaldúa, Gloria E. "Haciendo caras, una entrada: An Introduction." *Making Face, Making Soul/Haciendo Caras: Creative and Critical Perspectives by Women of Color.* Ed. Gloria Anzaldúa. San Francisco: Aunt Lute Foundation, 1990. xv–xxviii.

———. *Interviews/Entrevistas.* Ed. AnaLouise Keating. New York: Routledge, 2000.

———, ed. *Making Face, Making Soul/Haciendo Caras: Creative and Critical Perspectives by Women of Color.* San Francisco: Aunt Lute Foundation, 1990.

———. "Metaphors in the Tradition of the Shaman." *Conversant Essays: Contemporary Poets on Poetry.* Ed. James McCorkle. Detroit: Wayne State UP, 1990. 99–100.

———. "now let us shift . . . the path of conocimiento . . . inner work, public acts." *this bridge we call home: radical visions for transformation.* Ed. Gloria E. Anzaldúa and AnaLouise Keating. New York: Routledge, 2002. 540–78.

———. "People Should Not Die in June in South Texas." *Growing Up Latino: Reflections on Life in the United States.* Ed. Harold Augenbraum and Ilan Stavans. Houghton Mifflin, New York. 1993. 280–87.

———. "La Prieta." *This Bridge Called My Back: Writings by Radical Women of Color.* 1981. Ed. Cherríe Moraga and Gloria Anzaldúa. New York: Kitchen Table: Women of Color Press, 1983. 198–209.

———. *Prietita and the Ghost Woman/Prietita y La Llorona.* San Francisco: Children's Book Press, 1995.

———. "Putting Coyolxauhqui Together: A Creative Process." *How We Work.* Ed. Marla Morris et al. New York: Peter Lang, 2000.

———. "She Ate Horses." *Lesbian Philosophies and Cultures.* Ed. Jeffner Allen. New York: State U of New York P, 1990. 371–88.

———. "Speaking in Tongues: A Letter to Third World Women Writers." *This Bridge Called My Back: Writings by Radical Women of Color.* 1981. Ed. Cherríe Allen. Moraga and Gloria Anzaldúa. New York: Kitchen Table: Women of Color Press, 1983. 165–74.

———. Syllabus for "Conocimiento . . . inner work, public acts," class taught at Florida Atlantic University, Spring, 2001.

———. "To(o) Queer the Writer—*Loca, escritora y chicana.*" *Inversions: Writing by Dykes, Queers, and Lesbians.* Ed. Besty Warland. Vancouver: Press Gang, 1991. 249–64.

———. "(Un)natural bridges, (Un)safe spaces." *this bridge we call home: radical visions for transformation.* Ed. Gloria E. Anzaldúa and AnaLouise Keating. New York: Routledge, 2002. 1–5.

Anzaldúa, Gloria E. and AnaLouise Keating, eds. *this bridge we call home: radical visions for transformation.* New York: Routledge, 2002.

Aurobindo, Sri. *The Future Evolution of Man.* Pondicherry, India: Sri Aurobindo Ashram, 1963.

———. *Letters on Yoga I.* Pondicherry, India: Sri Aurobindo Ashram, 1988.

———. *Powers Within.* Ojai, CA: Institute of Integral Psychology, 1998.

———. "The Reason as Governor of Life." *Birth Centenary Library* 15 (1971).

Ball, Arnetha F. "Empowering Pedagogies that Enhance the Learning of Multicultural Students." *Teachers College Record* 102:6 (December 2000): 1006–34.

Bar On, Bat-Ami. "Marginality and Epistemic Privilege." *Feminist Epistemologies.* Eds. Linda Alcoff and Elizabeth Potter. New York: Routledge, 1993. 83–100.

Barabási, Albert-Lázló. *Linked: The New Science of Networks.* Cambridge, MA: Perseus, 2002.

Barthes, Roland. *A Lover's Discourse: Fragments.* Trans. Richard Howard. New York: Hill and Wang, 1978.

———. *The Pleasure of the Text.* Trans. Richard Miller. New York: Hill and Wang, 1975.

———. "Roland Barthes versus Received Ideas." *The Grain of the Voice: Interviews 1962–1980.* Trans. Linda Coverdale. New York, Hill and Wang, 1985.

Belenky, Mary F., Blythe M. Clinchy, Nancy R. Goldberger, and Jill M. Tarule. *Women's Ways of Knowing: The Development of Self, Voice, and Mind.* New York: Basic Books, 1986.

Benson, Bonnie and Jane Day, eds. *Anthology 2001: Conocimiento . . . inner work, public acts.* Unpublished collection of Florida Atlantic University student writings, 2001.

Berlin, James A. *Rhetorics, Poetics, and Cultures: Refiguring College English Studies.* Urbana, IL: NCTE, 1996.

Bernard, Ian. "Gloria Anzaldúa's Queer Mestisaje." *MELUS* 22:1 (Spring 1997): 35–53.

Bizzell, Patricia. *Academic Discourse and Critical Consciousness.* Pittsburgh: Pittsburgh UP, 1992.

Bohm, David. *Wholeness and the Implicate Order.* 1980. New York: Routledge, 1996.

Brennan, Teresa. *History after Lacan.* New York: Routledge, 1993.

Brereton, John C., ed. *The Origins of Composition Studies in the American College, 1875–1925: A Documentary History.* Pittsburgh: U of Pittsburgh P, 1995.

Butler, Judith. 1990. *Gender Trouble: Feminism and the Subversion of Identity.* New York: Routledge, 1999.

Butler, Octavia. *Parable of the Sower.* New York: Seven Stories Press, 1994.

Cajete, Gregory. *Native Science: Natural Laws of Interdependence.* Santa Fe: Clear Light Publishers, 2000.

Capra, Fritjof. *The Tao of Physics: An Exploration of the Parallels between Modern Physics and Eastern Mysticism.* New York: Bantam, 1977.

———. *The Turning Point.* New York: Bantam Books, 1982.

Caputi, Jane. "On Psychic Activism: Feminist Mythmaking." *A Feminist Companion to International Mythology.* Ed. C. Larrington. London: Pandora Press, 1992. 425–40.

Carse, J. P. "Shapeshifting." *The Encyclopedia of Religion.* Ed. M. Eliade. New York: Macmillan, 1986. 225–29.

Cassirer, Ernst. *Language and Myth,* New York: Dover, 1953.

Castillo, Ana. *Massacre of the Dreamers: Essays on Xicanisma.* Albuquerque: U of New Mexico P, 1994.

Cervantes, Lorna Dee. *Emplumada.* Pittsburgh: U of Pittsburgh P, 1981.

Cervenak, Sarah J., Karina L. Cespedes, Caridad Souza, and Andrea Straub. "Imagining Differently: The Politics of Listening in a Feminist Classroom." *this bridge we call home: radical visions for transformation.* Ed. Gloria E. Anzaldúa and AnaLouise Keating. New York: Routledge, 2002. 341–56.

Chalmers, D. *Towards a Theory of Consciousness.* Cambridge, MA: MIT, 1995.

Chaudhuri, Nirad C. *Hinduism: A Religion to Live By.* Delhi: Oxford UP, 1996.

Cheney, Jim and Lee Hester. "Truth and Native American epistemology." *Social Epistemology* 15:4 (2001): 349–34.

Chopra, Deepak. *How to Know God: The Soul's Journey into the Mystery of Mysteries.* New York: Random, 2000.

————. *Quantum Healing: Exploring the Frontiers of Mind-Body Medicine,* New York: Bantam, 1989.

Couser, G. Thomas. "Signifying Bodies: Life Writing and Disability Studies." *Disability Studies: Enabling the Humanities.* Ed. Sharon L. Snyder, Brenda Jo Brueggemann, and Rosemarie Garland Thomson. MLA: New York, 2002. 109–117.

Crowley, Sharon. *Composition in the University: Historical and Polemical Essays.* Pittsburgh: U of Pittsburgh P, 1998.

Daly, Mary. *Pure Lust: Elemental Feminist Philosophy.* Boston: Beacon Press, 1984.

Daly, Mary *Quintessence . . . Realizing the Archaic Future: A Radical Elemental Feminist Manifesto.* Boston: Beacon Press, 1998.

Dayananda, S. *Introduction to Vedanta,* New Delhi: Vision Books, 1993.

Dimmitt, Cornelia and J. A. B. van Buitenen, eds. *Classical Hindu Mythology*: Philadelphia: Temple UP, 1978.

Doty, Mark. "Elizabeth Bishop, *Croton,* watercolor, 9" × 5 ." *An Island Sheaf.* New York: Dim Gray Bar, 1998.

Dowd, Maureen. "Autumn of Fears." *New York Times,* Sept. 23, 2001. p. 17.

Ducornet, Rikki. *The Monstrous and the Marvelous.* San Francisco: City Lights, 1999.

Elbow, Peter. "The Cultures of Literature and Composition: What Could Each Learn from the Other?" *College English* 64: 5 (2002): 533–46.

Erikson, Eric. *Child and Society.* New York: W.W. Norton, 1963.

Fernandes, Leela. *Transforming Feminist Practice: Non-Violence, Social Justice and the Possibilities of a Spiritualized Feminism.* San Francisco: Aunt Lute Books, 2003.

Flax, Jane. *Disputed Subjects: Essays on Psychoanalysis, Politics, and Philosophy.* New York: Routledge, 1993.

Freire, Paulo. *Pedagogy of the Oppressed.* New York: Continuum, 1970.

French, Sally. *On Equal Terms: Working with Disabled People.* Butterworth-Heinemann: Oxford, 1994.

Fusco, Coco. *English Is Broken Here: Notes on Cultural Fusion in the Americas.* New York: The New Press, 1995. 25–36.

Garber, Linda. *Identity Poetics: Race, Class, and the Lesbian-Feminist Roots of Queer Theory* New York: Columbia UP, 2001.

Gates, Henry Louis. *The Signifying Monkey: A Theory of African-American Literary Criticism.* New York: Oxford UP, 1988.

Gilligan, Carol. *In a Different Voice: Psychological Theory and Women's Development.* Cambridge: Harvard UP, 1982.

Goswami, Amit. *The Self-Aware Universe: How Consciousness Creates the Material World.* Los Angeles: Tarcher, 1995.

———. *The Visionary Window: A Quantum Physicist's Guide to Enlightenment.* Wheaton, IL: Quest Books, 2000.

Grahn, Judy. *A Woman Is Talking to Death.* Oakland, CA: Women's Press Collective, 1974.

Hall, Stuart. "Ethnicity: Identity and Difference." *Border Texts: Cultural Readings for Contemporary Writers.* Ed. Randall Bass. New York: Houghton Mifflin Company, 1999. 295–306.

———. "Racist Ideologies and the Media." *Media Studies.* 2nd ed. Eds. Paul Marris and Sue Thornham. Washington Square, NY: New York UP, 2000. 271–82.

Haraway, Donna. *Simians, Cyborgs, and Women.* New York: Routledge, 1991.

Harding, Sandra. "Gendered Ways of Knowing and the 'Epistemological Crisis' of the West." *Knowledge, Difference, and Power: Essays Inspired by Women's Ways of Knowing.* Eds. Nancy Goldberger et al. New York: Basic Books, 1996.

Harjo, Joy. *The Spiral of Memory: Interviews.* Ed. Laura Coltelli. Ann Arbor: U of Michigan P, 1996.

Hawken, Paul, James Ogilvy, and Peter Schwartz. *Seven Tomorrows.* New York: Bantam, 1982.

Heidegger, Martin. *Being and Time.* Trans. John Macquarrie and Edward Robinson. New York: Harper & Row, 1962.

hooks, bell. *Talking Back: Thinking Feminist, Thinking Black.* Boston: South End, 1994. 98–104.

———. *Yearning: Race, Gender, and Cultural Politics.* Boston: South End, 1990.

Horner, Winifred Bryan. "Rhetoric in the Liberal Arts: Nineteenth-Century Scottish Universities." *The Rhetorical Tradition and Modern Writing.* Ed. James J. Murphy. New York: MLA, 1982. 85–94.

Hutcheon, Linda. *The Politics of Postmodernism.* New York: Routledge, 1989.

Ikas, Karin. "An Interview with Gloria Anzaldúa." *Borderlands/La Frontera: The New Mestiza.* 2nd edn. San Francisco: Aunt Lute, 1999. 227–46.

Irigaray, Luce. "This Sex Which is Not One." *New French Feminisms: An Anthology.* Ed. Elaine Marks and Isabelle de Courtivron. U of Massachusetts P, 1990. 99–106.

Jackson, Shannon. "White Privilege and Pedagogy: Nadine Gordimer in Performance." *Theatre Topics* 7:2 (1997): 117–38.

Jordan, Judith V. et al. *Women's Growth in Connection: Writings from the Stone Center.* New York: The Guildford Press,1991.

Kaup, Monika. "Crossing Borders: An Aesthetic Practice in the Writings by Gloria Anzaldúa." *Cultural Difference and the Literary Text: Pluralism and the Limits of Authenticity in North American Literatures.* Eds. Winfried Siemerling and Katrin Schwenk. Iowa City: U of Iowa P, 1996. 100–11.

Keating, AnaLouise. "Forging El Mundo Zurdo: Changing Ourselves, Changing the World." *this bridge we call home: radical visions for transformation.* Ed. Gloria E. Anzaldúa and AnaLouise Keating. New York: Routledge, 2002. 518–30.

———. " 'Making New Connections': Transformational Multiculturalism in the Classroom." *Pedagogy* 4:1 (2004): 93–117.

Keating, AnaLouise. "Message from G. Anzaldúa concerning D.S. & More." From author to members of WS 5013 eGroup. Oct. 15, 2003.

———. "Myth Smashers, Myth Makers: (Re) Visionary Techniques in the Works of Paula Gunn Allen, Gloria Anzaldúa, and Audre Lorde. *Critical Essays: Gays and Lesbian Writers of Color*. Ed. Emmanuel S. Nelson. New York: Haworth Press, 1993. 73–95.

———. "Risking the Personal." *Interviews/Entrevistas*. Ed. Gloria E. Anzaldúa. New York: Routledge, 2000. 1–15.

———. *Women Reading Women Writing: Self-Invention in Paula Gunn Allen, Gloria Anzaldúa and Audre Lorde*. Philadelphia: Temple UP, 1996.

———. "Writing, Politics, and las Lesberadas: *Platicando con* Gloria Anzaldúa." 14:1 *Frontiers* (1993): 105–30.

Kegan, Robert. *In over Our Heads: The Mental Demands of Modern Life*. Cambridge: Harvard UP, 1994.

Klepfisz, Irena. *Periods of Stress*. Brooklyn, New York: Out & Out Books, 1975.

Koethe, John. "Contrary Impulses: The Tension between Poetry and Theory." *Critical Inquiry* 18:1 (Autumn 1991): 64–75.

Kohlberg, Lawrence. *Collected Papers on Moral Development and Moral Education*. Cambridge: Moral Education and Research Foundation, 1973.

Kovel, Joel. *White Racism: A Psychohistory*. 1970. London: Free Association Books, 1988.

Kyburz, Bonnie Lenore. "Meaning Finds a Way: Chaos (Theory) and Composition." *College English* 66:5 (2004): 503–23.

Lashgari, Deirdre. "To Speak the Unspeakable: Implications of Gender, 'Race,' Class, and Culture." *Violence, Silence, and Anger: Women's Writing as Transgression*. Ed. Deirdre Lashgari. Charlottesville: University of Virginia P, 1995. 1–21.

Lather, Patti. *Getting Smart: Feminist Research and Pedagogy With/In the Postmodern*. New York: Routledge, 1991.

Leonard, George B. *The Transformation*. Los Angeles: Tarcher, 1972.

León-Portilla, Miguel. *Aztec Thought and Culture: A Study of the Ancient Nahuatl Mind*. Norman: U of Oklahoma P, 1963.

Lerner, Gerda. *Why History Matters: Life and Thought*. New York: Oxford, 1997.

Levi, J. H., ed. *A Muriel Rukeyser Reader*. New York: W. W. Norton, 1994.

Lionnet, Françoise. *Autobiographical Voices: Race, Gender, Self-Portraiture*. Ithaca: Cornell UP, 1989.

Lorde, Audre. *Sister Outsider: Essays and Speeches*. Freedom, CA: Crossing Press, 1984.

———. "Song for a Thin Sister." *Chosen Poems: Old and New*. New York: Norton, 1982. 78.

Love, Patrick G., and Victoria L. Guthrie. "Kegan's Orders of Consciousness." *New Directions for Student Services* 88 (1999): 65–75.

Lu, Min-Zhan. "Professing Multiculturalism: the Politics of Style in the Contact Zone." *CCC* 45:4 (1994): 442–58.

Lugones, María. "Hablando cara a cara/Speaking Face to Face: An Exploration of Ethnocentric Racism." *Making Face, Making Soul/Haciendo Caras: Creative and Critical Perspectives by Women of Color*. Ed. Gloria Anzaldúa. San Francisco: Aunt Lute Foundation, 1990. 46–54.

Lugones, María. *Pilgrimages/Peregrinajes: Theorizing Coalition against Multiple Oppression*. Rowman and Littlefield, 2003.

———. "Playfulness, 'World'-Traveling, and Loving Perception." *Women, Knowledge and Reality: Explorations of Feminist Philosophy*. Ed. Ann Garry and Marilyn Pearsall. Boston: Unwin Hyman, 1989.

Lunsford, Andrea and Robert Connors. *The New St. Martin's Handbook*. Boston and New York: Bedford/St. Martin's, 1999.

Macy, Joanna. *Mutual Causality in Buddhism and General Systems Theory: The Dharma of Natural Systems*. Albany: State U of New York P, 1991.

Martí, José. "Musa Traviesa." *Poesia Completa*. Madrid: Alianza Editorial, 1995. 63–69.

Martinez, Theresa A. "The Double-Consciousness of DuBois and the 'Mestiza Consciousness' of Anzaldúa." *Race, Gender, & Class* 9 (2002): 198–212.

Marx, Gary T. "The Ironies of Social Control." *Social Problems* February (1981): 231–46.

Maslow, Abraham. *The Farther Reaches of the Human Mind*. New York: Viking, 1971.

———. *Towards A Psychology of Being*. New York: Van Nostrand Reinhold, 1983.

Maso, Carole. *Break Every Rule: Essays on Language, Longing, and Moments of Desire*. Washington, DC: Counterpoint, 2000.

Menchú, Rigoberta. *Yo Soy Rigoberta Menchú, Y Así Me Nació La Consciencia*. Barcelona: Editorial Argos Vergara, 1983.

Miller, Patricia H. "The Development of Interconnected Thinking." *Toward a Feminist Developmental Psychology*. Ed. Patricia, H. Miller and Ellin Kofsky Scholnick. New York: Routledge, 2000. 45–59.

Miller, Patricia H., and Ellin Kofsky Scholnick, eds. *Toward a Feminist Developmental Psychology*. New York: Routledge, 2000.

Miller, Thomas P. *The Formation of College English: Rhetoric and Belles Lettres in the British Cultural Provinces*. Pittsburgh: U of Pittsburgh P, 1997.

Miller, Toby. *The Well-Tempered Self: Citizenship, Culture, and the Postmodern Subject*. Baltimore, MD: Johns Hopkins UP, 1993.

Mohanty, Chandra Talpade and Biddy Martin. "Feminist Politics: What's Home Got to Do With It?" *Femininity Played Straight: The Significance of Being a Lesbian*. New York: Routledge, 1996. 163–84.

Momaday, M. Scott. *The Man Made of Words: Essays, Stories, Passages*. New York: St. Martin's Griffin, 1998.

Mosha, R. Sambuli. "The Inseparable Link between Intellectual and Spiritual Formation in Indigenous Knowledge and Education: A Case Study in Tanzania." *What Is Indigenous Knowledge? Voices from the Academy*. Ed. Ladislaus M. Semali and Joe L. Kincheloe. New York/London: Farmer, 1999. 209–25.

Moya, Paula and Michael Hames-Garcia, eds. *Reclaiming Identity: Realist Theory and the Predicament of Postmodernism*. Berkeley: U of California, 2000.

Muñoz, José Esteban. *Disidentifications: Queers of Color and the Performance of Politics*. Minneapolis: U of Minnesota P, 1999.

Murrell, Annette. "Don't Take This the Wrong Way . . . You're Not a Token . . . Be Yourself . . . We Need a Black Perspective." Paper presented at CCCC Conference 2001, Denver, Colorado, March 14, 2001.

Needleman, Jacob. *A Sense of the Cosmos: The Encounter Between Modern Science and Ancient Truth*. New York: Doubleday, 1975.

Nicholson, Linda. *The Play of Reason: From the Modern to the Postmodern.* Ithaca, NY: Cornell UP, 1999.

Ogilvy, James. *Many Dimensional Man.* New York: Harper, 1979.

Oliver, Kelly. *Witnessing: Beyond Recognition.* Minneapolis: U of Minnesota P, 2001.

Organ, Troy Wilson. *The Hindu Quest for the Perfection of Man.* Eugene, OR: Wipf and Stock Publishers, 1998.

Ortega, Mariana. " 'New Mestizas,' 'World'-Travelers, and 'Dasein': Phenomenology and the Multi-Voiced, Multi-Cultural Self." *Hypatia* 16:3 (2001): 1–29.

Pagels, Elaine. *Adam, Eve, and the Serpent.* New York: Vintage Books, 1988.

Palmer, Parker. "Community, Conflict, and Ways of Knowing." *Change* Sept.–Oct. (1987): 20–27.

Parker, Pat. *Womanslaughter.* Oakland, CA: Diana Press, 1978.

Parker, William Riley. "Where do English Departments come From?" *The Writing Teacher's Sourcebook.* Ed. Gary Tate and Edward P. J. Corbett. New York: Oxford UP, 1988.

Partridge, E. *A Dictionary of Slang and Unconventional English.* London: Routledge and Kegan Paul, 1961.

Peavey, Fran. *Heart Politics Revisited.* Australia: Pluto Press, 2000.

Perry, Donna. *Backtalk: Women Writers Speak Out.* New Brunswick: Rutgers UP, 1995.

Piaget, Jean. *The Moral Judgment of the Child.* London: Kegan Paul, 1932.

Pinkvoss, Joan. Personal communication. September 1999.

Radhakrishnan, Sarvepalli. *East and West.* London: George Allen and Unwin, 1955.

Rainer, Tristine. *Your Life As Story: Writing the New Autobiography.* New York: Putnam, 1997.

Readings, Bill. *The University in Ruins.* Cambridge: Harvard UP, 1996.

Reuman, Ann. "Coming into Play: An Interview with Gloria Anzaldúa." *MELUS* 25.2 (2000): 3–45.

Rich, Adrienne. "Transcendental Etude." *The Dream of a Common Language.* New York: Norton, 1978. 72–77.

Rothenberg, J., ed. *Shaking the Pumpkin: Traditional Poetry of the Indian North Americas.* Albuquerque: U of New Mexico P, 1986.

Rushin, Donna Kate. "The Bridge Poem." *This Bridge Called My Back: Writings by Radical Women of Color.* 1981. Ed. Cherríe Moraga and Gloria Anzaldúa. New York: Kitchen Table: Women of Color Press, 1983. xxi.

Sáenz, Benjamin Alire. "In the Borderlands of Chicano Identity, There Are Only Fragments." *Border Theory: The Limits of Cultural Politics.* Ed. Scott Michaelsen and David E. Johnson. Minneapolis: U of Minnesota P, 1997. 68–96.

Saldívar-Hull, Sonia. *Feminism on the Border: Chicana Gender Politics and Literature.* Berkeley: U of California P, 2000.

———. "Introduction." *Borderlands/La Frontera: The New Mestiza.* Gloria E. Anzaldúa. San Francisco: Spinsters/Aunt Lute, 1999. 1–18.

Saldívar, José David. *Border Matters: Remapping American Cultural Studies.* Berkeley, CA: U of California P, 1997.

Sandoval, Chela. "AfterBridge: Technologies of Crossing." *this bridge we call home: radical visions for transformation.* Ed. Gloria E. Anzaldúa and AnaLouise Keating. New York: Routledge, 2002. 21–26.

———. *Methodology of the Oppressed.* Minneapolis: U of Minnesota P, 2000.

Schroeder, Christopher, Helen Fox, and Patricia Bizzell, eds. *Alt Dis: Alternative Discourses and the Academy.* Portsmouth, NH: Boynton, 2002.

Seccombe, Karen. *"So You Think I Drive a Cadillac?": Welfare Recipients' Perspectives on the System and Its Reform.* Boston: Allyn & Bacon, 1999.

Sedgwick, Eve Kosofsky. *Tendencies.* Durham: Duke UP, 1993.

Sejourne, Laurette. *Burning Water: Thought and Religion in Ancient Mexico.* New York: Random, 1976.

Semali, Ladislaus M. and Joe L. Kincheloe. "Introduction: What is Indigenous Knowledge and Why Should We Study It?" *What Is Indigenous Knowledge? Voices from the Academy.* Ed. Ladislaus M. Semali and Joe L. Kincheloe. New York/ London: Farmer, 1999. 3–57.

Sheldrake, Rupert. *The Presence of the Past: Morphic Resonance and the Habits of Nature.* Rochester, Vermont: Part Street Press, 1995.

Talbot, Michael. *The Holographic Universe.* New York: Harper Perennial, 1991.

———. *Mysticism and the New Physics.* London: Penguin, 1993.

"The 15th Anniversary Retrospective." *Sinister Wisdom* 43/44 (Summer 1991).

Thomson, Rosemarie Garland. "Integrating Disability, Transforming Feminist Theory." *NWSA Journal* 14:3 (2002): 1–32.

Torres, Edén E. *Chicana Without Apology: The New Chicana Cultural Studies.* New York: Routledge, 2003.

Trujillo, Carla, ed. *Living Chicana Theory.* Berkeley, CA: Third Woman Press, 1998.

Tsui, Kitty. *The Words of a Woman Who Breathes Fire.* San Francisco: Spinsters, Ink, 1983.

Walker, Barbara. *The Woman's Encyclopedia of Myths and Secrets.* San Francisco: HarperSanFrancisco, 1983.

Watts, Duncan J. *Six Degrees: The Science of a Connected Age.* New York: Norton, 2003.

Wendell, Susan. *The Rejected Body: Feminist Philosophical Reflections on Disability.* New York: Routledge, 1996.

West, Genevieve. "It Takes Time": The Generative Potential of Transgressive Teaching. *Radical Teacher* 58 (2000): 21–5.

West, Thomas R. *Signs of Struggle: The Rhetorical Politics of Cultural Difference.* Albany: State U of New York P, 2002.

Widman, Stepanie M. with Adrienne D. Davis. "Making Systems of Privilege Visible." *White Privilege: Essential Readings on the Other Side of Racism.* Ed. Paula S. Rothenberg. New York: Worth, 2002. 89–95.

Wilber, Ken. *Quantum Questions,* Boston: Shambala, 2000.

Wilkerson, Abby. "Disability, Sex Radicalism, and Political Agency." *NWSA Journal* 14:3 (2002): 33–57.

Williams, James D. "Rhetoric and the Triumph of Liberal Democracy." *Visions and Revisions: Continuity and Change in Rhetoric and Composition.* Ed. James D. Williams. Carbondale, Southern Illinois UP, 2002. 131–61.

Williams, Patricia J. *The Alchemy of Race and Rights: Diary of a Law Professor.* Cambridge: Harvard UP, 1991.

Wolf, Fred Alan. *Mind Into Matter: A New Alchemy of Science and Spirit.* Portsmouth, NH: Moment Point Press, 2001.

Woo, Merle. *Yellow Woman Speaks.* Seattle: Radical Women Publications, 1986.
Wright, Elizabethada A. and S. Michael Halloran. "From Rhetoric to Composition: The Teaching of Writing in America to 1900." *A Short History of Writing Instruction.* 2nd ed. Ed. James J. Murphy. Mahwah, NJ: Hermagoras P, 2001.
Yarbro-Bejarano, Yvonne. "Gloria Anzaldúa' *Borderlands/La Frontera:* Cultural Studies, 'Difference,' and the Non-Unitary Subject." *Cultural Critique* (Fall 1994): 5–28.
———. "The Lesbian Body in Latina Cultural Production." *Entiendes? Queer Readings, Hispanic Writings.* Ed. Emilie L. Bergmann and Paul Julian Smith. Durham: Duke UP, 1995. 181–97.

List of Contributors

Beth Berila is the interim director of the Women's Studies Program at St. Cloud State University, where she teaches courses in feminist, queer, and critical race theory, cultural studies, and social justice issues. She is the author of "Toxic Bodies? ACT UP's Disruption of the Heteronormative Landscape of the Nation," which appeared in *New Perspectives on Environmental Justice: Gender, Sexuality, and Activism* (Rutgers University Press, 2004). Her work focuses on gender studies, cultural activism, and community-based arts as a medium of social justice work.

Mary Loving Blanchard has published poetry and short fiction under the pseudonym *nia akimbo*. Currently she is working on a collection of poetry titled *making art, making love*. Mary received her Ph.D. in the School of Arts and Humanities at the University of Texas at Dallas; she is an assistant professor of English at New Jersey City University, where she teaches literature and composition courses.

Mark W. Bundy lives in Southern California where he is completing work on a Ph.D. in English as a Chancellor's Distinguished Fellow at the University of California, Riverside with emphases in Lesbian and Gay studies, the Gothic genre, and Contemporary American Poetry. Most recently, he has published an article in *Reading Sex and the City*, and his writing will be featured in a book of critical pieces on HBO's highly acclaimed show *Six Feet Under*.

Jane Caputi is professor of women's studies at Florida Atlantic University. She is the author of *The Age of Sex Crime* (1987, winner of the Emily Toth Award given by the Popular and American Culture Association) and *Gossips, Gorgons, and Crones: The Fates of the Earth* (1993). She also collaborated with Mary Daly on *Websters' First New Intergalactic Wickedary of the English Language*. Her most recent book is *Goddesses and Monsters: Women, Myth, Power and Popular Culture* (University of Wisconsin/Popular Press, 2004).

Amanda Espinosa-Aguilar is an assistant professor of English at Washington State University where she teaches rhetorical theory, composition, and ethnic American literature. She has presented papers at numerous national conferences. Her publications include "Linking Assignment Design to Paper Grading in Classes About Diversity," in *Contested Terrain* (2001) and "Analyzing the Rhetoric of the English Only Movement," in *Language Ideologies: Critical Perspectives on the Official English Movement* (2001). In 1999, Professor Espinosa-Aguilar was elected to the Executive Committee of the Conference on College Composition and Communication, and served as the co-chair of the Scholars for the Dream Award Committee in 2002.

Linda Garber is associate professor in the Department of English and the Program for the Study of Women and Gender at Santa Clara University. She is the author of *Identity Poetics: Race, Class, and the Lesbian-Feminist Roots of Queer Theory* (Columbia University Press, 2001), editor of *Tilting the Tower: Lesbians / Teaching / Queer Subjects* (Routledge 1994), and author of *Lesbian Sources: A Bibliography of Periodical Articles, 1970–1990* (Garland 1993).

Inés Hernández-Ávila, Nimipu (Nez Perce) and Chicana/Tejana/Mexican Indian, is a poet, cultural worker, and professor of Native American Studies at the University of California, Davis. Her creative and scholarly work bridges the Native American and Chicana/Chicano communities. She was chair of the Department of Native American Studies and is current Director of the Chicana/Latina Research Center at UC, Davis.

Simona J. Hill is an associate professor of sociology and codirector of the Honors Program at Susquehanna University in Selinsgrove, PA, and a former director of the Pickett Community School in Philadelphia, PA. In 2003, she received the university award for teaching excellence. She earned her BA, MA, and Ph.D. from the University of Pennsylvania. When she graduated with the doctorate in sociology in 1989 she was the first African-American woman since 1937 to do so. She has published essays in a number of anthologies and journals. Committed to higher education that enhances a person's abilities to think critically and act responsibly toward future generations, her academic mission is one of teaching activism, community leadership, scholarship, and mutual empowerment.

AnaLouise Keating's most recent book is *this bridge we call home: radical visions for transformation*, co-edited with Gloria E. Anzaldúa. AnaLouise is also the author of *Women Reading Women Writing: Self-Invention in Paula Gunn Allen, Gloria Anzaldúa, and Audre Lorde*; editor of Anzaldúa's *Interviews/Entrevistas*; and co-editor, with Renae Bredin, of *Perspectives: Gender Studies*. She has published articles on critical 'race' theory, queer theory, Latina writers, African-American women writers, and pedagogy. An associate professor of women's studies at Texas Woman's University, she teaches courses on U.S. women of colors, feminist epistemologies, feminist theories, and Gloria Anzaldúa.

Irene Lara received her Ph.D. in Ethnic Studies at the University of California, Berkeley. As an assistant professor of women's studies at San Diego State University, she teaches courses in her research areas, including Women's Health and Healing and Latinas in the Américas. Her publications include "Healing Sueños for Academia," *in this bridge we call home: radical visions for transformation*, and the coauthored "Fiera. Guambara, y Karichina! Transgressing the Borders of Community and Academy" in *Chicana/Latina Feminist Pedagogies and Epistemologies of Everyday Life*. She recently received a Ford Postdoctoral Fellowship for Minorities to complete her book *Decolonizing the Sacred: Healing Practices in the U.S.–Mexico Borderlands*.

Amala Levine was born and raised in Germany. She came to the United States as a graduate student, receiving a Master's Degree in English from The University of Texas in 1967 and a Ph.D. in Comparative Literature from UCLA in 1978. She has taught at Southern Methodist University, The University of Alaska, UCLA, and The Graduate Faculty of Political and Social Science at New School University in New York. Currently she is president of The Symposium, a not-for-profit educational institute, edits its journal, *Symposium*, and teaches in New York where she lives.

A fat chicana academic, **Elena Levy-Navarro** is interested in formulating attachments across divides of time and across the divides created by contemporary essentialized identities. In her essay here and in another entitled "Making the Impossible Possible: Imagining Alternative Experiences of Pain," she works to renegotiate her relationship with her body so that she can promote attachments with people like herself who would be made abject by our dominant culture.

María Lugones is an associate professor of Comparative Literature and Philosophy at Binghamton University where she teaches women's studies, ethics, political philosophy, and the philosophy of race and gender. Lugones is the author of *Pilgrimages/Peregrinajes: Theorizing Coalition Against Multiple Oppression*, "Playfulness, 'World'-travelling, and Loving Perception," and other essays on women-of-color philosophy and politics.

Lee Maracle is the current Distinguished Visiting Professor of Canadian Culture at Western Washington University. A member of the Sto:loh Nation, Ms. Maracle is the author of several books, including: *Ravensong* (novel), *Sojourner's & Sundogs* (novel and short stories), *Daughters are Forever* (novel), *Bobbie Lee* (novel), *I Am Woman*, (nonfiction), *Bent Box* (poetry), and has edited several works including the award winning *My Home As I Remember*. Ms. Maracle has published in over thirty scholarly journals, anthologies, and literary journals worldwide. She is Canada's most acclaimed and published Native woman author.

Carrie McMaster recently completed an MA in Women's Studies at Texas Woman's University and is now pursuing a Ph.D. in Family Therapy, hoping to practice gender-sensitive family therapy with alternative families following her graduation and temporary licensing. Her academic and professional interests include relationship and other forms of family violence, women and disabilities, alternative families, and cultural diversity and individual differences. Her fascination with the writings of Gloria E. Anzaldúa arose from her discovery of Anzaldúa's keen awareness of and illuminating commentaries on issues of diversity and human differences.

Zulma Y. Méndez is a doctoral candidate in the graduate school of education at the University of California, Riverside. Her interests include critical pedagogy, cultural and gender studies. Zulma is a fronteriza from the Juárez/El Paso area where she currently lives.

Caren S. Neile is founding director of the South Florida Storytelling Project at Florida Atlantic University, where she is Artist-in-Residence in Communication. She is the managing editor for *Storytelling, Self, Society: An Interdisciplinary Journal of Storytelling Studies* and social action coordinator on the national board of the Healing Story Alliance. Her publications include *Hidden: A Sister and Brother in Nazi Poland* (coauthor, University of Wisconsin Press, 2002) and a chapter in *A Beginner's Guide to Storytelling* (National Storytelling Press, 2003).

Mariana Ortega is an associate professor of philosophy at John Carroll University, University Heights, Ohio. Her research focuses on questions of self and sociality in Existential Phenomenology, in particular Heideggerian Phenomenology. She is also interested in U.S. Third-World and Latina Feminism, Multiculturalism, Latin American thought, and Race Theory.

Irene Reti lived upstairs from Gloria Anzaldúa as her friend, comadre in writing, and tenant from 1992 to 2002. Irene's most recent publication is *Out in the Redwoods: Gay, Lesbian, Bisexual, Transgender History at UC Santa Cruz, 1965–2003* (University Library, UC Santa Cruz, 2003). She is the publisher of HerBooks, a nationally known lesbian feminist press founded in Santa Cruz in 1984, which has published twenty-five titles to date. Her publications include *The Lesbian in Front of the Classroom: Writings by Lesbian Teachers*; *A Transported Life: Memories of Kindertransport*; *Childless by Choice: A Feminist Anthology*; *The Keeper of Memory: A Memoir*; and *Women Runners: Stories of Transformation*. She has a BA in Environmental Studies and Women's Studies from UC Santa Cruz, and an MA in History from UC Santa Cruz. She works as an oral historian at UCSC.

Chela Sandoval is chair of the Department of Chicano and Chicana Studies and an associate professor of critical and cultural theory at the University of California, Santa Barbara. She is the author of *Methodology of the Oppressed.*

Mónica Torres is an assistant professor of English at New Mexico State University. Her research and teaching focus on cultural constructions of identity, the rhetorics of film and popular culture, and "borderlands" epistemologies and pedagogies.

Edith M. Vásquez teaches as an adjunct instructor of Chicana/o and Latina/o Studies at California State University, Long Beach and at the University of California, Riverside, where she recently received her Ph.D. in English.

Eve Wiederhold, assistant professor of English, teaches in the composition and rhetoric program at the University of North Carolina, Greensboro. Her research focuses on the intersection between public rhetorics and feminist theory. She also co-edits *Lore: An e-journal for Teachers of Writing*, an online publication available through Bedford/St. Martin.

Kelli Zaytoun is assistant professor of English and Director of Women's Studies at Wright State University in Dayton, Ohio. She is past chair of the National Women's Studies Association's Women's Centers Caucus. She received an interdisciplinary Ph.D. from Miami University in 2003, drawing from the fields of psychology, women's studies, English, and education. Her current research focuses on identity and cultural issues in psychological development theory. She lives with her son in Yellow Springs, Ohio.

Index

Titles beginning with words "The," "La," or "El" have been alphabetized by the second word. For example, "Prieta, La."

Printed in the United States
102417LV00001B/65/A

9 781403 967213